GONE FERAL

Noel -

How a marine
handles the apocalypse!

Ted
Nulty
'17

GONE FERAL

Ted Nulty

STEALTH BOOKS

GONE FERAL

Stealth Books

www.stealthbooks.com

Edited by Sara Jones

Cover Design by Alexandre Rito

Selected graphic elements licensed from 123RF.com

ISBN-13: 978-1-939398-50-5

Printed in the United States of America

I would like to dedicate this book to all of my Kappa Sigma brothers, and to all the kids out there battling cancer. What you're facing is tougher than anything anyone in this book had to face. Keep fighting!

PROLOGUE

"Whiskey Three November…"

The transmission was faint, which was rare with the satellite technology used in the radios carried by the Marines of Hotel Company.

"Whiskey Three November, send it."

"Data link, new target, sending."

"Copy, out."

The three camouflaged figures remained perfectly still as the data stream updated the battlefield computer the team leader was carrying. After the alert sounded in his ear, CWO3 Mark Norris checked the new reference, updated his fire plan, and made sure both the sergeant and corporal with him were squared away on the new intel.

"Fuckin' Predator is trackin' their shit down today," Corporal Jake Derry whispered as he began plotting the stalk to their final observation point on the next ridge.

"Let's see if we can get some decent on-call air and light these guys up." Sergeant Arturo Sanchez was a solidly built brick of a Marine who could trudge along all day with 100 pounds on his back and barely notice it.

The sniper team spent almost two hours covering the mile-and-a-half trek to their next hide. The team had barely finished making sure the hide was secure when Derry pointed out the mule pulling a pickup bed across the valley in front of them. A head could barely be seen looking out from under the tarp tied across the top of the cut-in-half Toyota truck.

"Does he think he's being sneaky?" Derry asked as he laid the laser designator on the improvised cart.

Sanchez, who had been looking back down the slope behind them, said, "What?"

"Fucker's trying to hide under the tarp. Like we're not gonna see the damn thing."

"The Talis don't fully understand our technology. He thinks the drones won't shoot him if he's out of sight or his heat signature is removed. He doesn't understand that we get a return from the mule's heat," Norris said as he panned the area with his binoculars.

"Well, let's disabuse him of that notion right now," Sanchez growled.

Norris looked over at Sanchez and shook his head. The normally quiet sergeant became a regular chatterbox when he was only allowed to speak in whispers. The only other time he became verbose was when he was calling troops into formation. Then the creativity of his speech was admired by all the Marines present.

"Eagle One, Lima November 204 on station. Flight of four F-18s, cluster and precision. Over."

"Lima November 204, standby; only activity is a lone horse-drawn cart. The Predator should have a rocket for it. Over." Norris noted the flight's check-in time.

"Roger, Eagle One, standing by. Time on station will be twenty mikes unless diverted. Over."

"Copy, 204. Out."

"We gonna light his shit up, or what, Gunner?" Derry had the portable laser set up and was tracking the slowly moving cart.

"Easy there, Rambo; let's see what he's up to first." Norris was looking through the twenty-five power Leupold scope mounted on the top of his Barrett M107 sniper rifle. The .50 caliber special application scoped rifle (SASR) was capable of reaching out the 1600 yards to the target, but the Marine's job was to designate targets and remain hidden.

As the cart rolled into a slight depression and came to a stop, Sanchez noticed movement to their rear. He immediately pressed a button on his radio that sent an alert to the other two Marines, who immediately shut up and began scanning every foot of ground in their immediate vicinity.

"Two hadjis about 400 meters, five o'clock from line of march."

"If they're behind that finger, they'll get a good line on us, Gunner," Derry whispered as he carefully surveyed the terrain. The hunters could quickly become the hunted if the team became exposed to two enemy elements at once.

"You'd think the fuckin' Predator would have picked them up too," Norris complained as he maintained watch on the mule cart. "Let's ask the zoomies what's up."

"Skillet, Whiskey Three November, we have movement to our five o'clock, at least two individuals. Do you have a line on them?"

"Whiskey Three November, Skillet. Negative, we have you and the target in front of you; be advised that we may have civilians beyond the element we are tracking." The controller sounded bored.

"Skillet, say again. We have a mule-drawn cart to our front and movement of at least two individuals behind us." Derry was grinding his teeth so hard it could be heard over the radio.

"Oh shit! Whiskey Three November, we have you marked as the target element. Re-tasking the Predator." The controller sounded like he actually sat up and took notice. "Whiskey Three November, can you designate either target code 124, or ID your element?"

Norris had the PBL targeting laser ready to go and after programming the proper code, he said, "Skillet, cart is lit, code 124."

No sooner had he started to speak, when the controller came back with, "Whiskey Three November, ground contact; return 124. We have a better picture now. You have an element of five unidentified subjects 430 meters bearing 015, moving south."

"Shit—we have gophers out front, gents," Norris said as he watched several heads become visible next to the cart. Things were officially screwed up with the team being between two enemy elements, both of which outnumbered them.

"Skillet, the cart is in a depression, and it appears there is a cave opening in there. I have multiple contacts coming out of the ground. Can you have the Predator engage?"

"Whiskey Three November, affirmative. Will engage designated contact only." On the controller's screen, he had two groups of people—both on ridges overlooking the depression where the cart was located. Both had more than two people, which he thought was the number in a sniper team. "Whiskey Three November, say your element size. Unable to determine friendly unit."

"Skillet, Whiskey Three November is leading a unit of three Marines."

"Copy, Whiskey Three November. We have you now. Engaging target."

The Marines didn't have long to wait as the Predator on station, more than 12,000 feet above their heads, made a slight bank and fired a Hellfire missile. The AGM-114M followed the reflected laser dot to the side of the cart and penetrated the flimsy truck bed material before detonating. The ensuing blast flipped the cart over and killed everything in the immediate vicinity. The shockwave raised dust for over 100 meters in every direction.

"Poor mule," Norris said as he tried to see through the cloud of dust to do his TDA (Target Damage Assessment). There was literally nothing left standing in the blast zone; even the scrub bushes had been blown flat.

"That got them stirred up behind us, boss," Sanchez said as the group of men behind them highlighted themselves along the ridge in an attempt to see the devastation.

"They movin' on us?" Norris asked without looking back.

"Negative."

"Skillet, Whiskey Three November; I'm gonna designate the second group and see if you can positively ID. Then we'll see about engaging them."

"Skillet copies."

Norris had already slid the designator back and handed it to Sanchez.

"Don't paint the cow," he said, referring to Derry's nickname.

Sanchez smiled as he carefully lined up the optical crosshairs with a rock next to one of the Talis, who was still looking at the devastation caused by the Hellfire.

As soon as he began to paint the rock, the combat controller called out, "Contact, ground target, element of five individuals."

"Copy, Skillet; can you tell us what they're doing?"

"Element is deployed along the ridge, 500 meters from your location. No activity that I can tell; they seem to be just lying there."

"They probably can't tell if it was an IED or us," Norris whispered. Then he asked, "Skillet, do you have weapons visible?"

"Affirmative, multiple long guns. And they're all pointed your way."

"Copy, can you engage?"

"Negative, drone is Winchester; CAS is available."

"Lima November 204, Eagle One, I have an element approximately 500 meters from my location. Terrain feature adjacent target is painted code 124. Can you engage? Over."

"Eagle One, Lima November 204, ground contact code 124. I have good lock on the beam; say again target type and size. Over."

"Lima November 204, target element is five troops in the open. Predator confirms weapons. Over."

"Eagle One, copy. I can smooth out that whole ridge, if you like. Over."

"Negative, 204. We are less than 500 meters away. If you can engage with precision-guided ordinance, though, I'd appreciate it. Over." Norris could just see a four-plane element dropping bombs hither and yon.

"Eagle One, are we cleared to engage?"

"Lima November 204, affirmative. Cleared to engage target designated code 124. Over," Norris said as the Scout Snipers tried to make themselves smaller. They needn't have worried, because the flight leader was "switched on." The first two-plane element rolled in and placed a 1,000-pound GBU (Guided Bomb Unit) right on the laser. Again, everything for a hundred meters surrounding the laser's reflected dot was flattened. All five of the Taliban were killed instantly.

"Well, shiiiit!" Derry whispered loudly. "I guess that is that."

The Marines waited for the QRF (Quick Reaction Force) to arrive via their CH-53s then began walking down the hill to meet them as they secured the cave opening.

Their tour rotation was over in another week, and the Marines were ready to get back home.

CHAPTER 1

Miami, FL

Khaled Mehmanham watched the news in his Miami condo and shook his head in wonder. The major stations were all running stories on a homeless man who had chewed the face off of another man on a freeway overpass. He was pleased at the shock displayed by the talking heads on the news station. Although this was the first incident that had garnered national attention, it was actually the third time in two months that Khalid and his cell had distributed tainted PCP to homeless addicts. Although both previous incidents had resulted in violent outcomes, this was the first time the results had occurred in a predictable and spectacular fashion.

Khaled picked up his Android and sent a text to his controller.

Ciudad Juarez, Mexico

"Will we be able to count on this one, Jose?" Ibet asked the stocky young man next to him.

"Señor Ibet, we have delivered more than asked and at a higher success rate than promised." Jose was the distribution coordinator for the cartel in Ciudad Juarez. In spite of the preconceived notions of the public, the true brains behind the cartel's operations were very businesslike and professional. Even though he had made over six million dollars the previous year, Jose drove a late-model Nissan Altima and lived in a modest house to the west of the city. He was considered "middle management."

"I know; I have just received word, however, that our distribution network will be in place ahead of schedule." The two men were watching the loading of several tons of white powder into the bottom of a tanker truck.

The truck would travel into the U.S. by driving straight across the border. There was no stealth involved… just plain bribery and a lot of money.

San Diego, California

The two men finished their jog around Lake Miramar and stood in the parking lot, stretching. Both were sweating freely from the five-mile jaunt, and they took their time to catch their breath.

"The hill is closer than I thought," said the first of them.

"It will mean a higher drop, for sure," the man who went by the name of *Juan* said with a nod.

"Can't we just insert the bundles from the shore? I don't see the difference," said the second man, whose driver's license identified him as *Luis Castellano*.

"Only as the plan states, my brother."

"Yes, but as they used to say in the Corps, 'Improvise, adapt, and overcome.'" Luis had never spent a day in the Armed Forces of America, but the history created by his handlers showed him to be a college student using his GI Bill after serving a stint as a Marine.

"We will consider this if things dictate a change in the plan," said Juan as he stared to the west at the city, which was visible through the marine layer that blanketed the northern part of San Diego.

CHAPTER 2

Hill River State Park, MN

The Jeep Liberty was covered in mud up to its doorsills. It splashed through even more as it backed up to the edge of a creek that fed into a small lake. The rear seat of the four-door Jeep had been folded down to make room for the large bundle that sat in the cargo compartment. The two men casually climbed out of the Jeep and began to unload the seventy-pound bundle. After manhandling it out and onto the ground, one of them walked to the water's edge, removed a test tube from his pocket, and took a sample of the water next to the shore. After placing a stopper in it and making a few notes on the vial, he helped his compatriot unroll the bundle into the water.

As the last of the plastic ran out, the gel-coated brown powder slurped into the creek, with a few inches still protruding above the surface. Both men grinned at each other as they went back to the Jeep and got out a pair of poles with flat ends. They used these to push the bundle out into the creek, being careful not to tear the delicate coating. Once the capsule was completely submerged, they hopped back into the vehicle and headed back east, to Duluth.

Two days later, Dan Preston was driving his Chevy Silverado work truck down one of the fire roads when he thought he entered *The Twilight Zone*. The park ranger was moving slowly toward Fire Creek, looking for a couple of lost campers, when a small, whitetail deer bounced out of the brush on the side of the road. The young male was bucking and twisting like a rodeo bull. Then Dan noticed that two squirrels were clinging to the side of the wildly gyrating animal. Streaks of blood were smeared down the animal's flank, and the heads of the squirrels were completely covered in gore.

As he brought the truck to a stop, he watched as one of the squirrels lost its grip and was sent flying down the dirt road toward the truck. The young deer immediately pounced on the rodent and began slamming its hooves into the gore-encrusted animal at its feet. After turning its antagonist into mush, the deer appeared to notice the truck for the first time. It paused and stared for just a moment before resuming its wild gyrations. The second squirrel appeared to be frantically shaking its head but did not last more than another three seconds before losing its grip and suffering the same fate as its partner.

Dan got out of the truck and turned to retrieve his rifle from behind the seat. He had only turned away from the scene that played out in front of him for a split second when the door to his truck slammed painfully into his back, pushing his torso into the cab of the truck. The deer had slammed into the door with its hooves and continued to ram it with its head, causing the door to shove into Dan repeatedly. He used his hands to push backward against the door that had him pinned. He had just managed to turn his body around, bringing his rifle to bear, when he felt a searing pain in his lower left leg. Looking down, he saw that the deer had bitten him right above the ankle and was shaking his leg like a rat terrier. Using the interruption in the battering from the door, Dan turned the tables and slammed the door into the head of the creature that was still trying to chew through the top of his boot. The third time the door swung open, it missed the deer's head because the animal was lying on its side, and the door passed right over it.

Dan put the barrel of his Remington 700 to the side of the beast's head and pulled the trigger. The deer collapsed like it had been sledgehammered to the ground. As the echoes of the shot faded into the woods, Dan jerked his tender ankle out of the thing's mouth and poked it one more time with the barrel for good measure. After eliciting no response from the animal, he turned back and traded the .308 scoped rifle for his M4 carbine. The ranger slung the rifle, made sure a round was chambered and the safety was on, and then examined the body lying at his feet.

Thin strips of flesh were missing in several places where the squirrels had latched on and torn away the skin. In fact, the young buck looked like something out of a zombie movie; there were open, weeping wounds all over the torso and legs. Fearing rabies, Dan got the medical kit out and pulled on some nitrile gloves. When he leaned down and placed a hand on the carcass, he could feel the heat through the gloves.

"You were definitely running a fever," he said aloud as an uneasy feeling crept up his spine. *Radiation,* he thought. *This thing feels like a fucking piece of microwaved meat.* He went over to the squirrels and, after poking them to ensure he didn't get a violent response from their mangled little bodies, picked them up, but he was unable to determine if the bodies were unusually warm.

It was then that Dan noticed something was wrong. He stopped and listened and couldn't figure it out for a moment. Then he realized that the sounds in the woods were wrong—off somehow. He could hear birds in the distance, but the normal sounds of the woods were absent. His hindbrain was kicking in and alerting him to things his conscious mind couldn't grasp. There was also a low, almost subliminal growl floating on the air.

Now fully freaked out, he got on the radio and called the ranger command post to let them know he had multiple animals that were behaving abnormally. After informing them that he had been forced to kill an apparently rabid deer and that he would be bringing the carcass back for examination, he began gathering the animals for transport.

He wrote the date, place, and time on two plastic bags, put the squirrels inside, and sealed them. These, he placed in a red biohazard cooler, which was kept in the truck for specimen collection. The deer, he rolled onto a big, blue tarp and wrapped it with generous amounts of duct tape. After hoisting the 120-pound animal into the bed of the truck, he stopped and turned around to check his surroundings. The creepy feeling was back full force; he brought the rifle up to his shoulder and panned the wood line through the ACOG (Advanced Combat Optical Gunsight) scope mounted on top.

Nothing appeared out of the ordinary—no shadows out of place… no sudden movements to catch his eye.

Still, he could not shake the feeling of unease.

After securing the med-kit and making sure the deer carcass wasn't going anywhere, he climbed back into the cab, locked the doors, and placed the M4 on the seat next to him. It would not leave his side till he felt a lot more comfortable.

As the truck began making a four-point turn on the narrow firebreak, Dan failed to notice the two kit foxes on the side of the road. Although they were both torn literally to shreds, they had been dragging their brutalized bodies toward him. Only the massive damage to their tendons and ligaments had prevented them from attacking the ranger.

CHAPTER 3

Grand Rapids, MN

"They did what?" Scott Preston was looking at his younger brother as if he had grown horns out of his forehead.

"I'm not shittin' you. The little fuckers were latched on to the side of this young buck and it was going crazy." Dan was filling out a damage report for the truck. The deer had managed to put several sizeable dents in the door. "I bagged all the critters and gave 'em to Carol. She said she'd get back to me with a report on whether they were rabid or not. I've never seen anything like it. And that buck almost chewed through my boot!" He swung his foot up on the desk to display the victimized appendage. The damage to the boot was relatively minor, with a flap of the leather pulled loose from the stitching.

Scott walked over from the desk he was leaning against and peered intently at the boot. "Is that your blood?" he asked, noticing the brown stains on the leather.

"Nope," Dan said, leaning forward to inspect the stains. "I didn't see that." He reached down to untie his boot when Scott grabbed his hand.

"Better glove up, little brother. That could be infected with god knows what."

"Yeah, you're right." He started to get up, but his brother waved him back to his seat as he walked back to his desk, retrieved a pair of the blue gloves, and threw them at his brother's face. Dan, expecting this, was ready and snatched them out of the air. After removing the boot, he dropped it in a trashcan liner and hobbled over to his locker. He hung up his gun belt, grabbed his cross-trainers, and stumped back to his chair.

"So, did you find the lost sheep?" Scott was reviewing the incident report as Dan put on his shoes.

"Nope. And I'm not going back out there till Carol calls back. If we're gonna start running into rabid bears, I want to know about it first."

"Well, I'll have Glenn and Yavi check it out," Scott said as he threw the report back on Dan's desk. "You forgot to check the N/A box for Other Vehicle/Person."

"Thanks." He made the required notations. "And tell them to be careful. That place gave me the heebie jeebies."

"I'll pass on your concern about hormonal squirrels." Scott was already picking up the microphone from the radio sitting at the dispatch station. After plopping down in the chair, he began calling the other two patrol units.

"Patrol Three, Glenn, you there?"

"Yeah, Scott, what's up? Did your brother find the wayward souls?"

"No, he didn't, but he did have a run-in with some of the local fauna, and they dinged up his truck."

"Moose or bear?" Glenn asked, figuring those to be the only two big enough and capable enough to damage a full-size pickup.

"Neither. It was a deer and two squirrels."

After an extended pause, in which both of the Preston brothers could imagine Glenn rolling his eyes, they heard a Jim Carrey imitation of "*Reeeaaalllhehehe*."

"Yup, that's his story, and he's sticking to it."

The unbent paperclip went zipping across the office airspace from the rubber band stretched across Dan's fingers and impacted with the back of Scott's neck.

"Ow, shit!" he exclaimed as he slapped his hand to the back of his neck.

"Well, I'll tell Bambi and Thumper to behave. Did he make it to Fire Creek?"

Scott was hunched forward and peeking under his arm to see if there were any more incoming missiles.

"Thumper was a rabbit, you dumb shit!" Dan yelled across the room as Scott keyed the mic.

"Did you copy that last?" Scott asked as he gestured threats at his brother while continuing to duck the paperclips being fired at him.

"I did. Tell your brother I'm sorry I'm not as Disney literate as he is."

"He says he was about a mile out when Bambi and Chip and Dale decided to play WWF with his truck." Scott was now pointing a finger at Dan and giving him a look that said pain was on the way.

"Copy. Show me en route. I'll check in when I'm in the area."

"Okay; thanks, Bud." Scott put down the mic and turned toward his younger brother.

"Chip and Dale were chipmunks…" Dan attempted to duck, and was mostly successful, as a copy of the Yellow Pages slammed into his shoulder as he tried to twist away. The impact knocked him out of his swivel chair and sent him sprawling to the floor. He looked up at his older brother standing over him as the rest of the office acted like nothing out of the ordinary was happening, since it wasn't.

"Asshole," Dan mumbled.

CHAPTER 4

Buffalo, NY

"All is well, Satif?" the man asked as he was ushered into the entryway of the mansion.

"It is, my friend. And how have you done, Mohammad?" The two men began to stroll toward the back patio, where a table had been set for breakfast.

"Two days and it begins. Are you ready?"

"The supplies are in, and the staff arrives tomorrow. How long until the effects begin to manifest?" the slender man asked as he took a seat at the table.

"I am only awaiting word from our friends in Minnesota."

"And what word is that? I thought they had reported a successful delivery and they went back and received favorable results from the water test."

"Michael said he was going to examine the area and would get back to me today. The pilots are all ready to go and the planes are loaded and ready." Mohammad leaned back as he placed a slice of banana in his mouth and slowly chewed. "I think our 'diversion' will cause more panic than our operation."

"Inshallah."

"Inshallah."

CHAPTER 5

Hill River State Park, MN

The Jeep Liberty was pulled off to the side of the road, just on the other side of the small bridge that spanned Fire Creek. Glenn slowed and looked around for the owners but could only see where the grass had been pushed down by someone heading toward the water. He pulled his truck past the Jeep and turned off the motor. He started to type a patrol update into his video display terminal (VDT), but the cab of the truck began to heat up the moment the motor turned off and the AC stopped running.

Turning the key back on for power, he lowered the window; instantly, the stench hit him like a physical force.

"Whew, shit!" he exclaimed as his eyes began to water. The smell was so overwhelming that he immediately rolled the window back up. He grabbed a bandana from his duffle bag and smeared some Vicks VapoRub on it. After tying the bandana around his face, he opened the door and stepped out. The rangers routinely had to remove dead animals, so they all kept the bandanas and Vicks handy.

Glenn was about to head down toward the creek when a niggling sensation caused him to pull up short. He froze and began to turn in a full circle. It was then that the subtle clues indicating something was wrong hit him full force. Not only was the stench overwhelming, but the sounds from the surrounding woods were off. The bird noises seemed subdued, and he faintly heard what sounded like a catfight off in the distance.

Glenn and Dan had served together in Iraq; in fact, Dan was the one who had talked him into becoming a state park ranger when they both got out of the Army. Glenn's training taught him that if something looked wrong or felt wrong, it *was* wrong.

Well, I am definitely feeling the vibe now, he thought as he went to his truck and got out his M4 carbine. It was almost identical to the one carried by Dan. With the exception of being chambered for the 6.8 mm SPC cartridge, the ACOG-equipped rifles were identical to the ones they had carried overseas in the sandbox. They had elected for the larger, more powerful caliber because they sometimes ran into unsavory elements of the two-legged variety, as well as the occasional rabid wolf or other large predator.

Glenn threw his tac vest over his torso and secured it with the Velcro straps. The vest had numerous magazine pouches for both his rifle and pistol, as well as compartments for a compass, thermal blanket, 100-ounce hydration system, and a pouch with two "field-stripped" MREs. He was loaded down with an extra thirty-eight pounds of Kevlar and equipment, but he was, literally, loaded for bear.

"Central, Patrol Three, over." Glenn had leaned into the car and hit his EVA button on the truck's VDT. By activating the button, the truck would broadcast its GPS coordinates; it would also relay the coordinates of Glenn's handheld radio and act as a relay tower to boost the handheld's signal.

"Patrol Three, go." It was Scott's voice on the other end.

"Hey, Scott, your little bro was right. There is definitely some creepy shit out here. I saw several dead animals on the road, and I'm at Fire Creek Bridge right now. The smell is awful. Definitely multiple dead animals in the area." Glenn had walked over to the black Jeep and was looking inside. "I have a black Jeep Liberty parked here next to the bridge. Minnesota license number 26M3897. Isn't that the car we're looking for?"

The interior of the Jeep was in like-new condition and no wrappers or other trash littered the vehicle. As Glenn walked around the passenger side, he noticed a rental car barcode in the corner of the rear window.

"Central, does this come back as a rental?"

"Hey, Glenn, we're supposed to be looking for a dark blue Jeep Cherokee, Minnesota custom plate FZ4U2. I'm running the other plate now."

"Copy. I'm gonna look down by the creek for the occupants of this Jeep. Something is way wrong out here."

"Patrol Three, P-Two and S-One are en route."

"Copy, thanks." Glenn was already following the trail of smashed down grass toward the creek bank. After rounding some brush, Glenn froze in his tracks. The banks on both sides of the creek were covered in dead and dying animals, including two swarthy-skinned men who were lying next to a wolf and a bear. The wolf had been horribly injured but was still snapping and growling at one of the men who was lying next to it. Upon seeing Glenn, it began to scrabble toward him, hitching itself forward with its two front legs. The rear legs had suffered so much tendon damage and muscle loss that they were useless. Glenn backed away and raised his rifle. He fired one round into the wolf and watched it collapse on its side. The bullet hole was tiny compared to the horrific wounds covering the rest of the body. After making sure the animal was in fact dead, he turned to the two dead human bodies and, after gloving up, checked them for life signs. Finding none, he stood and slowly panned the area with his rifle at the ready.

There were dead fish floating on the surface of the creek as well as washed up on the shore. Every carcass showed signs of extreme violence. They looked as if they had all fed on each other. There were bite marks on everything, and blood and gore was smeared over the surrounding foliage and landscape. The rotting fish smell was so overpowering that he didn't notice the chemical tinge to it at first.

"Sam One, Patrol Three."

"Patrol Three, Central. S-1 is on his way out to his truck." The voice belonged to Kate Barry, one of the office staff and the usual dispatcher. "What's up?"

"Central, I need you to notify state crime lab. I have two dead bodies and multiple dead animals of widely different species. I need you to also have them notify CDC for a possible toxic or biological spill. Dead fauna numbers in the multi-hundreds."

"Patrol Three, Sam One. Say again last. Over." The tension had caused Scott to revert to mil-speak.

"Scott, I have hundreds of dead animals of all types and two dead males of Hispanic or other dark-skinned ancestry. I even have a small brown bear and a fuckin' wolf that was half chewed up and was still trying to fight. It's like *The Twilight Zone* out here. I'm going back to my rig and getting my NBC shit on. I'm gonna exfil about a mile out and close off the road. Then I'm gonna drive through and close it off about a mile past the bridge. The spill, or whatever, is right at the bridge. The bodies are just downstream of the bridge, but I'm telling ya, you're gonna need MOPP 4 stuff." The words came tumbling out in a rush as Glenn backed away from the carnage.

"Sam One, Central copies all; notifying state now."

"Glenn, just get the hell out of there. We'll meet up at Travelers Road and Fire Creek. If it's in the water, it would have traveled downstream, and we should be able to see anything out of the ordinary at the highway bridge." Scott had the lights and sirens going as he pushed his Excursion up to max safe speed.

"Central, Patrol One. Show me en route. Break. Sam One, where do you want me? The animals I found were over a half mile from the bridge, to the east." Dan was closing in from the north.

"Central, Patrol Three. Have them stay way back. I can smell some sort of chemical smell in the air, and I'm getting light-headed." The truck was about twenty yards away when a chittering sound made him look down at his feet. A small field mouse was latched on to his boot and was shaking its head back and forth, trying to worry its way through the edge of the opening by the tongue. He laughed out loud at the sight of a tiny mouse taking on a boot that was twenty times its size, let alone the man inside it. A quick shake of his foot sent it flying off into the brush. "Take that, you little shit! Come back and I'll stomp you into paste!"

"Oh shit! Central, get medical en route to P-3's location." Scott was driving with the mic in the same hand he was using to steer. With the other hand, he was scrolling through his contact list on his iPhone so he could call his captain. He had to swerve violently when a truck pulled onto the highway from a side road. He avoided the collision but lost his phone onto the passenger-side foot well. "Central, S-1. Can you call Ming and bring him up to speed, please?"

"Sam One, I copy. Scott, will do." Kate was already lining up little yellow Post-its on her desk and had written a note for each task. She also had a landline receiver pressed to her ear with her shoulder as she gestured frantically at the other two office staff members to gather around.

"Ellie, you call the CDC on the emergency contact number and tell them what's going on." She handed off one post-it.

"Trevor, I need you to call this number and tell the state crime lab that we have an emergency with multiple dead bodies and missing persons." She sighed at his funny look. "The other campers they were looking for—the reason they were out there!"

She made a conscious effort to calm down when she noticed her voice going up in pitch and volume. "Our agency ID is right here," she said as she shoved another yellow piece of paper at him.

As the word was going out, Glenn had staggered back to his truck. Being a veteran from Iraq, he had drilled extensively with NBC (Nuclear, Biological, Chemical) equipment. He and Dan both kept gas masks in the stainless steel gear lockers mounted in the bed of their trucks. Although his nasal passages were starting to sting, the chemical smell was not that bad and reminded him of a freshly chlorinated pool. He managed to get the mask out and over his head, and after a few deep breaths, his head started to clear.

Glenn pulled his phone out, snapped a picture of the Jeep's license plate, and then started the truck. As he pulled away, he noticed a small garter snake working its way across the road. The reptile didn't appear in any hurry and behaved normally.

"Well, there's *something* not trying to kill me."

CHAPTER 6

Montgomery Field Airport, San Diego, CA

The pilot walked out to the Cessna 310 and nodded to the fuel truck operator, who was rolling up his hose after topping off the tanks of the twin-engine aircraft. He waited as the only other passenger on the upcoming flight hustled across the ramp. The two men quickly took off all the tie-downs and finished the pre-flight inspection. After climbing over the dozen bundles that were in the main compartment, both men donned headsets and looked at each other with grim smiles.

"Montgomery ground, Cessna 397 Zulu. Request taxi and departure, VFR local. I have information Golf."

"Cessna 397 Zulu, cleared to taxi; hold short runway 28 left. Wait for final clearance," the controller's voice came back after a slight hesitation.

"Three ninety-seven Zulu copies. Hold short 28 left."

After taxiing out and waiting for a small plane from one of the local flying clubs to land, their plane was given clearance to take off and were soon climbing out to the west and heading over the ocean. As soon as they were off the coast by five miles, the man called Luis climbed in back and detached the door on the right side of the aircraft. It had been specially modified to be removed in flight and fell away, just missing the horizontal stabilizer.

As Luis moved over to the other side of the main compartment, the plane banked to the left and began to head inland. Over the next forty minutes, it flew over every major water reservoir in San Diego County.

Lake Hodges, located between the cities of Escondido and Poway was the first. Hodges was followed by Lakes Wohlford, Poway, Miramar, Henshaw, Otay, and then the San Vicente and El Capitan Reservoirs. The last two reservoirs received the biggest bundles shoved out of the small plane. By the time he took his seat up front again, Luis was sweating freely from manhandling the packages.

The plane was just east of Montgomery Field when they requested and received landing clearance from the tower. Again, the two men looked at each other and smiled. The smiles were much more grim this time.

"Montgomery tower, Cessna 397 Zulu; I'm having difficulties with my flight controls, and I have a vibration under the aircraft," the man calling himself Juan said, putting what he thought was a convincing note of panic into his voice.

"Cessna 397 Zulu, are you declaring an emergency at this time?" The tower controller had already gestured the control tower supervisor over.

"Tower, I am losing response to my control inputs. Aircraft is turning to port with full opposite control input. Yes, I'm declaring an emergency!" Juan yelled the last part as he banked the plane southward with no problem whatsoever. As he lined up the airplane's nose with his target building, he pushed the nose down toward the FBI field office located off Aero Drive and shoved the throttle forward.

The small twin-engine plane had two storage compartments over each engine nacelle. These had been packed with the latest binary explosives. The plane smashed through the fourth-floor window on the north side of the building and slammed through to the third before the binaries were detonated by the delayed impact fuses. The forty-three pounds of binary in each nacelle had a NEW (Net Explosive Weight) of more than 200 pounds of TNT. The blast blew everything out of the third and fourth floors, killing ninety-seven agents and staff.

CHAPTER 7

Phoenix, AZ

The Phoenix field office of the FBI sits on the intersection of 7th Street and Deer Valley Road, directly across from the Deer Valley airport. Aircraft in the pattern for runway 25L routinely fly right over the new facility. A Piper Seminole from a flying club at the field took off and flew around various parts of the Phoenix metropolitan area before coming back to the airfield and requesting clearance to approach the field from the south. After being granted permission to enter the left hand pattern, the mid-sized plane entered the downwind leg. As it approached the FBI building, the nose dipped and the plane plowed into the front of the building, right over the wall designed to prevent terrorist attacks. The explosives-laden plane almost made it to the middle of the building before it detonated in a blinding fireball.

The north, south, and west walls were blown completely out, while the east wall remained standing. The collapsed roof sloped down from the east wall into the pile of rubble that was once one of the FBI's newest facilities. Forty-two of the eighty-one agents and staff who were in the building were severely wounded or killed in the blast.

CHAPTER 8

Camp Pendleton, CA

"Hey, Gunner, you gotta check this out!" Sergeant Sanchez yelled out into the platoon assembly area. The "area" was not much more than a large garage attached to the back of the company building.

"Coming!" Mark said as he finished directing the Marines to stow the field gear they had been inventorying. As he walked into the company administration area, he noticed that the majority of the Marines were standing around the TV in the Geedunk lounge. "What's up?" he asked as he shoved his way past the junior Marines present.

"Fuckin' plane crashed into the FBI building," Arturo said, making room for him as he got to the front of the crowd. "Real mess. FAA says the plane reported an in-flight emergency, and an eyewitness says it looked like the plane had a piece of fuselage missing from the right side when it burned in."

The view on the screen showed a massive hole in the north side of the building. The reporter was talking to witnesses as the camera panned across the devastation. As it reached the end of its sweep and started back, Mark noticed something wrong.

"That looks like an outward blast effect!"

Sanchez looked closer at the screen as all the veterans in the room began to notice the same post-blast indicators of explosives. He went over and grabbed the remote from a lance corporal and hit the DVR record button. As the Marines all began to discuss the turn of events, the news cut away to the studio, where the anchors excitedly relayed that several other aircraft had crashed into various federal buildings around the country.

"Fuck! They did it to us again!" said one of the staff sergeants.

"Get your shit squared away and give me all hands on deck in ten mikes!" Norris said as he pushed his way out of the room. "I'm going to see the man!"

Mark strode rapidly down the hall as people began hustling to get a quick call made before running out to the company grinder. As he approached the door to the company commander's office, Captain Linde came barreling out, and the two men almost collided.

"Where's the Fitz?" he said, referring to the company gunny.

"He's over at dental. I just had Sanchez call formation. Captain, did you see the news?"

"No, but the Battalion CO did, and he just lit me up. Multiple planes into skyscrapers again?"

"Yeah, but they're small planes, and apparently they all crashed into public buildings, not skyscrapers," Mark said as he did an about-face, and the two men strode to the company assembly area. Marines were forming up in their platoons while the platoon sergeants tried to track down their lieutenants and get the troops organized.

"Platoon commander's inside, Gunner. Can you stand in until I get this figured out?" the captain asked as he held the door open for the staff to go inside.

"You got it! I'll get them on a war footing."

Norris nodded to one of the sergeants that he would be taking the formation. As one of the platoon sergeants was getting ready to call the formation to order, a gray Honda Accord skid to a stop at the edge of the parking lot.

Gunnery Sergeant Timothy Fitzgibbons was out of his car and storming across the sidewalk toward Norris when Captain Linde stuck his head out the door and motioned for Norris to come in and for Fitz to take the formation. As Norris hurried inside, he heard the gunny tell one of the platoon sergeants to take the formation. He then followed Norris inside.

"I'msh not g'na be huld well, sir," he said when the captain gave him the "what gives?" look. The gunny's mouth was full of cotton wadding from the dentist and half his face was numb from the Novocain he had received.

"Gotcha, Gunny. They can stand down till we get some word from on high, anyway." He turned to address the officers and staff. "Well, it looks like they shit on us again, and we were caught with our britches down, again. I don't know what the ramifications of all this are going to be, but I want to start a few things in motion. First, I want all the troops to get a call in to family and find out if we have any casualties in our house; if so, I want to get them whatever support they need. But we are all here for the duration.

"B: I want all our callout gear staged, and I want the troops who live off base to have it with them at all times. I don't believe there will be any civil unrest, but you never know if we'll be called on to render assistance to local law enforcement.

"Item the Third," he paused to let the chuckles subside at his trademark listing of items to accomplish, "I want Motor T to have all our vehicles on line and ready ASAP."

"No go, sir," said the Motor T chief. "I have eleven of our sixteen troop Hummers down and two of the C and C's down for routine. Of that eleven, three are major overhauls and will be ninety-six hours plus for parts, etcetera."

"Well, don't skip anything, but get us our wheels as fast as you can."

"Aye aye, sir."

"Admin, I want all leaves cancelled and a frost call out now. Fitz, I want 100 percent location on everyone in the next hour."

The gunnery sergeant nodded his head vigorously to acknowledge the order. He turned and grabbed his clipboard from his desk and headed outside.

"Mark, what's the status of our weapons and gear?"

"Well, all our small arms are good to go. I know the crew-served for a couple of the Hummers are at the battalion armory for maintenance. Belted 5.56 is low because we just had the FAMFIRE for the SAWs, and First Platoon was on the range last week. We are TOE for special ordinance; my guys are up on Lake City for the SASRs and M40s. I don't know about the inventory for the crew-served, but I'll find out about grenades for the MK19s and .50 cal for the M2s. I'll e-mail you a list."

"Thanks, get me that as soon as you can," he said, turning toward the door. "All right let's get the word out."

Across America, 157 aircraft had flown around over bodies of water and then crashed into various public buildings. Most of them federal buildings or FBI field offices. In some instances, the planes crashed into electrical power stations or water treatment plants. All five of the major railway bridges spanning the Mississippi River suffered extensive damage or completely dropped into the river. But that was not all; Britain and areas throughout Europe suffered a similar fate.

In addition to the air assaults, several trucks dumped gel packets into water supplies, where the chemicals dissolved into the drinking water, and then consumed by the populations. The chlorate-tainted PCP/LSD derivative crossed the blood-brain barrier in all the higher-order animals that ingested it.

This brought on a high fever, uncontrollable rage, and carnivorous behavior, including cannibalism. Within twenty-four hours, 12 percent of the first-world population was exposed. In forty-eight hours, the percentage jumped to thirty-six.

Society began to collapse.

CHAPTER 9

Rancho Bernardo, CA

Mark drove home at 2130. After all the preparations had been started and the inventories completed, there was nothing left for him to do. There were no further incidents reported. After being held over, the Marines had finished prepping for what might come and then had been released to go home and see their families. As he pulled his green Ford F-250 into his driveway, several teenagers, led by his two daughters, came flooding out the front door.

"Daaaaddy!!" was all he heard before the two blonde bodies checked him into the side of the truck.

"What's up, Coach?"

"Hey, Mr. Terry's Dad."

"Hi, Pops." This last greeting was from his son, who had remained standing on the front porch.

"Hey, you guys help me unload this stuff," Mark said as he walked back to the tailgate and dropped it. "Jimmy, put the water and MREs in the garage, and then bring the cans in to the pantry."

"Is it that serious?" he said, coming down the front steps. He reached out to grab his sister, who was making herself scarce at the first sign of work. "Come on, you can help too."

"He said for *you* to do it," his youngest sister, Melanie, said; however, it was halfhearted as she saw the look on her father's face.

The other teens all pitched in and had the truck unloaded in short order. As the last load was going in, Mark made a pistol with his hand and nodded toward the super cab. Jim went over and began taking ammo cans out of the back seat and putting them on shelves next to a massive American Liberty safe that was bolted to the floor of the three-and-a-half car garage. When he ran out of shelf space, he stacked the cans next to the safe. As he walked to the door and into the house, he turned off the light and hit the button for the automatic garage door. Mark handed him a folded sheet of paper. Jim briefly glanced at and headed over to the kitchen counter where the iPad was sitting. He opened a file and flattened out the sheet of paper. He looked at it once more and began updating the ammunition inventory file on the computer.

Mark, in the meantime, had walked into the den, where every seat was taken by a teenager. They were all watching the news with a surprising amount of concentration for high school kids. The Fox News anchor was listing the total number of attacks and the estimated damage.

One of the boys turned to Mark with an expectant look on his face. "Do you think they'll bring my dad back?"

"I don't think so, Chris; the attacks occurred pretty much worldwide. Even in Iraq and the 'stan. Even Egypt caught some. I'm pretty sure the countries that weren't hit are getting looked at pretty hard," he said as more faces turned toward him. "I don't think the operational tempo will change until we pin this on someone."

"This was a stupid attack," said a girl named Tia from across the room. "They didn't really hurt us like last time, and when we find out who did it, we'll really kick their butts!"

A chorus of *yeah* and *you betcha* echoed her feelings. Mark looked at them and shook his head.

"They managed to take out all our railway bridges. That will affect goods coming and going in a big way. The financial markets are already reacting strongly, and we've shut down air traffic again. No, they hurt us pretty bad, and we're still not sure what their objective was and if they were successful."

"I say we just level their whole country," a young man named Austin said. "We should just bomb them back to the Stone Age!" More expressions of agreement followed this statement.

"I hate to tell you this, but they pretty much do live in the Stone Age right now." Mark walked across the room, unbuttoning his cammie blouse. "Their living conditions are pretty medieval as it is."

"My dad says the same thing all the time," Chris said, turning back to the TV.

"And he would be right," Mark threw over his shoulder as he headed down the hall to the stairs.

After showering and putting on some Harley Davidson sweats, Mark went downstairs to determine which kids were staying and if anyone needed rides. His oldest daughter, Terry, and Jim both drove but became lazy about it. He had experienced more than a few phone calls from concerned parents trying to locate their kids, since the Norris household was a virtual youth hostel for Rancho Bernardo.

Once assured that all had communicated in some form with their parental units, including speaking with Tia's skeptical mother himself and assuring her that he would keep all ten fingers and toes attached to her daughter, he said goodnight and hit the sack. His two dogs were already on the bed. The 112-pound boxer and 150-pound Rottweiler were already on his side of the bed and both refused to look at him as he came in the room.

"Come on, you guys. Move over." The request was met by both dogs sprawling out even flatter. "Get your fat ass over, you stupid mutt!" he grunted as he pushed on Buster the Boxer. "Ugh. I hate dogs!"

He rolled the over-muscled dog off the bed. As soon as that was accomplished, he scooched under the covers and began to push on Thor the Rottie from under the covers. This resulted in a reproachful look and a bracing of paws.

"Dammit now! Move over! Let's go!"

With the tone of voice approaching the "I'm in trouble" setting, Thor huffed and flopped over, giving Mark enough room to slip under the covers and establish some space before Buster jumped up from the other side and promptly lay up against his side.

"I hate dogs," he muttered again with a final shove toward the 250-plus pounds of muscle that was taking up three quarters of his California king-sized bed.

CHAPTER 10

Hill River State Park, MN

The park rangers and county sheriff, along with state troopers from four different field offices, made a perimeter almost fifty miles in diameter as reports of animal attacks on humans skyrocketed. The park rangers and U.S. Forest Service rangers had put together a search team outfitted with full Racal suits. The team had been able to locate the two missing fishermen, a father and son, who had apparently killed each other. Both had stabbed and bitten each other in fits of orgiastic rage.

In Bemidji, a man walked out into the street and attempted to attack a passing car. When he bounced off the vehicle, the driver stopped and attempted to help him up. When he bent over the man, who was thrashing on the ground in agony, the man on the ground grabbed the driver and began to bite and pummel him. The driver's throat was torn out and he bled out as a small crowd gathered around. The man managed to attack three more people in the crowd before someone got a shovel and beat him over the head. The three surviving victims were rushed to the hospital with bite wounds and bruises.

After being identified, police went to the man's house, where they found his wife and daughter dead. Both had signs of being in epic battles. They found the wife with a mouth full of her daughter's flesh. One of the officers went around to the back of the house, where the family dog attacked him. The large mastiff had torn the officer's calf off by the time he un-holstered his pistol. It took seven shots to put the enraged beast down.

As the police supervisors began sorting out the crime scene, another report came in of a man attacking a group of children at a summer camp. The children and their camp counselor had made it back onto their bus with only one child being bitten. They were stuck inside the bus as the enraged, partially clothed man pounded on the outside of the vehicle. When officers arrived, several attempts at using electronic stun devices failed and the officers literally had to gang tackle and subdue the thrashing man. Two of the officers were bitten so badly that they required medical attention at the hospital. The third had been bitten on the outside of his clothing and had the wound cleaned and dressed by responding paramedics.

As the two wounded officers were taken to the hospital, the governor was being briefed on the reported chemical spill at Fire Creek. The briefing being conducted by the state police liaison officer to the governor was interrupted twice with office staff rushing in to inform him of the ever-increasing number of attacks. After the second time, he had his secretary call FEMA in Washington and stop with the interruptions.

The following morning, the wife of Steven Penny, one of the wounded officers, was sitting in the waiting room with their son and daughter when the doctor came out to inform her that, except for a fever and some scarring, Steve looked like he would be fine. They had kept him overnight because of the fever but were preparing to release him. They had been in to see him, but the kids were already starting to fidget and climb on their father, so Michelle took them down the hall to reduce the wear and tear on her already bruised husband. As the doctor stood to go, the news of the first plane attacks came on the TV.

All the hospital staff stopped and stared as the news of plane crashes around the country was broadcast. A nurse came in and told the doctor that they had incoming injured from a plane crash as well. As he strode down the hall to make sure the ER was ready, Ben Cline—an FBI agent—and two other people walked into the ER reception area.

“What the hell is going on, Ben? I’ve got cannibals and plane crashes in one day. The worst I’ve had in a month is a broken ankle from a tractor accident and a concussion from a baseball!”

“Rob, this is Ken Layver and Bill Palmer from the CDC. They’re here because of these attacks. People and animals all over the place are attacking and killing each other. Now while we’re on the way over here, I hear a plane went down and crashed into the power station up north.” Ben wiped his face with his hand and looked up wearily. “I have a sinking feeling this is going to be one hell of a long day.”

Rob shook hands with the two men from the CDC and asked that they follow him to the ER so he could answer their questions and prep the unit at the same time. They had just entered the ER when screaming broke out down the hall. They all turned in time to see a nurse stagger out of Officer Penny's room with her hand pressed to her face. Blood was running freely from her broken nose, and she was attempting to tell the other people in the hall to get back when Steve Penny leapt on her back and started pummeling her to the ground. As she slumped down the wall and curled into a fetal ball to protect herself, several other hospital staff attempted to pull the man off of the stricken nurse.

Paul Brannigan, the officer assigned to watch the crazed man who had attacked the bus from the day before, finally tackled Steve and got him into handcuffs. The injured man was snarling and attempting to bite everyone holding him. Steven's wife and children looked on in horror as their husband and father was pulled off of the sobbing nurse.

"I am having some very bad feelings about this," Rob said, looking at the men from the CDC. "That man was injured by another man yesterday through a bite. We held him overnight because of fever and were going to release him. Barb! Laura! Get some orderlies over here to restrain him. And I want full quarantine on every one brought in with an open wound injury! Especially bites! Those I want restrained!" He turned to the other three gentlemen in the hall. "Any ideas?"

The four men had just put their heads together when more shouting broke out even farther down the hall.

CHAPTER 11

CDC, Atlanta, GA

The short, dark-haired woman strode purposefully down the wood-paneled hallway. The carpeting muffled the sound of her conservative heels, which made a noticeably louder sound when she was traveling the tiled corridors in the lab areas.

Dr. Anna Napolitano passed by an anteroom; she nodded at the secretary there and stepped right in to the office of the director of field operations. She hadn't bothered knocking, and she didn't wait for an invitation to sit either. She marched straight across the office and dropped a folder on Gary Little's desk.

"Well?" he said, looking up as Anna plopped down in the leather-bound chair across from him. "What did you find out?" He noticed the concerned look on her face and waited patiently for her to gather her thoughts.

"Well, it's chemical and it's nasty. We've autopsied all seven of the victims, and three of them showed no abnormalities at all except for the trauma that killed them. Four showed signs of massive swelling in the prefrontal lobe and were definitely poisoned with some form of PCP. But the pathology reads like a massive overdose. They all showed signs of severe muscle strains and tendon and ligament damage. This damage was outside from the wounding trauma and was hard for us to detect because of that trauma. It's like they had no pain receptors at all and just strained until the muscles literally ripped loose from the bone. There is some form of thick serum in their saliva and tears. We are running a full battery of tests on it now. No viral or radiological pathologies indicated—"

"Wait… What?" Little looked back through some notes. "I thought we received reports of the victims being 'hot.'"

"Yes, the park rangers who had the first reported contacts with the affected animals reported abnormally high body temperatures." Anna looked through some notes in the other file she carried. "All the animals and people who have been a victim have displayed high fevers, but nothing radiological has been detected yet. According to the reports, the heat felt radiant, not nuclear."

"Well, thank God for small favors, anyway," Little said, looking over the new notes. "I'm going to see the director."

As he stood and began placing various file in his briefcase, he was violently thrown to the ground. The whole building shook as a secondary explosion occurred from igniting jet fuel. A Falcon 900 executive jet had just slammed into the building.

CHAPTER 12

San Diego, CA

Mark woke to the sounds of sirens as a fire truck and ambulance passed by one street over. He normally would have just rolled over and gone back to sleep, but with the recent occurrences, the sound left him uneasy. He rolled out of bed and looked at the two mounds of furred flesh still lying peacefully on the bed. Feeling no immediate threat with his two watchdogs being so vigilant, he stepped over to his closet and began to dress. After putting on jeans and an oversized bowling shirt, he slipped a Glock 19 in a paddle holster inside his right hand waistline and a spare holder with two extra magazines on his left hip. A quick look in the mirror to make sure nothing was "printing," and he went into the bathroom to brush his teeth.

As soon as he left the bathroom, both dogs were right on his heels as he headed downstairs. He looked into the family room as he walked by and noticed that just about every horizontal surface was covered by a sleeping teenager. As he turned into the kitchen, Cindy, who was Terry's best friend, walked in through the archway from the hall.

"Good morning, Cindy Loo Who. How are you?"

"I'm fine," she said in a very childlike voice. "Can I have some water, please?" Her blonde hair was coming loose from the high ponytail she had put it in to sleep, and she looked amazingly like the Dr. Seuss character Mark had nicknamed her after.

"Sure, honey; here you go," he said, handing her a bottle of Arrowhead from the fridge. "When did you guys get to sleep?"

"Don't know," she said over her shoulder as she headed back toward the den. "The boys were up late playing that war game." She paused long enough so that he could see the look of disgust on her face then turned back toward the family room. Jim was infamous for holding all-night sessions of *Call of Duty*.

Mark started to chuckle but was interrupted by a body check to his left thigh. Thor was up and, therefore, ready to be fed, watered, and let out. Further human conversation would not facilitate this, so it could wait until these more important prime directives could be met. Mark leaned over and slugged the dog hard enough to move it over a step, then went out the sliding glass door and retrieved the dogs' bowls. As he was outside, he could hear more sirens off in the distance. The sound was not uncommon, as they lived just a few blocks from the fire station and less than two miles from the hospital.

After putting enough food to feed a pack of wolves into each bowl, he added half a can of Alpo to the bowls and went outside. Both dogs were already seated with pious looks of innocence on their faces. He set the bowls on the ground and straightened up. Both dogs were now staring intently at him.

"Okay, go ahead," he said and both of them began to eat like they hadn't been fed in months. The sound was enough to startle people who had never witnessed it before. Mark stepped inside and closed the slider after making sure the water jug that fed their water trough had at least two gallons still in it.

Mark now faced the dilemma of cooking for some unknown number of kids or going for donuts. Justifying his choice by not counting the occupants of the house, he decided to get pastries. He walked over to the "key wall" by the front door, picking up water bottles lying around along the way, and took down the truck keys. As he was stepping out the front door, he heard Jim's voice behind him.

"Donuts?" Jim was standing in the doorway to the garage.

"Yup. Want to come?"

"Nah, I've got to get dressed and run Erin home. Her folks are leaving for some vacation, and they want to see her before they leave." Erin was another friend who tended to live at the Norris house whenever school was not in session. "Can I take the 'Car'?"

The 'Car' he was referring to was the dark grey 2009 Porsche GT3 RS parked in the far stall of the garage. It had been Mark's dream car ever since they first came out. It was the only vehicle worthy of taking garage space away from the other occupants of the garage. Said occupants included a Harley FatBoy, a Ducati Monster, several quads, and two dirt bikes. Parked on a cement pad on the side of the house was a custom trailer that held a ski boat and two jet skis.

"Nope," Mark said as he turned to snatch the keys from the hook.

"Why not?" There wasn't much of a whining note to his voice.

"Two reasons—one, I don't like you; and two, you have just reminded me that all my hard work defending this great nation of ours has earned me the right to enjoy life a little. I will, therefore, be taking *my* 'Car' to the donut shop!"

With that, he went out to the driveway and pulled the truck far enough back that he could get the RS out. After hitting the remote button in the truck for the garage door, he stepped down from the lifted truck and threw the keys at his son, who had come out to the front porch. He then climbed into the low-slung car, and after carefully avoiding the truck's massive tires, was off down the street.

As he made his way to the donut shop, Mark noticed the lack of traffic. *Well, that's to be expected, I guess. Everyone wants to see what's happening in the world.* He made a note to check the news and call in to Battalion Ops when he got back. *Can't be too bad,* he thought, looking at his phone for messages.

Nobody's bothered to call me.

The donut store was open and Lin was behind the counter. She smiled warmly as Norris came through the door. She finished helping the young mother who was in front of Mark, then gave him a once over.

"Where you been, coach? You trying to no longer be my best customer?"

Mark thought that she intentionally made her accent into "Movie Asian" just for the effect whenever he was around.

"I'm a working man, Lin. I have to earn the millions that I spend here!"

"Psst… Ha! Millions! Tran!" she yelled into the back bakery area. "Mr. Coach Mark say he spend millions dollars here! You been hiding all this money from me?" Several of the regular customers looked at Mark with knowing glances.

Her husband, Tran, stuck his head around the corner and smiled. "Yes, dear. I keep it hidden in back here so I can run away with Terry when she gets older." He smiled at Mark, referring to his oldest daughter. "We're making plans right now to run away to the Caribbean."

"Ha! She wouldn't give you the time of day, you lecherous old man! Go back and finish baking before I call police on you for child molestation! Mr. Coach Mark, how many kids today?" Lin said as she began folding a pink box and sliding tab A through slot B. "Jim is there?"

"Yes, ma'am… about eight kids, I think."

As soon as she heard confirmation of Jim's presence, she grabbed two maple bars, his favorite, and began filling two boxes with Mark's standard load out of donuts and muffins. She turned to the fridge and pointed with a raised eyebrow. Mark shook his head no.

"Hokay, that's $18.16 millions dollars, please," she said with a smile.

Mark handed her a $20.00 and was walking out the door when he heard a scream. Looking around the parking lot of the little strip mall, he saw the young mother who had just been in the donut store pushing aside another woman who was clawing at the back seat of a Toyota Sequoia.

Mark set the donuts on top of his car and began jogging toward the confrontation. The young mom had succeeded in throwing the other woman to the ground. She had turned back to her daughter when the other woman got up and jumped on her back, pulling her head back with her hair and striking her in the face. Just as Mark came around the open car door, the female attacker swung her head forward and bit into the mother's scalp. The mother began thrashing around, making it hard for Mark to grab a hold of the assailant. He finally got a handful of her hair and wrenched her head back. A strip of the young mother's skin peeled back with it. Mark twisted the woman's arm behind her back, but no matter how much pressure he applied, she kept struggling until her arm finally broke with an audible crack.

He got her wrestled to the ground and was kneeling on her neck when an SDPD cruiser pulled into the lot. As the officers got out of the patrol car, they noticed that Mark's shirt had ridden up over his holstered gun. They both drew their guns and began yelling at the two combatants. They had to rush forward and restrain the young mother, who had gone to the back of her car and was approaching Mark and her attacker with an upraised tire iron.

"I'm an off-duty reserve with the SO!" Mark shouted as he continued to try to subdue the wildly gyrating woman underneath him. "ID is in my back pocket! Can you guys help me get cuffs on her? She's 5150!"

The two SDPD officers rushed forward and began helping to restrain the woman who was screaming louder than the young girl in the back seat of the Sequoia. After handcuffing the woman, she was placed in leg restraints and a bite bag. The bite bag was a thick canvas bag that was placed over the suspect's head to prevent the officers from getting bit.

After they securely restrained the suspect, the officers began to treat the young mom, who was trying to console her severely shaken up daughter. Lin, from the donut shop, had brought out a first-aid kit and had a thick gauze bandage pressed to the wound on the mom's head. As the chaos began to settle down, Mark heard sirens for the third time that morning.

CHAPTER 13

CDC, Atlanta, GA

The heavily laden executive jet had come in from the north over Clifton Road and slammed into the CDC building right at ground level. The terrorists didn't have bunker buster technology, but they did have explosives—lots of them. And quantity has a quality all its own. The blast from the explosion leveled the upper floors of the building, collapsing it onto the underground labs. It also severely damaged the quarantine building next door. And although the labs survived the blast, it took rescue workers two days to get to all the survivors from the underground complex.

Anna Napolitano and Gary Little were trapped for seventeen hours in his office before a sound of moving rubble and a flashlight beam told them that help was there. Forty minutes of digging later, they were pulled through a narrow opening, sent down one of the tunnels, and then up to ground level to be processed at the FEMA center that had been set up in the parking lot. Anna looked around and noticed the lack of people.

"Where is everyone?" she asked a harried worker who was recording her name and work location in a ledger. "I thought there would be more people here."

"All non-essential personnel were ordered home when the attacks started. Martial law has been declared until we can figure out what happened."

"Attacks? We were attacked here?" Little came up beside Anna. "Who attacked us?"

"We were attacked everywhere! I'm sorry, I didn't even think about the fact that you guys have been underground for the better part of a day." She handed Anna's CDC ID back to her and took Little's. "Director Little, the U.S. was attacked by over a hundred kamikaze aircraft yesterday. They were all small aircraft but were packed with explosives. Most of them flew around dropping bombs or something into various lakes and stuff. Then they all crashed into either a federal building or FBI office. Some crashed into the railway bridges across the Mississippi. All five of the major ones were blown up. Several key government buildings were hit. But they left congress and the White House alone; I guess they finally figured out how worthless they are."

Little let out a short bark of laughter at that but quickly controlled himself. He nodded his thanks to the young lady and gestured Anna over to the side of the tent. "We have problems."

"Oh, yes we do!" Anna was still dazed by it all. "If these attacks are related to this toxin, and those planes were dumping it in water supplies before they crashed, we could have casualties in the tens of thousands!"

"Oh, kiddo, I think if they did all that with the damage to the infrastructure and federal law enforcement, we'll see much higher numbers than that!"

Little had his Blackberry out and was typing on the keypad. The cell phone had not had service underground, but the wall outlet had worked, so both of their phones were charged. "Have you called your kids yet? They must be frantic."

"I sent my mom and dad a text as soon as I got above ground. They're waiting for me at their house. They haven't heard from Troy yet." Anna's husband was a major in the Army and currently deployed to Iraq. "How about Laurie? You get ahold of her?"

"Nope, it just goes to voicemail. Sent her a text too. I have to get this info to Washington immediately." Although Little sounded calm, his stomach was doing flip-flops. His house was on a lake that supplied water to the city, and the house drew its water from a ground well that shared the same aquifer.

"Gary!"

He turned his head at the sound of his wife's voice, looking frantically for her.

"Gary! Over here!" Laurie Little was waving from the far side of a police barricade next to the tent they had just left. He ran over and hugged his wife across the barricade. Anna following at a slower pace. "Oh, honey, we were so worried. I didn't know what to do until Martin called and said they were still getting people out of the labs."

"Where are the boys?" Gary asked, looking around for his two sons.

"They're at the house. Claire's watching them." She held him back at arm's length, taking in his scratched and bruised face and the torn and dirty suit. "Are you hurt?"

"I'm fine. I need you to call the house, though, and tell them not to drink any water out of the faucets, okay? Nothing out of the plumbing. Don't touch the water. You got that, babe? I'm serious!" Gary looked down at his vibrating phone, then turned away to answer it.

"How bad were the attacks, Laurie?" Anna asked as Gary walked away from them for some privacy.

"Are you okay?" Laurie asked as she turned to Anna.

"I'm fine. I was giving a report to Gary when the bomb—"

"Plane."

"Sorry—when the *plane* hit. My lab area is under a bunch of rubble. I was down in Gary's office giving him a report on a chemical attack in Minnesota that we think might be related to these airplanes. One of the workers inside the tent said that the planes were flying over bodies of water before crashing into stuff. Is that true?" Anna flashed her ID and gestured at one of the police officers manning the barricade to let Laurie through.

"That's what was reported on the news. They said a bunch of the planes were flying without doors on them, and their flight paths showed that they had all flown over a whole bunch of municipal water supplies before crashing into buildings. The buildings were all federal courthouses or law enforcement offices. Almost five thousand dead at last count. Oh, and the railroads; they hit the railroad bridges across the Mississippi… like four or five of the main ones." She stopped to catch her breath. "It sounds horrible, but I don't think it was as bad as it could have been. Did you say chemical attack? We didn't hear any reports about them spraying anything."

Gary turned back around and walked over to them. "Did you tell them about the water, hon?" He had his face down in the Blackberry again.

"What? Oh yeah, just a sec." Laurie fished out her phone and scrolled through her contacts, then held it up to her ear.

While she was making the call, Gary pulled Anna aside and brought her up to speed on Minnesota. "The chemical was dispersed into several creeks, apparently by a couple of terrorists who didn't realize how it would affect all the animals. A bear got to them and tore them up. The FBI is trying to investigate, but they were the number one target of the physical attacks; they've lost a lot of agents. Layver reported in that the chemical was dispersed so widely that they are seeing the effects statewide. Also, the serum is transferable, like you said. They have had massive exposure to the toxin… animals attacking humans… humans going wild. If that is ground zero, and these guys poisoned as much of the municipal water supplies as I think, then the U.S. is pretty much hosed."

"Babe, Claire was just going to bathe them. I told her no. She says that she can use baby wipes, but they were in the lake most of the day and are covered in mud." Laurie stopped at the stricken look on her husband's face. "Oh no, don't tell me they're going to be sick."

"Babe, listen; I need you to do exactly as I say, okay? Exactly!" He took her by the upper arms and looked firmly in her eyes. "I need you to go to the store and get bottled water. I don't care if it's in big jugs or little bottles, just get as much as you can. I don't want you or the kids to drink any water from the tap. If one of the boys develops a fever, I want you to restrain him and make sure you use bite prevention. Do not get bit by them or anyone! Go by and get as much cash from the banks, first, now that I think about it. Credit cards services may go down, but use them first if you can; save the cash for if things get bad. Then get canned goods and as much non-perishables as you can. Get them at a couple of stores, and don't tell anyone where you heard about this stuff. There's already going to be a run on foodstuffs because of the attacks. Then I want you to go home and board up the house. I mean all the extra lumber from the boathouse and dock needs to be boarded across all the ground-floor windows and doors. Buy some extra batteries for the radios—they're AA, I think. Call me when you have all that done. Anna and I are going to Washington as soon as a car gets here. I'll call you when I'm on the ground. Do you have all that?"

"Okay, so basically prepare for the end of the world. Am I right?"

"That's about it. There is definitely going to be civil unrest in the next few days. And once you're in the house, don't open it for anyone. People are going to be reacting violently to this chemical. If anyone, even a friend is acting odd, do not let them in." Gary's shoulders slumped with fatigue. "You know the combo to my gun safe; get out your pistol and the AR-15. Babe, you are going to have to be able to defend the house. I'll call you as soon as I'm on the ground and update you."

"I love you."

"I love you too." With a last hug, Gary and Anna climbed into the waiting GMC Yukon and headed to the airport, where a USAF Gulfstream was waiting for them.

CHAPTER 14

Rancho Bernardo, CA

It was after 0930 by the time Mark got back to the house. After checking his ID, the two PD officers had loaded the thrashing woman into the back of their patrol car and interviewed all the witnesses. They told Mark that the first calls of weird and violent behavior had started at about 0400 that morning. At first, it seemed to be a few domestic violence disturbances, but it soon became clear that something else was at play. The calls were not "typical" domestic violence calls. Almost all of them involved some form of mutual combat and extreme violence.

He stopped at the CVS for a gallon of milk and a gallon of OJ, and then headed home. Mark pulled the Porsche into the garage and closed the door. After gathering all the donuts, OJ, and milk, he managed to stagger into the kitchen without dropping anything. He deposited everything on the counter and was putting the OJ in the fridge when the first of the living dead came through the archway from the den. Chris had bags under his eyes and looked worse than the corpses in most Romero films.

"Hey, coach," he said as he shuffled up to the counter. "Anything good in there?" He began rooting through the first box of donuts.

"Touch one of those maple bars, and Jim will pound you!" Mark said, pouring himself a huge glass of milk. He went over and pulled a couple of regular glazed from the box, put them on a paper towel, and went into his office. He turned on the TV mounted in the bookcase with the remote after setting the donuts and milk down. He plopped into his executive chair and leaned back to watch the news.

He was calling into the staff duty officer when the news was interrupted by an urgent broadcast. The Emergency Broadcast System activated and began scrolling information about tainted drinking water. The CDC announced that hundreds, possibly thousands, of municipal water sources had been contaminated with a substance that caused severe fever and violent behavior. People who were bitten by a person with a high concentration of the serum in their saliva suffered the same effects. The compound affected all higher-order mammals, and even dogs and cats should be approached with caution.

Mark bolted out of his chair when he heard the tap turn on in the kitchen. He flew across the room and sprinted into the kitchen to see Jim rinsing out a glass in the sink.

"Did you drink the water?" he yelled as he pulled his son's arm away from the sink.

"Huh?" Jim looked at him like he was crazy. "I had some OJ."

"Get all the kids down here now! I want everybody in here and no one turns on a tap! Do you understand?"

"All right, okay, don't freak out," Jim said, pulling his arm away. "I'll get them. What? Is our water poisoned or something?"

"It sure as hell is," Mark said, looking around. He spied the dogs' water tower and got a sinking feeling. "Where are the dogs?"

"Out back." He followed his father's gaze to the dogs' water bowl. "Oh shit! Tell me they'll be all right, Dad!"

Mark looked at his son and said, "I don't know… Don't go out there. Get the kids rounded up and in the kitchen."

Mark went out the back slider, thought about what he was doing, and drew his pistol. He moved to the edge of the patio and peeked around the corner. No dogs. He moved along the back wall of the garage, to the pad on the side of the house. He peeked around this corner, only to see both dogs down on the ground, peering under the gate at something on the street. He was just about to call them when buster growled. Thor let out a rumble a few seconds later.

Mark decided to wait and see what happened. If the dogs were just doing their normal protect-the-house routine, he would call them over. If they showed any signs of abnormal behavior, though, he would be forced to put them down. He kept his Glock at his side and waited.

After a few seconds, the growling stopped and the stubs that were the dogs' tails began to wag as they recognized someone familiar. Seeing them in a somewhat normal state, Mark let out a special lilting whistle. Both dogs immediately turned toward him and trotted over, wagging their stubs.

As soon as they were in front of him, Mark said, “Seitz!” and both dogs immediately sat down.

“You stay!” he said and went back around to the dogs’ water tower. The huge five-gallon Arrowhead jug was over half full. He tried to think of the last time he had filled it from his hose, decided *better safe than sorry* and was about to dump it in his garden when he thought, *That would be just smart. If I dump it and it is poison, I’ll just be leaving it in my garden.*

He picked up the jug, carried it into the sink, and turned it upside down to drain. He stopped himself and set it on the floor then went back outside, picked up the bowl, and dumped that back into the jug. Once it was all done, he dried the bowl with a clean towel.

By now, all the kids were packed in the area around the kitchen island and table. They were all looking a little concerned as Mark moved with an intensity that showed he was very serious. Most of the kids had been on one team or another that he had coached and knew when it was okay to ask questions. This was not one of them.

“Terry, I need you to take the dogs’ water tower into the garage. Set it up there and use a fresh, five-gallon jug of Arrowhead. If there are any empty jugs, fill them up but put silver duct tape on them and write ‘Flush water only’ on them.” He handed her the base and bowl.

“Jim, I want you to turn off the automatic sprinklers. Then I want you to go out to the street and turn off the water main to the house.”

He was just turning to the other kids when he had a second thought and said, “Belay that; wait until I’m done here and I’ll go with you as over watch.”

Jim immediately understood that to mean that their own front yard could be dangerous. He started looking out the windows. He jumped when the garage door slammed shut behind Terry as she went out to set up the dogs’ water.

“Mel, you’re my communications girl, okay? I need you to do the following things, and I need the rest of you to listen up as well,” he said, addressing the rest of the now scared teenagers. “I need you to call all the relatives in our phone tree. You tell them not to trust ANY municipal water supply. Only water that was bottled before two days ago. The water will be turned off here in the house. No one is to drink any water that came from a tap or faucet. Got it?” He made eye contact with every person in the room until they had all acknowledged him.

“Kids, I want you all to call your folks and tell them that all the city’s and county’s water supplies have been poisoned. Tell them that if they haven’t seen the news yet today, they need to watch it. This poison is making people act violently; I saw it myself this morning. We’re going to take you guys home in the truck in a few minutes, if that’s where your parents want you to go. If your folks aren't home then you are welcome to stay here. I need you to tell Mel so she can make a list of who needs to go where. Got it?" He again waited for every kid to acknowledge him.

"Okay, let's get it done!" He went to the garage safe and got out a Remington 11-87 automatic shotgun. He stoked the extended magazine with seven rounds of 00 buck, chambered a round, and then put one more in the tubular magazine. After grabbing a bandolier of shells, he checked the Surefire light mounted on the front (even though it was broad daylight outside), made sure the safety was on, placed the sling over his shoulder, double-checked the pistol on his hip, and then handed an identical shotgun to Jim.

After Terry told them she had filled all the available containers, they repeated the loading-out process then went to the front door and looked up and down the street. With no one in sight, they moved out to the corner of the truck. Mark went forward with the shotgun at the low ready. After another sweep of the street, he motioned Jim forward. He crouched down next to the water meter and turned off the flow valve. He was backing toward the house when he heard the scream from up the street. A second later, there was the sound of breaking glass and then a thud.

Mark moved out toward the sidewalk, far enough to see what had happened. Across the street and about eighty meters west, one of his neighbors stood over the body of a man on the ground. She was sobbing and holding a baseball bat that had a streak of blood on it.

"Cheryl! Are you okay?" Mark kept the shotgun pointed down at the ground, but it was still pointed in the direction he was looking.

Cheryl looked up, startled. Her head swiveled back and forth twice before she saw Mark with the shotgun.

"He was attacking Kelly!" she yelled as she dropped the bat. "He crawled through her window and just went at her!" She kept glancing down at the man on the ground.

"Is that George?" Mark asked.

"Yes. I've never seen him like that! He just started clawing at her and growling like a dog. She made it into the bathroom and locked herself in. When I came around the corner, he came at me."

"Is Sarah okay?" Cheryl had two teenage daughters. Both had played on a team Mark had coached at one time or another. Mark was slowly walking toward Cheryl.

"She's already at the pool for swim."

"Oh shit!" Mark looked around and closed the last few feet with the distraught mother. "Can you get a hold of her? Tell her to get home right away. The city's water supply has been poisoned. You guys need to get behind some closed doors and hunker down."

"Oh, you don't really believe that stuff on the news, do you?" Cheryl had a look of incredulity on her face. "I mean, really, people going crazy from the water…"

She stopped talking as Mark looked at her, then down at the unconscious form lying at her feet and raised an eyebrow.

"I'm pretty sure it's for real. I saw a woman attack a young mother and her baby this morning. I would take what the news says very seriously for the next few weeks." Mark was keeping his head on a swivel as he talked. "Get your daughter out of the pool for sure. Do what you like, but I'd be careful. People are freaking out over everything that's going on."

"Okay. What are we going to do about him?" she said, gesturing toward the prone form on the ground.

"I'll take care of him; you just get your girls safe." Mark turned to yell at Jim. "Jim, get my flex cuffs from my SO bag, please. And be careful coming over here!"

"Okay, Pop!" he yelled back and went into the house.

"Why were you in the front yard with a shotgun, Mark?" Cheryl had an eyebrow raised. Between the Marine Corps and his part-time job as a reserve deputy sheriff, Mark had a reputation as kind of a "gun nut" in the neighborhood.

"I was turning off the water main so no more tainted water can make it into the house."

"What are you going to use for water then?" Cheryl was looking askance at him.

"Well, we'll drink bottled water and use unsafe water to flush with. The sewer system should still accept flow."

"And how will you bathe?"

"We won't at first." Mark watched as Jim jogged across the street, looking around with wide-open eyes. "We'll use baby wipes until we know how to make our water safe. We may wind up having to distill it."

"You know, you never really notice all the hiding places and bushes in the neighborhood until you're looking for the boogeyman to pop out!" Jim said, handing over the "go" bag.

He covered the unconscious neighbor as Mark slipped a pair of flex-cuffs on the man's wrists behind his back. A roll of duct tape was used to cover his mouth. Mark, not being one to leave things to chance, wrapped it around his head several times.

"I bet you're enjoying the hell out of that," Cheryl said, referring to the fact that there was no love lost between the nosey old man and Mark. Mark grunted and grinned up at her as he rolled the overweight man onto his back. A large knot had formed on the left side of his forehead with a long gash running through the middle of it. Mark felt it and noticed the hot feel of the skin right away.

"Jim, help me drag his fat butt up to his door. We'll leave him just inside, in case any more crazies come around, and then we'll notify the PD." Mark had the senior citizen under his arms and was walking backwards with him. The shotgun banged on his hip and smacked the first step before he decided to unsling it. He handed it to Cheryl after making sure the safety was engaged. He then continued to drag the unconscious man up the three steps to his front door.

The door was locked, of course. Mark had Jim watch the front as he retrieved his shotgun then went around to check the back door. Everything seemed all right until he stepped through the open rear sliding glass door. The smell of blood was strong and two steps into the house, he was able to see the torn up remains of George's schnauzer. The dog was fully disemboweled, and gore was smeared over the entire dining area. Mark quickly made his way to the front door and opened it.

As they were pulling George over the threshold, he began to come around. At first, it was just a back and forth tossing of the head. As they laid him on the couch, he became fully conscious and began to thrash around. He managed to get to his feet and charge at Mark, who laid him out with one clean butt stroke to the head. Although he didn't lose consciousness this time, he was slow getting up. Mark and Jim flipped him on his belly and zip-tied his legs to his wrists. They left him lying on the floor in the living room.

Mark went to the back door and locked it, then moved everyone onto the front porch. He went back inside to the kitchen and gave the pantry a once-over, taking note of both perishables and non-perishables. He then searched the rest of the house and found George's gun cabinet and the stacks of ammo on a shelf in the spare bedroom. He found a Remington Model 597 in .22 long rifle and two 500-round bricks of CCI ammunition for it. He ran downstairs to check on George, who was struggling with his bonds, and passed the rifle and .22 ammo out to Jim.

"Cheryl, I need you to go back inside your house and lock up. I'm going to have Jim go with you and show you how to operate this rifle." He was handing the three magazines he found to Jim. "James, my boy, I need you to show her everything. How to load the magazines, how to load and chamber the rounds in the rifle, and how to unload and clear it—everything."

"Okay, Dad. What are you going to be doing?" Jim was stuffing the magazines into his pockets while still looking around.

"I'm going to loot George's cache of weapons and ammo. I don't know what state of mind he's in, but I don't want him having access while he's like this." He looked over to see a disapproving look on Cheryl's face. "I'll leave a receipt, okay?"

"I'm sorry, I'm just having a hard time getting my head around this," Cheryl said, dropping her gaze and refusing to meet Mark's eyes.

"It's all right." Mark turned to Jim. "I want you to have her snap in, okay? I want you to set up a target and have her start through dry-practice training."

"You got it, Pop." Jim brought his shotgun to his shoulder and panned the street. Mark let him lead off across the yard toward Cheryl's front door. As they came up on the front porch, Kelly opened the door for them and stepped aside as they came through.

"You okay, kiddo?" Mark asked as he turned and bolted the door. "Did he bite you?"

"Yes, sir, I'm okay." Kelly had dried tears on her face but otherwise appeared in good shape. "He didn't bite me, just a scratch."

"Jim, it's marksmanship 101 for both of them, okay?" Mark said.

"Okay."

"You guys lock this house up tight, and I'll be back in a few minutes. And remember NO water from the taps," he said, pointing toward the kitchen. "Do you have bottled water?"

"About half a case left, I think," Kelly said as she looked in wonder at all the guns.

Mark stepped out on the front porch. "Lock up after me."

He looked back toward his house to see a Honda Odyssey mini-van pulling into the driveway. Tia came walking down the sidewalk from the front door as if she didn't have a care in the world. Mark jogged over to see Alan, Tia's father, step out of the driver's door with a .357 in his hand. Mark slowed and kept the shotgun ready as he approached.

"Oh, thank God you're all right," Alan said, wrapping his daughter up in a hug.

"Yeah, like something could happen with Coach Rambo here, Dad. Really!" Tia exclaimed as she wiggled out of the embrace. "Coach has been running around like he's back in Afghanistan." She pointed out the shotgun and other accoutrements.

"Well, I'm glad he has," he said, nodding to Mark. "We had about a dozen people at work go crazy and attack other people in the office. I got out of there and went home. I couldn't get a hold of your mother, so that's when I called you."

"You know about the water, right?" Mark asked, keeping an eye on the street.

“Yeah, something about boiling it, right?” Alan was also looking around and noticed the panorama of faces at the living room window. “Do you need me to drive kids home?”

“I don’t know. Go inside and ask Mel what’s up. She’s been contacting parents and such,” Mark said, gesturing toward the front door. “I’d appreciate it if you could hang out for a few till I get my neighbor squared away.”

“No problem; I was going to go by and check on Tia’s mom, but her not answering my calls is pretty typical,” Alan said with a grimace.

“Great, I’ll be back in a few.” And with that, Mark was jogging across the street again. He was less than halfway back to George’s front door when movement to the right caught his eye.

Mary-Beth Peters lived half a block farther up the street. The female bodybuilder was normally the sweetest person on the block. That perception was immediately erased by the blood-soaked jog bra and horribly stained clothes she was wearing. She had come out from around the side of her house and, upon seeing Mark, turned right toward him. She let out a low rumbling growl as she sped up to a full sprint in Mark’s direction.

“Freeze, Mary-Beth!” Mark screamed at the top of his lungs. This usually brought most people up short, as Mark had done time on the drill field as a drill instructor for the Marines before becoming an officer. It only served to focus Mary-Beth’s attention on Mark.

Without hesitation, Mark raised the Remington, picked up the sight picture through the EoTech Holo sight, and fired a round of buckshot at the lower torso of the charging woman. The nine pellets struck her in a pattern centered just to the left of her belly button. One pellet punched into the top of her femur, splintering it, while another shattered the pelvis above the hip socket. Two of the .30-caliber balls were stopped by the substantial muscle of her abdomen and barely made it to her bladder. The trauma was massive, and with the shattering of the bones, Mary-Beth fell face first to the street and rolled forward to stop about forty feet from where Mark was still moving toward George’s house.

Mary-Beth continued to try to pull herself forward on her stomach, leaving a blood trail eight inches wide as she did so. Her growls never changing in pitch, she followed Mark’s movements with her eyes. As he continued to jog past, she turned to attempt to follow him. Mark gave her a wide berth and continued up to the front porch, telling Jim, who had poked his head out of Cheryl’s front door, that everything was fine.

Mark almost received a bite on the leg as he stepped into George’s house.

George had worked his right hand loose, tearing away most of the skin, and was just inside the front door. With his hand free, he was able to rip most of the tape from his mouth; then using his liberated hand and still bound legs, he lunged at Mark and almost sink his teeth into his right leg. Mark leapt back and lashed out with the butt of the shotgun in almost the same movement. The descending blow finally completed what the three blows earlier that day had started. George's skull split open and he sank to the floor.

Mark shook his head and stepped across the threshold; he was just closing the door when he heard the popping sound of .22 fire from outside. He looked out the side window by the front door to see a blood-covered teenager lying in the front yard. Another pop sounded and Mark saw the .22 round impact the boy's head. He could tell by angle of the shot that it had come from Cheryl's second story. Mark ran up to the guest bedroom on the second floor, pulling a 00 buck round from his bandoleer and shoving it in the magazine tube of his shotgun along the way. He looked out the window to see Jim coaching Cheryl as she aimed out at the street. He noticed Mary-Beth crawling toward the downed teenager and watched in fascination as she began biting and chewing on the corpse. He looked over at Jim and Cheryl, who were also staring at the surreal scene below them. When Jim looked up, Mark nodded, and Jim put a round through their former neighbor's head.

Mark again searched the upstairs, finding the key ring to the gun cabinet and all the cable locks. He pulled out everything and laid it out on the bed. He then pulled out all the ammunition and laid it out, matching the firearm it was for at the foot of the bed. There were seven long guns and three pistols.

The long guns consisted of a nice over/under 20-gauge shotgun with 50 rounds of target load and another 35 of birdshot. There was also an old lever action Marlin in .30-.30 with over 200 rounds and a Savage .308 bolt gun, which was equipped with a mediocre scope. The Springfield M1 he found was also in .308 and had about 300 rounds for both. He was pleased to find a Winchester Model 70 bolt gun in 375 H&H Magnum with a much nicer Nikon scope, even though it had only about 60 rounds of various types of ammo for it. A Ruger Mini-14 in .223 with two full ammo cans of 420 rounds of Federal 62-grain ball and a Bennelli Super 90 Tactical with two ammo cans (360 rounds) of Winchester 00 buck rounded out the collection.

George's collection of pistols wasn't quite as extensive as his inventory of long guns. There was a Colt Commander Series 80 in .45, a Springfield .45 standard, and a Ruger GP100 .357 magnum revolver. There were over

1000 rounds of ball ammo for the .45s and almost 200 rounds of .38 special +P for the Ruger.

"And they call me the 'gun nut'!" Mark muttered as he headed down to the garage.

Mark found several hard and soft gun cases and two old sea bags, which he brought inside the house. He went through the garage and noted the tools and some camping supplies for later use if things got bad. Finding nothing further of immediate use though, he took the cases and one of the sea bags up to the bedroom, leaving the other sea bag in the kitchen.

He packed the M1, Mini-14, and Bennelli into cases and put all the ammo into the sea bag, which made it very heavy. He put the pistols in their cases and added them to the sea bag as well. Hoisting the bag on his back with the backpack straps on the side, he put the tactical sling for his shotgun over his shoulder. He was going to be a very slow mover. He waddled over to the guest bedroom window and shouted across to Jim.

"I'm gonna haul all this crap over to our house in a few minutes. I have to load up some food downstairs," he yelled across to the two faces in the window. "Cover me, please!"

Jim nodded and took the rifle from Cheryl as she moved out of the way. He took up a good firing position and shouted back, "I gotcha!"

Mark went back and grabbed the three cased long guns, letting his shotgun bounce against his chest as he went downstairs. He set the cases and sea bag next to the front door and went to raid the pantry. Being a bachelor, George had a lot of prepackaged food in both his fridge and pantry. Mark could not find any bottled water and remembered a conversation where George had stated that anyone who paid outrageous prices for bottled water when it came out of the tap for free was an idiot. He did find several bags of pancake mix and three unopened boxes of Bisquick. He split these, putting half in the duffle from earlier and half in the second sea bag. He divided the rest of the spoils up evenly and took those two bags to the front door as well. George's corpse was starting to smell and the bowels had let loose. *Should have taken him out back when he was fresh.*

Mark checked the front through the windows and stepped out on the porch with the shotgun up and ready. After making sure there were no threats out front, he turned, grabbed the small duffle, ran the few steps to Cheryl's porch, and left the supplies there. He ran back and managed to make two trips across to his own house when a shout from Jim warned him of impending trouble.

He looked down the street in the opposite direction from George and Cheryl's houses and saw a disheveled figure shambling toward him. He was just going to turn back and continue running for Cheryl's house when another crazy person came sprinting out from the same side of the street as Mark's house. The running figure slammed into the slower moving one and they both went to the ground. What followed was nothing but sheer savagery.

The shambling figure had heard the approach of the other feral and turned toward it, but it was too late to avoid the full-body impact of the collision. Clawing and snapping at each other, the two combatants rolled over twice before coming to a stop, with the slower larger one on top. They continued to rip into each other until they both collapsed from the grievous injuries they had inflicted. After a few moments, the larger man staggered up and began shuffling up the street with an even more pronounced limp. Its injuries caused it to stagger back and forth. Mark stood mesmerized until Jim yelled down to him.

"Do you want me to take him down, Dad?"

Mark shook himself loose from the grisly scene and nodded.

The pop of the .22 was followed by the collapse of the man. He toppled over onto his right side and finally came to rest. A second pop resulted in a round just missing the other man who was still lying down the street. Mark was just turning to ask Jim what that was all about when a third shot from the .22 struck the cranium of the smaller downed man.

"Just making sure, Dad," Jim said as he pulled the magazine from the rifle and gave Cheryl and Kelly a now redundant lesson on refilling the mag.

Mark jogged up to Cheryl's door and was let in immediately.

"He didn't have any kind of bottled water," Mark said, gesturing toward the bag of supplies on the ground. "I put half of his food stuffs in here except for his perishables. We still have power, so we might as well let his fridge keep it cold. If the power goes out, we'll have to recover it and use it right away, but it's fine where it is now. I brought you one of his pistols and the ammo for it." With that, he took out the GP100 revolver and several boxes of the Winchester hollow points.

Mark gave them a thorough lesson in operating the pistol, explaining the difference between double action and single action. Another session of dry practice, and Mark pronounced them competent enough to get themselves in trouble. He walked through the house, making sure it was as secure as he could make it. With that done, he and Jim met the girls at the front door.

"Cheryl, I hope you can get this place squared away. Okay, I have a bunch of kids to take care of, so we're out of here. I know you have to go get Sarah. I'll walk you out to your car and make sure you're off okay. I would suggest getting bottled water if you can, but be careful when you get out of the car. Let me know if you need anything." Mark and Jim escorted Cheryl and Kelly out to a Hyundai SUV after Kelly closed and locked the door. They then trotted back across the street to see a window full of faces watching them.

Mark watched Cheryl drive down the street; she had to swerve to avoid the two corpses that still lay in the middle of the road. He then walked to the small gate on the opposite side of the garage and put the padlock on it. He did the same to the large vehicle gate next to the garage. As they walked into the garage from the outside door and secured it, Mark said, "Let's get the fire panels down."

In 2007, a series of wildfires had devastated San Diego County. Hundreds of homes had burned down, including three on the same block that Mark lived on. Part of the fireproofing improvements had been lag bolt-mounted, steel shutters. The three-eighths-inch thick shutters each had a small view slit in them and were mounted on bolts that were countersunk into the concrete surrounding the window molding. The shutters would be a deterrent to any unwanted company.

As Jim and Terry were bringing the shutters down from the loft in the garage, Mark checked in with the other kids to see how the phone calls were working out and to have Mel attempt to notify the police about the violence that had occurred in the street out front. Mel had taken over the end barstool at the kitchen counter and created a new document on the iPad. She was furiously typing with her phone to one ear.

"I think we've got it all, Mark." Tia was next to her and texting on her phone. "Mel called all your family she could and left messages or spoke to someone. We tried calling 9-1-1, but the message says all circuits are busy and to hang up and call 9-1-1 if it's an emergency. I wonder what genius thought of that? She can tell you all the particulars. She's on the phone with Erin right now. I guess some people freaked out in her neighborhood. Her parents went to Target to get some stuff, and Erin says she's seen like five fights in front of her house. She's totally freaked out!"

"Okay, let me make a phone call and then we'll get this house locked down." Mark strode into his office, noticing Alan standing watch at the front window and made the call he had failed to complete earlier in the morning.

He got through to the staff duty on only the second try. He was informed that there had been many incidents of violence, and they were in complete lockdown. No one was to come or go. As they were talking, Mark actually heard gunfire in the background. The duty officer explained that the word had gotten out too late about the water and several units had filled up from municipal supplies. Any unit that had a Marine go berserk was immediately quarantined. Because this involved restraining all the personnel, some of the Marines in several units actively resisted the quarantine. Since there was no way yet to test for exposure, they were not allowing anyone on the base.

Mark gathered the kids in the den and stood in front of them.

"Okay guys, this is what we're gonna do…"

CHAPTER 15

Bemidji, MN

So, this is the apocalypse, Dan thought as he looked at the wreckage of what had once been his and Scott's childhood hometown, the city of Bemidji. Several fires were burning unchecked. There were bodies lying in plain view. One house on the outskirts of town had literally piles of bodies in a ring outside of it. The owner and his son had two .22-caliber rifles with little bitty scopes that they had used to kill over forty feral people that had tried to rush their house. The sound of the gunfire had only brought more crazies running. Dan and Scott pulled up in front of the house and used a bullhorn to ask the two men if they needed anything.

"If you get to the Walmart and there's any .22 ammo left, we could use some. But we got another four or five thousand rounds in bricks right now, and then we'll start using our real guns!" Dan and Scott acknowledged the request with a wave and headed farther into town.

"That's not a bad idea, you know. Raiding the Wal-Mart," Dan said as he drove the truck around the corner slowly.

"We'll see about that. I don't think we're down to the level of looting stores yet."

"What the hell do you mean 'not at that level'?" Dan was staring at his brother like he just grew an elbow out of his forehead. "One-third of the population is infected, or poisoned, or whatever you call it. And they've eaten another third of the population! That only leaves a third of us left, Big Bro! We are definitely at the loot-for-survival level!"

"We have plenty of ammo at the district office; let's go there first and see what we can. Then we'll talk about Walmart." Scott was constantly scanning their surroundings. Most people were inside and following the instructions given to them. Some had ventured out for supplies and run into trouble. The population centers were where the most person-on-person casualties occurred, but because animals were reacting to the chemical agent as well, people were dying from animal attacks. Dogs turned on their owners and cats would jump on unwary passersby if they weren't already engaged in a fight.

The two rangers had to be hyper-vigilant wherever they were. Attacks came from all directions and at any time. They had donned full tactical armor and wore long underwear, in spite of the heat. With only their faces exposed, they would have cooked quickly if not for the truck's air conditioning, which was going full blast. They were still sweating buckets, which was not good for their hydration. They were going through Gatorade and bottled water at an alarming rate.

"There it is," Scott said unnecessarily. He pointed to the brownstone building. "Pull around back and let's see if we can get in without attracting any attention."

"Roger that." Dan was already heading for the open gate to the back lot when there was a loud thud at the back of the truck. As both of the men looked in the rearview mirrors, they saw a crowd of about fifteen people running toward the truck. One of them was hanging on the tailgate and attempting to pull himself into the bed. Scott turned around and opened the rear-sliding window.

"There goes our cool air," Dan said as he felt the hot air on the back of his neck.

"Well, you don't want me to shoot through it, do you?" Scott said as he aimed at the face of the man who was pulling himself over the tailgate. "Round out."

The hollow-point bullet left the barrel at a scorching 1250 feet per second. It impacted the man right on his nose. Because of the angle that his head was to the bullet's flight path, the hollow point blew his front two teeth down into his tongue and sent shards of bone upwards into the nasal cavity. By the time it had expanded to a diameter of .68 inches, it had impacted the spine and ricocheted off to the right-hand side, leaving a gaping wound in the back of the man's neck. The bullet wasn't done causing damage though. It then penetrated the left side of a teenage girl, passing between two ribs and puncturing her lung before becoming wedged against a rib in her back. She managed to take a few more steps before she collapsed from the lack of air. She would have struggled on for another several minutes before dying, but two of the other pack members immediately turned and began to eat her.

"Well, do you want to drive around the block and try to lose them, or do you want to just pull in the yard and deal with them there?" Dan asked as he picked up just enough speed to keep the enraged runners behind them.

"Might as well just deal with 'em." Scott holstered his pistol and worked his M4 out the window. "Take me on a wide slow right, and I'll take care of them."

As the truck bounced through the entry gate, Scott hitched himself so that the ejection port of his rifle would spit the brass outside the truck. He then waited as the crazed crowd stumbled into the equipment storage lot. Dan had slowed the truck to almost a crawl when Scott opened fire. He was aiming for the pelvic area. It was a lot easier to hit and was a blood-rich area. Also, physics was physics, if you broke the "bone bridge," the person could no longer stand. He fired seven shots when a crazed man came running out from between two road-salting trucks and tackled the woman he was aiming at. The ensuing fight was brutal and quick. The others in the pack fell on the man and ripped him to shreds. Then two of the pack started fighting with each other and total chaos ensued. In a matter of seconds, all the affected people were dead or incapacitated. Only one could stand up afterward, and Scott put a bullet in her brain as soon as she did.

"Let's drive around the yard a few times and see if there are any more in hiding," Scott said, changing magazines.

"I think they all would have heard that, don't you think?"

"Humor me."

Dan drove up and down through the rows of vehicles. They only saw one other body, and it was apparent that it was suffering from some form of paralysis. It seemed that once a person was in the throes of the poison, their body no longer stopped itself from overexerting. Many of the affected people literally tore the muscles and ligaments from their bones by straining too hard. Once the tendons were destroyed, the body would lie there and die from exposure, or whatever came along and killed it.

They backed the truck up to the rear entrance of the building and turned the motor off. They left both windows down and went over to the door. The power was still on and the electronic card reader showed a green dot when Dan put his ID up to it. They entered the rear of the building and went to the top floor. They searched every room from the roof down, finding one feral that they put down easily. They scavenged everything they thought would be useful and brought it to the bank of central elevators on each floor. Once they had their mound of supplies moved down to the mechanic bays at the back of the building, they took a break in the small break room. A rifle butt to the glass of one of the vending machines yielded a couple beef and bean burritos, and Dan actually paid for a couple of cokes from another machine.

They sat at the break table and discussed where the world was going, planned on contacting relatives, and generally shot the shit for almost an hour. After cleaning up their mess (Dan even picked up the broken glass from the vending machine), they set about organizing their stash. When they were done with that, it was time to head downstairs.

The firearms range was for the administrative types who were sworn to get in their quarterly qualifications. The facility was also the ammunition and arms storage point for the entire northern half of the state for the park service. Scott, having previously served as a firearms instructor, had an intimate knowledge of the facility and knew where the keys and combos were kept for the entire facility. It took them the rest of the day to bring up all the pallets of ammunition and weapons boxes from down below.

"It looks like I'll be going back to 5.56," Dan said as he wheeled a pallet of the ammunition up to the closed warehouse door. His M4 was chambered for the 6.8 SPC round.

"Ahh, it won't be that bad." Scott was pushing a dolly with a dozen Pelican cases full of standard M4s. "And you still have, what—ten, twelve million rounds of your personal stuff? Please!"

"I wish ten million! Shit, I barely have two case lots of service stuff and maybe five cases of standard ball range stuff!" Dan was pulling the hand lift out from under the pallet and heading back for another load. "I don't know if I'll be able to scavenge enough reloading supplies to make more than a couple thousand rounds."

After checking on the truck, they raided the vehicle key storage box and took all the keys with them up to an interior office on the third floor. They pulled a couch and a comfortable chair into the office then closed and locked the door. They decided one of them would stand watch while the other slept until daylight. Any light at all during the night brought the ferals out.

CHAPTER 16

Quantico, VA

Anna rubbed her face and leaned back on the tall stool she was sitting on. Her eyes were burning and her neck was in serious need of a massage. The muscles were tight from leaning over the microscope for the last three hours. Sleep was so far in her distant past that she had forgotten what it was. And she smelled; that was what bothered her the most. She hadn't showered since right before the last time she slept.

The sample of brain tissue in front of her had yielded about as much of an answer to the mystery chemical as she was going to get. It was time to figure out how the body was concentrating the chemical in the saliva. She took the slide, replaced it in a tray of similar slides, and headed for the fridge to trade it for another tray.

The base hospital for MCB Quantico had been secured and put back into use. Over twenty staff members from the CDC had taken over a set of rooms next to the toxicology lab. After setting up their work area, the staffers had gone about collecting samples for study. The human tissue samples were abundant, but Anna wanted to see the effects of the toxin on all mammals, so teams were dispatched to collect dogs, cats, and rats. She got more than she bargained for when the Marines took her request literally and began pulling up to the hospital with all sorts of wildlife, both alive and dead.

The first day, she received several dogs and cats. The second day, she was called to the loading dock and found several kennel containers with rabbits, squirrels, mice, and a young horse tied up to the rail. The following day found more animals, including a very hog-tied young black bear. After dealing with the irate hospital staff, a small area was set aside in the open field to the west of the medical center, where the animals were euthanized and the necessary samples collected. She was stunned at how the Marines just went and accomplished their mission.

Anna had been studying these samples, along with those taken from cadavers, and the outlook for a preventive compound was poor, but she was making headway on recovery methods. The body wanted the toxin out and made every effort to do so, but the psychosis induced while under the influence prevented any type of reasonable treatment from being self-implemented. The brass wanted a drug, a magic pill, and there simply wasn't one out there yet. She and Gary had finally come up with some protocols, but she knew the answers she had weren't going to be well received.

She had just finished compiling her notes when Gary walked in from the adjoining lab. He was unshaven and smelled just as bad as she did. Anna looked over at him with a grim smile as she stuffed the notes in her briefcase.

"Well, I'm not going in there till after I shower." She looked him up and down. "You could use one too."

Gary, who had bloodstains on his overcoat, looked down at himself and shrugged. "Hey, I have to live like this; they can put up with it. I don't want some armchair general thinking he's the only one working around here!"

"Well, I refuse to be seen like this, so you'll have to just represent for us lab rats." She pumped her fist in a power-to-the-people gesture then handed him her case. "I'm going to hit the staff showers, and then I'll meet you in Conference Room B."

"K, you want me to bring you some coffee?" The question was purely rhetorical, and he got no response as she walked down the hall. He hefted both his and Anna's briefcases and headed off to the cafeteria.

The conference rooms were on the ground floor administrative area. The room they were using had a large projection screen TV. Outdated technology compared to today's flat-screen Plasma TVs, but it was big. Gary connected his laptop to the TV and got his PowerPoint ready.

The brass began to trickle in with their lackeys carrying their cases. Gary watched the almost comical way the hierarchy was displayed by the military members of the conference. The middle-ranking officers always showed up first in an attempt to get the most favorable seat possible, but they didn't know how many higher-ranking officers would be there, and it was embarrassing to have to get up and move for someone of higher rank.

But you didn't want to leave any gaps or some general would move a captain closer than a lieutenant colonel. Next came the lower ranks who just knew to stand at the back of the room. Finally, the big cheeses would show up and take their rightful thrones.

The meeting was scheduled for 1000, and everyone was there by five after, except Anna. Gary was about to send one of the staff to see if she had fallen asleep in the shower (something he had done just the other day), when she walked in with her long black hair still wet. Her shirt halfway down her back was wet from the undried locks. She shot him a grin and walked up to the screen to stand next to him, gratefully accepting the cup of coffee he handed her.

"Ladies and gentlemen, we're going to get underway." Gary nodded to his assistant, who dimmed the lights. "We have identified the toxin and its method of harm. We know how it was delivered into the environment and how it was dispersed into the population. We have also discovered its propagation factor, which is about the same as the flu. It has an R-nought of about 2.3. This means that for every person who suffers direct exposure to the toxin, he or she will expose approximately 2.3 more persons through direct contact, mostly bites. This isn't a viral or bacteriological infection, but because the body is constantly eliminating the toxin by flushing it out, it does have a waning period of time during which the concentrated toxin can be transmitted through the bites. Remember, repeated exposure to the tainted water sources will re-concentrate the toxin in the body, sometimes fatally so.

"The toxin is a concentrated form of PCP laced with LSD. It is then 'cut' or diluted with chlorates instead of bicarbonates. This chemical compound allows the drug to cross the blood-brain barrier and concentrate directly in the prions of the cells in the brain. The result is uncontrollable hunger fueled by rage with no self-control. You have turned the person into a very hungry, modern-day cannibalistic berserker.

"The human body appears to half-life the toxin in about six to ten days; this means that the body ejects half of the toxin within it during that time. This time variance is due to several variables, such as percentage of body fat, metabolic rate, amount of fluids the body has to flush the toxin out, and, of course, length of exposure period." Gary looked at his assistant. "Next please." The screen changed and he continued.

"If the person is exposed to the toxin over time, the body shunts it into the fat cells and it is stored for longer periods of time versus one large dose in which the body tends to express symptoms and eject a majority of the toxin shortly thereafter. The problem is that the individual suffers from complete psychosis during that period and tends to immediately fulfill its basic needs and with all that physical activity comes thirst. They drink more contaminated water and the toxin gets re-concentrated.

"If the exposed person is successfully restrained and immediately given massive amounts of de-ionized water, the flushing occurs more rapidly and will probably be out of their system in about 3 months. During that time, periods of lucidity will become more and more frequent. We don't know if the person will make a complete recovery or will suffer from bouts of psychosis for the rest of their lives. Obviously, we haven't been able to conduct long-term studies yet. I'm going to turn the floor over to Anna Napolitano, who will brief you on the toxin's transference factors and some more of the chemistry side of things. Anna…"

Anna stepped forward and nodded for the screen to be advanced. "Okay, let me first make it clear that I am a bio-chemist and there are aspects of this compound that really require a hard chemistry background. The toxin is very effective per micro gram. Toxicity is achieved at the 30 to 40 parts-per-billion levels. Remember that this chemical is concentrated at the cellular level far more efficiently than if some street user smoked it. The estimated size of the packets dropped would have concentrated the chemical in the five or six parts-per-million range… "

A hand shot up from the side of the room. Anna turned and nodded. "Yes?"

"I thought you said the toxin needed 30 to 40 parts? Does that mean they have to drink a lot of tainted water?" The young Army Major stopped when he realized that everyone was staring at him, including a three star Admiral.

"I'm sorry if I misspoke…" Anna began.

"It's quite all right, Miss Napolitano," Admiral Huff said. "You said 30 to 40 parts per billion for poisoning to occur. Someone will explain to the good major here that water tainted at six parts per million is almost 600 thousand times more concentrated than you need to achieve toxicity. Please continue." The sheepish look on the young soldier's face was priceless. His bid to look good at this meeting gone up in smoke, he meekly shrank back into his chair.

"Okay, so we have 750 plus municipal water supplies that are tainted. The outdoor supplies—lakes, reservoirs, etcetera are all degrading the toxin. Again, I can't give you a definite time frame because there are so many variables… temperature, soil absorption rates, oxygenation levels, fluid agitation. We're just going to have to wait and see."

"So have you come up with a cure? A way to detect the toxin? A treatment besides more ion water?" Brigadier General Daryl Branson was by far the most obnoxious person Anna had to deal with. He was from the Army's Finance Corps and had been in DC when the attacks began. He had been shuffled around until the pentagon put him in charge of logistics for the Dream Team that was tasked with finding a cure.

"I think we have come up with—"

Again, Anna stopped as Admiral Huff looked over at Branson and raised his hand. The three star was well liked and very respected.

"I'm interested in what Miss Napolitano has to say, and I think we'll save our questions for the end, hmm?" The implied question was understood as the order it was and Anna continued.

"There just isn't going to be an effective cure. I mean, sure, we could tranquilize the subjects that are observed displaying symptoms of toxicity; then we have to restrain and care for them. I have tested counteracting agents, but so far, even minute doses have caused such bizarre blood chemistry that the test subjects—animals so far—have all expired. As for a way to test the water, that's easy. Any cop can just test for PCP; it will react the same way. Removing the toxin will require that the water be distilled at least twice, and don't hold me to that, because the chemical does go airborne and can re-taint the water during the process. A very specific refining protocol will have to be followed. But a third distilling has resulted in a consistent purity level that is acceptable for consumption. The chlorates evaporate too much to maintain their effectiveness in transferring the toxin to the brain cells.

"Treatment is going to be de-ionized water; if I come up with something better, I'll let you know first thing." She took a deep breath. "Now for the bad news…" She waited for the groans to die down. "The toxin contained in the serum saliva that the victims produce is: A, concentrated; and B, durable in the environment. This means that any saliva that gets smeared on a surface will still maintain its toxicity even when the saliva dries up. As soon as the residue is exposed to moisture, it will revert to its nasty state. In fact, concentration through bites will keep the toxin in the environment long after it has disappeared from the water supplies. As long as mammals keep biting each other, the toxin becomes more embedded in the ecosystem. This 'serum toxin' will stay active for about two years."

"So we can expect animals to be dangerous for that amount of time?" the Marine colonel sitting next to Huff asked.

"Yup; any more questions?" Anna watched the hands go up. "Yes, General Branson…"

CHAPTER 17

MCB Camp Pendleton, CA

The base was in chaos.

So many Marines and sailors had been exposed to the toxin that no one trusted anybody else. After the first day, there were hundreds dead. By the end of the second day, it was thousands. Those few Marines who could, banded together and stood in small knots of humanity among a sea of insanity. Command and control was reduced to small units.

Major Joseph Henkel was able to assemble a unit of LAVs and keep them and the Marines inside them secured. By using water from a series of tanker trucks that had been positioned the week before for a training exercise, he was able to ensure his troops got untainted water. He then set about securing one of the mobile desalinization plants. It took him three hours to round up the personnel to operate the plant. They were able to fight their way to the coast at Red Beach. It was the usual area that the plant was set up for training and the Marines had it up and running in another hour.

Henkel was standing on the beach looking out over the surf when a young corporal jogged up and was just coming to attention when the major glanced over his shoulder and said, “Yes, what is it, Corporal?”

“Sir, we have comms with an infantry unit up in the 52 Area. They say they were able to get their unit mobile with all their gear. They want to know if we need any water bulls. They say they have the tow capacity for four bulls, sir, but they don’t know how to verify if they’ve been contaminated or not. They don't want to approach any of the equipment in case the toxin, or whatever it is, is airborne." Corporal James was looking around nervously. "Do we know if it's airborne, sir?"

"We most definitely do not, Corporal. Tell them that only Marines in MOPP gear should be next to any large amounts of water. Tell them we have a clean reliable source here and we can keep them supplied during limited ops." The major turned away from looking out at the ocean and began heading back to the camp. "Let's get this sorted out, James. Maybe if we can unfuck ourselves, we can start helping the civilians."

Colonel Tom Neal was not feeling very manly as he hid in the space above his drop-down ceiling. He had crawled up there when he saw Sergeant Palmer, a six-foot-four-inch, 255-pound mountain of muscle, rip the stomach out of Lance Corporal Dern and eat her entrails. Dern had been the colonel's administrative assistant. She had been working on compiling a list of units that were operational. An unrewarding task, as the status of the units were changing faster than she could record and classify them.

A loud crash and screaming brought heads popping out along the hall. Sergeant Palmer was pummeling the young MP who had been stationed at the end of the hall. The young MP had allowed the massive sergeant to get too close before realizing the man was not behaving rationally. By then, it was too late and Palmer had slammed him into the wall. As the smaller Marine struggled to draw his M9 pistol from his holster, he was hit twice with fists the size of Volkswagens. The young MP lost consciousness and slid to the ground.

Several people had begun yelling all at once, and Palmer turned his bloodshot gaze down the hall. Several of the heads popped right back in the doors they had popped out of as the huge Marine turned and started down the hall. One young lieutenant had charged forward and actually managed to tackle the giant man to the ground before being battered into unconsciousness. Dern and another young Marine had rushed into the hall and tried to help, but by then the lieutenant had lost his life, and they followed shortly thereafter.

Neal had witnessed the carnage and decided discretion was the better part of valor at the moment and hid. Palmer had stormed up and down the hall, trying locked doors and smashing things. He then went back and brutalized the body of the Marine that had tried to help Dern, biting him on the face and neck. Neal was hoping the giant would wander up to the second deck so he could get to the MP's sidearm and put an end to this chapter of the nightmare.

After about five minutes, the noises outside his office stopped, and Neal heard the sound of heavy boots clomping off down the hall. He waited five more minutes and was just reaching his foot down onto the desk when he heard the screaming start upstairs. Neal scrambled down off of the desk and eased his head out to look down the corridor. The blood and body parts looked like they were from a B horror movie set. Neal scrambled down the hall and began searching for the gun belt the MP had been wearing. The entire thing was covered with blood and bodily fluids that were already starting to congeal. The radio was a shattered mess.

Neal took the pistol from the holster and, keeping the gun belt with him, went into the bathroom. Turning on a trickle of water, he first washed the blood off the M9 pistol, then he rubbed the gore off the belt. He checked the magazine holder and only found one fifteen-round magazine for the 9mm Beretta. He recalled the asinine discussion he'd had with the bases' provost marshal one night at the O-Club about how he only issued one spare magazine to his troops, claiming that he had less lost rounds at the end of the year. Neal said he thought the lessons of the Marine barracks in Lebanon were too easily forgotten. If the PM were standing in front of him now, Neal would have punched him in the face.

After performing a function check on the weapon, Neal stuck the spare magazine in the front pocket of his Charlie trousers and moved out. Carrying the pistol at the low ready, Neal went to the stairway at the end of the hall. He kept the weapon pointed in front of him as he slowly worked his way around the landing and up to the upper hallway. Slowly slicing the pie, the upper corridor came into view. Again, he was met with the sight of dead bodies and gore-smeared walls. No mutant giant psycho killers were visible though. He held still a minute and listened.

Neal had just stepped out into the hallway and begun to step carefully forward when he heard the sound of a diesel engine outside. As the sounds of Marines getting out of the vehicles drifted up, Neal heard a shuffling and a loud bump in the room ahead and on the left. This was the front side of the building and whoever was in there would be able to look out the window and see what was happening out front. A loud grunt was followed by the sound of someone pushing furniture out of the way and moving hastily toward the hall.

Neal pushed himself up against the wall and had the pistol out in front of him as Palmer flew out the door and turned away from him. Neal took careful aim and was pulling the trigger when the spongy feel and long stroke told him that the safety was still on. Palmer had taken three steps down the hall when the click of the safety being taken off brought him up short. As he spun around, a 9mm ball round hit the rear of his right bicep and creased a line across the muscle of his back. He glared at Neal and looked around behind him like he couldn't figure out where the pain was coming from.

The delay gave Neal a chance to get off another round. This one was aimed a little better and Palmer wasn't spinning away from the aiming point. The second round entered the big man's upper left chest. It cracked a rib and ended up lodging under the scapula. The impact caused Palmer to jerk to the side, but only slowed him down. Neal got off one last shot before the behemoth was on him. The fight was one sided as the 185 pound, fifty-two-year-old, 5'10" colonel was bowled over by the 255 pound, twenty-five-year-old, 6'4" sergeant

The last shot had struck Palmer in the left side of his torso as well. This one went between two ribs and nicked the top of his left lung. Blood started to enter the plural cavity but the wound wouldn't be incapacitating for a while. As both men tumbled to the ground, the slide of the Beretta was pushed out of battery by the body pressed against it. Although Neal pulled the trigger repeatedly, the weapon would not fire. He managed to get his left forearm under Palmer's chin and hold off his snapping jaws, but he was taking a brutal beating from the mountainous fists that were slamming into his side. He felt his right shoulder pop out of its socket and was about to lose consciousness from the pain when a loud thud resulted in Palmer slumping off to the side. Neal groaned and looked up at the barrel of a Bennelli M2 twelve-gauge automatic shotgun.

"I need you to say something other than a groan, sir, or I'm gonna waste you." Jake Derry had the barrel trained on the colonel's head, and it did not waver a millimeter.

"Get me out of here, corporal, if you please. I am not crazy yet."

"Right away, sir!" Jake rolled the huge slab of beef that was Palmer over, grunting with the effort. "Boy, they fed that fucker right when he was little! What a monster!" Jake looked at the relatively diminutive colonel, and his respect went up several notches. "Sir, you should have shot him some more before playing patty-cake with him."

"I'll take that under advisement. Unfortunately, all I had was this Beretta and it did not seem to be very effective." Neal groaned as he sat up. "I think my arm is broken or out of its socket."

"Shit, sir, if you're gonna shoot someone, you should at least do it with one of these." Derry gestured at the holstered .45 on his hip. "We've got a couple of med battalion nurses, and I think even a doc, out at Red Beach, sir. They'll fix that right up. That's where we have a compound set up. I think we're moving it over to the LCAC compound soon though. Better walls and the water POGs can still get us safe H2O." Derry was trussing up Palmer as he spoke.

Neal heard the other Marines call out "clear!" as they searched each room. The rest of the entry team finally gathered around the colonel with Marines facing outwards. The team was well equipped and one of the Marines offered the colonel a drink from a bottle of water. Neal noticed they all had plastic water bottles and a few canteens to supplement their Camelback hydration systems.

After hog-tying and dragging the huge Marine into one of the offices, they closed and locked the door. One of the Marines painted a big black "X" on it, and another made a note on his phone of the location and number of occupants, even though the gunshot wounds would kill the huge Marine in a few minutes. The colonel watched all this as Derry gently set his arm into a sling he had fashioned from a standard medical dressing. They went downstairs and met three other survivors who had managed to escape the carnage in the building.

"Hey, Jake, we got bars again," one of the Marines said, lifting up his cell phone.

"Well, try for the gunner and see what happens!" Derry had been trying to get a hold of Norris since early that morning.

"On it." The young Marine was already dialing.

"Let's get you over to see a doc, sir, but I have to ask, sir… have you had any water from a fountain or other communal source, sir?" Derry was looking intently at the colonel and it was then that the colonel noticed not all the Marines were pointing their weapons outwards. Several had them pointed down at the ground, but in his direction.

"I only drank bottled water since the day before yesterday. In fact, I can't remember the last time I drank from a fountain." Neal noticed a bit of tension leaving the Marines' bodies.

"Perfect; thank you, sir. I'm gonna take you at your word and let you ride up front in the Humvee, sir." Derry gestured to the troops to mount up. As they were all piling in the Hummers, a half-naked woman, covered in gore, came around the side of the building. Upon seeing the Marines, she began sprinting in their direction. The slight limp from her previously overstressed muscles caused her to run with her body at an angle.

"Contact rear!" one of the Marines yelled. Neal had no sooner spun around to look when two M4s and a shotgun blast threw the woman to the ground.

"Gunner's up on my phone, Jake," said the Marine who had been trying to make the call.

"Gunner! Holy shit, sir! Are you okay?" Derry asked while gesturing for the Marines to continue piling into the Hummers.

"Sitrep, Derry." Norris had sat down and taken a break from putting homemade armor on his truck.

"Well, sir, we have a desal plant started over at Red Beach, but I'm pretty sure we're moving it over to the LCAC area and we're gonna fortify that. Most of Hotel Company made it to the beach and are reinforcing the unit there. I just came by Regimental HQ and we found Colonel Neal. He's a little chewed up. I found him rolling around with that steroid fucker we always see at the gym. He was in the shit with him, sir, and now he's a little dinged up. There were three other survivors at Regimental HQ; everyone else was dead or crazy, and we had to put them down, sir. We have survivors streaming in from base housing, but we have to take our time processing them."

Derry was now sitting behind the colonel. He didn't want the colonel to see that he had his pistol out and ready, just in case the colonel had been contaminated and did freak out. The convoy was heading back out to the beach to drop off the injured colonel then they were going back in for more sweeps of the battalion and regimental areas. As the corporal finished his report, Neal turned around and put out his hand for the phone.

"Is this CWO-3 Norris?" Neal asked, interrupting the orders that Mark had started to give Derry.

"Colonel Neal?" Mark asked.

"Gunner, your young corporal here just saved my ass from getting eaten. I am very appreciative and his sitrep was accurate, as far as I can tell. I was in the process of compiling a list of combat-capable units in the regiment and trying to coordinate with other outside units including the Navy, when the shit hit the fan. I can tell you that one of the artillery units managed to gather its personnel and take over the main side PX. There are little pockets holding out all over the place, but their status changes very quickly. The Navy is pulling all their ships that have water purification capability away from the docks. They will be able to supply on-shore units with fresh water if they can set up beachhead supply points. We'll use the LCACs to ferry supplies back and forth until then. We don't have large-scale rioting, but there are so many affected people throughout the base that no real perimeter has been established. I'll see what is going on when I get to you at the beach."

"I'm out in town, sir. I got cut off and I never made it back to base. I'm holed up at my house in Rancho Bernardo. I have a house full of kids and neighbors, and they're all scared. The shit has really hit the fan out here; we have observed hundreds of affected people just in my neighborhood."

"Well, shit; who's in charge out at the beach then?" Neal looked outside and noticed they were passing under the I-5.

"You'll have to ask Corporal Derry, sir."

"Okay, well, can I expect the pleasure of your company soon, or do you have other orders?" Neal watched as they approached a sentry point. A Marine on the right side was from H 2/5 and recognized Derry. He waved the small convoy through.

"You're the next up in my chain of command, sir," Norris said with a slight wince. Usually when a colonel expected the pleasure of your company, God himself took it as an order to be where ever that company was expected. If Neal ordered him back to base, he was going to have to leave a bunch of civilians behind at his house. His kids were going with him no matter what. "I'm unsure of my ability to make it to the base, sir. I don't know the road conditions, and I am securing twenty plus civilians here. That includes my children, Colonel."

"Well, shit! Okay then, what's your situation, Norris? How are you set for holding out until we can get to you?" The Hummer had come to a stop at a GP tent and a major was standing there waiting for the colonel to finish his phone call. Derry stood next to him, along with the Marine whose cell phone he was using.

"Sir, as I said, I have twenty plus civvies at my house. I am extremely well armed and supplied with beans, bullets, and Band-Aids, sir. Every adult person is armed with mil-grade weapons and that includes my kids. I have a little more than forty gallons of fresh bottled water in five-gallon jugs, and one of the adults here at my house has the keys to a storage room at his work that has many more. I am currently making ready to recover that water. I have dry goods and MREs to last us at least thirty days, which is twice as long as the water will last if I don't get to the stuff in storage.

"I have two generators and sufficient fuel for them for about ninety days of rationed operations—just running them enough to charge comm gear, batteries, and other essentials such as refrigeration for my perishables. I am good to go on vehicles with a four-wheel-drive truck, one all-wheel-drive SUV, and a minivan. All have fuel and are in good shape mechanically. I have no injured, but we have had to kill several of our neighbors. I have sufficient ammo to sustain major combat operations on three continents if necessary, sir!"

"Outstanding!" Neal chuckled at the joke, realizing it probably wasn't far from the truth. "Well, then, my orders are as follows… survive… and save as many civilians as you can along the way. I'm going to check with this major who's standing here patiently waiting for me, and once I know better what we are capable of, I will get back to you. Cell phones are working right now, but if they go out, are you going to be able to talk to us?"

"Yes, sir; if you could tell Corporal Derry there I'll be up on the team net at sevens, sir, he'll know what I mean. I have my team gear, sir." Norris turned as Alan walked into the garage. "Is there anything else, sir?"

"No, Gunner. I'll pass anything I have to your young Marine here."

"Aye aye, sir!" Norris hung up the phone.

"Sergeant Derry!" Neal said, turning toward the young Marine and handing him the cell phone.

"Uh, it's corporal, sir," Derry said, feeling only slightly uneasy correcting a full-bird colonel. "What can I do for you, sir?"

"First of all, you cannot argue with me when I call you 'sergeant,' Sergeant!" Neal waited for his meaning to sink in. "Next, you can pass on to your team 'good job!' from a very thankful old man. The gunner said he'll be up on sevens?" Neal raised an eyebrow in question.

"That means he'll be monitoring the radio at seven minutes past the hour and half hour, sir."

Neal patted the big Marine on the shoulder with his good hand and turned to the major.

"Pardon my call there, Major. Do you, perhaps, have someone who can put a Band-Aid on me while we talk?" Neal said as he gingerly hefted his wounded arm up.

"This is the med tent right here, sir," Henkel said as he gestured to the tent they were standing next to. "Doc's waiting for you. I can wait to brief you, sir."

"Nonsense. It's not every day that you get to watch a Bird Colonel squeal like a baby. You should cherish these moments."

Colonel Neal had a resigned look on his face as he trudged into the tent. "C'mon, let's get this over with so I can be of some use around here."

CHAPTER 18

Rancho Bernardo, CA

The big Suburban on huge tires rolled slowly down the block toward Mark's house. The lifted gold behemoth had all the windows rolled down, and the barrels of rifles and shotguns protruded from every opening. Because the driveway was full of Mark's truck and Alan's mini-van, the suburban rolled up the curb and positioned itself right on the lawn with the front facing the street. The driver's door opened and a tall grey-haired man used the sideboard to hop to the ground. Noticing the steel fire panels in place over the house's windows, he stopped himself from pulling out his rifle and instead closed the door gently.

Keeping his hands in plain view, he began to approach the front door. He was just about to take the first step up when the front door opened a crack and a grenade rolled out toward him. It clunked along the porch, and the man was just about to turn tail and run behind the truck when he realized the reason the grenade was clunking around so much was that the spoon was still attached. He stopped in mid-turn and looked up at the door. Mark and Jim were looking at him expectantly.

"Son of a bitch! You took ten years off my life, you assholes!" Clifford Barnes was an old fishing buddy of Mark's. "I swear to God I will get even with you two for this!"

Mark and Jim were grinning ear to ear. They threw open the door and rushed out to tackle Cliff. They had him up against the side of the

Suburban when Cliff's son, David, came around from the passenger's seat and started laughing at his dad's misfortune.

"I thought for sure you were gonna tell him before you guys got here." Jim spoke in a subdued voice. Loud noises tended to attract the ferals.

"I did. I told him you guys were really stressed and to approach the house with caution. I might have said the words 'booby trap' too!" David was grinning as well.

"You knew about this, you little shit?" Cliff turned toward his son and made a fist.

"We were texting about it on the way over, Dad." David was holding up his cell phone and pointing to it. He made sure to stay out of the incredibly long reach of his father's fist.

Jim picked up the smoke grenade which not only still had the pin in it, but the safety cap was in place. He tossed it in the air and put it in the tac vest he had commandeered from his father as the rest of the crew climbed down from the giant four-wheel drive. Cliff's daughter and wife all hustled inside and locked the front door behind them. The impromptu reunion was held in the foyer, with most of the other kids knowing David and Jamie from school. The gaggle of people slowly moved into the living room.

"Nice," Cliff said, looking around. "I like what you've done with the place!"

The living room furniture had been pulled away from all the exterior wall windows except for a few pieces that were placed near the window peepholes for people to use while looking out the observation slits. The main picture window was three panes and fifteen feet wide. Each steel shutter had a slit in it, giving the room three forward-facing observation ports. Each of these had a barstool in front of it so the person on watch could comfortably view their assigned area. A gun rack had been placed next to the archway leading to the foyer. The rack was full of M-4 Carbines, AR-15 rifles, and shotguns. Cliff also noticed that all the kids over about fifteen wore sidearms.

"Well, you know I've been looking to remodel," Mark said, slugging Cliff in the arm.

"Mark T. Norris, if you don't offer your guests some hospitality, I'm going to make you sleep with the dogs!" Jen said, using their time-honored joke about their sleeping arrangements. She came out of the den with some folded linens in her arms. She went straight to Cliff's wife, Jessica, for a half-hug. "I swear that man is such a crud! Can I get you guys anything, a drink of water?" She pointed at the tap, jokingly.

"Oh, shit man, the middle initial came out and I just got here!" Cliff said, gesturing toward the front door. "Come on, kids, let's go; Coach

Mark is about to get his butt kicked." He swiveled away from another punch aimed at his shoulder.

"Come on in the den and tell me what's up." The two men headed down the hall as Jess and Jen went into the kitchen to talk. The kids all gathered around to swap stories about what had happened to them since the outbreak of violence. The population at Mark's had grown since that first morning. Some of the people were parents of kids who had realized they were totally unprepared for what was happening. Two Marines from Mark's unit had made it to the house, one bringing his pregnant wife and four-year-old daughter. All in all, there were twenty-one people in the large house.

"Man, you've got quite a crowd going here. Last bastion of humanity, or what?" It was more of a statement than question. As they made their way into the den, Cliff noticed the hide-a-bed couch had been pulled out and made up. "How many folks you got here?"

"Twenty-one by last count," Mark said, pulling out his chair behind the desk and gesturing for Cliff to sit in one of the chairs facing it. "Some showed up with supplies from their houses, and some came by to pick up kids and realized they were safer here. I brought home a good amount of gear from the base, and a little ammo too. We're going to head over to Alan's work and try to get at the stores of bottled water there. We have no way of knowing what water is safe, and until we get some word on that, we're only drinking bottled water and canned juices. How are you guys holding out?"

"Well, we had some water and David had a camping filter we were going to use, but then we heard from the Stallmans that even boiled water isn't safe." Cliff leaned back in his chair. "I was coming by to see if you wanted to head up Scripps Parkway and hit the Costco with me. And maybe the Walmart. I could use the extra guns in case we run into unfriendly people, and I'm not just talking about ferals. They have a lot of bottled water there."

"And, although you can fit a lot in that 'burb, you can haul more in my truck!" Mark gave Cliff a pointed look. "I can hook you up with whatever weapons you need. I have been scrounging the neighborhood, and I've got a lot of stuff stored here. Some of the weapons I've come across are odd calibers, but I've taken anything that chambered a common caliber."

"Of course!" He laughed. "I'm not stupid! Besides, I'm going to hit Home Depot too. I'll be hauling my work trailer and moving slow. I'll take whatever weapons you've got. I have three families at the house, and I don't even have a gun for everyone. The Baileys have two families with them and they are way short. I think Kyle has one pistol and his kid's .22 and that's it. We do need your help, buddy."

"I'll make you a deal. Jim, Alan, Terry, and I will come with you. We'll bring Alan's van and my truck. But we go get the water first from Alan's work and you help us haul it back here. We'll split it with you. Then we stop by your house on the way up to Costco and drop off your portion of the water and some weapons and grab the trailer. We stop by Kyle's and get them armed up, then get up to Costco and pack as much stuff as we can if it hasn't already been picked clean." It was common knowledge that, in the event of an apocalypse, Costcos were on just about everybody's list as the place to hole up.

"You got it. I'll take David with me, and we'll leave the girls here while we do it."

"I'm going to have Jim ride with Alan and Terry with me. We're going to the industrial park off of West Bernardo Drive. Alan says he has keys and knows exactly where the water is. He says the first storage room is about twenty meters from the main entry and the other is by the cafeteria loading dock, just inside the rollup door."

"Let's do this."

CHAPTER 19

Bemidji, MN

The Courtyard Hotel had only one vehicular and one pedestrian entrance along the front of the hotel facing the street. There was a small hallway leading to the physical plant area behind the building and other than the ground floor windows, the building was a veritable fortress.

Scott and Dan, along with Yavi, Glenn, Kate and her husband, Rich, and their daughter, Elle, had chosen the building for its defensibility. They had parked a Forestry Service panel-sided pickup across the drive and boarded up the ground-floor windows on the exterior walls. The rear exterior hallway had been barricaded with some furniture and plywood but could easily be moved out of the way for escape if needed. The hotel's front glass door had been busted out (attracting three ferals that had to be dealt with), and the frame had been sandwiched between two more sheets of fitted three-quarter-inch plywood. This whole setup had then been braced with two-by-twelves screwed into the wall studs and cross-braced with two-by-fours. It would be easier to hack through the wall than to get through the front door or windows.

There were almost fifty survivors living in the hotel. It was off the highway, just outside of town to the southeast, so the population was substantially less in the surrounding area than it was in downtown. They had been making forays into downtown, when possible. In fact, the largest group recovered had been from downtown between the medical center and the university.

Two state police officers had been moving their families out of town when they ran into a mob of ferals fighting in the street in front of them. Before they could get turned around, the ferals began attacking their vehicles. The press of bodies was so thick that they had to run over some of them to get away. In the process, a broken thighbone punctured the sidewall of a tire on the Ford Explorer that one family was driving.

It wasn't long before the car was mobbed and the windshield was broken. The GMC Acadia the other family was driving had barely gotten free, and they were about to get out and start shooting at the mob when Yavi, Glenn, and Dan came around the corner during one of their patrol/looting missions. They took in the scene and immediately set to rescuing the beleaguered family.

Glenn and Dan got out of their truck and began laying down rifle fire. There was a group of almost fifty ferals in the road, but they were packed in tight. Both men made sure that they kept their fire away from the Explorer. As the ferals noticed the fire from the men, some charged toward them. These were immediately engaged. Both Glenn and Dan went through their first magazine in about twelve seconds. They each took a knee and yelled "reloading" at almost the same time. Dropping their spent magazines while they still had a round or two in them, they slapped home full ones from their vests and continued to fire.

Yavi had climbed out of the driver's seat, leaving the truck running, and hopped into the back of the bed. From this perch, he provided 360-degree security for the two rangers standing below him. He only had to engage one feral, who came sprinting around a corner, attracted by all the noise. He watched in awe as another feral jumped off the building to his right, also trying to get to the source of the noise.

"Heads up!" he cried, trying to warn Dan and Glenn of the falling man.

Glenn glanced up too late to move out of the way, and the falling body struck him on the right shoulder, driving him painfully to the ground and causing him to twist his knee. The feral had jumped from the roof of a five-story building and shattered seventeen bones in its body, including its jaw, which it tried to work open and closed. Dan turned and put a round through its head and leaned over to help Glenn up.

"Fuck! My leg is toast, dude! Help me back to the truck!" Glenn was using his free hand to push himself along the chassis toward the cab. He continued to put out rounds by firing the rifle with one hand from the hip. Although far less accurate, he still managed to hit several ferals.

"We good?" Dan yelled up at Yavi.

"Clear for now. You want me to drive? Or do you want me to come clear that out with you?" Yavi was pointing at the Explorer, where the sounds of shots coming from inside it were accented by the sound of shots coming from the cross street. "Sounds like they have some other help too."

"I'll go. Just stay ready to pull my ass out if the shit hits the fan."

"If you die, I'm taking your Winchester!" Glenn teased as he grimaced at the pain in his knee.

"Oh yeah, and if you get into trouble just toss the gimp out to feed them if you need to get away," Dan said to Yavi as he jogged toward the Explorer, changing out magazines again as he moved. This time, he made sure to insert the expended mag back into his vest. Even though they had several hundred back at the hotel, magazines were a commodity worth more than gold.

Yavi looked down at Glenn. "That's cold! But a good idea!" he said brightly, raising his thick bushy eyebrows. Glenn's face paled slightly at the joke.

As he reached the side street that the other fire was coming from, Dan engaged the last few ferals he could without endangering the occupants of the stranded SUV. There was a ring of bodies around the car, and only two were left trying to get into it. Dan approached carefully, stopping to butt stroke a wounded feral. As he got near the car, he could see the windshield had been shattered, but the safety glass was in one piece—it was just pushed in on the dash. A young boy of about fourteen, who had gone feral, was kneeling on the hood of the SUV, trying to get his hands around the edge of the windshield. Dan moved to get a safe angle on him, while making sure that all of the bodies he was stepping over or around were in fact dead and not going to take a chunk out of him.

As he approached from the passenger side, he kept the other feral, a large woman in a floral-print dress, in sight. She was pressed up against the rear window on the driver's side, clawing at it and scaring the hell out of the three-year-old little boy strapped into a car seat. The driver was frantically reloading a pistol and trying to roll down his window as his wife screamed at him to do something while shoving back on the windshield.

Dan put the aiming point from his ACOG on the head of the feral on the hood and squeezed the trigger. The young boy's head snapped to the side and he rolled off the hood. Dan saw another man approaching from the cross street and, observing that he was holding a pistol in a somewhat proficient manner, kept his attention on the fat lady. As he moved around to the back, the other man fired two well-aimed shots at the woman. This caused her to spin around and fall on her rather large derriere but did not put her out. The man stepped forward to fire another shot but was grabbed by a wounded feral on the ground. It grabbed his ankle, pulled his foot to its mouth, and bit down. The man let out a surprised yell of pain and began trying to shake it loose. Dan stepped up behind the woman, and after making sure the other man was not in jeopardy of being hit, put a round right through her head. He then stepped forward and yelled, "Wait!" as the man was about to shoot toward his own foot. Dan took out the machete that he had taken to carrying and, after getting the man to hold still, brought the heavy blade down on the skull of the offending critter.

They both turned as the door to the Explorer swung open and the driver stepped out. He stepped forward to introduce himself as his spouse went around the car to console the still screaming toddler in the back seat.

"Chris Colander," he said, putting out a ham-sized fist. He was 5'11" with a buzz-cut flat top of reddish blonde hair. His stocky build showed a barrel chest with just a little bit of weight beginning to appear around his middle. He nodded to his friend. "The pistolero here is my partner, Roy Jones."

"Dan Prescott," Dan said, shaking hands all around. "Let me call my compatriots over here." With that, he waved the other two rangers over. "That was a little close there." Dan had bent down to look at the femur sticking out of the tire.

"Yes, indeed. We might have really been screwed if you hadn't shown up."

The sound of bodies being squished under large tires interrupted any further conversation as Yavi pulled the truck up to the scene of carnage. There were so many bodies on the ground that he couldn't get close without running some over.

"Hey, numb nuts." Dan gestured at the flat tire. "Think of that next time before you drive over too many corpses! This is Yavi. If you speak slow and grunt some between words, he can usually understand English. The lazy one being chauffeured around is Glenn. He's the smarter of the two but he still has to take off his shoes to count higher than ten."

Glenn nodded and was about to speak when Yavi cut him off.

"Just call me Novocain nuts," Yavi said, shaking their hands and scanning the area as he went to the back of the truck and began pulling out a heavy-duty floor jack. "You have a spare for that thing, right? I'd like to get moving before the rest of the city gets here." He nodded his head toward a feral in the distance that was jogging toward them.

"I got this," Chris said as he opened the rear hatch of the Explorer and pulled out a rifle case. He took out a beautiful Weatherby in 7mm magnum and turned in the direction of the oncoming feral. He pushed his arm through the sling and took careful aim. The loud report started the baby crying again and earned him a reproachful look from his spouse, who immediately went back to cooing at the child. The 7mm bullet covered the 400 yards to the running feral in just under a second and impacted its sternum. The hydrostatic shock turned every organ in the chest cavity to mush. The body fell forward from its momentum and slid to a stop.

Roy's wife pulled the GMC up next to the disabled Ford and got out. Introductions were made all around, and after a little discussion, both families agreed they would follow the park rangers back to their Hotel Haven. Yavi helped change out the tire on the Explorer while Dan checked on Glenn's leg. After the tire was fixed and all the gear was repacked into the back of the Explorer, they set off for the hotel. The only stop they made was at a Ford dealer to swap out the Colander's old Explorer for a new one… and an extra spare tire.

CHAPTER 20

MCB Camp Pendleton, CA

Colonel Neal was beginning to truly understand the state of the world as he got off the radio with a rear admiral down in San Diego. The city itself had practically burned to the ground. The Navy ships that had been in port at 32nd Street Naval Base had all pulled out to sea and anchored off of Point Loma. All of them had suffered some crew loss to either tainted water or attacks by ferals. Some had suffered damage to some extent, and one frigate had been abandoned at the dock due to a fire that started below decks when the crew was attempting to fight some feral crewmembers.

The city of Coronado was almost entirely intact. The island (which was actually a man-made isthmus) that formed San Diego Bay only had two access points: the Coronado Bridge and the Silver Strand. After learning of the water danger, the CO of NAS North Island had called the police chief in town and made a plan. The city's water supply was turned off at the inlet pumping station. The two aircraft carriers at the dock turned on their desalinization plants and began to supply Coronado with clean water. The only ferals that cropped up were people who drank water outside the city before coming over the bridge or up the strand. Both avenues had been quickly secured by Navy SEALs from NAB Coronado. The Naval Special Warfare operators were able to secure the peninsula down near Imperial Beach and on the San Diego side of the bridge. They had placed barricades across the freeways and simply shot anything that did not follow their orders to a tee. A rescue mission had retrieved several hundred patients and staff from Balboa Naval Hospital, and a medical quarantine area was being set up to check out the tide of incoming people.

Refugees were already flooding across the bay to escape the packs of ferals that were forming in the city of San Diego. Some people swam across the bay to get to Coronado. Others used boats, rafts, and any other floating conveyance they could find to get to the safety of the island. A few even attempted to make the mile-long trip across the bay using surfboards and boogie boards. Naval security vessels and Coronado police boats were able to pick up most of the people seeking refuge, but there were far too many to get them all. Occasionally, one that slipped by would turn feral and bloodshed would ensue. The quarantine area often broke out in bloodshed as well, and any new bite victims were isolated until they, in turn, succumbed to the toxin coursing through their blood.

By now the third and fourth generation bite victims were beginning to show up. The toxic serum they received from their bites was diluted enough for them to just suffer from hysteria, mild fits of uncontrolled anger, and/or weeping. Some of these people went feral as well. Children who were relatively easy to subdue became nightmares to care for. Because they would thrash uncontrollably, they had to be fully restrained. This included bite protection for the caregivers, which quickly ran out, and they had to resort to duct tape. Some of the kids still fought so hard, they threw up and choked on their own vomit. Any that were left with their mouths exposed had to be placed with a clear area around them so caregivers wouldn't get bit. Also, the padded restraints ran out and kids would literally struggle so hard with their bonds that they would strip the skin off their arms to get free. By the fourth day, there were hundreds of children thrashing their de-gloved appendages.

Neal had all of these problems, but on a smaller scale. The LCAC compound was fully fenced except for the beach, which was easily patrolled from the end of the fence to the water. The Marines had started cramming survivors inside the compound's fenced area and set up a regular security watch schedule. The Navy's medical battalion from the base hospital was filling up tents with wounded as fast as they could be found and erected. Marines and their families were trickling in or being found by the patrols.

All of the access gates to the base had been abandoned. Some when the Marines on duty there had gone feral and turned on their companions, and others when the Marine MPs ran out of ammunition and could no longer defend themselves from the ferals, which attacked them from both inside and outside the gates. Neal's first order of business was to push the safe zone out to the base perimeter. To do this, he assigned teams of his best-trained infantry mixed with Recon and FAST Company Marines to go out and re-establish the base perimeter. He then began forming interior security teams from whatever units he could and the clearing process began.

“Gunny Fitz, I want you to take two platoons to the main gate with the engineers and Seabees and get it fortified properly. I need you to establish a storage area for supplies that is easily accessible in case we start seeing human wave attacks by the ferals. They are starting to hunt in packs and I need these Marines to be able to hold. I’m sending Derry and his team out to the back gate to do the same. Staff Sergeant Brown has a resupply schedule set up for the gates as we re-establish them.” He turned to the young Navy lieutenant from the Seabees. “Remember, they have to defend in 360 degrees; they’re just as likely to have a feral come at them from inside the base as from outside.”

“Yes sir!” The young Sailor was chomping at the bit.

“Carry on!” Neal said, dismissing the group in front of him before turning away from the group.

“Uh, sir, I have a Lieutenant Colonel Barrent here to see you, sir. Says he has keys to the PMO armory.” Staff Sergeant Warm had an unreadable look on him. Neal had made it clear that he was very upset with the fact that the gates had been overrun so quickly because of an administrative policy for restricting ammo.

“Really? Well, by all means, send him into my office right away.” With that, Neal went to his office and took several deep breaths. He sat behind his desk and felt that he was moderately composed when there was a knock on the door.

CHAPTER 21

Carlsbad, CA

Kirk Barrent was in Carlsbad when the world went crazy. The newly divorced provost marshal for Camp Pendleton was enjoying his new-found bachelorhood (even though he had been behaving like a single man since long before his divorce) with a new condo right up the street from the beach.

Pizza Port was hands down the best pizza on the planet, and they were a damn fine microbrewery too. Barrent had been sitting at a table drinking and eying a young lady when a disturbance at the door distracted him. After a few more seconds of yelling and cursing, a young man dressed in a bathing suit and flip-flops burst through the door. His face and chest were covered in blood and gore, and his arms and legs were covered in scratches. He looked around and jumped on an elderly man who was the closest to him. They both went to the ground and the young surfer savagely began chewing on the man's face as he began to scream. Two other young men immediately tried to tackle the attacker and pull him off.

The fight that ensued eventually encompassed nine people, all of whom were bitten. By the time the police showed up, calls were coming in from all over the city. Barrent stayed to serve as a witness, but then decided to call it a night. He went home and didn't even bother to check his messages on his home phone and was so distracted that he left his cell phone in his car.

The seven beers he had consumed ensured that he slept through the chaos until the following morning. By then, buildings were burning out of control and the world had sunk into a Mel Gibson movie.

Kirk woke up with a throbbing head, made worse by the blaring sirens passing his house. Shielding his eyes, he looked out his window to see smoke rolling through his neighborhood. The bright haziness didn't keep him from noticing the shapes of what appeared to be several bodies lying in the street and on the sidewalk. The landline phone went straight to a busy signal, and he had to think about where his cell phone was. After recalling that it was in the car, he walked right outside and down to his covered carport.

The BMW 5 Series sedan was where he left it but ash covered it. A streak of blood and several scratches ran along the passenger side. This made him so mad that he kicked his neighbor's POS Nissan, putting a dent in the door. The cussing and noise attracted some unwanted attention; a fourteen-year-old girl with a torn shirt and shorts came around the corner and stared at him. Kirk recognized her as one of the neighbors and immediately dismissed her from his mind. It was almost his undoing. He went to his trunk to get out the car care products that he kept there. The open lid blocked his view as she climbed up on the Nissan and hurled herself at him. The open lid saved him as it slammed into his head, causing him to jerk back and renew his cussing. The girl's jaws slammed shut with a *clack* right above his face and she tumbled off to the side of the BMW.

A thin trickle of blood flowed into Kirk's eyes as he tried to regain his balance. The girl scrambled to her feet and immediately launched herself at Kirk as he was wiping the blood out of his eyes. In spite of the ferocity of the attack, the young girl stood no chance against the trained Marine. He easily redirected her momentum into the side of the Nissan. The impact snapped her head to the side and cracked her skull, dropping her to the ground. Barrent slammed the trunk shut and went back inside.

After spending fifteen minutes cleaning the gash on his forehead and changing his soiled clothes, he realized his cell phone was still in his car. It was then that he noticed the blinking light on his message machine and saw the red *thirty-seven*. He sat down, pressed play, and listened as the messages went from isolated reports of violence to full-scale panic as various gates and posts were overrun. The last three messages were from a young corporal who was holding out at the Mainside armory and had locked himself in to prevent all unauthorized Marines from getting a hold of weapons.

His attempts at calling the base were fruitless and he decided to head in. After showering and shaving, he had a light breakfast then put on a cleaned and pressed Combat Utility Uniform—something he rarely wore—and even put on his Sam Brown belt with his holstered M9 pistol. He chambered a round and ensured that both of his magazine pouches had fully loaded magazines, and headed out the door. The smoke drifting up the street was thicker, and several buildings closer to the beach were on fire.

Barrent made it the four blocks to the freeway onramp when he ran into his first pileup. How so many cars had smashed into each other was beyond the laws of physics. There were cars piled three high, and he wondered at the energy required to get them up on top of each other. He looked over his right shoulder as he started to back away from the mass of wreckage. It was a good thing he did, because there was a red Toyota pickup barreling down the road toward him. He backed to the side of the road and watched as the truck skidded to the wrecked cars. The driver was a little late getting on the brakes and nosed into the pile with a crunch. The driver was a young man, who got out and stared at the damage to his front end.

The noise was enough to get the attention of three ferals who immediately ran toward the truck. Kirk was about to get out and talk to the driver when the young man heard the sound of running feet and looked around. Spotting the threat, he turned and climbed hastily into the cab. Two teens flashed past Kirk's window and slammed into the truck, both smashing at the glass and snarling. The third was a large man who walked up behind them and pulled one of the kids down from behind. Soon all three were rolling around in a tangle of limbs.

Kirk got out of his car and approached the snarling ball of arms and legs just as one of the kids let out a yell and went slack. The other kid only lasted a few seconds longer before he too was being devoured. The large man looked up and snarled as Kirk approached. Kirk fired three quick rounds into the man's face and watched him topple over. The driver of the truck just sat there with his mouth open.

"Do you know if any of the onramps are clear?" Kirk asked. He had to repeat himself twice to get through to the young man.

"Huh? Oh, yeah… um, no. The ramp south of here is blocked too; that's why I came this way." He looked around nervously. "Do you think it's like this everywhere?"

Barrent was already turning away and heading back to his car. The young man jogged quickly after him.

"Hey wait! Where are you going? Do you know of someplace safe?"

Kirk glanced over his shoulder at the approaching young man and placed his hand on his recently re-holstered pistol. The action was not lost on the stranger and he pulled up short.

"Hey! I was just trying to be friendly." He slowly raised his hands. "My name is Doug Stone."

"Well, nice to meet ya there, Doug, but I have to get to Camp Pendleton right now and I don't have time to screw around. If I were you, I'd find a nice place to hole up until some order is restored, but I have to go." With that, Kirk turned and got into the BMW and drove away.

"Well, thanks for the help, asshole!" Doug yelled at the car as it sped away down a side street. He immediately regretted it as he heard a scream from up the block and saw a gore-covered woman start in his direction. He got back in his truck and took off in the same direction as the BMW.

He didn't have to go too far to catch up. Two blocks away, he came upon the BMW smashed up onto the curb by another pickup truck. Kirk was leaning against the rear passenger door, reloading a pistol. Two bodies were at his feet. As soon as he finished the reload, he turned around and approached the driver's side of the Silverado that had run into him. The driver was slumped over the steering wheel unconscious. He considered shooting the idiot, anyway, when he noticed Doug sitting in his truck looking at him. A quick once-over showed that the BMW and Silverado weren't going anywhere unless it was on a flatbed. Kirk turned toward Doug's Toyota. Doug considered just putting the truck in reverse and leaving, but the asshole in camouflage did have a gun.

"So now you want a ride?"

"It's that or I take your truck," Kirk said, putting his hand on the pistol again.

"Dude, do you always have to threaten people to get what you want?"

"No, but I don't have time to fuck around, so let's go. We need to get on 5-North."

"You know, we could just go up the 101. Might be easier. That way, even if it is blocked, we can just go around. If the freeway gets clogged, we might get stuck on it."

Kirk thought about it for a minute then nodded his head. "All right, but don't stop for anyone. You can get to Harbor Drive and the main gate from the 101."

"Got it." Doug put the truck in gear and began to ease his way past the wreckage. The going was slow and they had to make several detours around other wrecks. They avoided one street entirely where a hedgerow was burning fiercely right up to the sidewalk. Several people on a rampage charged the truck, but Doug usually just accelerated away. There were two incidents where some of the more athletic ones actually caught the truck, and Kirk had to shoot them off before they could climb into the bed. This left Doug with ringing ears and the start of a bad headache.

The 101 leaves Carlsbad and crosses a short bridge over a lagoon before entering downtown Oceanside. Their luck ran out when they reached the bridge and found the way impassable. Two flaming wrecks had the bridge completely blocked, and there were several feral humans eating victims on the road.

"Why the hell is everything on fire?" Doug was staring at the mess in front of them. "I mean, car wrecks don't usually catch on fire, do they?"

"Well, probably only one in twenty, but how many have we seen today? A hundred? Just the law of averages catching up with us."

"Well, let's leave it behind again!" Doug grimaced as he backed the truck away from the unfriendly stares he was starting to get. They tried several different routes to the freeway but were stymied at each onramp. Doug had just remarked that his gas was getting low when a feral that had been sitting in a tree came smashing through the windshield.

Kirk was able to shove the broken body back out, but the damage had been done. The steering wheel had been snapped loose from the nut, and it was stripped beyond their meager means to repair it. Kirk had to use two precious rounds of ammo on a woman who sprinted at them from between two houses.

Kirk was furious that they had doubled back so far. They were now about a mile farther from the base than when he had started out that morning. He decided to head back home and regroup. He would try the phones again and get some more ammo. He had a rucksack too and he would not venture out again without being better equipped and supplied.

As he prepared to leave, Doug asked, "What do we do now?"

"*We* don't do anything. I am going back to my house to pick up some supplies, and then I'm heading to the base."

"Well, are you just going to leave me here after I drove you around all day? That's fucked up, man."

"Life is fucked up." Kirk checked up and down the street then began working his way toward the ocean and his condo. Doug tried to move with him in a tactical manner but was untrained. Kirk turned on him and put his hand on his pistol. Doug backed slowly away but couldn't help flipping him the bird. Kirk just snarled at him and continued on his way.

It took him twenty minutes to make it back. He only encountered two crazy people on the way, which was good, but a cat jumped on his arm as he was passing by a fence. The feline clawed up his sleeve pretty good before he was able to grab it by the back of its neck and throw it back over the fence. He got to his front door and had to use his hide-a-key because he had left his regular ring in the BMW. Once inside, he locked the door and collapsed on his couch.

He spent ten minutes trying to come up with a plan on how he was going to get back to base. He had his full set of combat gear that every Marine is issued. He had thought the pistol would be sufficient protection to get him the few miles to the front gate. That obviously wasn't the case, so he pulled it all out of the closet in his spare room and laid it on the floor.

He didn't have all the latest gear. Some Marines had received newer body armor and other equipment. He still had the older LBE (Load Bearing Equipment) harness, or "Deuce" gear, and a flak jacket instead of one of the newer plate carrier-type vests. The LBE had two canteens and two magazine pouches for the M-16. He transferred his pistol and magazines to the pouch and holster on it.

He almost filled the canteens up with water from his tap before remembering that it was a bad idea. He used the last half of a bottle of Arrowhead from his fridge and then put a bottle of orange Gatorade in his other pouch. His bachelor's pantry didn't yield much in the way of travel supplies, but he wasn't planning on taking more than a few hours to get to the base.

He waited for the sun to set and began his trek. He decided to parallel the interstate until he reached the main gate. Two days of running and hiding later, a patrol picked him up just inside the main gate.

"Lieutenant Colonel Barrent, come in," Neal said, trying keep the frown out of his voice. Although he was usually a pretty easy person to get along with, he remained seated. The message was clear that this was going to be a superior/subordinate conversation. Barrent came in and, seeing the colonel seated with a stern look on his face, immediately approached the desk and came to attention.

"Lieutenant Colonel Barrent, reporting as ordered, sir!"

"At ease." Neal saw a quick look of surprise cross the man's face as he placed his hands in the small of his back. The expected invitation to sit was not forthcoming. "We have a fucked up base, Mr. Barrent. Due in no small part to some very questionable leadership decisions at the PMO office. I have personally interviewed five MPs. All five of them reported that, not only were they not issued the appropriate ammunition according to Marine Corps order, armory access was placed off-limits to the staff NCOs, including the watch commanders, in violation of COMCAB West standing orders. Those Marines who were on duty when the shit hit the fan were quickly overrun. They did not have the ammunition or support from their command to complete their mission. And when the PMO office attempted to reach their CO, he could not be reached for three fucking days!"

Neal's voice had slowly risen in volume as the anger he felt came spilling out. He took a deep breath and held up his hand when Barrent started to reply.

"I see it as a severe lack of leadership that NCOs and junior officers aren't trusted with access to equipment they need. There are Marines dead because of those decisions—no ifs, ands, or buts about it. These policies have been removed from our SOP. Is there anything that is going to prevent you from re-establishing the security of this base?"

"No sir!" Barrent, who had not received an ass chewing like this since he was a boot lieutenant, swallowed before asking, "Sir, will I be able to communicate with my chain of command at COMCAB West?"

"I'm it for the West Coast. We have one general in the hospital, and the rest are missing."

Neal looked Barrent in the eye. "I am acting commander of 1st Marine Division and acting base commander. Do you need to communicate something to me?"

"No, sir."

"Get those armories open, Colonel. And if you can assist us in accessing the ASPs on base, it would make my day."

"Um, sir, the keys to all those areas are sealed in the PMO armory."

CHAPTER 22

North San Diego County

The convoy of vehicles rolled slowly through the entrance gate to the industrial campus. The Suburban and Mark's truck pulled up to the front door of the manufacturing building and formed a protective bracket that Alan backed his Odyssey into. Mark, Terry, Jim, and David formed a perimeter while Cliff walked Alan up to the door.

Since the key card still worked, he swiped his way into the building and they went inside, leaving David and Jim to watch the vehicles. They entered the foyer and were just turning right down the main hall when a feral came running around a corner from the left. Terry raised her shotgun and fired one round of twenty gauge, striking the sprinting feral in his left shoulder, spinning him to the ground. Mark stepped up and fired one round from his silenced MP5SD. The 147-grain subsonic slug entered the right eye socket and ended any threat.

The shotgun blast did not go unnoticed though. Sounds of movement could be heard from several parts of the building, including over their heads. The thuds of running feet and various bumps and thumps told the team of scavengers that company was on the way.

They continued to move down the hallway until Alan pulled up short in front of an unmarked door. Pulling out a key ring, he unlocked it, revealing a storage room for the bottled water jugs kept there for the various water coolers throughout the building. A quick count showed there to be seventeen five-gallon jugs with the sealed plastic caps still in place. There were nine empty jugs being stored there as well.

"See!" Alan said proudly. "And there's more in the storage room by the cafeteria."

"Beautiful!" Mark said as he and Cliff kept watch in both directions. Some of the sounds were getting closer. "Alan, if you and Terry could please move those out to the hall here—Contact left!" Two quick shots from the HK, and another feral slid across the hall with its head a misshapen lump.

"Company!" Cliff said as he fired a twelve-gauge round at the feral that had appeared at his end of the corridor. No sooner had the first flopped to the ground than another appeared a little farther down the hall. "More company!" A second blast from the Mossberg 590, and the feral's head jerked back from multiple impacts in the face, jaw, and neck. It flopped on its back and began rolling around in a fit of rage and pain. Because it was over thirty yards down the hall, Cliff held his fire and waited.

"Okay, we know the water is here now. We are going to clear this building then see what we can recover. We will clear rooms just like we discussed back at the house. Terry, hon, I need you to take over vehicle watch with five-minute check-ins, okay, babe?"

"K, Dad." Terry didn't seem fazed at all with the violence that had occurred around her. She swiveled her shotgun on its sling and hefted two of the full jugs. Alan grabbed two. Mark grabbed one with his left hand and kept the MP5 elevated with his right. They headed back to the front doors and, propping one open with one of the full jugs, began carrying all the jugs—both full and empty—out to the trucks and van. Five minutes later, they had all the water out and loaded. Mark looked at Jim as, on his last trip out, he carried two reams of printer paper.

"What?" he said with a grin. "We need some computer paper."

Mark just smiled and shook his head as the loot was tossed in the Honda.

"Okay, do we clear and scavenge, or go to the cafeteria?" Mark asked as everyone gathered around. They didn't quite form a circle, as they were all looking outwards in a perimeter.

"Well, you're in charge, Dad," Terry said. She had just assumed her father would be the leader of any endeavor. He always seemed to be in charge wherever they went.

"Well, my two cents is, we have water as a top priority, then food. I think we'll find both at the cafeteria. I don't know what other office supplies ya'll need, but I prefer burgers to paper any day," Cliff said, nudging Jim. "We can always come back."

"I agree." Alan was nodding along with the suggestion.

"Me too," David said, which was a given. He fairly worshipped the ground his father walked on.

"Okay, then, I had similar thoughts, but I want you guys to know that everyone has a voice. The only time I insist everyone listen to me is in a tactical situation." Mark had a habit of making eye contact with everyone when he was addressing a group. "Let's do this."

As they were loading up and preparing to drive off, they were startled by the sound of breaking glass over their heads. Ducking and preparing for ferals to leap on them from the upper floors, they were surprised to hear a feminine voice.

"Wait! Please, can you help us?" An attractive, dark-haired woman was waving a dark piece of clothing from a third floor window to get their attention. "We're trapped up here, and there's a… Alan? Is that you?"

"Hey, Jean," Alan said, giving the woman a small wave. "Is there someone up there with you?"

"Yes!" she said breathlessly. "Richard attacked half of the office staff! And then he tried to attack me! I'm in the conference room with Becca and Ron. Thank God the fridge and water cooler were full. We had just had Subway brought in when everything went crazy. We finished the sandwiches this morning. Thank God the power is still on, or the food would have spoiled."

"Ma'am, we'll be right up. Can you tell me how many ferals there are outside your door?" Mark had taken a few steps back so he didn't have to crane his neck up to see the window the lady was leaning out of. "Can you hear anything? Any movement?"

"Hold on a moment..." The head disappeared back inside and was immediately replaced by two more popping out. Both people started waving and smiling. Alan waved back. A few seconds later, a commotion resulted in Ron's and Becca's heads ducking back inside to be replaced with Jean's.

"He's still out there… I can see him down by the elevators, staring at them like he's waiting for one to open up. Be careful, he killed almost everyone on the floor! Alan, you know how much he liked to work out. It was awful… just awful!" Jean obviously had a flair for the dramatic. "Alan, are you carrying a gun?" Her head poked farther out. "Are you in a militia?"

"Yes, Jean, I'm carrying a gun. No, I'm not in a militia. This is Mark Norris. He's a Marine, and these are his friends. We came to get the bottled water from the storage room down here. Only bottled water is safe." Alan looked at Mark and raised an eyebrow, then turned back to look up at Jean. "We'll be right up."

"Oh well, we have plenty of bottled water up here. Be careful." Her head disappeared to be replaced by the waving Becca and Ron again.

"Terry, you and your brother stay here and watch the cars. We'll be right back. Try to make some room for the additional passengers we have and organize the cargo space for the rest of the water bottles. Alan, you're number two in the order of march; you tell me where to go. And where we're going is up a stairwell, away from old Mr. Richard. David, you have our flanks, son, and your dad will bring up the rear." Again eye contact was made. "Questions?"

"The stairways are at both ends of the building as well as next to the elevator," Alan said, gesturing in both directions. "We have to go back through the building, though, because they are locked from the outside. We can get to the stairwells from the fire doors on the inside first level, and then work our way up from there."

"Why don't we have two of us split up and make a distraction at one of the other fire doors and we can come at him from two directions?" Cliff asked, taking in the layout.

"We don't split up. I don't want to risk a crossfire, and we aren't a tactical team. There's too few of us to support each other if we run into multiple ferals." Mark shook his head. "KISS, right? Keep It Simple, Stupid"

"Yup, you got it. Didn't think of that." Cliff reloaded his shotgun. Mark made a mental note to talk to everyone about immediately reloading weapons whenever possible.

They entered the foyer again and made their way to the west end of the building, since it was afternoon and it would put the slanting rays of sunshine at their back once they were on the third floor. The smell was awful, but not as bad as it could have been. The building's fans and air-conditioning unit kept the smell of the dead bodies down. Most of the corpses had been eviscerated and consumed as well. There was a strong odor of urine and feces from where the ferals had just stopped and done their business.

Being as quiet as possible, the rescue team made their way to the fire door. Slowly pressing on the crash bar, Mark eased the door open and listened for a moment before they entered the stairwell. Keeping to the outside wall, Mark "cut the pie" up the four flights of stairs to the fire door on the third floor. As they were waiting and listening on the landing, the earpiece in Mark's ear crackled.

"Dad, the lady says that Richard is back outside the conference room door." Terry was speaking in a low voice.

"Copy, honey," Mark said and relayed the information to everyone else. It didn't change their plan, but it did mean the feral would be closer and have to be dealt with quicker. If any other ferals attacked, it would get very interesting, very quick.

Mark had made each person in the group go over basic room clearing before they left. They stacked the door with Cliff in front, followed by David, Alan, and Mark bringing up the rear. They all had their rifles and shotguns pointed outwards, alternating left and right throughout the line. Everyone went silent and hunched down slightly.

"Ready?" Mark asked. "Wait for the squeeze up."

Several mumbled "yeahs" reached his ears. After checking the stairwell behind him, both above and below the landing, Mark turned and gently but firmly squeezed Alan on the back of his upper thigh. Alan did the same to David, who repeated the process with his father. Cliff immediately turned the handle and pulled the door all the way open. He stepped through the doorway and took five steps to the left before stopping and panning his Mossberg left and right, looking for threats. David stepped through and pivoted right, taking four steps before coming up against a partition. He then turned to face the room before him. Alan followed Cliff to the left but stopped after two steps and turned to face the room. Mark was the last one through and stepped two paces straight into the room with his submachine gun raised in front of him. He glanced over the sea of cubicles for a brief moment but kept his attention focused on the feral that was thirty yards in front of him.

Richard was a mess. They needn't have worried about any other ferals on the floor because he had torn every other living thing on the floor to pieces, including the potted plants from the employees' desks. His white shirt was encrusted with two-day-old bodily fluids and blood from when he had eaten his fellow coworkers. He had removed his pants and underwear but had not cleaned himself very well after evacuating his bowels. His hands were filthy from scratching at the various fluids caked over his body. Dirt from the potted plants just added the final layer of grime on top of it all.

Richard had, however, been very fit before succumbing to the toxin. At 6'2" and a muscular 240 pounds, many of the women in the office swooned over the good-looking man.

Upon hearing the door open, he turned immediately and rushed toward the people spilling out of the stairwell door. But something in the back of his mind told him these were not easy prey. He attempted to duck in between two cubicles just as a 9mm round slashed across the back of his left buttock. This elicited a grunt of pain as he ran farther into the maze of cubicles, making several turns before coming to a stop and feeling the back of his leg. He pulled his bloody palm around to the front of his face and looked at it, the smell of his own blood eliciting another angry grunt.

"I didn't get him!" Mark said as everyone kept a vigilant eye on their assigned sector of responsibility. "Shit, stay on line, guys. David, you come forward and clear around to the front windows. Cliff, stay there. Alan, slide this way with me."

As the four of them were orienting themselves to better face the room, Richard began heading toward the north wall of the building. He saw a binder lying on the ground and threw it like a Frisbee over the cubicles at the intruders of his domain.

The only effect it had was to give the four rescuers a better idea of where the feral was; although, Cliff almost shot the binder when it came flying over the cubicle wall.

"That's a smart one, Mark," Cliff grunted. "We better be careful."

"Yeah, I see that," Mark replied. "Okay, folks, let's move along the front here. And clear these offices as we go. There's no way in hell I'm going to try and clear that office space." He gestured at the open area full of desks and partitions.

They made their way toward the conference room, clearing the executive offices along their right and keeping a sharp eye out to their left. They made it to the first of the conference room's two doors and knocked. Jean informed them that this door was blocked by furniture and could they go to the other door. Mark looked at Alan with a face that said, "You've got to be kidding me!" Alan just shrugged and gestured up the hall. The four of them moved to the other door and knocked.

"Are you sure it's safe?" Jean asked through the door.

"Ma'am, it is most definitely not safe out here, but it will be even less so when we leave! Are you coming or not?" Mark rolled his eyes at Alan and mouthed, *"What the fuck?"*

"She's a total pain in the ass," Alan whispered back as the sound of arguing drifted out from under the door. There was a sound of moving furniture, which elicited another eye roll from Mark, and the door opened. Mark gestured for the occupants to come out. Ron stepped out and slid along the wall. Becca was about to follow when Jean grabbed her arm and pulled her back into the conference room, slamming the door shut again.

"What the… are you crazy?" Mark whispered over his shoulder as he heard another thump over in the cubicles. "Come on, guys, we have to leave now. Your friend Richard is still out here, and he's not too happy."

There was a loud bump from the conference room as the two women on the other side began arguing loudly. The four rescuers and Ron all exchanged looks of disbelief.

"What the hell, Ron?" Alan was glaring at his former coworker.

"Alan, she's fucking nuts! If Becca wasn't in there, I'd say leave her!"

"I heard that, Ron!" The door flew open to show Jean's face livid with anger. "I'm not going out there as long as Richard is out there!"

At the sound of his name Richard let out a yell and threw a computer monitor over the partitions. It smacked into the wall near Cliff and crashed to the ground. Cliff sent a buckshot reply into the nearest cubicle which sent Richard scampering away.

As Cliff lowered the shotgun, Richard popped his head above the intervening partitions and looked at the group. He dropped back down again before anyone could aim in on him. Jean tried to slam the door again but David was ready and jammed his work boot in the jamb to prevent it from closing all the way.

"Just leave it open, please," he said forcefully, as Becca forced her way past and out into the hall.

"She's afraid because Richard was screaming that he was going to kill her when he started going nuts!" Becca went over and huddled next to Ron. "He kept saying, 'I'm gonna kill her if it's the last thing I do!' and other stuff."

"I'm likely to kill her myself if she endangers anyone else." Cliff was looking pointedly at the woman who still had her hand on the door and was looking like she would slam it at her first opportunity. Jean looked up at this and blanched. She turned toward Becca, looking for some support, but the younger woman just turned away.

"I thought you wanted the water," she said finally, stepping back into the room and pointing off to the side.

"We do have a couple of unopened five-gallon jugs of water in there." Ron was nodding.

"Okay, David, yell out the window to Jim that we're okay. You three newbies, grab all the jugs you can carry; they're your cab fare. Any other supplies in there?" Mark was trying to interpret the noises Richard was making on the other side of the room. "Food, weapons, anything?"

"Other than the water, we were down to the Perrier and crackers we keep in there." Becca was shaking her head. "The only weapon we had was a broken table leg and a can of defense spray." She held up the tiny can of mace and smiled.

David barely choked back his laughter as he took in the arsenal. Cliff elbowed him gently, not wanting to lose focus on the open area in front of him.

"I'm sorry," David said at the crestfallen look on Becca's face. "I just hope you never have to rely on that stuff, because it doesn't work on these guys. A friend of mine's mom found out the hard way." His look took a serious turn as he spoke of the tragedy.

"All right, get the water. We're wasting time." Mark's Spidey sense was tingling; Richard was being a little too quiet.

They began moving back toward the stairs they had come from when Alan said, "Why not just go down the central well? It's closer, and we can go right out the front door. And we don't have to go past the cubicles." He gestured at the danger area.

"You're right." Mark stopped in his tracks, causing Ron to pull up short to avoid running into him. "Going your way, Cliff!"

"Gotcha," Cliff said. He had been walking backwards to cover their rear as they left. He merely stopped and began inching forward. Everyone in the middle of the line turned around and the whole circus began heading toward the central elevator bank and stairwell.

They made it to the elevator alcove, where Ron and Becca set down the two jugs each they were carrying. Jean was only carrying one, and no one had said anything in an attempt to avoid a verbal confrontation. Ron and Becca set theirs against the wall, while Jean just let hers drop from her hand in the middle of the alcove. It toppled over and began to roll away. David put his boot on it and pushed it back to Jean with a warning look.

Cliff glanced over his shoulder at the disturbance as he opened the stairwell door. He had just turned back when the door was ripped out of his hand and a female feral drove her shoulder into his upper thighs, knocking him off balance. The woman had been crouched down low and went right under the barrel of his shotgun. The feral was in among the group in an instant and immediately pulled Ron's left leg out from under him, sending him crashing to the floor as she turned on Becca and struck her twice in the stomach. Everyone was yelling and cursing as what had been a tiny Asian woman in a pantsuit wreaked havoc among them.

Mark stepped forward and was about to slam the butt of the HK into the back of the whirling dervish when a slight noise behind him caused him to duck. The small two-drawer file cabinet slammed into the back of his right triceps and across his back. The force of the blow drove Mark to his knees, falling on top of the female feral. She turned and tried to snap at him when Richard jumped on Mark's back and sent them both sprawling flat.

Mark went into survival combat mode. He jammed the muzzle of the HK up under the chin of the feral he was lying on top of, pushed off of her a little, and pulled the trigger twice. Both rounds went under her jaw and ruined her face. She immediately slumped back and was still. Meanwhile, Richard was attempting to fend off the flurry of blows that David was raining down on his head and back. David was swinging his shotgun back and forth like a pugil stick. This was not as effective as he would have liked because Becca had fallen back into him. Richard was trying to keep his balance with Mark thrashing around beneath him when Cliff stepped up and, holding the barrel of his shotgun, swung for the bleachers. The stock of the Mossberg glanced off of Richard's shoulder and slammed into the side of his head. The blow would have caved in the skull and broken the neck of a normal man. Richard's well-developed trapezius muscles prevented his neck from breaking, and the upward angle of the blow from bouncing off his shoulder reduced the force enough to keep it from being instantly fatal. It did lay him out cold though.

Cliff and his son pulled the monster the rest of the way off of Mark and were just pulling him to his feet when he let out a yell. The female feral had woken up and, although the left side of her jaw was shattered, had bitten down on Mark's wrist. A bone shard from her shattered jaw penetrated the Nomex Tactical glove he wore, and it cut into his skin. David did not hesitate and slammed the butt of his shotgun down on her temple, ending her for good. Mark stood up and looked at his wrist. *Well, now I'm fucked,* he thought.

Mark walked over to where Richard was laid out and put two rounds through his head. He turned and did the same for the female. He then went to the knocked-over water jug and pulled the plastic cap off. He held his hand under the water and removed the glove. The bone fragment came out as the glove was removed. It had only penetrated about a quarter of an inch, but it was obvious that the female's blood and some thick, clear yellow fluid had gotten onto his skin next to the wound. He held the injured hand under the water and gently scrubbed the blood away from the small tear in the skin. He massaged the area roughly until blood was flowing freely from the wound. Another good rinsing and a regular-sized Band-Aid covered the damage.

"All right, let's go," he said, standing up and kicking the still half-full bottle away. Mark took point this time and opened the stairway door. He cleared the landing and stepped through the doorway. They started down the stairs but came to a stop when they saw the mess on the second-floor landing. Someone had been eaten in the doorway. What remained of the corpse lay across the threshold, preventing the door from closing. Sounds of movement came from just the other side. Mark held up his fist, signaling everyone to stop just as Cliff fired a round from the landing above them. The silence following the shot was only broken by the sound of the feral's body he had shot sliding down the rest of the stairs to the third-floor landing.

Mark was just about to ask what happened when a face popped around the doorframe. As the feral's eyes got wide, Mark fired twice, putting a round right between them, and one through the cheek, causing the body to flop out of sight. Done taking chances, Mark advanced through the carnage-covered landing to the door and peeked out. The damage to the feral's head was catastrophic. He pushed the corpse the rest of the way through the door and closed it.

They continued down to the first level and back out to the trucks. Jim and Terry had looks of mild concern on their faces that quickly changed to alarm as they saw the looks everyone was giving them. Jim immediately went to his father and began looking him over.

"What happened?" Terry cried as she also picked up on the vibe.

"I just got scratched, guys." Mark's glove covered the Band-Aid and there were no other apparent injuries.

"Where?" Terry asked.

"Show 'em, Mark," Cliff said as he nodded for the four remaining jugs to be put in the bed of the truck.

Mark pulled down his glove and pulled the Band-Aid off. There was only a small spot of blood on it. Jim examined the wound and looked up with a confused look on his face.

"It's from the bone of a feral, son," Cliff said. "It had fresh blood on it when it penetrated his skin."

"Oh no! Daddy!" Terry began to cry. Jim's face took on a hard look.

"Look, guys, I'm going to be fine. I don't think that limited exposure is going to kill me or turn me into a loony tune, okay?" Mark was hugging Terry and had Jim by the arm. "Come on now, we have work to do." With that, he gave them each a gentle shove toward the vehicles, then he faced Alan.

"Where to for the cafeteria?" he asked, pulling the glove back on without replacing the Band-Aid.

"Look, Mark, we don't have to keep going…"

"We came here to do a job; let's get it done." Mark's very direct stare would brook no argument.

"The loading dock is back around that side of the building and across the parking lot," Alan said pointing out the way.

"What the hell is she doing?" Jim asked, gesturing with his rifle.

Jean was marching off across the parking lot toward an Audi. She hit the remote access button and the car chirped. Alan and Ron jogged over and caught up to her just as she was reaching for the door handle to the car.

"Jean, where are you going? And what the hell are you doing? These people are here to get us somewhere safe," Ron said, gently grabbing her arm.

Jean spun away from the grip and let loose a verbal tirade.

"I am going home! Where I am going to shower and change my clothes. After that, I'm going to take a nice long nap in MY bed. I smell and I'm hungry for some real food. I haven't heard from Deron since this all started, and I'm sure he's worried sick about me. And since you cretins would have gladly left me here," this last with a glare at Cliff, "I'm not going to make myself any more of a burden!" She turned back around and climbed into the car.

"Let her go," Cliff said, gesturing for them to return to the other vehicles. "Ron, Becca, what kind of cars do you drive?"

"I have a Toyota Corolla," Ron said, pointing out a tiny silver car.

"Acura MDX." Becca pointed to an all-wheel drive SUV.

"Nice!" Mark said, admiring the Acura. "We'll take that along for sure…" he stopped in mid-sentence. "Well, if you'd like to join us, that is. No one is going to force you to do anything…"

The sound of Jean's Audi peeling out of the lot caused a break in the conversation as they all watched her drive away. The car bottomed out going out of the driveway and even fishtailed a little as she put her foot in it, accelerating up the street. There was another squeal as she took the corner at the top of the hill, and the car was gone.

The small convoy, which now included Becca's Acura, went around to the roll-up door by the cafeteria. The electronics manufacturer employed almost 800 workers, running two full-time shifts and a skeleton crew at night. The dining facility was capable of feeding all of them. The steel shutter door was down, and the standard door next to it, closed. Mark and Cliff backed their vehicles down into the loading dock while Alan and Beca were directed to park by the smaller door. As they were getting out of their vehicles, a feral came jogging around the corner from the parking lot they had just crossed. Cliff was raising his shotgun when Mark said, "Wait."

Two much quieter rounds from the MP5, and the body collapsed to the ground. Mark followed his own mental note from earlier and changed out his half-full magazine. He had just finished stuffing the partially full one back in his vest when two more ferals rounded the corner of the building. Two more sets of double taps, and they, too, were on the ground. The one that had been on the left was not dead, however, as it let out a scream and began thrashing around. Mark thumbed the selector down and sent a three-round burst into its body.

They had Cliff and David take up positions at the end of the loading ramp, and Terry stayed at the vehicles, watching over Ron and Becca. The rest stacked at the door and, after Alan opened it, disappeared inside. Thirty seconds later, the bay door began to roll up. Thirty seconds after that, Alan appeared with two five-gallon water bottles in his hands. It took them another ten minutes to fit the forty-nine full bottles they found into the vehicles. Next was every bottle of anything drinkable: soda, sports drinks, vita-water—if it was drinkable, it was packed into the trucks and trailer.

They still had some space left, so Mark and Alan raided the storage room for bulk supplies. It would take a semi two trips just to haul the dry goods out of the storage room and another to empty the freezer. They did grab a huge box of steaks, about eighty pounds of hamburger patties, another forty of hot dogs, and four boxes of what had become semi-fresh produce. They stuffed bulk containers of condiments and spices into every nook and cranny. Other bulk goods such as sugar and flour were piled on top of everything in the bed of the truck. Bags of baked goods were placed on top of other items inside the other vehicles to keep them from blowing away.

By the time they finished and re-secured the building's doors, even Cliff's suburban was sitting low on its suspension. They all piled back into the vehicles, and the convoy began its trek back to Mark's. As they were leaving the business park, they saw a group of ferals lying on or next to the road. One of them was trying to pull its broken body toward the approaching convoy. Cliff slowed to look at the poor creature then sped up and ran it over, running over a few more that were not moving along the way. The trip back to Mark's house was uneventful. Only a few ferals ran at the convoy, and they were all left behind.

CHAPTER 23

Rancho Bernardo, CA

The convoy returned from the business park. They backed the vehicles up to the house and formed a bucket brigade to get the supplies in quickly. Mark reloaded the two magazines that were short rounds, and replaced them on his vest and in his weapon. He had Cliff trade in his shotgun for the M4 Jim was carrying and had Jim take the other MP5SD, giving them two silenced long guns. Using the universal clips on his vest, Mark attached a long holster under his left arm that held a Ruger .22 pistol with an AWC silencer attached. Mark put four spare magazines for the .22 in special pouches and was ready to go.

As Mark was doing a "Battle Rattle" check, jumping up and down to check for noise, Jen burst through the garage door with Melanie on her heels. Both looked like they were about to start crying. Cliff was next through the door with an apologetic look on his face. Jim brought up the rear.

"Where is it?" Jen demanded as Mel pulled up beside her with her hands on her hips. "You show me, Mark Norris—this instant!"

Mark knew better than to say, "Where's what?" He lifted his sleeve and pulled his glove down. The penetrative wound was only slightly swollen but very hot to the touch and bright red for about four inches all around it. He had forgone a Band-Aid, and there was a slight weeping of clear fluid. The wound was not sore though, and Mark demonstrated this by pushing on it to show them it didn't hurt.

"You guys settle down. It's not that bad. I rinsed it immediately and I'm up on my shots. It was a bone fragment from a jaw—"

"So it was from its mouth, Dad?" Mel was giving him her most intense stare, the one reserved for the dogs when she was disciplining them.

"Yes, honey, but—"

"And you were just going to go back out without telling us?" Jen had her hands on her hips too now.

"Well, yes. We have to get to the Costco and the—"

"We don't have to do that, bud. The rest of us can take care of it if you want to rest." Cliff put in his two cents, wincing slightly at the glare Mark gave him.

"You guys are not going out there without—"

"We can handle it Dad, we—" Jim started.

"Stop!" Mark's command voice had been honed on the drill field, and never once had a troop complained that they couldn't hear him, even during a firefight. "I am fine; if I ever become 'unfine,' I will inform you all immediately. I have things that need to be done to ensure the safety and security of you guys and the rest of the people here. WE are going to go to Costco and Home Depot over on Scripps Parkway, and WE will return with as much supplies and equipment as we can transport. This matter is now closed from further discussion!"

He took Jen and Mel in a hug, pulling them in tight. They stood like that until Cliff and Jim started to fidget. He let them go slowly, and they all made their way inside the house. As they filed through the doorway and toward the living room, Mel peeled off and went to the counter in the kitchen. She grabbed a yellow legal pad covered in her neat handwriting and came back over to her father.

"Just some stuff before you go, Dad," she said, looking up at Mark.

"Okay, honey, what have you got?"

"Well, Corporal Jake says he's a sergeant now and the rest of us should now bow down before him. Do you guys really have to do that? I thought you just saluted." She shrugged. "He also says that they have the base 80 percent secure and that they are going to try and get here by the day after tomorrow. The salinization…"

"*De*salinization, honey."

"Whatever… plants are all working fine and they are filling up the 'bulls,' whatever that means, so they can start sending patrols out into Oceanside and San Clemente. He says Colonel Neal has his 'stuff'—I used that word instead of the real one he used—together and they will begin major off-base ops tomorrow if the gates hold. There are reports of the ferals actually banding together now in groups larger than twenty. That info came from back east somewhere. Aunt Carol says hi and she and

Uncle Bill are doing fine at the cabin. They have two families with them, and they're set with their well water since the cabin is up so high and none of the water tested as tainted. Which brings me to the last thing… you can test the water with a 'Dope Kit'? I guess whatever it is in the water tests positive for PCP. Uncle Bill is running your reloading press like there's no tomorrow. The rest of this can wait until you come back." She finished, slapping the pad against her thigh.

"Thanks, Mel, and good job," Mark said, giving her another squeeze. "Babe," he said, turning to Jen, "how is everything else around here? I know you guys have to organize stuff and put together a watch schedule. Is there anything you need specifically that I should look for while I'm out and about slaying dragons?"

"Just feminine products," she said with a grin. The girls were always trying to embarrass him by asking him to pick up feminine hygiene products at the PX or the CVS.

"I live to serve!" he said, looking over at the front door lookout who nodded the *all clear*. And with that, he was leading the team out the door.

CHAPTER 24

Buffalo, NY

"I think the first phase of our plan went rather well," Satif proclaimed. He leaned back from the dinner table and wiped his mouth. "The Infidels are lost, over 50 percent of their population is destroyed, their military is useless. I think we have done well!"

Ibet was furious at the fat man across from him. "We are seeing thousands, maybe millions, of believers die too! The toxin has virtually wiped out Egypt."

"Some sacrifices were necessary; you knew this—" Satif started.

"And the toxic carriers have—" Ibet cut him off.

"And some of those losses are for the better!" Satif interrupted right back.

"The Great Satan still has its fangs though, Satif." Khalid joined the conversation. He had been on the last plane into the Buffalo Airport. The toxin had spread its disaster faster than they had planned for. "The nuclear arsenal will always hang above our head like the Sword of Damocles."

"Then we shall parry the sword strike if it should fall!" Satif had no idea what the "Sword of Damocles" was, but he wasn't about to let them know it. He had made his tutors study for him most of the time growing up, and he was somewhat less educated than he professed. He leaned forward. "They say they could bomb us back to the Stone Age, yet where do you think they will be in ten years, ha? By the time the cowards crawl out of their caves, their countries will be wastelands of thugs and outlaws.

Like my *Road* movie..." He snapped his fingers at Mohamed for assistance.

"*Road Warrior*," Mohamed supplied.

"*Road Warrior*!" Satif yelled. "They will be living like the scavengers they are!" He leaned back again with a satisfied grin.

"And Phase Two?" Ibet Asked. "When do we start?"

"In six days, my friend. We will let the toxin kill off some more of the non-believers, then we will have the teams ready and…" He paused at the sound of gunfire from outside. He glanced over his shoulder out the window but could see nothing. The fact that there was actually danger outside the walls of the estate and the security contractors actually had to defend them was unsettling for Satif, and it showed. His face went slack and a little pale. In a few moments, he would be sweating. "We will begin to poison the land as we poisoned the people, and this time, it will not make its way to our lands." He pushed back from the table and nodded to the rest of the terrorists gathered there. "I will retire now, my friends."

As soon as Satif left the room, the other three men pushed their chairs together and began to discuss the plans for the following days in earnest.

CHAPTER 25

San Marcos, CA

Albert Castillo was a badass.

The twenty-three-year-old gang member had grown up in San Marcos, California. His mother had come across the border illegally while she was pregnant with him, not knowing which of a half dozen men were his father. Albert had been a very skinny little kid who learned early that you had to be tough to survive. He began taking martial arts classes at the YMCA when he was six. The discipline taught took hold but not in the way anyone could have anticipated.

Albert did stay out of trouble, but only because his discipline and intelligence kept him from making the same mistakes other gang members his age were making. He refused to sell or transport drugs. Instead, he became an enforcer, administering beatings to those who failed to show proper respect to his gang. He kept his face concealed as much as possible and worked mostly at night. By the age of sixteen, he had killed three rivals and was a much-respected member. He earned the name "Nosferatu" after slitting the throat of an addict who had stolen from one of his runners. As the man bled out, Albert whispered in his ear, "I will suck the lifeblood right out of my enemies!"

"Man, that's some scary vampire shit right there, homie!" said Ricardo, his number two. "You be that Nosfertu guy on *Blade* man!"

"Nosferatu, Rico, Nosferatu." Albert pondered the name for a moment and decided it fit. From that day forward, he had everyone refer to him as Nosferatu. No abbreviations, no shortening of the name, always Nosferatu.

Nosferatu had been poisoned by drinking water from the tap in his mother's apartment. He had gone feral and killed his mother as she herself was turning. A rampage through their apartment complex left seventeen people dead, and another twelve so horribly maimed that even with the toxin coursing through their system all they could do was flop around and crawl feebly toward the street. The toxin didn't quite destroy his ability to reason. He had faint memories and thoughts. It was these memories that saved Ricardo from being torn apart when they encountered each other on a street corner two blocks from his apartment.

Ricardo, however, had attacked Nosferatu at first and suffered some grievous injuries before rolling over in a submissive posture. Nosferatu would have ripped the guts out of anyone else, but something in the back of his mind stayed his hand. As he walked away, Ricardo rolled over and began to follow his leader. Two days later, the pack numbered eighteen. By the end of the week, he was leading forty ferals as they hunted prey. This included any ferals that did not join the pack, as well as animals and people.

Nosferatu's memory served him well in feeding his pack also. He remembered that grocery stores held food and doorknobs turned. This gave his pack an advantage in staying alive. They went from house to house eating everything they found. Because they were well fed and took shelter to sleep instead of always being on the hunt, their wounds healed better and faster. The pack became more cooperative and fights between members less frequent. They became more efficient at getting into buildings or other places where survivors had barricaded themselves.

A fourteen-year-old survivor had been found by the pack's scouts. She had been run to ground and finally took shelter in a parked minivan. The pack pounded at the car for half an hour before Nosferatu looked around and spied a metal pipe lying in the gutter. In a fit of rage, he picked it up and began swinging it at the van. The third hit cracked the window. By the fifth, understanding had dawned in his now primitive brain.

Ten seconds later, the street echoed with the screams of the young girl as she was torn apart.

He kept the pipe.

CHAPTER 26

San Diego, CA

The convoy pulled into the Costco/Home Depot parking lot and stopped. Two ferals began jogging across the lot, in the direction of the trucks. Mark stepped down from the passenger seat and fired two rounds. Both ferals went down, but one got right back up again. Mark had to wait for it to get around some cars for a clear enough shot to put it down. All the other passengers in the convoy got out of the vehicles and formed a line, five abreast, with about ten feet between each person.

They took their time approaching the Costco building, making sure there were no ferals hiding behind cars. They stopped to finish off several that were either so wounded they couldn't move or had incapacitated themselves by overexerting their muscles. It took them almost 20 minutes to secure the parking lot, which was surprisingly empty of cars.

The steel shutter doors of the Costco were all rolled down. Someone had tried to ram a car through one of the doors by backing into it at a high rate of speed, and it was still wedged in the door opening. The driver had managed to rip the door out of its left-side track before being attacked and killed. The partially eaten corpse was still belted in the driver's seat. The opening the car had formed was more than big enough to allow people to climb over the roof of the car and into the building.

The vehicles were all backed up next to each other in front of the building, and the tailgates were open. Everyone gathered by the Buick that had been bashed into the door. The opening showed that there were some lights still on in the building, but it was mostly dark.

"Terry, you're out here, please," Mark said, gesturing at the vehicles. "I need you to watch over Alan as he scavenges gas from the cars. Alan, no more than forty meters out, okay? I want her to be able to cover you."

"I thought we were going to siphon the gas station tanks," Alan said, getting a bag of equipment out of the back of the Suburban.

"We are, but I want to siphon as much as we can from cars that are abandoned. Also, look for keys on the corpses, if you can, without getting too mucked up. Another four-by-four would be nice to have. If you do get one, gas it up and remember to top off all our fuel tanks as well." Mark waved toward the convoy vehicles. "I think Becca's Acura only has half a tank. Then all the gas cans, please. Remember, you have to prime the pump with the bulb on the electric pump before using the batteries."

"I got it," Alan said as he left the others and began to scour the parking lot, being careful as he stepped around cars, so that nothing could reach out and grab him.

"Let's go." David was next to the door opening and had been peering into the interior of the building. "We should be able to just roll up the door and turn on the lights."

"All right, stick-boy," Mark said, gesturing David through the opening. "Jim, cover him."

The two fathers waited anxiously while the two young men entered the building by climbing over the roof of the car. A few seconds later, Jim's head popped out, and he asked for the bolt cutters. After disappearing back inside, there was a metallic clank and the next door over started to rise. It was only up about four feet when a screech filled the air. Both Mark and Cliff rolled under the door and were getting to their knees when the sound of Jim's MP5 spitting out rounds brought them up short. Both David and Jim were facing into the warehouse with their weapons to their shoulder. Lying next to the checkout registers, some forty yards away, was the body of a female feral.

David walked over to a bank of light switches and began turning them on. No more screams broke the silence, so they proceeded to clear the checkout area. They then systematically cleared the outside walls and the back storage room. After that, they formed a paranoid bubble and went up and down the aisles with guns and eyeballs pointed in every direction. They found some linens and other items piled just outside the air curtain leading into one of the refrigerated areas. It had been made into a makeshift nest. Torn open packages of meat and other foodstuffs were thrown about. They found that the feral had been using the women's restroom, just not the toilets in it.

“Why would she make her bed right here, where it’s freezing?” Jim wondered. He was standing in the middle of the makeshift nest. “It’s got to be fifty degrees here.”

“Might be ‘cause of the fever they seem to have.” David was poking through the trash strewn about the area.

“Shit, I never expected to find this place even halfway intact,” Mark said, looking around at the thirty-foot-high racks of everything you could ever want in a survival situation. “We should just move in here and live forever… or until the power goes out!”

“I’m thinking we should leave it.”

Every head turned to look at the person who had just committed blasphemy. Cliff stood there and returned everyone’s stare for a moment, and then continued with the sacrilege. “We should take the few essentials we need and lock it back up.” He turned his gaze on David. “Close your mouth, son; you can breathe through your nose and not look so stupid.”

David, whose mouth was, in fact, hanging open, closed it with an audible clomp. Mark, who also had a look of incredulity on his face—albeit without the jaw dropping—thought about it for a few more seconds and nodded. Jim’s head pivoted back and forth, realizing he’d missed something and finally said, “What?”

“Cliff’s right. We should take what we need, especially the perishables and enough frozen goods to fill our storage space, then seal this place up if we can. The power is still on and the refrigeration is still working. This place has two emergency generators, right? Isn’t that what Nate said, Jim?” Mark looked at his son who was nodding in agreement. “That means we’ll have two days to get here and recover any food stuffs we need if the power does go out. We leave a note for any other survivors who come along, telling them how to contact us and how to get in and get to the supplies they need.”

“But Dad! What about raiders? What if they come and take it all away?” Jim looked confused. “And you’re gonna tell them where we are?”

“Well, son, I don’t think we have any more right to the goods here than anyone else, and we’re a lot better off than most. We are definitely better armed than most militias, so I’m not too worried about them contacting us. Besides, we have Derry coming tomorrow, and I don’t know what supplies they’re going to need for the survivors and refugees on base. We’ll take what we need and leave a method of communication for any other survivors, bud. My last standing orders were to survive and help others do the same.”

The sound of a big V-8 had everybody turn toward the doors but nothing came into view. They divided into pairs, with one person carrying a load with their weapon slung while the other kept overwatch, and then they'd switch. Mark was using a hand forklift to wheel a pallet of canned vegetables out the front door when he stopped dead in his tracks.

"Really?" He was staring at a bright orange Ford F-150 Raptor four-by-four with black graphics. Alan was grinning from ear to ear as he poured gas into the tank from one of the twenty plastic VP fuel cans they had brought along. "That is the most un-tactical vehicle I have ever seen! And orange… Really?" he asked again in disbelief.

"Dude, this thing is awesome! Six point two liter, 411 horsepower, high output motor! It's already lifted," Alan said, putting the can down and patting the side. "It only has 830 miles on it! Is it safe to go in there?"

"Yeah, take someone with you though, why?" Mark said as Alan sped past him, grabbing Jim along the way.

They were back out a few seconds later. Alan had a four pack of Clorox wipes with the plastic already torn off. He opened one of the tubs and pulled a few wipes out and scrubbed some blood out of the interior. He then spent a moment wiping down the dash since the car had obviously been sitting for the past few days with the door open. When the dust was gone, he turned to look at the crowd that had gathered and said, "What?"

It took them more than two hours to load everything they were going to take on this trip into both of the trucks, Becca's Acura, Alan's minivan, and Cliff's suburban and trailer. In spite of everything they took, it was less than 2 percent of what was available. They used Mark's truck to pull the Buick out of the door then used tools they had brought along to bash and wire the damaged door closed. They then rolled down the other door, secured it from the inside, turned out the lights, and propped open a side door. They planned on getting a combination lock from Home Depot and coming back to secure it.

The Home Depot posed the same tactical challenges as the Costco had. The front roll-up doors were open and the glass was shattered. They cleared the building slowly and carefully. Although they did not find any ferals, they did find many more bodies. The store had been looted a little more as well. All the portable generators were gone except for four of them on a top shelf. Mark found the forklift and lowered them to the ground. They would only take two of them, as Mark already had two at his house and Cliff had one at his.

"Jim, I need you to get me all the diamond blades for the gas cutoff saw you can find. Check the warehouse section too… better yet, Terry!" he yelled, only to find her standing right next to him. "Who's outside?" he asked, looking around.

"'Who's on *first*,' Dad, not outside," she said, quoting Abbot and Costello. "David is outside with Alan, drooling over that ugly truck."

"Oh, okay. Do you think you could look up the location of some saw blades for me? And grinder blades too? I know we are going to need them big time in the future. Jim will get the ones I need off the shelf and give you a part number. If you could tell us where they are stored in back, I'd appreciate it." He turned to Jim. "I need the diamond blades for the cutoff saw and grinder, both diamond and masonry bits for the RotoHammer too. In fact, if they have a new Bosch, grab one. Ours is a little long in the tooth. Cliff, you know what you need, so take Becca with you."

Another hour saw the convoy again riding low on its springs. The shutters were lowered over the broken doors and padlocked with big industrial combination locks. They went back to the Costco and padlocked it as well. Using a Sharpie pen, Mark wrote a note on the door itself, telling anyone who might come along after them the combo to get in, and instructions on how to contact them. He also explained that they would send a rescue team if there were ferals around or the party was unable to travel the seven plus miles to Mark's house. *Not that I'm going to have room for them,* he thought. *But that's what the base will be for.*

CHAPTER 27

Bemidji, MN

Yavi and Chris were patrolling along the SR 71 at the Highway 2 intersection south of town, when Yavi stood on the brakes and slowly climbed out of the truck. Chris, who had been scrolling through an iPad he had picked up to see what apps were working, looked around in confusion. He hopped out of the truck, brought his rifle up, and started panning his side of the road. He worked his way around the front of the truck and stopped to stare as well.

Coming up the Paul Bunyan Expressway was a column of Minnesota National Guard vehicles—two Stryker AFVs, eight Hummers, and two trucks, followed by another two Strykers. The column came to a halt about two hundred meters short of the pickup. Yavi made sure his M4 was pointed at the ground, then raised one arm and waved slowly. The lead Humvee pulled away and drove slowly toward them, making sure it stayed off to the side so that the gunners in the AFVs could keep a clear field of fire on them. After stopping, the Hummer idled for a moment, and Yavi could see the person in the front passenger seat talking on the radio. A minute later, the door opened and a young lieutenant stepped out and approached.

"Hello, gentlemen," he said, stopping a good thirty yards away and still giving his gunners a clear field. "Lovely day."

"It sure is now!" Yavi exclaimed. "Man, are we glad to see you! My name is Yavi and this is Chris." He pointed needlessly at the man standing next to him. “We’re with a band of survivors that’s holed up in a hotel about two miles north of here.”

“My name is Lieutenant Crowe.” The lieutenant smiled. “I’m with the National Guard. Could you tell me how bad the city is?”

“Well, Bemidji is pretty much fucked!” Chris gestured at the city behind him. “Downtown is completely overrun. We were getting one or two survivors out of there a day, until recently. The ferals have started to form packs and are learning to use tools. They no longer just rush at us and attack blindly. They wait in ambush and use some rudimentary cooperation. There are a couple dozen ranches and homesteads in the outlying areas that have held up pretty well. Water is a definite problem. But we have found that if we distill it a couple of times, we’re good to go.”

“Well, you seem to be well-armed and supplied,” Crowe said, pointing at their slung M4s and pistols.

“I was with the state park service as a ranger, and Chris was a state trooper. We were able to gain access to our agency armory and get pretty well supplied.” Yavi patted the state park GMC. “We have almost eighty survivors at the hotel and we’re working on setting up another building for sheltering more,” Yavi said as two more guardsmen approached from the Hummer. “How is the rest of the world?”

“Well, it’s like Bemidji: pretty much fucked.” Crowe gestured to the two men joining them. “This is Master Sergeant Lovell and Sergeant Giles—this is Chris and Yavi.” The men all came together and shook hands. “The numbers we have received from National Command Authority is over 60 percent of the world’s population is dead or gone feral. No real numbers from Africa or the Middle East. Europe was almost completely wiped out. Britain is in contact with us, but they suffered almost 80 percent losses. We come across groups pretty consistently that are holding out okay. This upper part of the state, though, has had it pretty bad. We think the whole thing started here… well, over in Hill River.”

“That was us. I’m out of the same office that first discovered it. In fact, those rangers are back at the hotel with the two guys from the CDC who came out to analyze this.”

“Would that be Ken Layver? We have orders to find him, if we can.”

“Well, look no more!” Yavi smiled brightly. “For I shall serve him up to you on a platter!” The cannibalism all around him had no effect whatsoever on his humor.

“Yavi isn’t very PC,” Chris said, frowning at the always-smiling ranger.

“Well, let’s go meet them, then.” Crowe waved the soldiers back to the Hummer. “We’ll follow you gents.”

The drive back to the hotel took ten minutes. Chris got a hold of Glenn on the radio and filled him in on the morning's events. Glenn, in turn, got a hold of the other vehicle that was out on sweeps and had them return to the hotel as well. The courtyard was overflowing with people when the roof lookout yelled down that the National Guard convoy was in sight. Several people went out into the street and set up a perimeter. Standing rules said no one outside without security.

Yavi pulled his truck into the hotel parking lot. Crowe had his Strykers park across the street at both ends of the block with the rest of the convoy spread out. The troops all dismounted, except for those on the gun turrets, and began to stretch their legs. They walked into a hero's welcome and were virtually mobbed by the crowd greeting them. Crowe introduced his company commander, Captain Nelson, and began getting the troops squared away as the park rangers brought the captain up to speed on their situation.

"Quite the set up here. Are any of the other buildings secured?" Nelson asked, gesturing toward the buildings across the street. "The open space would be hard to secure though. Are you seeing any large groups of ferals?"

"We are getting them barricaded slowly but surely. We only recently gathered enough people to need it and to have enough of a labor pool to get the construction done." Scott waved toward the crowd. "We have been encountering larger groups with less infighting among them and we have observed larger cooperative hunting packs. We've also seen tool use. I think this is in third or fourth infection-level ferals. But sometimes, once they go a little feral, they drink from whatever water source they can find, and then they go completely overboard."

Nelson was nodding and actually taking notes. He would wind up grilling everyone he could corner and document everything he could about the behavior of the ferals. Crowe had some troops clear all the buildings along the block before allowing half of them to stand down and mingle. The survivors were hungry for news from anywhere and were not above bribing the troops with some fresh cooked meals. A BBQ was laid out along with as much fresh produce as they had.

"Well, this beats Mr. E's anytime," Lovell said, referring to the military MREs they had been living off of since leaving the National Guard armory the previous week. "I'm surprised Nelson is letting us even eat this."

"He did say we have to stick with our own water until further notice." Giles had pieces of corn on his chin from the half-eaten cob he was waving around. "I think he'll be cool though. These folks have a rooftop garden and rain catch. They also have two stills going to purify water. That Yavi guy said the power went out two days ago. They have a couple of generators—"

Gunfire interrupted him as the gunner in the northern Stryker fired a short burst at something in the twilight. A few seconds later, the lookout on the roof of the hotel called out that she had movement to the north as well.

Lovell looked at the smoke drifting up from the grills and saw that the smoke was drifting northeast. "I think that's what's bringing them in." He pointed out the smoke to Giles. More gunfire from the north Stryker and then a single shot from the hotel roof signaled an end to the festivities. As the troops headed back to their vehicles, a scream sounded from somewhere to the north of the hotel.

One of the troops had snuck off to take a piss and had stepped between buildings. A feral had snuck between the lookouts and jumped him while he was using both hands to unzip his fly. They both fell back out into the street and began rolling around. Two other troops rushed over and delivered, crushing butt strokes to the feral's head, but it was too late. The feral had bitten half the face off of the young soldier. He was taken to the medical Humvee, but the slightly yellow serum on his face showed that the toxin had been delivered into his bloodstream.

"What is your procedure for this?" Scott asked Crowe.

"We've been letting the victim decide, actually. Most of the time we just sedate them until they turn violent. Then an injection." Crowe shook his head at the loss. "They did try to put them in a prison yard down in Minneapolis, but they would just tear each other up at first. Then if they survived they would form packs and work like mad to escape and attack anyone they could. They just started sedating them and then pushing morphine until they expired."

The young soldier said goodbye to some of his squad mates and was moved into a Radio Shack that had been cleared across the street from the hotel. The rest of the soldiers were preparing sleeping quarters when more gunfire broke out. Scott and Dan jogged to the perimeter, followed by several of the other survivors. They joined the guardsmen already stationed there and filled in any slight gaps. Crowe had the security force spread out evenly and told them not to group too tightly at the north end. It was good advice, as three minutes later, there was gunfire from the east.

At first, the ferals showed up as individuals, but at 2240, the roof watch saw a small pack of about twenty. The pack stalked back and forth about 150 yards out, not daring to get any closer once one of the rooftop snipers dropped one that got a little too curious and came in close. This pack stayed along the eastern perimeter patiently working their way back and forth. Word was sent to Scott and Glenn, who had become the de facto leaders of the group. Glenn and Dan, along with Chris and his Weatherby made their way to the roof.

The sentries had been instructed not to fire on anything outside of the 150-yard mark for fear of wasting ammo. Both Dan and Glenn were expert marksmen and Chris had been a sniper on the SWAT team. A small armory had been established on the roof, and both Dan and Glenn kept scoped rifles there. They had zeroed and practiced with the rifles over the past week, setting up and measuring range markers from their shooting positions. Glenn used an accurized AR-10 with a Nighthawk scope. He would engage targets out to 400 yards. Dan, using an HS Precision .308 topped with a Leupold scope would cover out to 800 yards. Chris and his 7mm was responsible for anything out beyond that.

They had just set up their positions, Dan and Glenn with bipods, and Chris using a pair of sandbags, when the sentry on the west side of the building called out that he had another much larger pack approaching from that direction, but they were about half a mile away. Chris immediately pulled up his sandbags and went to that side of the roof. Several other survivors with scoped rifles joined them.

Scott informed Nelson of the situation, and he sent two of his designated marksmen to the hotel roof and two more to the roof of the Radio Shack. Everyone was put on alert status. Guardsmen were hustling back to their vehicles and survivors were preparing positions at the hotel windows when Chris fired the first shot at the pack approaching from the west.

They had observed that a definite pack leadership rapidly evolved when the ferals banded together. An alpha usually established its dominance quickly, and if he or she was successful, the pack would soon swell. Eliminating the alpha usually resulted in the pack disintegrating if another did not come forward.

Snipers in combat are trained to look for indicators of leadership and target the individuals who display them. Chris saw the feral that was obviously the alpha of the pack approaching from the west. The huge man wore overalls and some kind of leather sleeves over a plaid flannel shirt. The sleeves had protected him from other ferals' attacks. He would point and a scout would run off in the direction indicated. That was all that was needed to put a bulls-eye right on his chest. Chris waited until the pack reached an intersection that they had doped out for his rifle earlier. They had actually used the stop sign on the corner to zero his rifle.

Chris made the adjustment on his scope for 820 yards. He laid the crosshair right on the alpha's chest, took a breath, and let it all the way out. As the crosshairs settled back on the center of mass, Chris slowly pulled the trigger to the rear. The shot broke and the 7mm match bullet streaked away. The alpha never knew what hit him. The 150-grain bullet slammed into his sternum and crushed the bottom of both ventricles before impacting the spine. The deformed bullet then blew out the back and punched into another feral, knocking it down and killing it as well.

On the other side of the roof, Dan and Glenn identified the pack members most likely to be alphas and opened fire. After five shots, some of the pack broke and ran away, but some actually dove behind cover. These were engaged if any part of them became exposed. Both of their rifles were magazine fed with ten-round box magazines. After the first twenty rounds, there wasn't enough of a pack left to recognize. They both picked up their rifles and gear and went to help Chris.

One of the guard snipers had set up a Barrett M107 .50-caliber sniper rifle. He let the big gun roar, and a line of ferals went down, the 671-grain bullet smashing through six bodies before traveling down the street. The sniper would aim at the head of a feral closest to them, and because of the downward angle, the bullet would first pass through a skull, then a chest, then a stomach, then a leg. The first ten rounds killed or wounded twenty-five ferals before they were running for cover. With the pack leadership gone and confusion taking over, the pack began to disperse. By the time all the rest of the snipers had fired a few shots, targets in the open were getting scarce.

The gunfire slowed down to a few sporadic pops and finally died off. The troops began policing up the fired brass and storing it away. No one knew when manufacturing facilities would produce new ammo, so they would have to start reloading eventually. It didn't seem that pressing of a matter with several hundred thousand rounds being stored in the hotel, but the long run Scott was thinking of could last years.

The sentries went to 50 percent watch while one half cleaned weapons. Chris only got off eight shots since the internal magazine in his rifle only held four rounds. He only took a few minutes to punch the bore with a brush and Hoppes #9, then a few patches. He went over to watch one of the guard snipers clean his massive Barrett.

"Man, I'd sure love to have one of those," he said with longing in his eyes. "How far out can you shoot with that thing?"

"I haven't tried anything over 1600 yards," the young soldier said as he broke down the weapon. "That's a beauty you've got there too, sir. I bet you could stretch her out real good." There was a look of admiration in his eye for the Weatherby.

"Well, you let me know when you want to trade, son, and I'll call it a done deal."

"Really?" The soldier looked around. "I'm Rob. If you're serious, I'll hook you up. I can't give you much ammo, though, since we're kind of limited on that. But we have four complete spare 107s, including the light intensifiers, and I can probably get ya two or three hundred rounds." He was looking at the gun case and the accessories there. "How much ammo you have for it?"

"I have one-and-a-half case lots, about seven hundred fifty rounds of Federal match. Are you serious you can do that and not get court martialed?" Chris was actually licking his lips in anticipation.

"Shit, for that rifle, I could make it happen. And if you're gonna give me all that ammo, I'll hook you up with some more from my end." Rob stuck out his hand. They were shaking hands when Giles led a work crew up on to the roof to put up an antenna.

CHAPTER 28

Vista, CA

Nosferatu heard the convoy coming long before he could see it. He had started having the pack hang out by the 78 Freeway. People had started to travel again as supplies grew short. Since the freeways had been pretty clear since the day of the attacks, people were traveling them both on foot and in vehicles. Even the occasional bicyclist became a victim to the pack's hunger.

Gesturing toward one of his scouts, Nosferatu made a "Guh" sound, sending her off to gather information on the size and direction of the many vehicles he could now hear. The pack had not yet run into any prey that they could not overcome, so when the scout came back waving two open hands, Nosferatu thought his ship had come in. He began waving at the other pack members to get up. The pack made it to the overpass, which was their usual ambush point. Some began climbing down onto the green signs mounted on the overpass, while others hid off to the side of the road. Nosferatu hid at the corner of the overpass, ready to run down the embankment.

The convoy of up-armored Hummers was slowly working its way east along the 78. Sergeant Sanchez was in the first vehicle. Derry was in the third. They had only seen the occasional feral since leaving the newly re-established base perimeter. Sanchez was in the front passenger seat of the Hummer, going over the surface street routes they would take once they got off the freeway in Rancho Bernardo. His head was down, looking at

Google maps on his laptop when the driver tapped him on the shoulder at the same time the gunner up top said, "Contact front. Movement on the overpass. Looks like a couple of folks have been ambushed here."

The convoy immediately spread out to the sides of the road and slowed. Normally, they would speed up to get out of a kill zone, but the fighting ferals had changed the way they operated.

"I see some hanging on the back of the road signs!" Corporal Koch said from the turret. "They're hiding along the overpass too, Sergeant! I can see their heads popping up!"

"Company, prepare for contact!" Captain Johnson was the convoy commander. "Sanchez, see if we can go around. I don't want them dropping bricks on us. Break. Base, Gypsy One-Six, we have contact with a group of ferals that have taken up ambush positions on the 78 at the Rancho Santa Fe overpass, we—"

"Contact right! Contact right!" The sound of gunfire broke out all along the column. "Contact rear!" The gunners in the top turrets began putting out rounds as a wave of feral humans broke out of the cover on the right side of the freeway and charged down the embankment to jump on the slow-moving vehicles in the convoy. There were over 100 of them and sixteen made it in among the convoy vehicles. Some of these began to jump on the hoods of the Hummers in an attempt to get at the gunners in their cupolas. The rest pounded on the vehicles and pulled at anything they could get a grip on. Some of the Hummers had windows down, both to cool the occupants and to allow them to point their weapons out the side. One feral managed to pull the driver's side rear door open on one of the vehicles and began clawing at the Marine sitting there. The young lance corporal was able to shove the feral back out but was dragged along with it. A furious scuffle ensued, resulting in the feral lying there with a broken arm on one side and a dislocated shoulder on the other. Lance Corporal Sullivan untangled his rifle sling and shot the injured feral twice in the head.

"Well, you Kung Fu'd the hell out of him," Derry said, coming around the Hummer and standing next to Sullivan, looking down on the corpse. "He bite ya?"

"No, Sergeant, just some scrapes." All the Marines were "sleeves down and covered," which meant there were no areas of skin exposed except for the face. They all wore their knee and elbow pads, along with their leather-reinforced gloves. Most of them had riot shields and big, polycarbonate face shields attached to their helmets. All this made it tough to chew through to the Marine underneath. Sullivan dusted himself off as more firing broke out at the front of the convoy.

The ferals along the overpass stood up to get a better view of what had happened, so the gunner in the front Hummer, who had an M2 .50-caliber machine gun, opened up on the overpass. He hosed along the concrete retaining wall, hitting five of the curious onlookers, before shifting his aim to the green highway signs hanging from the overpass. Eight bodies fell down onto the highway. Another burst, and two more joined their brethren lying on the blacktop below. The rest of the pack on the overpass looked at Nosferatu for guidance. Some started to run away, back to the shopping center they had been sleeping in. Others charged down the slope toward the convoy, in spite of Nosferatu gesturing for them to run away. These were shot and killed in short order.

Derry was holding his rifle, looking over the hood of a Hummer when Nosferatu's gesturing caught his eye. He shifted his aim and watched the muscular feral herding his pack away from the freeway. Derry fired just as the feral turned to trot after his pack. The round caught him in the hip, just grazing the bone. Nosferatu spun to the ground but popped right back up and turned toward his assailant. Their eyes met across the 200 plus yards separating them. Nosferatu snarled and took a step, ready to fight. Derry just raised his rifle to fire again, but as soon as he saw the movement, Nosferatu dove to the ground and rolled behind cover. He crawled over to an abandoned car and looked back at the Marines who were getting ready to move out.

As the convoy rolled under the overpass, Derry's Hummer was hit with a rock. He turned and looked at the feral standing on the overpass, glaring at him. It ducked behind cover again as another gunner opened up on it with a M240G machine gun. Derry was just turning back to face forward when he saw the feral running along the frontage road for a few yards before disappearing.

"Persistent bastard," Derry mumbled as the convoy moved on.

Mark Norris had a fever. His muscles ached and his head throbbed. Even though he had the thermostat set at a frigid sixty degrees, he couldn't seem to get cool. The kids all came in to check on him, and the constant intrusions were making him angry. He was going to snap at the person coming through the door until he realized it was Jen. The nasty remark died on his lips and he looked over at the TV. He had the Sherlock Holmes DVD playing to distract himself. Even Robert Downey Junior's cool humor couldn't get rid of the feeling of anger and frustration. And knowing that it was probably due to the toxin in his system was just making him angrier.

"Well, aren't we a bit testy, Mr. Norris?" she said, setting a bottle of cold water on the nightstand next to him. "They're just worried about you."

"I'm fine, dammit! I just need a little rest. And I can't get it with a head poking through the door every five minutes!" Mark grabbed the bottle and chugged it down without stopping. He tossed the empty bottle into a half full trash bag of similar discards. "You know how I am, babe, when I get sick. I just want to be left alone to burn the fever out."

"You can be nice and let the kids get you things when they ask," Jen scolded as she was putting away some of Mark's clean underwear. She turned to see him pointing the TV remote at her, he was pushing the "Mute" button in an exaggerated fashion. "Very funny, Mr. Cranky Pants!"

She walked out of the room, but before the door closed, Mark could see several concerned faces trying to peer in at him, including Alan's. He had made Alan promise to stay close by and stay armed in case Mark turned feral. This had taken a few minutes of fierce whispered argument before Alan finally relented. Jen nodded to him as she passed. "You should go get some rest yourself, Alan. You were out with them."

All the others were exhausted. After bringing back the water from the business park and the supplies and materials from the Costco and Home Depot, the vehicles had to be unloaded and the supplies stored in the garage and backyard. Mark had pulled the boat trailer out and parked it down the street, since the street in front of the house had become crowded with their convoy vehicles. The entire pad on the side of the house was stacked with nonperishables. Some of the tools they had taken from Home Depot were stacked there and in the backyard. The Home Depot had also contributed two extra-large barbeques and a dozen propane tanks to the cooking facility.

They had noticed that ferals tended to start showing up about twenty minutes after every meal. All of Mark's neighbors who owned property directly adjoining his had either turned feral, or were nowhere to be found. So the hedges between the properties were trimmed down low. The kids had built two sandbag emplacements on the roof for the lookouts. One of Mark's Marines or one of the deputies was always on watch with the high school kids, who were in charge of securing the house. Most of the kids used a pair of Ruger 10-22 rifles that stayed on the roof with the watch. Equipped with inexpensive scopes and Butler Creek 30-round magazines, they were perfect for eliminating ferals out to 100 yards. Mark had more than ten 500-round bricks of Winchester .22 hollow points. The 36-grain hollow points were perfect for engaging the ferals in small groups. The .22s weren't as loud as other rifles and the hollow points were plentiful enough. Mark also had more than a dozen bricks of other .22 ammo that he had picked up here and there. So far, the .22s had accounted for more than two dozen ferals that had come around.

The bodies of the dead had begun to be a problem, so they started taking them down to the end of the road and burning them in the drainage culvert. The toxin was bad enough; they couldn't afford to start losing people to disease. They had started with plenty of hand sanitizer, but it was running low. The CVS was the next place for a supply run.

At 4:23 pm the lights flickered once. At 5:19 pm, they died all together. The house went dark and a couple of the girls made small squeaks that were quickly shushed by the others. Being quiet was now a survival mechanism.

Jim immediately went to the side of the house and started one of the generators. He switched the refrigerators over to generator power. He started each of the spares and let them run for a minute but then shut them off. Next, he propped open all the window shutters that faced the backyard area. This let enough light in with the skylights that they didn't need to burn candles during the day inside the house.

Terry checked the oven, which was on gas, and confirmed that it still worked. The plan was to conserve expendable resources as long as possible while the power and other utilities still worked. The way things were looking, it might be awhile before public utilities would come back. There was a brief flurry of activity as most everyone did some chore or assignment. Since it was summertime, there were still a few hours of daylight left. They made plans to have dinner done by dusk from now on.

Mark noticed the power going out and called for Alan, who told him to stay in bed and that everyone was doing what was planned. Mel came in and told Mark that Sergeant Derry had called over the radio and that the rescue column was through Vista and headed their way, ETA one hour or less. She left, and Jim came in to report that all the power-out procedures were taken care of. Terry came in, marched up to him without saying a word, gave him a huge hug, and tried to turn away before he could see the tears forming in her eyes. Jen came in with two ice packs wrapped in towels. She put one under each arm, turned, and marched out the door as well. Mark was considering installing a revolving door when gunfire sounded from the roof.

The gunshots picked up in intensity and, after thirty seconds, it wasn't just the .22s; the sharp bark of an M4 joined the cacophony. When the boom of a sniper rifle sounded, Mark got up and started pulling on his utility trousers. He was in the middle of pulling on his boots when everything went quiet. He made his way to the door, but it opened as he reached for it. Jim stood there a little breathless, his M4 slung over his shoulder.

Mark stared at him for a minute, waiting for him to speak and finally said, "Well?"

"Pop, you are really red!" Jim was still staring at the flushed skin on his father's neck.

Mark slapped him across the noggin, a little harder than he intended, and asked, "What happened outside, you numbskull?"

"Ow!" Jim said, flinching back. "It was a pack of about forty, Dad. They were up the street when some of the kids saw them start our way. Even after we dropped a few, they kept coming. Staff Sergeant Kyle came up top, and we had to shoot most of them. We can still hear a few of them around us, but they aren't showing themselves. We are putting the shutters on now."

"Okay, have Mel—"

"Mark Norris, you go get back in bed right now!" Jim was grabbed by the collar and swung by the neck away from the bedroom. He left without another word, knowing that discretion was the better part of valor. Jen then spun back around and placed her hands on her hips, squaring off with the Marine in front of her. "Everything is taken care of, and we need you to get better!" The tears were starting to flow as she stared at the angry red patch of skin, which had spread from his arm up to his neck. "Please! We really need you to just get better!" And with that, she was in his arms, the sobs wracking her body.

Mark, who was never very good at being in touch with his feminine side, just stood there like a statue and slowly put his arms around her. They stood there for a while until the crying subsided. Mark let her go, set his rifle back next to the bed, and began unstrapping his belt and thigh holster. He climbed back into bed and meekly asked, "Can I get a few more ice packs? It doesn't feel so bad when I get cooled down."

"Sure, coming right up." Jen nodded and went out the door.

The convoy finally made it past Lake Hodges and got off of Interstate 15. Going west, they moved into Mark's subdivision. When they were two blocks away, they saw several ferals hopping fences, moving toward Mark's house. They decided not to engage, in case anyone from the house was outside. Derry got Mel on the radio as they turned onto Mark's street.

"Mel, this is Jake, is your dad there? We're coming up your street now."

"Hi, Jake. Dad's in bed; he's pretty sick. The roof lookout called down that they saw you get off the freeway." The tears were evident in her voice. "Please come help my dad."

"Did he get bit, Mel?" Jake punched the Hummer's dashboard in front of him. "Shit, shit, shit!" he said, without keying the mic.

"No, but he got some bones in him during a fight. Alan said the blood got mixed. He's running a really high fever, and he has a rash." The words rushed out as Mel began crying. "I don't want my daddy to die, Jake!"

The anguish in Mel's voice tore at Jake's heart. He had known Mark since he first joined the unit. Mark had been a newly promoted WO1 and Jake was a private first class, straight from the school of infantry. Mark had gotten Jake to become a Scout Sniper and was truly his mentor in the Corps. He was also very close to the kids, especially Mel, who he treated like a kid sister and who had somewhat of a crush on him.

The convoy pulled up in front of the house, stretching from one end of the block to the other. As they climbed out of the Hummers, the lookout on the roof hollered down, "Watch out! We have some ferals in the area!"

The convoy had picked up fourteen survivors on the way down, and they had to be hustled inside quickly. There were a few minutes of confusion and milling around as the refugees were hustled inside the already overcrowded house.

"We saw them on the way in!" Captain Johnson yelled back up as the chaos settled down.

Derry had already bulled his way through the crowd on the porch as the front door opened. He stepped into the foyer and saw Jen just stepping out of the kitchen. It was obvious she had been crying. He went to her for a quick hug and asked, "How is he?"

Jen shook her head and was about to burst into tears again. She managed to gain her composure and pulled him off to the side so the kids and new arrivals couldn't hear. "He's got it, Jake. His fever has been going up, his skin is getting flushed, although not all over like they said in the news. He's also been getting really irritable… like unreasonably so. I'm scared, Jake. Really scared!"

"All right, let me talk to him. He in the bedroom?" Jake turned at her nod and went down the hall. He noticed all the modified living arrangements and people in the house. He nodded to Corporal Price, one of the Marines who had holed up in the house with Mark.

He climbed the stairs and said "Hey" to Alan, who was sitting in a chair outside the room. Jake noticed the shotgun leaning against the wall and the pistol on Alan's hip. He rapped on the door three times sharply.

"Come!"

Jake opened the door to see Mark propped up in his huge bed with ice packs all around him. Because this room was on the second floor, they hadn't closed the fire shutters yet. With all the people in the house and now no A/C, they were going to have a hard time keeping the room cool.

"Sergeant Derry, one each, reporting as ordered, Ma'am. I have brought the Marines and the situation is well in hand. They have us surrounded, which is good; it means we can attack in any direction!" He came to a splayfooted mockery of attention, started a British palm-up salute, changed his mind into a Nazi *Heil* straight arm, looked at his hand like it had a mind of its own, and then rendered a parade rest rifle salute without the rifle that was still slung around his shoulder. This resulted in him saluting from his crotch.

"At ease, maggot!" Mark couldn't help but grin at the buffoonery. "Sergeant, my ass! Don't think because you stole some rank insignia that you are now a sergeant in my beloved Corps! You couldn't even tie your own shoes last week and now you think you can lead men? I don't fuckin' think so!"

"You wound me, sir!" Derry was about to continue with the shenanigans when Johnson appeared in the doorway. Derry stepped to the side, stood up straighter, and said "Gunner, this is Captain Johnson. Sir, this is CWO3 Norris."

"Hey, Hey! Get back down, Gunner!" He said as Mark tried to get to his feet. "We didn't know you'd been bitten. How long ago was it?" He was looking closely at Mark's neck. The redness had actually decreased with the ice packs but was still blotchy.

"Yesterday, Captain, but I wasn't bitten. I had a very slight amount of blood contamination." Mark proceeded to tell them about the incident at the business park. He showed them the contact area on his wrist.

"So a contaminated bone penetrated your skin? Just that little bit?" Johnson then added, "And it's Dave."

"That's all, Dave. I was able to wash the wound right away and disinfect it. I don't think disinfecting it helps since what we know is that it's a chemical, right?" Mark received nods from the two fellow Marines. "I think the flushing removed a good amount of the chemical before it could get into my bloodstream. Close the door, Jake, please."

Mark waited until they were alone then went on. "I need you to get my kids and Jen to safety, Jake. And everyone else here. I may turn feral soon, and I can't let them come to harm, especially at my own hand. Promise me, Devil Dog, Your word as a Marine."

"And what? Leave you here alone?" Derry was looking back and forth between the captain and Mark. "I don't fucking think so! You're coming with us, Mark. No ifs, ands, or buts about it. We have base medical up and running. We'll take care of you!"

"No, I'm not Jake. I'm not the type to have someone put me down like a rabid dog. I'm going to try and fight this, and if I can't, then my last conscious act will be to eat my gun. I don't want my kids around to see it. You will get them to safety, dammit! Don't make me get out of this bed, or I will disassemble you in place, do you copy?"

Derry looked pained. There were few men that the sergeant feared, but Mark was one of them. Although Derry was an inch taller and weighed twenty pounds more, Norris had put him in the dirt on more than one occasion during hand-to-hand drills. A pissed off Mark Norris was not to be taken lightly.

"We'll get them to the base, Gunner," Johnson said, patting the air to calm things down. "I understand how you feel, but we do have the medical center up and running, and we are in contact with what's left of the country, including assets from the CDC. We would make sure you were cared for."

"I'm telling you, if I just got left alone for a couple of days, I'd be fine." Mark was shaking his head. "I just can't even take the slightest risk with Jen and the kids. I'll keep a radio here and contact you when I'm better. Then you can come and get me. Derry has always wanted to be useful, Captain. This would be his big chance to show that he's not a waste of good oxygen."

"That's all well and good, Gunner, but the colonel asked us to bring you back."

"I spoke to him twenty minutes ago. His exact words were, 'I'll leave it up to you.' Call him, Jake." Mark nodded toward the team radio on the nightstand.

"I'll just do that! Cause you are high on crack if you think I'm leaving you here alone!" He snatched the radio off the table and marched out of the room, mumbling in four letter words as he did. Captain Johnson had to step lively to avoid being run over by the 6'3" mountain that went storming past him.

"That kid really likes you," Johnson said as he went over to the chair that had been put beside the bed. "All he kept saying was wait till the gunner's here and he'll fix it."

"His hope may be a little misplaced. I am not doing shit for a couple of days."

The sound of gunfire in the distance prevented further conversation, as the Marines at the northeast end of the block came under attack by several ferals. Johnson had to respond to various radio calls. Mark's house radio used by the roof lookouts came alive with reports as well. They reported seeing movement in several directions, with the ferals numbering in the hundreds.

This time, Mark made it downstairs, and he got the house defenses in order. The Marines were fully engaged out front, and the roof sentries were reporting movement in the yards adjacent to Mark's. The sound of small-caliber rifle fire drifted down from the roof but could not compete with the sound of M4s and Squad Automatic Weapons from out front. Mark got his radio back from Jake and was headed out the back door when he glanced into the living room.

Several of the kids had begun to cry, and a couple of them were so frightened that they started to panic. Mark went over to calm them down. Tia especially was in a great deal of distress. Mark approached and put an arm around her to console her.

"Here, kiddo, come on now, everything's going to be okay. The Marines got here. Come on."

"It's not going to be enough! It's just like in the movies; we're going to run out of ammo, and then we'll get overrun!" Tia was shaking with fear. "How can we fight off hordes of them? It's just like all the zombie movies! And what about the Red Ball Theory? They are going to outnumber us before we can get organized!"

Mark laughed out loud, causing Tia to stare at him. He tried to calm himself but the laughter felt good, so he laughed until it was just a snicker.

"Bad math, honey; that stuff could never happen," he said giving her shoulder a squeeze. "Are you talking about that theory that if you put one red ball in a box with a bunch of blue balls, and then move the box around, the balls will collide, and every time the red ball touches a blue ball, it turns red. And then every time one of those balls touches a blue ball, it turns them red as well and pretty soon, they're all red? What movie is that from?"

"It was in a book," Tia said, looking at him in wonder. "How did you know about that?"

"They used it to show us how Ebola could be spread once." Mark pulled her up to a chair and looked her in the eye. "But the guy who tried to apply that to zombies got it wrong."

"How come?" one of the other kids asked.

"He forgot about the green balls!" Mark said with a smug look on his face, which was returned with a bunch of "what" and "huh" from the kids who had gathered around them. Soon, all the teenagers were in the living room, listening as Mark held an impromptu class.

"Okay, look, let's just say we have a million blue balls." He had to wait as the high school giggles subsided. "And we have not just one but a hundred thousand red balls. You'd think it would all be over really quick, right?" Heads nodded in agreement. "But what about the green balls? Not everybody who comes into contact with a red ball is infected. Some are armed and trained to protect themselves. They have guns and know how to use them. Now, every time a red ball runs into a green ball, the red one not only doesn't turn the green ball red, it gets taken out. All of a sudden, the red ball threat is reduced substantially, right? And not every red ball wins. Sometimes the red ball dies trying to get a blue ball."

"I guess so." Tia and a few others were nodding.

"Now think about this! What if every green ball had a force field?"

"What? You don't have a force field!" one of the kids said.

"Ahh, but for purposes of accuracy, I do!" Mark looked at the skeptical faces around him. "Not only am I a green ball, but I've been protecting you guys, right? Jim and Terry and Mel and I have been keeping you guys safe. And the Marines have been securing the base for survivors. And going out to rescue them… Us. So we have green balls with force fields, and…" He held up his finger for the Coup de Gras. "Sometimes the blue balls become green! You guys are all getting better trained and learning how to survive, right?'

Again he was met with nods as the kids all looked at each other with a little more respect and a lot more understanding.

"But what about ammo?" Tia asked again. "There's thousands or even millions of them. We don't have that much ammo."

"Who says?" Mark looked around at the crowd that had gathered. "The entire population of California was just over thirty-seven million when this all started. Guys, I have over 200 thousand rounds just here at my house. Camp Pendleton has literally tens of millions of rounds. There is far more ammo than ferals, or even the entire human population. And the whole wave attack thing doesn't work. Unless you're stupid like they are in the movies and only carry one or two magazines of thirty rounds, in which case, you might be in trouble. We engage the ferals out at more than two football fields away. And that's you kids on the roof! Some of us do it at a far greater range. There is little chance of the bodies piling up so high they can come through the skylights!

"Think about this, there were 300 million people in the U.S. There are over 100 million registered gun owners with over 500 million guns! Look at the stuff I got from George's house. Now there are eight more people armed and supplied with ammo. Sure some people got caught away from their guns and may have perished in the beginning, but that will stabilize soon. And we have one more thing we don't have to worry about with these people. They aren't zombies! They can die from a shot to the chest and be killed just like anyone else. So we are sitting pretty with 200,000 rounds of ammo."

"Really? Two hundred thousand?" Tia looked skeptical.

"Yes, would you like to see it?" Mark gestured toward the door.

"Um, yeah. It would make us feel a lot better," she said, getting nods of support from the other kids.

"Come on," Mark said, standing up. "Listen… the gunfire has already died down."

They all got up and trooped into the garage, where Mark showed them the shelves of ammo and the gun safe. He explained how many rounds of ammo each can held. He then had Mel show them the ammo inventory file on the laptop in the kitchen. They were all suitably impressed and felt a lot better when the brief tour was over.

Jim came down and reported that, between the Marines and the sentries, they had killed or wounded about a hundred ferals. Mark asked Jim if the sentries had enough ammo. Jim gave him a funny look and said of course. They hadn't even gone through two tiny boxes of .22 ammo. He didn't know about the Marines, but he didn't think they were going to run out anytime soon. He said the few rounds fired from the .50s on top of the Humvees were devastating. One bullet would kill several ferals if they were lined up right.

Johnson came in at the end of the report and asked if Mark needed any extra ammo. Mark laughed and told him no, they were fine for now. In fact, he offered to supply the convoy with replacement ammo for any they had expended getting there.

Johnson also looked at him funny, and all the kids in the hall started laughing.

"Did I miss something here?" Johnson asked.

"Hey Dad!" Mel yelled from the kitchen before he could explain. "Someone's at Costco." Mel leaned around the archway holding one of the radios in her hand and shaking it at him.

"Okay, Mel." Mark walked over to her and took the walkie-talkie from her. "Hello, my name is Mark. Who's this?"

"My name is Gilbert Cabrerra. I'm at the Costco off of Scripps Poway Parkway. I found your instructions. I'm here with fifteen other survivors, but we're trapped. We were coming here to see if there were any supplies left when a group of crazies attacked our cars. We managed to outrun them here, but we had just pulled into the lot when the first of them caught up to us. My wife saw your message on the door and we came inside, but we only have two guns and about forty bullets left. There has to be at least a hundred of them."

Mark waited, expecting the man to say over, then realized he was a civilian. "Okay, Gilbert, I'm with the U.S. Marines and we have a rescue column that can come and get you guys if you just stay holed up. We're only about ten miles from you, but it will take us about thirty minutes to get set up and get there. Can you folks hold on for that long? The food in the coolers should still be cold. The power just went out and they have backup generators. We left tons of food there. Over."

"The generators are working all right; in fact, the crazies are pounding on the shed where the generators are running. We already started to eat... we were pretty hungry. Over. And we have dogs too. We're feeding them."

Mark again waited since he didn't think ol' Gilbert quite had the radio protocol down. He was about to speak into the radio again when Gilbert came back with, "Hello? Did you hear me?"

Johnson shook his head and went outside to prepare the troops for the mission. Jim went back up to let the lookouts know what was going on and Jen was helping everyone else pack their things and load the vehicles for the trip up to the Marine Corps base. Mark moved into the kitchen to finish the conversation.

"I was waiting for you to say *over*," Mark began. Before he could go on, Gilbert was back on the radio.

"I did. OVER. I hope you guys have some serious guns because there are a lot of them out there!"

"We have plenty of guns." Mark couldn't keep the chuckle out of his voice. "The convoy is on its way. Keep the place locked up and you'll be fine, out."

"Roger, over." Mark and Mel could hear someone in the background giving Gilbert a radio lesson. They looked at each other and grinned. "Hon, could you call Cliff and tell him Uncle Sam's Misguided Children are here. The convoy will escort the families with him back to the base when they're done collecting the people at the Costco."

"K Dad; do you want them to come here?"

"Ask them if they can. If not, the convoy can swing by on the way back from Costco." Mark turned to head back to bed. He was feeling flushed again, and if it hadn't been so comical, he knew he might have snapped at Mr. Cabrerra. He made it back upstairs and was climbing into bed when Alan stuck his head in the door.

"You feeling okay? Your rash was really faint when you climbed out of bed, but it's an angry rash now." He said in a mocking tone. "Just so you know, I heard what you said earlier. I'm sending the kids to the base, but I'll stay here and help you out. I owe you, Mark."

"No you won't. Your kids are going to need you. You don't know where their mom is and you know what that probably means. They don't need to lose another 'rent." Mark used the term the kids used to describe their parents. He looked at him long and hard. "That's what this is all about, buddy; I need you to be there for them, including my kids, and they're not going to be in a good place if I go. I think I'll be fine, but I would hate it if you stayed and I injured you when you could be safe up at Pendleton taking care of my kids."

Alan nodded his consent and went back out to the hallway. Up on the roof, Jim leaned against the skylight, thinking about the conversation he had just eavesdropped on. A plan began to form in his head and he went down to the garage to make some preparations. He was in there with the dogs when they started to growl at one of the floor vents. He got down on his hands and knees and looked at the vent. He saw a strange face staring back at him as the dogs went to full alert, giving out their short, sharp barks that indicated a bad guy was near.

Jim scrambled to his feet, grabbed his rifle, and sprinted to the door. He burst out into the hall yelling, "Perimeter breach! Ferals in the backyard!"

Since the front door was wide open and a line of people were in the hall carrying belongings out to the convoy vehicles, mayhem ensued. Jim went out the front door and around the front of the house to the side gate. Two Marines came over with their rifles up and asked what was going on. Jim, who had been trained by his father, made the appropriate hand signs to indicate *eyes on enemy, other side of gate*.

They pushed the gate open in time to see Nosferatu slipping over the fence into the neighbor's yard. They held their fire for lack of a clear shot.

"Who's on watch up there?" Jim yelled up at the sentries on the roof. "Look north!! Contact north!" He jumped up on a pallet of canned goods and aimed his rifle into the adjoining yard. He didn't see anything, but he heard the sounds of something running away.

"We saw him for a sec!" One of the sentries hollered down to them. "Mexican guy with tattoos, wearing a wife beater."

"I just saw his face through the vent, and then jeans!" Jim turned toward the two Marines. "I wonder if he was even feral."

Everyone was starting to calm down when a rock flew over the roof of the neighbor's house and hit the sandbag wall on the roof. It was followed a few seconds later by another. A few more and Jim and the Marines were ready to send out a team to deal with the pest.

"Rocks? Really?" Jake said as another flew overhead. "Okay, that's it. You said it was a feral, Jim?"

"Yeah, I saw his face looking at me through the vent in the garage." Jim pointed up. "The guys up top said he was a Mexican guy with tattoos, wearing a white tank top and jeans."

"White tank and jeans?" Derry got a sick feeling in his stomach. "The tats, were they like fancy script along his neck up to his jaw?" Derry demonstrated on his own neck.

"Yeah, how'd you know? Did you see him?"

"We had a run-in with him earlier today." They walked out front. As soon as they cleared the front hedge, there was an animalistic scream from up the street. Every head turned to see Nosferatu as he pointed at Derry then dove into some bushes with bullets chasing him.

"I think he has a hard on for you, Sergeant," Captain Johnson said, walking up to them.

"I think you're right, sir. That's the pack leader from up in Vista. He followed us all the way down here!" Derry shook his head. "That has to be what? Like twelve… maybe fifteen miles! How the hell did he keep up?"

"Well, he sure is motivated. We need to tell these folks to be on the lookout while we pick up other groups of survivors." Johnson went back inside to brief Mark and supervise the last of the loading.

The Marines got back in their vehicles, with the exception of Sergeant Derry and two others who were going to stay behind and augment the house's security. Cliff had been notified by radio that the Marines were there for extraction and he was packing up the survivors who were at his place and they would be over at Mark's by the time the rescue mission returned. Jim gave Sergeant Sanchez detailed directions on how to get to the Costco and how to lock it back up again when they were done. The plan was to get the survivors at Costco, make it back to Mark's, and spend the night. Then the entire circus would head back up to Pendleton.

Derry took two large Pelican cases out of the back of one of the Hummers along with several ammo cans of Lake City match ammunition. He got it all hauled inside as the convoy left. He went to the garage and left one case there. He opened the other and put the M107 into a soft case and slung it over his shoulder. From the other case, he took eight 10-round box magazines and a light intensifier. These went into the custom harness he was wearing. With his M4 still slung, he was carrying over a hundred pounds. He trudged up to the roof and began setting up his gear. Jim joined him a few minutes later, and since it was getting crowded, he told the sentries to take a break. They put the .22s back in the makeshift rack and climbed down.

"I bet your old man has been dingin' those fuckers out at a fuckin mile! I bet they don't even know what hit them!" Derry was gently pressing the massive .50-caliber rounds down into the magazines. "I saw him hit this Tali once at 1700 yards. Kicked his ass right off the fuckin' mountain."

"Um, Jake, Dad prefers that we not use any major calibers up here." Jim pointed to the Rugers in the rack. "They're too loud and it attracts unwanted attention."

Derry stopped and slowly turned his head to stare at Jim. "You've gotta be shittin' me! How far out are you hitting them with those peashooters? Fifty yards? Come on!"

"I swear," Jim said, raising his hand to God. "If Dad hears that Barrett go off, he'll be up here in a heartbeat, chewing ass!"

"Oh well, I'm just gonna have to straighten the good Gunner out on that! We just had a minor firefight out here. Everything in ten miles heard it. We might as well take them out before they get close." He turned to go back down, only to find Jen at the top of the ladder, staring him down. This was quite a feat, as she was only 5'9" tall and was several rungs down on the ladder, looking up at the huge man.

"And just what do you think you're going to straighten out, Mr. Derry?" She took two more steps up the ladder, forcing him to retreat. "I know you wouldn't want to disturb Mark's rest over some egotistical macho bullshit." She raised an eyebrow in question.

"I, uh… well, you see, we need to be able to engage these ferals at a much longer distance than these rifles here are capable of." He pointed to the rifles behind him. "We can start eliminating threats much farther out with this!" He said patting his Barrett.

"Well, that may be, but he shall not be disturbed at all for the rest of the night. Do you understand? You can ask tomorrow about that whatever it is!" And with that, Jake was staring down at a bobbing red ponytail.

"Come on, it's actually pretty challenging to get a good headshot with one of these. We're working well out to about two hundred yards. You pretty much have to hit them in the temple for a sure kill. Anything in the front of the face is hard to tell because their mouths are usually covered in gore and stuff." Jim walked over and got his personal Ruger off the rack. He set his M4 in its place and took out another for Jake. "It takes a bit of skill to put them down from two to four hundred yards. Dad clipped one in the leg over by the Lake Hodges Bridge with this." He held up his .22.

Jim's rifle had a much nicer 3x9 power Bushnell scope. The Ruger had been his competition rifle in the Boy Scouts. It had a bull barrel and some other modifications. The rifle he handed Jake was a plain old factory rifle with a cheap 6x power scope on it. Jake's rifle had an absurd-looking Butler Creek 30-round banana mag. Jim's had the flush 10-round rotary magazine. There was an open box of Winchester 36-grain hollow points sitting on the top board of the rifle rack. They were sold in bulk boxes of 555 rounds in some form of marketing ploy that Jake could never figure out. There were several spare loaded magazines lying about.

Jake leaned his M4 up against the parapet, started to put away the Barrett, but then thought better of it. The sun had just set, and it would be dark very soon. And without the streetlights, it would be very dark. The starlight capability of the Barrett would come in handy. He took the .22 and went over to the parapet wall. Setting the rifle on two small sandbags made of old socks, he got into a good firing position.

"Do you guys have range cards made up?" Before he had finished the question, a stapled-together booklet was slapped against his arm. After looking back and forth between the scope and the booklet he said, "Not bad, you do this?"

"Per Pop's instructions."

"I notice you have stuff marked out to 2500 yards."

"Again, per Pop's instructions."

Derry took the data book and began to study it intently. He looked out over the landscape and began to match the image with the drawing in front of him. After getting acquainted with the layout, he looked at the ballistics tables that Jim had included in the booklet.

Jim, who had long ago memorized the details, sat down facing north—the direction the feral had last been seen. He made sure there was a round chambered, pulled the rifle up to his cheek, and began panning the landscape by quadrants. He would peer into what appeared to be good hiding places, taking his time and letting his eyesight penetrate the shadows, looking for things that were out of place from the last time he had looked there. It was while doing this that he realized there was a set of eyes staring back at him from the shadows next to a house. He slowly pressed the safety off with his trigger finger and moved the crosshairs over to the eyes. They were barely visible, looking out from under some shrubbery. Just as Jim squeezed the trigger, the eyes moved back into the brush. The shot broke and Jim saw the bushes move violently. The thrashing only lasted a moment.

"Got you, fucker!" Jim mumbled under his breath.

"Got who?" Jake asked, panning his scope over to the general area that Jim's rifle was pointing.

"I got that Mexican fucker, I think." Jim was staring hard at the area and was rewarded with a flash of white, and then he could make out a patch of blue jeans through the leaves. "There he is again!" he whispered.

"No way, really?" Jake had seen the movement, but because his scope was inferior to Jim's, he was having a hard time seeing through the brush. "That guy is pretty crafty. I caught your movement though."

Jim again slowly squeezed the trigger. This time, he was rewarded with a howl and more thrashing. The blue jeans rolled out of sight. A second later, they caught a flash of movement as a body ran across the street on the next block over. Everything was still for several minutes, so they started looking around through all the sectors. It wouldn't do to have another feral sneak up because they had tunnel vision.

Two blocks over, Ricardo was in bad shape. Jim's bullet had struck him just under the nose. It had punched through the skin above the upper lip and bounced off the bone right where his teeth were anchored. The bullet skidded off to the right side of his face, creating a furrow under his cheekbone. The impact knocked out his incisor and loosened three other teeth. He had fallen to the ground with his hand over his bloody mouth only to be shot in the ass less than a minute later. This bullet hit him in the pocket of his jeans, luckily, since the extra material of the pocket slowed the bullet enough to prevent it from going too far into the buttock. It still hurt like hell and caused massive cramping. Ricardo almost lost it and went fully feral again. Only Nosferatu holding onto him and grunting kept him from flying into a rage and charging at his tormentor.

They retreated all the way to the Lake Hodges open area. They had to think, and that was hard. This prey fought back and had guns—something Nosferatu knew instinctually to be dangerous. What was left of his pack had followed him, strung out in a long line of stragglers. Over half the surviving pack was still north of the I-15 Bridge over the lake. Some of the pack lost focus and drifted away or were distracted. Hunger would send them off on a hunt, and then out of sight became out of mind. The younger and more fit pack members made the trek easily. The old and injured fell by the wayside. The pack that formed on him now was smaller, but it was much more capable.

CHAPTER 29

San Diego, CA

The Marine convoy reached the Costco in less than twenty minutes from the time it left Mark's house. The Hummers pulled up to the edge of the parking lot and formed a line. There were over a hundred ferals; some had gathered around a mini-van, while others pounded on the rollup doors. Johnson had the vehicles move so they could shoot across the face of the building instead of toward it. It would be a shame to have the survivors last this long, only to be shot by friendly fire.

Several ferals noticed the convoy, and one of two things happened. They either charged or ran away. The ones that charged the convoy were brought down first. As soon as the first shots sounded, the rest of the pack turned and, like the others, either ran away or charged. The troops held their fire as long as they could, but sometimes they had to fire toward the building. Several of these shots penetrated the rollup doors. After a three-minute fight, the parking lot was free of the ferals. They could still be seen moving in the distance, but the Marines had very strict rules of engagement. The human race had been decimated; there were to be no chances taken if there was a possibility that the body moving in the distance wasn't feral.

The Hummers formed a protective perimeter around the doors, and Sergeant Sanchez went to open them. As he was unlocking the door, two gunshots and screaming broke out inside. Several Marines nearby heard this and stacked outside the door. They burst into the dimly lit interior and began panning their weapon lights around. Several survivors could be seen huddled by the checkout area.

"U.S. Marines! Coming in!" they all shouted as they rushed to the survivors. One of the men huddled in the group was startled and turned the pistol in his hand at the camouflaged figures running toward him. He realized his mistake and turned the gun away just as one of the PFCs was drawing a bead on him. He turned back to the shelving and pointed. It was unnecessary, as there was movement plainly visible. The ferals inside the building climbed through the gaps in the products on the shelves or just plain ran to the back of the store, chased by bullets from the Marines and screeching as they went.

"They came through the roof! They are climbing up in the racks!" one of the women screamed. She was clutching a bleeding child to her breast. "I thought this was a safe place!" The fury on her face was evident. "You said it was a safe place!"

"Get on line!" Sanchez had to ignore the survivors for a moment as he organized the Marines to clear the building. "Watch out above! They're up in the storage racks! First squad on the left, second up the middle, third on the right! Clear an aisle then get someone up high to clear that shit out. I don't want some feral dropping down on us! McGuire, you copy?"

A corporal at the far end of the line gave a thumbs up. The Marines moved forward and cleared a section before a small lance corporal was sent up into the storage racks. He spent a few minutes climbing back and forth like a monkey before reporting in.

"Sergeant Sanchez, the ferals came through the roof. There's some kind of opening about forty meters back from where I'm sitting. I saw one climb out and I've seen two drop in. This is definitely their access point. We need to secure the outside of the building, Sergeant, and secure the roof. We need to see how they're getting up on the roof!"

"Roller Six-One, this is Two, the ferals have a hole in the roof that they're using for access. Need to secure outside of building and roof," Sanchez reported to Captain Johnson. "They have some type of access, and Jones says they are moving freely between the roof and the storage racks. Suggest we clear from the outside in. Over."

"Roller Six-Two, copy. Will get it done." Johnson turned and began issuing orders to the Marines.

"Contact roofline!" Gunfire from a couple of the gun turrets broke out. A wounded feral jumped from the thirty-foot height to land right in the cupola with one of the gunners. The body slamming into him broke the Marine's neck and caused him to slouch into the harness, blocking the feral from climbing down into the Hummer. As the gunner's body was forced down, the M240G machine gun pivoted on its pintle mount until it was straight up. As the wounded feral scrambled for a grip to pull itself up, it hooked a finger inside the trigger guard and sent a burst of 7.62mm rounds into the air. The noise so startled the wounded feral that he yelped and began thrashing around, which sent more bursts into the air. This cycle increased until the violent actions of the enraged feral twisted the ammunition belt and caused the weapon to jam.

This did little to resolve the dilemma the feral was in. It was now tangled in the dead Marine's harness, and as it tried to push itself up, the hot barrel of the machine gun laid a blistering wound along its back, causing more thrashing and screaming. Its head finally popped out over the cupola armor, and one of the unit-designated marksmen shot it in the face. The driver backed the vehicle away from the building to prevent a repeat of the fiasco, and two Marines climbed up the outside to remove both of the bodies.

As they set the two bodies down, a German shepherd leapt out from between two cars and attacked the Marines. The ticking of the dog's nails gave them just enough warning to face the threat before it was on them. Lance Corporal Sullivan was able to butt stroke the dog before it could latch onto him. His partner shot it as it flew off to the side.

The Marines found where the ferals were climbing up to the roof on the backside of the building. The small room housing the generators stuck out off the back wall next to a roof access ladder. A brief, one-sided firefight, and the Marines secured the area. There was a lot of movement visible along the roofline, and Johnson was loath to send his troops up the ladder, needlessly exposing them to the danger of attack. The DDMs were dropping the few ferals that stuck their heads up above the roofline, but the roof was huge, encompassing over twenty-three thousand square yards of open space. There could be hundreds of them up there out of sight.

Sergeant Sanchez faced this same problem from the inside. He had managed to get several Marines stationed up in the racks and stop the traffic through the breach. The rest of the Marines were ferreting out the ferals that had managed to get into the building. The survivors were taken outside and loaded into the Hummers. There were only eight left alive, and two of them were severe bite victims.

"Roller Six-One, Two. Sir, do we really need to secure this building? We're probably going to take casualties trying to project force through to the roof." Sanchez' Marines had finally cleared the interior of the building. He was looking up at the open roof hatch. Every once in a while, a feral would poke its head into the opening and have to duck back as a Marine took a shot at it. The noise coming from the roof was increasing as the ferals became more agitated.

"Roller Six-Two, Roller Six-One, I really want to, but not at the risk of losing another Marine. Let's see if we can figure this out. I know we're smarter than these things." Johnson had pulled his perimeter out. Just as he was going to order a team up onto the roof of the Home Depot to see if they could get a field of fire on the roof of the Costco, all hell broke loose. Ferals began dropping through the roof hatch to the inside of the building while several jumped onto the rear utility shed and then down to the rear lot. Although the assault was sudden, the Marines were able to finish off the thirty-seven ferals quickly.

"I think that was as close to a coordinated assault as we're going to see, sir," Sanchez said, walking up to the captain's vehicle. "They're still hearing movement on the roof though."

"I was going to see if we could get 'eyes on' from the Home Depot roof. Think it's high enough?" They both turned and spent a minute looking back and forth.

"I have an idea, sir. Standby a moment." Sanchez walked over to one of the squads and, after spending a minute briefing them, walked back over to the captain. "Let's see if this works."

The squad disappeared inside the Home Depot building and a few minutes later, appeared on the roof. The Marines passed up the tallest A-frame ladder they could find and set it up. A PFC went up to the top of the 16-foot ladder and started looking across to the roof of the Costco through the ACOG scope on his rifle.

"Roller Six-Two, Roller Three-Five, the only ferals up there appear to be either dead or severely injured. There are fifteen bodies in sight. I only have movement on two of them. Other than that, it looks clear. Over"

"Three-Five, Roller Six-One, can you engage any moving threats? Over."

"Six-One, Three-Five, standby."

The Marine fired twenty-four rounds, placing each shot in the head of every body he could see on the roof. He reassessed the targets and fired twice more just to be sure. He kept the roof under observation for another minute before coming back over the radio.

"Roller Six-One, Three-Five, roof appears clear but I do have a few blind spots. I can see both the exterior ladder access and the roof hatch opening. I should be able to provide cover fire from here, over." Another Marine had climbed up the ladder as well and the two of them watched as Marines climbed up from the backside of the building and secured the roof. Two shots sounded as ferals that had been out of sight were taken care of, then the all clear was given.

"Outstanding!" Johnson went over to check on the survivors. "See what we can do about securing that roof hatch. And get the bodies off now. I don't want cholera developing around here."

The troops on the ground pushed two dumpsters up against the wall, and the troops on the roof tossed the bodies into them. A five-gallon jug of diesel was poured into the two dumpsters and lit on fire. Greasy smoke began to curl up into the air. The roof hatch was repaired with supplies from the Home Depot. While this was going on, both buildings were locked up, and once the roof was repaired, the convoy headed back to Mark's house.

As the convoy disappeared down the road, a feral loped up to the dumpster, pulled a body out, and began to eat.

CHAPTER 30

MCB Camp Pendleton, CA

Colonel Neal strode into base ops. No one called the room to attention, per his standing orders. He walked over to a staff sergeant at the communications console. The staff sergeant, who had been focused on the secure e-mail screen he was staring at, jumped in his seat to see a full-bird colonel looking over his shoulder. Nelson set a hand on his shoulder, preventing him from rising. "At ease," he said gently. "What do we know?"

"There are sixty-four bases that have reestablished safe zones of some sort. Major population centers are no more, sir. The toxin just got distributed too well. There are huge patches of country that weren't hit at all. National Command Authority is safe but in hiding. We have suffered a population loss of almost 40 percent. That is catastrophic for infrastructure, sir. The word from the Pentagon is that we can look at about a twenty-year reduction in technology. Because of our centralized manufacturing, the loss of skilled labor is going to reduce our ability to replace a lot of manufactured items. They say that the catastrophic loss of the population will result in a surplus of major items for about seven to ten years. Everyone can go get a new car, sir, because right now, there's about five new ones for every human left alive.

"The toxin is already being eliminated from the environment naturally. Because of the multi-species death toll, disease is going to be a problem for at least the next eight months. The amount of dead and rotting flesh in the environment will render water supplies unsafe long after the toxin is gone. Water will have to be distilled for the next two years. That's it for the national news, sir; you want the military update?"

"Give it to me."

"On our base, we have a good perimeter, and we've only had two incidents of small packs being found. There are probably another forty or fifty solo out there. We'll know more once the birds are up. Speaking of birds, we have managed to get the airfield operational. We have enough maintenance, aircrew, and aircraft to operate one squadron of heavy-lift helos, two squadrons of medium-lift VERTREP-capable birds, six Hueys—for transport or search-and-rescue functions, and two full squadrons of AH1-Ws, plus some extra crew and birds. We also have four Harriers on the deck that were here for some integrated training with the ANGLICO guys. They are Winchester for iron bombs, but have their Sidewinders and Gunpods.

"We have four MV-22 Ospreys from Miramar here at our airfield. We are in contact with some aviation assets at Miramar, but they report their base is not secure, something about too much perimeter to hold onto. Their F-18s are grounded because ferals keep fouling the deck on the runways. They are going to try to get them to Coronado or here. Their helos and Ospreys are operational, but it's tough for them to get missions off because they get swamped every time they begin flight ops. They are going to try to get them here also. We told them to bring their own gas. The FBO here has enough fuel to sustain about 120 days of medium ops. We do have some problems with access to the bunkers, sir. We don't have keys or combos to gain access to a lot of ordnance. The chaos hit too quick and we lost too many key personnel. We used a civilian locksmith company to change out the locks on a lot of those safes and doors. Needless to say, they aren't answering our calls.

"The various chow halls are stocked for at least ninety days with diminishing perishables, after those consumables are gone, we have about twenty-six months' worth of MREs. The engineers say that some of the training ranges that won't be used for a while would make great organic farms. One of the recon missions is slated to gather seeds and farming equipment the next time it's in town.

"We have the equivalent of four regimental combat teams returning from their foreign commitments. They left a good majority of their gear overseas, but they are still 90 percent on manpower, just 40 percent TOE. They will be landing at Miramar or Coronado over the next two days. CENTCOM also issued a warning order for an interior mission. Further on, that will go direct to you, sir.

"San Onofre called and said the grid will be up again tomorrow. The demand has dropped enough now for them to shuffle the routes, whatever that means, and enough of their personnel have been recovered to affect the necessary repairs. So Cal grid will be up by tomorrow at noon." The staff sergeant was surprised to see the colonel furiously taking notes. "That's about it, sir. General Morse is still at medical and will be down for at least a week. You're still the man, sir."

"Well, I don't know about that, son, but I need to know about on-base fuel supplies for vehicles." Nelson looked at his notes. "We'll have to hold off on everyone getting a new car, but replacing old or worn out vehicles from dealerships out in town will probably have to happen eventually. I'm not too worried about the water because that was the first thing we set up on the beach, and the Navy has ships anchored and supplying us enough to start pumping out the base supply lines. Eventually, we'll pump into the civilians off base as well.

"I'm a little concerned about not having access to the bunkers. Call the recon guys or the engineers; they like to blow stuff up. Let's put their skills to work, but only on the bunkers we absolutely have immediate need to access. Have a party of volunteers organized to search all the administrative space around the safes and bunkers. People are lazy and I know a lot of those combos are written on a piece of paper taped to some POG's desk. Have them square away the office spaces and look for dropped keys. Also, have Lieutenant Colonel Wilson screen and classify the skill sets of incoming refugees. We might have a locksmith in there somewhere.

"I hate to say this, but I'm going to want one of the Hueys for myself. I can get more done if I can get around quicker. I'm also going to want to check out the city and get to Coronado so I can coordinate with their command for rescue ops. Make the heavy-lift birds available to the recon guys for refugee extraction, with the Super Cobras as escort. Don't we have someone from MAGTAF planning over at the airfield?"

"Major Burns, sir."

"Yeah, him. Tell him he's in charge of assigning the rest of the assets. As long as we can VERTREP the ships when needed, he has free reign. I will be sending him missions soon.

"I'm glad to hear about the power grid; I would really like to get away from running the diesel generators. The Navy is patching power from the carriers' nuclear plants into some of the grid. I know Coronado is set. Gas is a concern though; who knows how long it will be before we start getting fuel shipments?"

"Um, I do, sir." The staff sergeant was grinning. "There are nine tankers slated to make landfall on the East Coast over the next two days.

They were waiting it out off the coast. We have four off Long Beach now, there are two off of Bremerton, and two in San Francisco Bay. Pentagon issued a warning order that securing the refineries and port facilities will be a mission priority."

"Thanks, Staff. When was the last time you had a break and some chow?"

"I just came back from twelve off, sir. I'm good to go. I had some hot chow with my family this morning."

"Very well, carry on. Good brief," Nelson said, walking over to the small desk he had commandeered in the corner. He began to organize the various understrength and fragmented units into larger composite ones. The task of fitting each Marine into their occupational field was tough. And there was going to have to be some change. He was pretty sure, the last time he checked, there was no Marine Corps MOS for farmer.

CHAPTER 31

Buffalo, NY

The four Bell Jet Ranger helicopters took off from the compound and headed west. Two smaller A-stars followed them into the sky but turned south. Each bird went to a different civilian airfield within 200 miles of the compound. A team of four well-paid and highly skilled contractors got off of each helicopter and went to work. The airfields were scouted, fuel bunkers checked, ferals eliminated, control towers secured, and certain buildings occupied. Radio calls were made with encrypted gear, and six cargo planes were dispatched. Soon, each airfield was brought up to limited-operational status. A few survivors approached the fields when they saw the activity, thinking it was the government restoring order. Those who did were shot out of hand.

Again, the helicopters took off—this time, from the newly acquired airfields. They continued leapfrogging across the country until they had twenty-three airfields occupied. The teams then began to ferry pilots out to every agricultural area that had a crop duster. These aircraft were recovered and brought back to the occupied airfields. Here, the crews began the task of getting them serviced and their tanks loaded with one of two different cargos.

"There they go again, sir, and they're still not responding to any calls. We've tried 121.5 and 243.0; we even looked up the approach plates for the airfields they're using and tried the published frequencies. A broad channel scan picked up some burst type static, which means they're using encrypted gear." The Air Force technical sergeant was looking at the real time satellite image of an airfield in Bassett, Nebraska. The small airport consisted of a concrete runway (13/31) that stretched away from the airport itself, and a turf runway (2/20) that ran across the concrete one. "For a general aviation airport that only did 2000 flight ops last year, according to the FAA, it sure is busy. We have another twenty airfields with the same MO, sir."

Brigadier General Trevor Grubbs looked at the image without saying anything. He scrolled through several others before looking in an airport guidebook for civilian general aviation. He then looked through a similar reference for military aviation airfields. After flipping back and forth he said, "I need a list of operational military flight assets that can do flyovers of these airfields and tell us what's going on. And see if we can get UCAV assets on it as well. I don't think anyone will complain about our conducting surveillance domestically, but if they do… fuck 'em."

"I'll compile that right away, sir." Technical Sergeant Willis was already punching keys on the terminal in front of him. "Sir, the drone drivers let us know that they have seven surveillance birds coming back CONUS. They are launching overseas and have the range to fly here direct. That's some long fucking legs, sir! They'll be here day after tomorrow. Those are the Global Hawks, sir. They are only bringing two Predators back with them, but we have over a dozen available domestically. This will give us some better intel locally."

"Okay, we'll definitely be using them soon."

Grubbs stood up straight and stretched out his back. He could sit up in the "emperor's booth" with all the data fed to him up there in a nice executive chair, but he liked to be down among his technicians, where the real work was done. These airmen and women were all he had left. When the attacks had first occurred, he called his wife and told her he would send a security team to get them. When the team reached the general's house, they found his wife and his son, who lived nearby, dead on the front lawn. They had been killed by a feral just minutes before the team got there. They collected his daughter-in-law and grandson and barely made it back to the base. He was now on a mission to unravel the mystery behind the attacks, and he swore he would see vengeance done upon the perpetrators.

A few trunk twists and side bends and he moved down the bank of monitors to talk with a young female first lieutenant. Willis looked at the man sitting next to him and grinned. The general was very well liked by the airmen who served under him. Both men began preparing the report for the "Old Man."

CHAPTER 32

Bemidji, MN

The National Guard troops were thankful for the impromptu base that the hotel provided them to work out of. As the guardsmen made more patrols and came across more survivors, the surrounding buildings were taken over and the "base" expanded. The survivors from the city made up 90 percent of the refugees. Most of the rural population was a hardy and self-sufficient lot. Only those without a reliable water supply came in to the camp from the outlying areas. The rangers had raided the Wal-Mart and a few other sporting goods stores and distributed firearms, ammunition, camping, and other survival gear to survivors near and far.

Reliable water was getting to be a problem though. The relief column had brought two Army Corps of Engineers technicians along. A platoon was detailed to secure the water treatment plant and get it up and running. Another was sent to secure the power station and make modifications to the grid. Because it was discovered that more of the population had survived in rural areas, the power to the city's grid was reduced or eliminated. So far, with the exception of a few minor glitches, most of the population of Minnesota had not lost power. They were used to long winters and power outages, anyway.

As the refugees began to take over more of their own security duties, the troops were able to spend their energy on recovering the city. The biggest packs of ferals were only about a hundred individuals strong. Any bigger, and they tended to hunt out an area and start to starve. Pack loyalty was only assured till the next meal was due. As these packs cleared out an area, they would migrate out of the city. The patrols would make contact with them at the edge of town, and after a brief fight, the ferals would flee back into the city.

The city of Bemidji sat on the western shore of Lake Bemidji. A small waterway connected Lake Bemidji to Lake Irving at the south end of the city. Only four bridges spanned the waterway, effectively dividing the urban area. Bemidji State University sat along the shore in the middle of town. So far, Captain Nelson had concentrated his efforts in the southern section of the city. The patrols were effective at breaking up the packs and driving them out toward the north along the eastern edge of the lake. The ferals were lucky to escape in a group bigger than five. More often, it was singly or in pairs that they escaped their hunters.

Captain Nelson was catching up on the various reports coming in from the outlying posts when a young specialist came pounding down the hall. Since the captain's room was the last in the hall, he knew it was some kind news for him, and anything was more interesting than checking food consumption. He called out, "Come on in!" before the young soldier could knock on the door.

"Sir, there are helicopters flying over the city! Papa One and Two both reported seeing them flying westbound, then Papa Two reported seeing one going east. They said it could be the same one. It's one of those private ones, sir, like the news channels use." The young soldier was flapping his hands in excitement. "I thought there weren't going to be any air ops for a while. Do you think they're gonna open the airports?"

"I don't really know." Nelson was able to keep his amusement to a smile. "Did the comm guys get anything from higher up?"

"I didn't wait around, sir." The specialist turned to go, stopped himself, and turned back to see the captain waving him away.

"Carry on!" Nelson was laughing now.

"Yes, sir."

Scott and Dan were out on patrol with two National Guard Hummers following them. They were heading north along Lake Avenue, on the east side of Lake Bemidji. Today's patrol was supposed to clear out some ferals that had taken up residence in a wooded area adjacent a recovering neighborhood. The residents had contacted Scott on the CB channel that he left with them a few days before. What had initially been a few ferals seen between the trees had turned into a pack that killed one of the residents who had gotten careless.

As they passed Greenbrier Lane, Scott glimpsed movement off to his left. He slowed his truck and pointed.

"Over on the left there, brother, do you see her?" He picked up his walkie-talkie and called the Hummer behind him. "Papa Three, I have movement in the tree line, ten o'clock. Over."

"Ranger One, copy. We saw her too. Do you want to dismount? Over."

"Yeah, let's spread out along the road here and see if she leads us to the pack or if they come running to her." He accelerated up the road then stopped about 100 yards past where he had seen the female ducking into the bushes. "Let's get on line."

The two Hummers each carried five troops. Four would dismount and the gunners would stay with the vehicles to provide heavy firepower. The eight guardsmen and two rangers spread out and walked west toward the lake. A narrow band of woods separated the road from a hiking trail and then the water. As they moved into the woods, they could hear movement in several places.

"Contact front!"

"Contact front."

"Contact right!"

All came over the radio at the same time. Because the area was known to have survivors, the rules of engagement were very strict. They would not shoot at any target that was not clearly identified. They would not fire toward buildings that could be occupied, and they would not fire unless they had a clear backstop for their bullets. Unless the ferals attacked en masse, it would be discretionary shooting.

The team made sure to stay on line as they swept through the trees. When they were about ten meters in, the first feral broke cover from in front of the middle of the line. It snarled and charged straight toward one of the guardsmen, who fired two quick shots with his M4 then a final, aimed shot at the head. The sound of the shot was still echoing in the distance when the next pair charged the same man. He was alert and good, but they were too close, and he only got off one shot before they tackled him. He got a second shot off as he went over on his back, killing the muscular teenager that was trying to bite his face. The other feral, a preteen boy, was able to get to his off side and latch on with both arms. Although the trooper was fully covered, the feral managed to dig a filthy finger into his eye. He released his grip on his rifle with one hand and, while pushing the feral's hand away, exposed his wrist. The feral closed his jaws on the exposed flesh and began shaking his head violently, tearing away a strip of flesh before a rifle butt slammed into the side of its head.

"Kerry's down, Kerry's down!" The trooper who had come over to help kicked the feral over to get it away from the wounded trooper and fired two rounds into its skull. The team began to contract its line to form a perimeter around the downed man when it was assaulted all across its front. Shots rang out on all sides as the team engaged over forty ferals that had lain in wait. Seven of them charged the southernmost vehicle but were too close together, and a quick dose of grazing fire dropped all but one of them. The gunner put the front sight on this last one and gave it a burst, stretching from hip to chest. A few more sporadic shots, and the woods went quiet. The team brought the injured man back to the Hummers and started to bandage his arm.

"Papa Three, Bear One." The voice came over the radio.

"One, Papa Three, we have one WIA and are RTB at this time. Over."

"Papa Three, we have multiple reports of aerial activity to your north. Papa Two says it's a civilian helicopter and has gone back and forth across the lake to the north of their position. How close are you to the shoreline?"

"Standby." The Sergeant in charge of the patrol looked at Dan.

"There's an access to the lakeshore trail just up ahead," Dan replied, holding up a hand with splayed fingers. He mouthed, "Five minutes."

"One, Papa Three, our rangers say we can be there in five mikes."

"Papa Three, get some eyes northward on the lake. Papa Two says there might be a boat out there as well. Over."

"Bear One, Papa Three copies all. Out."

It only took them four minutes to run the three vehicles off road through to the lakeshore. As they pulled up along the shoreline, the gunner in one of the Hummers reported a boat out on the water. Dan had just put a pair of binoculars to his eyes when the gunner reported seeing a civilian helicopter as well.

CHAPTER 33

Lake Bemidji, MN

Carol and Richard Hines were in trouble. The married couple had been completing graduate studies at Bemidji State University when the violence started. They both made it to one of the campus cafeterias and managed to seal the building. They kept quiet enough to avoid detection, first by the individual ferals, and then the packs that formed later.

They rescued and brought in seven other survivors over the past week. The small group had witnessed some looting and lawlessness by unaffected people at first, so they resisted making contact when they heard the occasional National Guard convoy go by. When they saw the helicopters out over the lake, they reasoned that they had to be from the government. They put a message on the roof, but the helicopters never came close enough to see it. The group decided that Rich and Carol would go down to the boat docks on the other side of Tamarack Hall and make their way out to the lake in an attempt to flag down a passing helicopter.

The number of ferals they had been seeing had dropped off dramatically in the previous two days. Rich and Carol were both avid runners and easily the two most capable of the survivors to attempt the mission. The school maintained a few boats for student recreation, and they were familiar with the dock area.

Richard and Carol left the cafeteria and made their way stealthily to the Cedar Hall apartments along Birchwood Drive Crossing. This road would expose them to the greatest chance of being seen. Their concern was unwarranted, as they made it all the way to the water without being observed by unfriendly eyes. They reached the dock and were looking for keys to a small motor boat when their luck changed.

Richard tugged on a small lockbox, which he thought held the keys. The box was not secured to the shelf it was sitting on and crashed to the floor, spilling the keys everywhere. Carol shot some daggers out of her eyes at him and continued filling the boat's gas tank. Richard shrugged sheepishly and began digging through the pile of keys on the floor.

"What number is that one?" he asked.

"SSHHH!" Carol hissed and rolled her eyes at him. "Two! And can you keep it down?" she whispered fiercely.

"Ah ha!" He held up a key ring with a float on it—the number "2" plainly visible. "If anything heard us, it's on its way; let's go."

He turned toward the boat and, as he was handing his wife the key, noticed movement outside through the window in the door. "Babe," he whispered, "there's an infected outside." His whisper was very low and urgent now. He pulled a butcher knife he had taken from the cafeteria and stepped to the side of the door. Carol put the cap back on the gas tank and stuck the key in the ignition, then she hunched down as low as she could.

The long, slow creak of the door slowly opening was straight out of a horror film, right down to the shadow that preceded the feral into the boathouse. The smell preceded it as well, and Rich almost gagged. The creature that came into view was caked with dried blood and gore all down the front of its flannel shirt. The filth was so thick that it cracked and flaked off as it moved. It had wounds on its face and arms that were open and weeping.

Rich wasn't taking any chances; as soon as the feral was past the door, he swung the knife, delivering a backhanded blow. The eight-inch blade plunged into the surprised feral's neck. The result was entirely unexpected, as the intruder turned to Rich like nothing had happened and launched his body right at him. Rich was slammed back into the counter and both bodies slid sideways to the ground. The feral was pummeling Richard's face and shoulders but the blows were not very effective, as Richard was doing a good job of covering up with his arms.

The feral opened its mouth to scream, but all that came out was a spray of blood and other material that Rich didn't want to know the composition of. He managed to get his hand on the knife handle and rip it forward, tearing a huge gash in the thing's throat. The feral fumbled off of Richard and stood, finally acknowledging its wound by placing a hand over its throat.

Carol, who had risen out of the boat, was about to stab it in the back with her own knife when it swept its hand around in an arc, knocking an oar into Carol's head. The blow tore a gash in her scalp and sent her sprawling. The swing of her knife was knocked off course and got tangled in the feral's shirt.

The tug on its shirt distracted the feral long enough to allow Richard to send his knife up through its abdomen and into its diaphragm, paralyzing it. The feral got a stricken look on its face and toppled over. Rich shoved the body out of his way and tried to stand up to go to his wife. His ankle let him know that this was not going to happen. It was severely sprained. He crawled over to Carol, who was groggily sitting up and holding the bloody wound above her ear. She leaned over and pushed the creaky door closed. Rich looked around for the first-aid kit he had noticed earlier and slowly got to his feet and hobbled over to it. He pulled out some gauze as Carol stood up and leaned against the counter.

After Richard applied a ridiculously large bandage that wrapped around her head, she started to help him hobble over to the boat. All of a sudden, his body began to shake, and she pulled away from him in alarm. It took Carol a second to realize that Richard was laughing but trying to keep it in. He looked over at her and finally burst out with a guffaw that he tried in vain to muffle.

"What in the hell is so funny?" Carol was glaring at him.

"All we need is a flute, a flag, and a drummer!" The laughter was becoming contagious as she realized the visual he was describing.

"What was that? The Civil War or the Revolutionary War, where the three guys are walking down the road and one has his head bandaged and the other one is limping with a flute..."

"I know what you're talking about, genius. It's the Revolutionary War, I believe." Carol shook her head and smiled as she climbed into the boat and began to untie the bowline from the dock cleat. Rich climbed unsteadily into the boat and squeezed the bulb on the fuel line to prime the small outboard motor. He then stumped to the driver's seat and turned the key. The motor turned over but didn't start. It took three tries, with Carol getting more frantic with each noisy failure, until the small outboard sputtered to life. Carol had been holding on to the dock cleat and gave the boat a gentle shove toward the open lake.

Richard pulled up on the throttle button and gently pushed the lever forward until the prop engaged. The boat surged a little and then stalled. Rich looked at Carol and shrugged as the boat drifted out from under the cover of the boathouse. He tried to turn the key, realized the boat had to be in neutral, pulled the throttle back, and tried again. By that time, the boat had drifted clear of the dock area and was in plain view to anyone or anything along the shore. A scream sounded from the shoreline to the south as they were spotted by some unfriendly eyes. Richard got the boat started again and this time, the motor didn't stall as he pushed the throttle forward and slowly pulled out on to the lake's smooth surface.

They turned north and cruised farther out, away from the shore. For the first time in nine days, they felt somewhat safe. They took a few minutes to just relax, and Richard gave Carol's head wound a thorough cleaning and rewrapped it. They ate from the meager supplies in their backpacks and shut the motor down when they were in the middle of the northern part of the lake. Rich took his tennis shoes and socks off. His left ankle was swollen and already turning a dark purple. He sat on the back of the boat and dangled his feet in the cool water.

They had been relaxing for forty minutes when they heard the sound of a chopper off to the northeast. The sound got louder as a Bell Jet Ranger came over the treetops of Lake Bemidji State Park. The helicopter was passing to the north of them when it pulled up into a climbing turn and flashed past them as they stood and waved their arms.

The helicopter came around again and began to hover just fifty feet away. It turned broadside to the boat, and Carol and Rich saw the side door open. A man in military-style fatigues was looking at them through a scope on his rifle. This made Rich a little uneasy and he stopped waving. With the helicopter this close, he shouldn't need the scope's magnification. Carol, however, kept waving until the man waved back.

Up in the helicopter, Johan Treutz took the rifle from his eye and contemplated shooting the man and taking the woman with him. His only problem was getting her to be compliant on the way back to base. There wasn't enough room for both of them in the helicopter. His dilemma was solved when his team leader came over the headset and told him to sink the boat immediately. The contractor from South Africa had been a mercenary for years, and had no problem opening up on the two helpless victims. He put the rifle up to his shoulder again and was about to fire when the first .50-caliber round smashed into the helicopter's rotor housing.

The bird shuddered as warning tones began to blare in the cockpit. The pilot asked if it was the people in the boat shooting at them. Johan informed him it wasn't and began to pan the shoreline. The helicopter started to rise and turn toward the west in an attempt to get to the Bemidji Airport. Johan saw the boat slipping past and let loose with a burst from his HK G3 assault rifle.

A second .50-caliber bullet smashed into the rotor housing, and the transmission gave up the ghost. The rotor blades began to wind down without the power of the turbine engine, and the helicopter lost lift. It had only gained about twenty-five MPH's worth of momentum and was fifty feet in the air when it lost power, and the rotors became unresponsive.

Because the pilot had been trying to accelerate, the helicopter was in a nose-down attitude when it struck the water. It immediately flipped over and started to sink.

Johan had been in an open doorway and was thrown clear. All the other people on board were so disoriented that they couldn't make their way out until it was too late. One of the other mercenaries made it out of the sinking bird, but his weapons and gear pulled him under before he could get free of them. Johan hit the water and was nearly killed by a rotor blade slamming into him. The blade just hit his backpack, ripping it to shreds, and driving him underwater, where he nearly lost consciousness. He released his rifle and shook loose from his pack and vest. He was keeping his pistol and the magazines for it though. With the weight gone, he managed to stay afloat.

Carol and Rich were caught completely by surprise when the man in the helicopter opened fire. The bullets had stitched a line of destruction across the boat, punching holes in everything and everyone. Rich was hit in the shoulder, the bullet passing low into his armpit and out the back without hitting any bone or major blood vessels. Carol was struck in the right shin. The bullet broke the right shinbone and tore through her calf. They both fell to the bottom of the boat and tried to find some form of cover. They heard a second boom off in the distance and the loud metallic impact on the helicopter. They both watched as the helicopter impacted the water a hundred yards from where the boat was floating.

Rich, again, got out the first-aid kit and attended to his wife's wounds. He felt the broken bone, but it seemed to be in the right place so he fashioned a splint by breaking the lightweight aluminum emergency oar and tying it to her leg. Two more bandages to cover the entry and exit wounds, and he was done with her. He then placed a bandage on his shoulder, sat back and said, "Shit! That did not work out at all like I thought it would!"

Carol was about to reply when they heard a splashing in the water. They looked to the west and saw the man who had shot them sidestroking slowly in the direction of the boat. He was obviously in trouble, and even the lake water hadn't washed away all the blood that was seeping from various cuts and scrapes.

"Oh, hell no!" Rich said, plopping into the driver's seat. He turned the key and started the motor. "We are not letting that guy on board!"

"But he might drown." Carol turned to keep her eye on the swimmer as Rich turned the boat away from him.

"Babe, I don't think he would have cared if we drowned." Rich was steering the boat eastward, away from the wreckage in case any more bad guys popped to the surface. "In fact, I have half a mind to go back and run his ass over!" He looked back to his front and saw a white truck and two military vehicles driving toward them on the eastern shore of the lake. "I think these are our saviors, honey."

Carol turned from looking off the rear of the boat and saw the three vehicles coming up the shoreline to meet them. They drove the quarter mile to the shore, and Rich pulled the throttle back to idle and let the boat drift in. The site of Dan and Scott in their park ranger uniforms took some of the edge off of seeing the guardsmen in their uniforms; the last person they'd seen in a military uniform had shot at them.

"Are you folks all right?" Scott asked, looking at Carol's head. "We saw the guy in the chopper shoot at you. We have some medical facilities back at our temporary operating base."

"We're both hit, and we suffered some injuries earlier today. There's a survivor from the chopper still swimming out there. We left him because he was the one shooting at us, and we don't have any guns." Rich was helping Carol off the bow of the boat as he explained their situation. "We heard and saw the helicopters earlier today and thought they would be from the government, so we set out to get their attention. It didn't go so well."

"You said there's a survivor still out there?" Master Sergeant Lovell was looking out over the water with binoculars. "Oh yeah, there he is. Did you see if he was armed?"

"We sure didn't," Rich said smugly. "We left him to drown."

Lovell looked at Scott with a raised eyebrow then turned back to Richard. The guardsmen had both of them on the ground and were treating their wounds. After ascertaining that none of the wounds were bites, they were carried up to the vehicles.

"You don't mind if we borrow your boat to go pick him up, do you?" Scott asked Richard as he was gently set on a stretcher in the back.

"It's all yours if it floats. There's a few bullet holes in it." Rich leaned back. "I may take a hammer to his knee caps though, for what he did to my wife."

"I'll let him know how concerned you are with his state of well-being," Scott said with a smile. He went to his truck, grabbed a backpack out of a side panel, and met Dan and another guardsman down at the shore. They shoved the boat off and cruised out to where Johan was feebly trying to backstroke to the shore.

"Keep your hands on the surface as you tread water!" Dan ordered as they approached the foundering man. "Are you carrying any weapons?"

Scott was driving the boat as both Dan and the trooper were covering Johan with their rifles. They kept the boat pointed at the swimming mercenary in case he started shooting. This would protect the motor and would also allow Scott to just run the swimmer over.

"I have a pistol in a leg holster that's about to bloody drown me. My left shoulder is broke, I think." Johan knew there was no way out. "I can't stay up with only one hand."

"I'm going to throw you a flotation device; you will put it under your chest and then keep both hands out of the water, or we will shoot you. Do you understand?"

"Well, come on then." Johan waved impatiently.

Dan threw the square life preserver out to Johan and waited until he was floating with both hands clearly visible. He gestured to Scott and they came alongside the injured swimmer. Dan took his hand as the guardsman kept his rifle pointed right at his head. They put the handcuffs on him while he was still in the water. He was then hauled halfway out on his belly at the rear of the boat and searched with his legs still hanging in the water. His belt was removed, along with his holster and other equipment. He was then pulled the rest of the way into the boat, none too gently, and again searched. He was stripped down to his T-shirt and trousers. Even his boots were removed and checked. While still lying on his stomach, his hands were cuffed behind him and he was finally allowed to sit in one of the seats as they headed back to shore. Dan asked several questions but the prisoner didn't make a peep.

After landing the boat, Johan was passed out to the troops on the shore, where he was searched again. All his belongings were placed in a bag and put in the ranger's pickup. Johan was loaded into the Hummer not being occupied by the Hines.

Master Sergeant Lovell called in a situation report and they had an uneventful drive back to the hotel.

CHAPTER 34

Rancho Bernardo, CA

The rescue mission was preparing to head back to Camp Pendleton. Cliff had brought over the survivors from his house and vehicles were prepared to transport all the survivors and their belongings up to the safe zone. Mark had finally gotten a good night sleep and the redness, while still noticeable, was much lighter. He'd eaten breakfast with his kids and told them that he would be along shortly, the Marine Corps wanted him to rescue a few more survivors, and then he would join them at the base.

The kids had listened stoically as Mark told them they would be going to the base while he stayed behind. They immediately protested, saying they could help keep the house secure and run the "Norris Way Station" while Mark and the Marines were out rescuing people. Several of the families volunteered to stay as well to keep it operational as a safe place for refugees. In the end, Mark told everyone, including Jen, that they had to go. Only Jake and four other Marines would be staying to take care of him. Cliff and his family were staying at their house as well, so there would be some help close by if needed.

The dogs would also be going; they had been cooped up in the garage for days and only got walked right in front of the house. This was tough on them, as their exercise routine usually involved several miles a day in the open space preserve near the house. They had not been taking any chances on the dogs being exposed to the toxin.

Terry, Mel, and Jen all packed their bags and loaded them in a GMC Denali. The top-of-the-line SUV had belonged to one of the neighbors down the street. Jim recognized the bodies when he was removing them to the drainage ditch for cremation. He and three Marines went to the house and found the keys, the SUV, and some other supplies. Jim tossed a large sea bag in back. He then went and got the dogs ready to go.

Jen was driving, with Terry riding shotgun and Mel in back with the dogs. Jim had wrangled a seat in one of the Hummers. There were plenty of open seats as the convoy had more civilian vehicles than military ones. The convoy consisted of six Hummers (the other two would be staying behind), and twenty SUVs, trucks, or vans. Alan's bright-orange Raptor was right up front with Tia in the passenger seat, looking embarrassed.

Cliff, David, Mark, and Jake stood outside to see the convoy off. As soon as it started moving, they went inside, secured the house, and went up to the roof. Jake and Mark had their 107s already set up to provide rifle support for the convoy. Cliff and Staff Sergeant Kyle were looking through spotting scopes while David kept a 360-degree watch. They kept the convoy in view as much as possible until it reached the I-15 Bridge across Lake Hodges. As the convoy was entering the freeway on-ramp, they began to see movement along the side of the bridge.

"Gypsy One-Six, Eagle One, you have movement all around you. It looks like they're gonna rush you as you get on the bridge. I am engaging at this time. Over." Mark took his hand off the mic and lined up his first shot as Jake did the same next to him. Neither one of them saw Nosferatu.

"Eagle One, Gypsy One-Six actual, copy all. We're ready. Break. Heads up, contact imminent, all quadrants. Out."

In the hands of a trained sniper, the M107 was a devastating weapon—and with it, Mark and Jake began doing what they did best. Jake got the first round off, and it literally slammed a feral into the embankment it was climbing. Mark's shot followed a split second later, striking a feral in the shoulder then transited the body laterally, blowing the collarbone out the other side and leaving a channel of torn flesh and bone in its wake.

Both men fired all ten rounds in their magazines and had reloaded when Kyle shouted, "Contact west!" and began firing his M4.

Two loud *booms* signaled Cliff and David to get into the fight. A group of ferals, about twenty strong, had snuck up to the house during all the commotion of the convoy leaving. They had waited patiently until Nosferatu gave them the signal to attack. Then they rushed the house, using all available cover, and fifteen of them made it into the yard. Three ran to the side pad and, using hand stirrups, were able to fling the smallest of their group up onto the roof.

This feral landed right in front of Jake's rifle, and he merely shifted his aim and squeezed the trigger. The feral was fast though, and the round only tore a small piece of flesh away from its side. It immediately leapt over the sandbags and attacked Jake. He was ready for the attack but not the ferocity. The 107 was a behemoth to try to use for any kind of close-quarters weapon, so he left it and used his left hand to keep the feral's mouth away while his right hand reached for his KA-BAR combat knife. He ripped it out of his sheath and was stabbing it up under the feral's ribs when another feral popped over the edge of the roof.

Mark had no chance at hitting this one and immediately stepped away from his rifle and drew his pistol. The HK .45 barked twice, sending the feral right back off the roof and into a third one that was being hoisted up. All four ferals fell off of the pallet of canned goods they had been standing on and crashed to the concrete. They were trying to untangle themselves when a soft *buuuurrrrppp* sounded from the backyard, and a stream of 9mm rounds killed them all.

Mark looked to his left to see Jim standing at the corner of the garage with his MP5 pointed at the pile of still twitching corpses. The young man turned around to face the flood of ferals climbing over the back wall and began firing. The roar of Cliff's shotgun drowned out everything as he fired six rounds of buckshot across the fence line in less than four seconds. The fifty-four pellets of buckshot and seventeen rounds of 9mm swept the wall clean of their attackers, sending anything on the wall back over into the neighbor's yard. Only one pitched face forward into Mark's backyard.

Jim started moving toward the back door but stopped to reload. A chunk of concrete slammed into the side of his head, sending him sprawling to the ground, unconscious. Both Cliff and David yelled out and attempted to scramble down from the roof to get to him. Mark grabbed both of them by the collar and swung them back into the sandbag emplacement, gesturing and yelling at them to continue to provide security. He then leapt off the roof, landing right in front of two ferals that were heading for his downed son. One of them began to scream but was cut off by Mark's roar of fury. Mark had left his long guns on the roof, but he had his knife and pistol. The feral looked stunned for a moment and that was all it took for Mark to punch it square in the face.

The other feral watched this and turned to go after Jim, who had still not moved. Mark's left hand shot out and grabbed its shirt, pulling it back and off balance. The KA-BAR appeared in his hand as if by magic, and it sliced down through the clavicle opening and into top of the chest cavity. A quick back and forth to sever all the important stuff, and the knife was twisted out. Blood exploded from the feral's mouth and out through the neck wound as the air in its lungs coursed its way past the destruction in the esophagus to escape.

Mark had already turned back to the feral that had its nose broken from his fist. Feral or not, physics cannot be denied. The blow to the face had broken the nose and caused the eyes to water. A shake of the head cleared the eyes, but the pain was so great that it reached through the foggy brain functions and let the feral know it was hurt. The message didn't have long to sink in, as Mark backhanded the blade into the side of its throat. A knee to the ribs sent the dying thing tumbling away as the KA-BAR ripped out the front of its throat.

Movement to Mark's right brought him around to face Nosferatu standing over Jim's still inert body. The muscular feral roared a challenge that was immediately drowned out by Mark's response. In a flash, Mark's hand dropped to the Safariland holster at his right thigh. The rotating hood slid forward, and the .45 was rotated up and out in less than a half a second. The HK went off three times as Mark closed the distance and jumped straight across Jim's body to slam into the threat to his son.

The first round grazed the outside of Nosferatu's left thigh. The second punched into the hip just outside the socket, the Corbon 200-grain hollow point removed a tunnel of flesh but missed the bone. The third round was a little more effective as Mark's aim tracked toward the center of mass. It punctured the abdominal wall, tearing through the large intestine and coming out the back below the floating rib. The damage would have eventually been fatal without medical attention, but it failed to take the alpha out of the fight.

As their bodies crashed together, some of Nosferatu's martial arts training came back to him. He twisted away from Mark's attack and attempted to slide step into a better position. He was only partially successful as his foot caught on Jim's body and he stumbled. Mark managed to rake the KA-BAR across the feral's chest, leaving a fourteen-inch gash across his pecs. Nosferatu had never been served up so much pain and injury so quickly. His enraged brain trying to keep up with the constant assaults and injuries pushed him to overload. He tried to take a step back and gather his wits to attack the source of all the agony when a 5.56mm slug tore through his back. He spun around to look at the roof, where the shot had come from. The motion saved his life; the next .45 round from Mark's pistol missed his center of mass but did hit him with a glancing blow that shattered a rib on his right side.

That was enough for the feral's self-preservation circuits to kick in. He only made it a step, though, before the .45 sent one last round through his lower back. He collapsed to the ground with legs that no longer followed orders. He hitched himself forward with his arms, trying to get around the corner and away from the constant assault his body was taking. He heard Mark's footsteps as he approached and turned to snarl at his attacker. His face turned only to meet the KA-BAR as it slammed into his right eye and into the brain cavity, ending Nosferatu's reign of terror.

Mark bent over the still unconscious form of his son and felt for a pulse. It was strong enough for him to feel over his own pounding heart. The side of Jim's head was speckled with blood from the scrapes the chunk of concrete had made, and the entire left side of his head was starting to swell and turn purple. Mark gently checked his neck for bulges and broken bones. Not finding any, he gently rolled him onto his back and checked him for other injuries.

Cliff and David came down from the roof. The firing had almost completely died down except for the occasional boom of Jake's .50 whenever a feral exposed itself near the lake. They helped pick Jim up and take him into his bedroom. They took off his gear and set him in his bed. David got a cool, wet washcloth and washed his face while Cliff got an ice pack, wrapped it in a towel, and placed it on the side of Jim's face when David was done.

Jake came down from the roof, took one look at Jim, and said, "Oh shit!" He turned around and went back outside.

"Gypsy One-Six, Eagle Two. Over."

"Eagle Two, Gypsy One-Six, send it. Over." It was Sanchez' voice on the radio.

"Hey, Art, Jim's hurt real bad and needs medical attention. Over."

"Eagle Two, how do you know that?" Sanchez looked at the rearview mirror then at his driver. "Did he fall out of his Hummer?" He gestured for the driver to pull over.

"Gypsy One-Six, I think you guys took off without him. We got hit pretty hard when we started to give you guys long rifle support crossing the bridge. We were being swarmed and he just showed up in the middle of the fight." Jake took a deep breath. "That Mexican guy that's been following us from Vista hit him in the side of the head with a cinder block. He's been unconscious since."

"Oh, the gunner is going to shit on someone! Eagle Two, Gypsy One-Six copies. All will RTB for a pickup." Art looked at his driver who had been filling Captain Johnson in on the conversation.

"Eagle Two, Gypsy One-Six actual, what is your tactical situation now?" Johnson wanted to know if he could just send a single Hummer back.

"Gypsy One-Six, Eagle Two, we killed about twenty here at the house, and between us and you guys we probably killed another forty at the bridge. We have no observable activity at this—"

"Belay that! Tell him we're taking Jim out to him. Get a location and tell them we'll meet them." Jake jumped as Mark silently appeared behind him and started shouting orders. As he relayed Mark's instructions, Cliff, David, and Mark took Jim out to one of the Hummers that was left behind and put him in the hardback's stretcher. After strapping him in, Mark jumped in the driver's seat while Jake climbed up into the gunner's cupola. David got behind Mark and his dad took shotgun.

"Gypsy One-Six, Eagle One rolling. Over."

"Eagle One, Gypsy One-Six, copy, we are just at the I-15/78 Junction, where the freeway is really wide. We have circled the wagons and are waiting for you. Over."

"Eagle One copies. Out."

As Mark's Hummer approached the Lake Hodges Bridge, they saw several ferals going cannibal on the bodies of the ones that had been killed earlier. Jake sent a few bursts from the 240 to scatter them. He only hit two, killing one, and wounding the other. They sped north along the mostly empty freeway, only having to change lanes twice to avoid abandoned vehicles. They reached the convoy seven minutes later.

The I-15/78 Interchange was next to a huge shopping center, and the convoy's presence had been noted by a few of the local predators. Most of the ferals had shed their lower clothing by this time, although some retained enough sense to keep their shoes. Art called them "The Pantless Army." Several came up onto the freeway and were immediately gunned down by the Marines.

Mark brought the Hummer next to a similar one and told the driver to leave Jim in the back, grab their gear, and they would exchange vehicles. Jen jogged over to ask what happened and came upon Mark holding a young corporal up against the side of a Hummer.

"You have exactly twenty-seven seconds to explain to me why my son was not in this Hummer when you left! The reason had better be good because at twenty-eight, I will begin to disassemble you in place, and at thirty, God himself will not be able to recognize what's left!" The rage in his eyes was causing the young Marine, who was familiar with Mark's reputation, to shake uncontrollably. "Begin!"

"Uh, well, sir, he came over right as we were going to leave and said he was going to ride with his mom." The young man pointed to Jen. "I watched him take his bag over to her car and everything!" He sent a pleading look at Jen for confirmation. "She saw it, sir, and even waved to me!"

"Mark! Mark!" Jen was pulling his hands away from the terrified young Marine. "It's true! Jim came over and said there was no room for the bag in the Hummer. I did wave to this young man, but it was to acknowledge taking the bag. Honey, I think Jim played us. He said he was going back to the Hummer and I didn't see him after that."

"Well, fuck!" Mark turned away and stalked toward the perimeter. He turned back to see Jen coming up behind him. She stopped when she saw the bright red skin along his neck.

"Oh, honey! Won't you please come with us? You need to get some help too!"

Mark was about to explode into a rant but, instead, took a deep breath and said, "Okay."

They sent a Hummer back to the house to maintain the number of Marines there, and they loaded up to continue to the base. Mark rode in back, holding his son's hand all the way.

CHAPTER 35

Bemidji, MN

Lieutenant Crowe squatted in front of the bound prisoner and shook his head. The man's wounds had been tended to, but his muscular build and the way his eyes never stopped moving and taking everything in, made Crowe nervous. He had made sure that the man was double shackled at all times and the bonds were rechecked every four hours. This was to make sure that not only was he not making progress in getting out of them, but to deprive him of any long-term sleep as well.

"I am entitled to legal representation, Lieutenant. I would like to speak to the person appointed to represent me at this time, please." Johan maintained a calm voice, in spite of the discomfort the two sets of handcuffs and leg chains were causing him.

"Well, in case you haven't noticed, there isn't much of a legal system right now, so I'll tell it to ya straight. We're going to check out the wreckage and check the aircraft ID numbers. We may just hand you over to some CIA guys. I don't think anyone would get mad at a presidential pardon if we violated your civil rights. If you are a part of this whole mess, I am going to come back in here and cut your fingers off knuckle by knuckle. Then I'm going to use a dull knife to cut off your eyelids and lips. I will keep you in such personal agony for so long, you'll try to take your own life at every turn. Then when it's really bad, I'm going to give you some very special water, you know… made with the stuff you guys put in our water supply. Then once your eyes are nice and milky, I'm going to let you go out into that big ol' world. Blind and in pain for someone who was innocent once to eat." Crowe stood up.

"Well then, you'd best hope I don't get free first." Johan was tough, but he couldn't help swallowing because of his suddenly dry mouth. He still put on his best tough guy routine though. "It's best not to make threats when interrogating a prisoner. It only stiffens their resolve. And since your behavior indicates to me that you are part of some misguided militia and not a real Army man, I am going to make every effort to escape."

"Have some experience interrogating prisoners, do ya? Or have you been trained on how to resist the interrogating?" Crowe stared at the man for another minute then left the room.

Crowe went down the hall to confer with Lovell, Giles, Scott Preston, and Captain Nelson. The four men were staring at a small laptop screen, watching as Johan hitched his way around the utility room in the Radio Shack, looking for any tools he might find to facilitate his escape. They had found pinhole cameras and set them up to cover several angles in the room. Johan rolled to his side to peer at something against the wall where the electrical panel met the floor. He then hitched around to get his hands on whatever it was.

"Industrious little fucker, isn't he?" Lovell said. He was the only person who could rightly call Johan *little*. "He went right after whatever the hell that is. And I bet if we go in there, he'll Houdini whatever the hell that is, and we won't find it!"

"Well, Master Sergeant, you may call him little, but that guy is a serious operator. Look how he's slicing a place in the waistband of his trousers for whatever that is in his hand." Crowe had pushed his way closer to the screen. "Well, do we tip our hand that we have the place wired by going in there and taking his toy away, or do we see what he tries to do with it?"

"If he's that good, he'll always assume that we have eyes on him. Then if we don't, he'll be pleasantly surprised when we make a mistake." Lovell was an old school Green Beret. "We should always squash any plans he makes. It will demoralize him."

"I agree; who's doing good cop?" Crowe asked.

"That would be me," Giles said, heading toward the door. "How nice do I have to be?" He didn't wait for a reply since the question was rhetorical and went down the hall.

The rest of them turned back to the screen in time to see Giles walk in and deliver an openhanded slap across Johan's face. The blow caused him to roll on to his side as the stars came out around his head. He knew better than to try and sit back up. Giles sent a kick into his gut with a combat boot, causing him to attempt a fetal position, but the leg chains were connected to the cuffs, and he couldn't get his legs very far forward. His torso did double over a bit. Giles leaned over and stepped on the handcuffs, which crushed Johan's wrists, then stepped on two of his fingers. The pain elicited a brief shout before Johan could clamp down and grit his teeth.

"Oh, sorry there, pal; I just need this." Giles pulled out the small nail that he found stuck in the man's waistband. He held it up in front of Johan's eyes and acted like he might jab him with it. "This, young man, is not being on your best behavior! If I didn't know better, I would think you might get up to no good with this. That would not show the proper appreciation of our warm and caring hospitality." Giles pivoted on the foot that was on the handcuffs, bringing another grunt of pain from the South African's lips.

Giles went back down the hall to show the others the small nail. Johan had not moved from his curled up position on the floor. Everyone turned to look at the sergeant as he came through the door. He held up the small nail and returned the stares. "Oh, come on now! I beat my kids worse for getting lousy grades!"

"Is that why they're so well behaved?" Lovell grinned back at the sergeant

"I didn't break anything, at least not bad enough to stick out through the skin!"

"Gents let's keep a close watch on him, and I don't want anyone going in there alone. He doesn't eat, drink, or shit without two guards watching him. In fact, let's cut the clothes off him. He can stay in his skivvies. Showers via bucket and brush. Got it?" Nelson looked them in the eye. "And no permanent damage. NCA will be interested in him."

Nelson went to the comm room to see if anyone had gotten back to him regarding the prisoner. The specialist manning the radio said there had been nothing yet, so he headed downstairs to eat. He hadn't made it down half a flight when the specialist yelled at him from the end of the hall.

"Sir! There's some zoomie admiral on the radio, sir!" The specialist grinned at his own joke. "He says he has a priority mission for us."

"Zoomie admiral, huh? Well, let's not keep the man waiting."

Nelson plopped down in the desk chair and picked up the mic. "This is Captain Nelson with the Minnesota National Guard, who am I speaking with? Over."

"Captain, this is Brigadier General Grubbs, U.S. Air Force. I run the show here in Colorado Springs for SATCOM. We have been monitoring several airports that show increased activity. I was notified that you are in Bemidji and have made contact with the crew from a helicopter; is that correct?"

"Affirmative on the location, sir. We are just outside the city's southern section. We observed several overflights of civilian helicopters. We believe them to be Jet Rangers, from the descriptions. When we sent a patrol to see if they could make contact, the helicopter was observed firing on unarmed civilians. The patrol had a DDM who engaged the bird with an SASR, sir, and brought down the bird. One passenger was recovered, not believed to be flight crew. He was the one seen firing at the civilians. He was thrown clear when the bird went in the drink. Over."

"Hold on, for clarification. What's a DDM and an SASR? Remember, son, I'm an old Air Force guy."

"Sorry, sir, a DDM is a Dedicated Designated Marksman, sir, they're snipers who operate in support of infantry. The SASR is the Barrett M107 .50-caliber Special Application Scoped Rifle. Over." Nelson looked at the specialist and shrugged.

"Okay, I got it. So the helicopter went in the drink? Where were the civilians you were talking about?" Grubbs had a tech bring Bemidji up on the main screen.

"The bird went down at the north end of Lake Bemidji, sir. The civilians had gone out on the lake in a boat to attract the attention of the helicopters. They had seen the birds earlier and thought they were rescue birds. Over."

"Captain, how well equipped is your force? I need a straight answer because I need you to recon the Bemidji Airport on the west side of town." Grubbs gestured for a tech to put the images up on the big screen. "My satellites are showing that it has become an active airfield again. If this is going to place your troops in jeopardy, then I will route a request through Washington. At this time, you are the only force close enough to one of these active airfields."

Grubbs studied the screen. "There are approximately twenty ground-force personnel, with two, I mean one now, helicopter in support. Three turbo prop aircraft have flown in and out of the airport. The other helicopter is out over the lake right now, by the way, looking down on the wreckage from the other bird, which is plainly visible. The water must not be very deep. Do you have anyone in the area?"

"Negative, sir. We pretty much roll up the carpet at night. The ferals just get too close to us, even with night vision gear. Do we have any word on air support from Minnesota National Guard? Or Air National Guard? I am a reinforced company with Stryker-armored vehicles. We have established a base of operations with a group of survivors that is centered around several law enforcement personnel. Most of these are prior service, and they really have their shit together, sir. We have been running joint operations with them because of their knowledge of local conditions."

Nelson was taking notes as the specialist brought over some maps. "I'm looking at a map now, sir. We can probably get good eyes on target and get you real-time intel. I can lay on the recon mission for tomorrow. It will be two days before we can get a combat op going, sir, unless it's real urgent. If they have air and any anti-armor, we'll be a bit challenged. My shooters are good, and two or three of the local cops are snipers. If we had air, it would be a lot easier. Over."

"I'll check on the air, but get me some eyes on that airfield. I can see it from overhead, but I need to know what they're doing." Grubbs jotted down a note on a sticky and gave it to Willis. "Tech Sergeant Willis will get up with you for communications protocol. Good luck, Captain."

"Thank you, sir. Out." Nelson swiveled the chair around to face the small crowd that had gathered there. "Platoon leader warning order; I need the four sneakiest sons of bitches we have, and if that includes some of the locals, then so be it! But I want stealthy people, got it?" He waited for the appropriate "yes sirs" to die down. "I want a recon element in place as soon as safely possible."

"Hey, Captain, Dan and Glenn were both super snoopers in the Army, and Dan is a pilot for us. He is really familiar with the airport and its layout." Scott waved toward the two rangers. "I think they both still have their Ghillie suits. They like to dress up and follow each other in the woods. It's a childhood thing; they used to hold each other during sleepovers… took till high school to break them of it. The reason I suggest this is not only because I'm trying to get rid of the two biggest mouths we have to feed, but also because if we can get our Cessna up, we'll be able to cover some ground."

"All right then, if you think the two of them can be persuaded to put the cuddling thing on hold, they're on the team. I'll need them to brief the rest of the recon element, anyway." He turned to Lovell. "Well, Master Sergeant, any snake-eater wisdom you can contribute would be appreciated."

"Roger that, sir. I'll have them ready." He looked at the two former soldiers. "Well, it looks like you're back in the Army now!"

"Not likely! But we'll get the recon element right up close. We are going to have to act like the birds are thermal equipped, and that's going to make it slow going." Glenn had stepped over next to Dan and put his arm around his shoulders. "I'll be okay, though, as long as I have my life partner here!" And with, that he turned and kissed Dan on the forehead.

Dan's look of long-term suffering had everyone in the room laughing. The group broke up and began to prepare for the upcoming mission. Scott and Glenn had turned toward the door when Scott yelped, slapping his hand to the back of his neck. The snap of the rubber band told him he had been the victim of another paper clip attack. Glenn attempted to step to the side but was unsuccessful in evading the next missile; it hit him in the back of his bicep. Scott ducked and made it another three steps down the hall before the next one hit him in almost the same spot on his neck.

"Ow, shit! How the hell does he do that?"

The recon teams did a standard stealth separation from a larger unit, each four-man team slipping into the shadows and sneaking away from a patrol. One of the patrols was a rescue mission and went to the university to recover Carol and Rich's friends. They had increased the size of a marksman/observer team, in case they made contact with any ferals. Quick reaction teams were stationed in buildings as close as they dared. The Bemidji Medical Center was still very popular with the ferals, so they worked their way farther west before heading north to the airfield. They had managed to scrounge up some suppressed weapons, and each team had at least one. They hoped they could eliminate any hostile contacts without alerting whoever was at the airfield.

Dan was approaching from the west, Glenn worked his way around to the north, and Lovell led a recon/assault team and took up residence in a building just south of Adams Avenue. He then worked his way across the highway to the BCA building south of the airport. Sergeant Green had a team located in some trees right near Gillet Drive, almost on the runway itself. They took all night getting into position and didn't see any air traffic in or out. The helicopter was on the ramp when they got there. The sound of generators could be heard faintly in the distance and there were lights visible in the terminal. Dan knew the light was coming from the flight planning office, where the charts and publications were kept.

"Rocketman, Mamba One, data upload." Glenn was familiar with the BDS equipment. He laid the crosshairs on the building and sent his uplink with the push of a button. The Ballistic Data Scope's laser rangefinder measured the range and the magnetic heading to the target, took a GPS position fix of the BDS itself, and plotted the target's position in latitude, longitude, and elevation. It converted this to the military grid system and snapped a high-resolution photo. All of this data was encrypted and sent via a burst transmission to a satellite overhead.

"Mamba One, Rocketman, we have the data." Tech Sergeant Willis again had General Grubbs leaning over his shoulder.

"Rocketman. Mamba Four, data upload."

"Rocketman, Mamba Two, data upload."

"Rocketman, Mamba Three, is in position, no uplink at this time. Over"

"Mamba Three, Rocketman copies. Out," Willis said.

"We couldn't come up with something better than Rocketman?" Grubbs was shaking his head at Willis.

"I suggested 'Supreme God Overlord' but the ground guys said no call signs with the word *over* in it were allowed. It messes with their little doggie brains, and they think they can talk after they hear it, sir." Willis grinned up at him. "Rocketman was their concession. They don't like call signs longer than two syllables, either, sir."

"Well, I guess we have to keep it simple for our green brothers."

"They're more like distant cousins, sir, like distant back to the apes!"

Grubbs chuckled and continued with his rounds. It would take awhile for the intel to start flowing in, and he had the ability to look up at the main screen from anywhere in the room. The entire operation would be on constant display there until it was over. Little green triangles appeared around the airport image with call signs attached underneath. A slightly larger red square appeared right over the airport terminal itself. Soon the aircraft were being tagged red or blue as Dan indicated which were hostile and which were friendly. If an airstrike was called, they didn't want to damage any civilian aircraft unnecessarily.

The updates continued through the early part of the morning. At 0923, a ground crew fueled the helicopter. At 0952, four men prepped it and took off. As soon as it was in the air, the radio intercept officer announced another encrypted burst transmission. The helicopter sped off to the west.

"Lieutenant Simmons, would you please track that bird for us on screen two?" Grubbs asked.

"Yes, sir!" The attractive young lieutenant looked a little frazzled. Her boyfriend had not been heard from since right after things went bad. She and Tom had been dating since the academy and had both managed to catch Colorado Springs as a first-duty station. She was on the ball, though, and managed to keep the helicopter centered in the screen as it curved slightly southwest and landed at a small private airstrip.

Three of the men got out of the helicopter and approached a hangar. Several ferals could be seen approaching, obviously attracted by the noise. None of them got closer than fifty yards before falling to the ground. A few seconds later, the men disappeared inside the building.

"Get me everything on that airfield and building." Grubbs was up in the "Emperor's chair" by this time. "What's going on at these fields?" he muttered to himself.

CHAPTER 36

Bemidji Airport, MN

The airport had been relatively calm since the Jet Ranger took off earlier that morning. Very little movement in and around the buildings could be observed. A feral wandered off of the Paul Bunyan Expressway and into the terminal area. The security element took it down and disposed of the body in a quiet and professional manner. The recon teams did not see anything until a small cargo plane landed at noon. Four men and some crates were unloaded and the plane turned around and left.

The helicopter returned at 1700 and only the pilot got out. At 1820 a small, funny-looking aircraft landed and taxied over to the one of the hangars where activity had been observed. Several men swarmed all over the aircraft, opening hatches and performing other tasks. As they were doing this, another plane landed; this one was a different make but equally odd looking.

"Rocketman, Mamba Two, I have eyes on two crop dusting aircraft that have landed." Dan was snapping pictures of the tail numbers. "The ground crew here are performing thorough maintenance on one of them. There are several metal containers on pallets visible inside the structure. Over."

"Mamba Two, we are tracking another aircraft inbound your location, ETA three minutes. This airframe also came from same airfield as other two. Over."

"Rocketman, copy one more inbound. Over."

"Mamba Two, what are the chances of you getting inside that hangar and checking out those containers? Over."

"Rocketman, the security here is on the ball. If we make it an assault with long rifle support, we can do it no problem, but we'll be blown. I am concerned with these aircraft being crop dusters. If they are planning on spraying more of this toxin into the environment, it could be the nail in the coffin for the remaining population. Over."

"Mamba Two, Rocketman actual, I am authorizing you to take whatever action is necessary to A: ground those crop dusters, and B: secure those containers. We need to know what this is all about."

"Rocketman, Mamba Three, we'll need a couple of hours to set this up and get the appropriate MOPP gear staged. The snipers can ground the airframes if they try to take off, but I'd like to plan a coordinated assault if possible. Over."

"Mamba Three, at your discretion, just don't let those planes back up in the air."

"Mamba Three copies all. Break. Base, can we get the MOPP gear en route to my location and a team suited up and ready to handle those containers? We have a couple of NBC guys; they should earn their paycheck like the rest of us. Over."

"Mamba Three, Base, they were on their way five mikes ago. ETA is one hour. Can you coordinate an assault in that time? Over."

"Base, affirm. Out." Lovell started looking at maps and conferring with the other teams. The snipers began identifying and designating targets. The assault team was briefed on the locations of bad guys and the containers. The terminal blue prints were studied and all the primary target aircraft, including the one that just landed were identified, and a plan began to form. Once the NBC team arrived, it took ten minutes to brief them and another ten to stage the vehicles.

The plan called for a sniper-initiated assault. All exposed personnel would be engaged by the snipers from all sides at the same time. The immediate loss of so many personnel would hopefully cause enough chaos that the door kickers could get right up to the terminal and make entry. Another assault team, led by Master Sergeant Lovell and containing the NBC techs, would work their way around to the hangar and secure the containers. The sniper teams would then collapse on the airfield and help secure it.

"Rocketman, Mamba Three, we are ready to initiate. Do you have any last-minute intel for us? Over."

"Mamba Three, Rocketman, the skies are clear. I have one body, probable sentry, moving between the terminal building and the building right to the east of it. I show an updated location for you of the BCA building, is that correct? Over."

"Rocketman, affirmative, our LOD is from here. We are ready to initiate. Over."

"All teams, Rocketman actual, you are cleared to go!"

"Guns up."

"Mamba One up." Glenn had his crosshairs on the sentry standing next to the helicopter.

"Mamba Two up." Dan was aiming at a sentry inside the hangar.

"Mamba Three up." The sniper with Lovell's team was aiming at the sentry by the front of the terminal.

"Mamba Four up." Giles only had one person in his field of view.

"All guns up, standby…" Dan gave everyone a second to make last minute adjustments.

"Ready, Ready, Ready, Fire!"

On the long *eerrrr* sound of "fire," all four rifles went off. All four of the targeted personnel dropped. The observers who had designated targets also fired as soon as the sniper rifles went off. Dan and Glenn each got off three rounds before there was no one left standing. The assault teams immediately rushed their objectives. The main assault force drove their Hummer and one of the Strykers up Moberg Drive toward the terminal as Lovell led his team out of the woods and around the west side of the terminal building.

The estimated size of the enemy force occupying the terminal was twenty. In truth, there were only eighteen, thirteen of which perished in the first hail of gunfire. Four more were inside the terminal building.

Klause Werner was one of the last of the mercenaries hired to protect the operation. He was stationed inside the front of the terminal to provide heavy weapons support to the outside sentries. When he saw his friend Eddie drop to the ground with half his head missing, he knew he was facing normal people, not ferals.

Klause had an RPG ready to go when the Hummer came around the corner. As the vehicle straightened out, he pulled the trigger and sent the rocket into the front grill of the doomed Hummer. The shaped charge warhead impacted on the driver's side of the front grill, sending a superheated jet of plasma through the firewall and into the cabin. The primary and secondary explosions killed all four occupants of the vehicle before they heard the cry of "RPG!" from the Stryker.

Corporal Maggio was the Mamba Three sniper and saw exactly where the RPG came from. He shifted his aim and was looking through his scope at the open window when he saw movement inside the room. Klause had picked up a replacement rocket and reloaded. He was swinging around to aim at the Stryker. Maggio put the crosshairs on him and sent a .50-caliber slug through his left upper chest. The left arm was nearly torn off and the mercenary was dead before his ravaged body hit the ground.

The rest of the assault team reached their objective, only having to engage one more person. One of the aircraft mechanics had a pistol and took a shot at the guardsmen as they approached the hangar. The terminal was cleared and three more mechanics were discovered hiding in a storage room.

"Rocketman, Mamba One, we have fourteen enemy KIA, three EPW. We are going to clear the rest of the terminal building and flight line. NBC is checking the containers in the hangar at this time." Glenn nodded to the re-formed assault team and sent them on their way. "There were four Blue KIA. Over"

"Mamba One, Rocketman actual, I'm sorry to hear that, son. Update from Washington, the CIA is sending out two field agents to take charge of the prisoners and interview you gentlemen. Please photograph and document as much as you can for them to collect. They will be taking all the intel materials you guys recover, including the metal canisters if they are safe to travel. Is the airfield secure?"

"Rocketman, Mamba Three, we should have the field cleared in short order and we will be able to secure for future flight ops. We do not have the manpower to secure the airfield on a long-term basis."

"Mamba Three, copy."

The assault team was very thorough and the terminal was secured in short order. However, they did not search all the planes on the parking ramp. Willie Braun was one of the aircraft mechanics, who loved anything with wings. During his breaks he had taken to exploring the other aircraft at the field. He had found a large ExecuJet parked at the east end of the ramp and, upon discovering the luxurious bed in the aft cabin, had taken to living in it. Having worked the night before, he slipped off unnoticed and crashed out in the king-sized bed. The sound of firing didn't concern him, as he thought the security team was just dealing with a small pack of ferals. He merely lifted his head, and after the short burst of gunfire ended, he plopped his head back down. The sound of the RPG explosion had him right back up.

Willie looked out a window as the airfield was taken over by a mixture of soldiers and police officers. He considered firing upon them with his assault rifle but realized that would get him nothing but dead. Instead, he picked up his radio and sent out a report of what had happened.

In Colorado Springs, a technician looked up at his screen as the HF monitor detected the burst of encrypted radio waves. He raised his hand

and sent the information to one of the main displays on the wall. He then called his supervisor and sent word up the chain of command.

"Mamba Three, Rocketman, we have detected encrypted radio activity that just occurred at your location." Willis was taking notes. "Our RDF is not accurate enough to pinpoint, but we believe it's coming from the terminal area. Over."

"Rocketman, Mamba Three, copy." Lovell turned to the newly returned search team and said, "You missed someone! They're calling for help right now! The zoomies say it's from somewhere in the terminal area. So search the building again and the bushes around the outside. Did you guys check the roof?"

"Affirmative top, we have Sergeant Giles up there with his rifle looking around," one of the Guardsmen answered. "We'll get it done." And with that, the troops hefted their rifles and made their way to the top of the building so they could clear it from the top down.

Willie, in the meantime, had received instructions to stay hidden and report back on the size and strength of the attackers. The contact back at his base informed him that help was on the way. He was told that if he could prevent them from removing the chemical containers that would be great, but he was not to expose himself to capture. *Well, I guess that means I can just stay put for a day, till help gets here.* Willie had no intention of exposing himself at all. Although he couldn't see into the hangar itself, he could see the comings and goings of the soldiers there. He had water and food in the plane with him, so it was his intention to just sit and watch.

CHAPTER 37

MCB Camp Pendleton, CA

The main hospital on MCB Pendleton was busy, but not from treating patients, although there were a few of those. It was busy being cleaned up and restored to full working order. When the first casualties of the violence caused by the toxin started to come in, the facility was almost immediately overrun. Not only because the patients would attack the staff, but because some of the staff were poisoned as well. In a matter of hours, the facility devolved into total chaos. The few surviving patients and staff who escaped were pursued until they were able to hole up with other pockets of survivors, or died.

Once the base had been re-secured, the task of cleaning up and re-opening the facility fell on the shoulders of the Medical Battalion. The Navy doctors, nurses, and corpsmen were tasked with getting things back up and running. "Volunteers" from the refugee pool were put to work cleaning and repairing damage to the building and its equipment, where possible. The flow of casualties had dropped off dramatically and things were coming to an even keel.

Mark and Jim had been given a private room together in the critical care area. The staff had done blood work on him and found only slight amounts of the toxin still present in his blood. Although he would spike a fever at the first sign of physical exertion, the effects were gradually wearing off. Jim had been X-rayed and multiple fractures had been set, including his cheekbone. He had regained consciousness for a few minutes after arrival, and the nurses kept waking him every four hours to check on his concussion. This was making him as irritable as his father. Very few of the staff stayed long in that room.

Jen and the kids, however, were permanently installed and had taken over the vacant room next door. Mel was still communicating with the Marines back at their house and doing what she could to stay busy. Terry, on the other hand, was suddenly very fascinated by the medical profession; it was believed that the very cute Navy corpsman stationed down the hall had something to do with this. Jen was helping out in x-ray and physical therapy, which is what she had done prior to the attacks.

Mark was sitting up in bed, looking over a document on the iPad that Mel had just handed him when he heard the guard who was stationed at the door come to his feet. As he looked toward the door, he heard "at ease" and Colonel Neal was standing there with several other Marines. Mark started to get to his feet when Neal gestured for him to sit back down.

"I was told in no uncertain terms by a redhead in the hall that if I, in any way, disturbed or upset you, I would be reduced in rank to something less than private and then shot." Neal walked over to a seat on the other side of the bed from the one Mel was sitting in and shook Mark's hand. "I have decided to take the threat seriously and have stationed my security team in the hall to prevent such an outbreak of violence. How you doing, Gunner?"

"I'm fine, sir, other than the pincushion effect from being stabbed by every person who walks by. I apologize for the redhead; she still thinks she's the boss." Mark eyed the two Marines standing in the doorway. "Garret, Hernandez, what are you doing here? They let you out of kindergarten early? Come on in, Devil Pups. This is your security team, sir?"

Neal looked at the two Marines as they smiled. "Hello, sir," they said to Mark then sat down at the foot of the bed. It was starting to get crowded, so Mel grabbed the iPad from her dad and said, "Excuse me." Then she went back next door. Jim mumbled and turned his back on everyone in the room.

"Kids got no manners these days," Mark said, still with a look of concern on his face for his injured son. "I'll beat him later. How goes the recovery, sir?"

"Well, there's good spots and bad spots, Mark. We are doing well for immediate survival needs here on the base. Sixty-four other bases have been re-established and are working on setting up safe zones. The population centers that got hit have taken massive casualties, virtually eliminating the populations in them. The rural areas remain almost untouched. Power comes back on any time now for the So-Cal grid. Our biggest challenge will be transportation and agriculture. The per acre population dependence has obviously dropped, but keeping those acres producing and then getting the foodstuffs to the surviving people is going to be a challenge."

Neal took a breath and leaned back. "We are getting some intel on the attacks. The terrorists used a creek in Minnesota as a test bed. They launched two days later. We have established a Middle Eastern connection, but every country we know of so far has suffered massive casualties. We have a group of survivors that took over an airfield in Minnesota and captured some of the people we believe are responsible for all this. They were preparing for another chemical attack, and our imagery shows that there are twenty-plus airfields that are doing the same. We need to get those airfields secured and the chemicals under our control or neutralized. I'm putting together teams…"

The lights flickered and then all the electronic devices in the room began to beep and come to life. "Well, San Onofre wasn't lying; our power is back. Anyway, as I was saying, I'm putting together Special Operations capable teams to go after these airfields. And since that was your unit's specialty, I'm going to need you for planning and training. I just don't think we have much time. The airfields that show activity give them the ability to disperse NBC agents over 75 percent of the country. And most of those are areas that were not affected in the first attacks. We think the first attack was to reduce the population in the cities and disable our investigative ability. Now, they are going after the remaining population, and remember, with 60 percent dead or feral, any follow-up attacks could reduce the U.S. to the Stone Age."

"I'm game, sir. We just have to convince these witch doctors that I'm okay to leave." Mark sat up straighter in the bed. "I can start operational planning from here, and brief the team leaders if you can—"

"Hold on there, hard charger," Neal chuckled, interrupting the beginnings of Mark's grand plans. "I'm going to see what the 'witch doctors' have to say and we'll go from there. I have some things to look into, then Major Henkel will be in here to brief you. Just get better; we need you and the rest of your FAST company guys."

"Aye aye, sir." Mark shook his hand, and watched him leave.

"You know Terry, Mel, Jen, and I would be fine back at the house, helping to recover other survivors while you're gone, Pops." Mark looked over to see Jim lying in his bed with his eyes still closed.

"Oh, yeah, 'cause that worked out so well for you last time. I swear, if the doctor hadn't confirmed your concussion, I'd give you one right now! What the hell were you thinking? Why weren't you with the convoy?" Mark was shaking his head in exasperation. "Do you know how devastated your sisters would be if they lost you? Christ, your mom's missing to God knows where, if she isn't feral or dead, and here they are getting moved up here without me. They need you, son, and I need to know that you're taking care of them. Not sneaking off so you can stay in the action. How fucking irresponsible was that, huh?"

Jim slowly sank further and further into his pillows as his father's volume got louder. He did meet Mark's eyes throughout, though, and had a grim set to his lips. "Jake was going to stay and help. I could have helped too. I'm a better shot than most of the Marines there, and I'm fully capable of taking care of myself."

"Since when?" Mark's drill instructor voice was coming out. "Those Marines have been through years of training. Just because you've come out with me a couple of times to the range, you think you're better trained than one of my Marines? I don't fricken' think so! They have ingrained muscle memory skills that will save their lives. They have trained as a team and know how to react when things go to shit. Just because you know a few hand signals and can shoot pretty good does NOT make you an operator!"

"He has a point, you know." Jake was standing just outside the door with Alan. "I think you're a pretty good kid, and you'll make a great Marine someday if you keep your head on straight, but your father is dead nuts-on about being able to operate, Jim. You have many years to go to earn that right."

"Right?" Jim looked at Derry as he and Alan came in and took the seats next to the bed. "I could be out there helping to recover those other survivors. I'm a 'Green ball' too, you know! I have the 'right' to help. I still have friends out there who need help. I could help find Mom too!" The firm set of Jim's jaw looked so much like Mark that Jake couldn't help but chuckle.

"Son, no one is trying to deny you any 'rights.' The *right* Jake was talking about was earning the responsibility to hold a fellow teammate's life in your hands. It's a privilege that Marines earn, and I'm sorry, son, you haven't earned it yet." Mark took a deep breath before continuing. "And Marines know how to follow orders. Something you would have failed at! Miserably!"

"Jim, I'm an okay shot with a pistol, and I can run laps around your dad." Alan was a marathon runner. "But I do exactly what he says because following orders is important. I've never spent a day in the service in my life, but even I know that you have to follow a chain of command or people can die."

"Well, since it's gang up on Jim day—"

"We're not ganging up on you, squid; we're educating you," Jake said, using the term that only he and Mark used for Jim when he did something stupid. "Besides, if you really wanted to help out, you'd be giving marksmanship classes to the survivors here on the base, helping to make them more self-sufficient."

"It's just like when I go on deployment, bud. I need to know you're here taking care of them. I have a job that really needs to be done and knowing that you're there to protect them takes a load off of my mind. I know you'd give your life for them, and that really does make me breathe easier." Mark ran his hand over his face, feeling the stubble. "This is how you contribute the most, son, really."

"All right. I just didn't want to leave you alone, Dad."

"Hey, Gunner, I think Staff Sergeant Quinones is setting up some ranges to start training some of the civilians. I know he's going to need help."

"Oh great! Now I can be a 'range bitch.'" Jim sighed heavily. "I'll be pulling butts all day."

"Everyone pulls their own butts, you know that." Mark didn't like the whining tone in Jim's voice and everyone in the room, including Jim, knew it. "But you will field day the ranges and do whatever you're told. Got that?"

"Yes, sir."

Terry bounded into the room and flounced over to her father. After a hug for Jake, she went over and set her head on Mark's shoulder, and without saying a word, stared up at him with big blue eyes, blinking them on occasion.

"No! Whatever it is, I'm saying *no* right now!" Mark sent a pleading look at Alan and Jake, who both burst out laughing.

"I didn't even ask anything, Dad!" Terry turned a pouty face on the two men at the foot of her father's bed. "And you guys laughing isn't helping!"

"Helping with what, Terry?" Jake asked innocently.

"I just wanted to go to a party down in the cafeteria with some people. I wouldn't even be out of the building!"

She stared back and forth at the two laughing men, before turning back to her father. "Dad, everyone's going to be there and it's right here. Tia can come too!"

Mark grinned as Alan suddenly shut up and stared at Terry. He was about to open his mouth when Mel popped her head in and said, "It's okay, Dad; Jen will be there. Terry just wants to go because Kenny is going."

"It's Ken, dork. And that's not the only reason." She turned back to Mark and, not one to miss a point in her favor, said, "See, Dad? Jen will be there!"

"Who's this Kenny guy, and where is he so I can give him some instructions?" Mark asked Mel. The stricken look on Terry's face was priceless.

"He's just down the hall, Dad," Mel said brightly as she pretended to ignore the lasers Terry was shooting from her eyes at her. "I can show you who he is!"

"Dad! No!" Terry was trying to put a pious look on her face for her father while glaring at her sister. The two looks were mutually exclusive, and she wound up just looking confused. "He's in the Navy—"

"What?" Mark did a convincing job of looking outraged. "I'll be damned if I'm gonna let some swab date my high school daughter! Where is he?"

"Oh, just forget it!" Terry was on the edge of tears. "I won't go! There, are you happy?"

"Oh, stop it!" Mark said, laughing at her alligator tears. "You know we're just messing with you."

"Thanks, Dad!" The tears were gone and so was Terry about a nanosecond later.

"I think I'll have a talk with old Kenny and make sure he understands a sailor's place in life," Jake said as he walked out the door. "I hope you feel better, Gunner. I'll let you know what's up when I get back from Base Ops."

He paused and looked over his shoulder at Jim. "*Green ball*, huh? I'll ask later."

"Thanks, Jake." Mark considered what was about to happen to the sailor down the hall as Jake, who was wearing his full tac vest and carrying his slung M4 went stomping down the hall. The six-foot-three-inch tall, well-muscled Marine was an imposing sight.

A few seconds later, Mark heard, "Come here, thing! I have some questions for you!" He leaned back in the bed with a small smile, knowing that things were well in hand.

CHAPTER 38

Bemidji, MN

The four helicopters swooped in from the north and landed on the parking ramp near the hangar. Fourteen mercenaries jumped out and assaulted the terminal. Two of the birds immediately took off again and provided top cover. They found nothing in the terminal and, upon inspecting the pallet of containers in the hangar, found them to be commercial water filter canisters. A second search revealed no one present at the field at all.

Willie came out of the Lear jet and made contact with the assault team leader, informing him that he had not even seen the canisters being switched out. The meeting was not a pleasant one and ended in both parties stalking off in different directions.

"So that's where that little bugger was hiding," Dan whispered to Sergeant Giles as they watched the two helicopters land again. Neither pilot got out of their helicopters though. Glenn and Giles were both fully camouflaged in Ghillie suits and were looking at the hangar and terminal from across the runway. "I wish we had another four or five rifles on this, we could ground these birds too."

One of the NBC guys had come up with the idea of swapping out the canisters when he found a bunch of Culligan water filters in a storage room. The guard troops had transported the gas cylinders back to an industrial park at the south end of town, not knowing what, if any, rescue team was coming, Master Sergeant Lovell had decided to err on the side of caution and evacuated the field. They had thoroughly disabled the crop dusters, ensuring that they would not be completing any missions in the near future.

Dan had fueled up and flown the park service's Cessna Skymaster to a large field on the south side of town just off of Roosevelt Road SE. They strung some camouflage netting over it and added some natural brush, just in case the mercenaries started flying around. A small pack of ferals showed up just as they finished concealing the plane, attracted by the noise of the planes landing. The gunner in the Hummer, who came to pick Dan up, sent them back into the woods with a few well-aimed bursts from his machine gun.

The next thing they did was string more netting on the top of the hotel, which they immediately took down when they realized it just made the roof of the building look suspicious from the air. They mounted one of the M-2s from a Hummer on the roof, along with two other crew-served weapons for anti-aircraft guns. The "safe zone" was now two full city blocks centered around the hotel, and some of the survivors were moving out into other buildings. The hotel itself was becoming more and more of a command post/social center, rather than refugee shelter.

Captain Nelson was again sitting in his office when he heard the sound of boots pounding down the hall toward his office. He yelled for the specialist to come in before he could knock on the door.

"Sir, we have Minneapolis on the line, and they're sending up some air later today," Specialist Jenkins said, coming to a stop in front of Nelson's desk. "They want an up-to-the-minute sitrep on the airport, sir."

"Very well, let's go." Nelson was already out from behind his desk.

Chris, Roy, Yavi, and Glenn were in the communications room when they walked in. The two local cops had been briefing some of the troops on the roads around the airport. The small crowd followed Nelson over to the radio.

"Mack One, Nomad Six, how copy? Over."

"Nomad Six, Mack One. Five-by-five, how me? Over."

"Mack One-Five, loud and clear. Over."

"Nomad Six, we have a flight of four Black Hawks, two Chinooks, and two Apaches en route your AO. ETA is thirty-eight minutes. We are coordinating their approach with Colorado so they will not be observed by your OPFOR. They will land at the strip where you parked the park service Skymaster. The two Chinooks are bulk fuel birds and are going to be mobile gas stations until the airfield is permanently secured and the available fuel there is tested. Both Apaches are air-to-air capable. We would like to assault the field and gather more EPWs. The Black Hawks have a platoon of infantry and two intel specialists to collect evidence and the EPWs. They also have the requested items from your shopping list. Over."

"Mack One-Five, good to hear. I will have a convoy waiting for them." Nelson gestured to Lovell to get it going. "At this time, I have two scouts with eyes on target. They have been updating Rocketman regularly. We will be able to assault six hours from now. Over."

"Nomad Six, Mack One-Five copies all. Out."

Nelson got up from his seat and looked at the local cops, who were standing there with expectant looks on their faces.

"Well, do you guys want to do it again, or what?"

"You'll have to ask the 'Crime Fighting Pickles' here," Chris said, gesturing to Glenn and Yavi, using the derogatory term that the state cops had for the rangers' all-green uniform. "I'm in."

"Me too." From Roy.

"Just call me the Magnificent Gherkin!" Yavi smiled brightly.

"Well, let's go then, gents! Time waits for no man!" Nelson said with faux enthusiasm.

"Not worried about it; pickles are timeless," Yavi said as they all grabbed gear and began trooping down the stairs.

The two Apache helicopters were eight miles in front of the formation of Black Hawks and Chinooks.

Tomahawk One was a Longbow Apache flying to the northeast of the aerial convoy. It would sprint forward for a few miles then drop behind some land feature, or even trees, with nothing sticking up but the ball on top of the rotor head. After scanning the area in front of it for hostile air activity, it would pop up and do it all again.

Tomahawk Two was not performing any theatrics. It was flying at a steady ninety knots on a heading of 355, with the pilot and gunner being just as vigilant. The entire flight had taken off from Camp Ripley north of Minneapolis for the short hop to Bemidji. As they approached their destination, the radio came to life.

"Tomahawk One, Rocketman, we have enemy aircraft taking off from Bemidji Airport at this time. Flight is two Bell Jet Ranger helicopters. They are heading east over the city at this time. Mamba One reports birds have armed men with automatic weapons on board. Over."

"Rocketman, Tomahawk One copies all. Will advise radar contact. Over."

"Tomahawk One, Rocketman, roger. Out."

The Apache banked slightly to the left and climbed about forty feet when the sophisticated radar picked the two enemy helicopters up. The radar and infrared systems identified and labeled the birds in the pilot's heads-up display. The Longbow's data sharing network projected the information to Tomahawk Two and the four Black Hawk pilots eight miles behind them.

"Rocketman, Tomahawk One, radar contact, two helicopters bearing 352, heading 075. They are just heading out over the lake. Correction, birds have turned south are now heading 185 along the lakeshore. Over."

"Tomahawk One, we have them real time. Can you engage if they assault Nomad HQ? Over."

"Rocketman, we can engage now while they're over the water. Over."

"Tomahawk One, Nomad Six, are they going to see you when you land? Over." Nelson and the convoy were waiting at the field. They couldn't see either the National Guard birds or the enemy helicopters.

"Nomad Six, Tomahawk One, they won't see us unless they fly right over us; we're down in the weeds. They will definitely see the 'Shithooks' if they get anywhere near here."

The pilot was looking at the digital mapping screen. "I'm going to have them go low and loiter twenty klicks south until we sort this out. Break, Badger One, did you copy? Over."

"Tomahawk One, Badger One copies all, wilco. Over." The flight of larger helicopters flew down to an altitude of sixty feet and began slowly circling south of Guthrie Road. The troops inside the Black Hawks began preparing their weapons in case they had to deploy. The Chinooks could do nothing but wait and see if they were going to have a safe place to offload.

To the north, the Jet Rangers turned west over the city and began a slow circle back to the airport. The mercenaries inside were looking for signs of the military unit that had caused so much trouble. The next phase of the plan became less and less effective the longer it was delayed. They had to deliver the next attack before the Americans and their ponderous bureaucracies could pull themselves together. The loss of the Bemidji team was a major setback. Those aircraft had been slated to deliver the *coup de grace* to the entire Great Lakes region, including Ontario.

The Jet Rangers circled back out over the lake and headed farther south. As they reached the southern end of the lake, one of the mercenaries noticed some movement to the southeast. He told the pilot, and the helicopter banked to the left and headed straight toward Nomad HQ.

"Tomahawk One, Nomad Six-Two, we're blown! Enemy helicopters are heading our way!"

"Nomad Six-Two, standby…" The pilot of Tomahawk One popped his bird up twenty feet and fired two sidewinder missiles. The sensor mast had been feeding data to both of the AIM-9s since they had first been designated as targets. They both left the rails and were still accelerating through Mach 2 when the proximity-fused warhead detonated. The explosion and wreckage of the missiles impacted the helicopters, wiping them from the sky. Two balls of flaming wreckage fell into Lake Bemidji, one of them only twenty meters from the shore.

The guardsmen on the roof manning the M2 machine guns and sniper rifles were totally surprised when two streaks flashed by them and impacted the two helicopters that were just a mile to the northwest of them. Both missiles had destroyed their targets without them even knowing they were in danger.

The Black Hawks and Chinooks flew into the temporary airfield. The bulk fuel bladders were off-loaded, and security was established. With the shooting down of the two enemy birds, they were on a short time line to get to the airfield. Tomahawk One landed and was re-armed while being refueled. As soon as that was accomplished, Tomahawk Two came in for gas as well. It was decided that the convoy drivers and the bulk fuel personnel would ride back to the hotel while the Chinooks took the Nomad assault teams, and an operation would be launched immediately to secure the airfield.

The birds had just gotten back in the air when Sergeant Giles reported increased activity at the airport. The two Apaches were streaking toward the field when the pilots of the Bell A-Star rushed out to the helicopters and began start-up procedures. They were followed by several mercenaries carrying machine guns.

"I really want one of those birds. I would love an A-Star for us to fly around in," Dan whispered to Giles as they watched the mercenaries running out to them. "Those Apaches are going to blow them out of the sky too!"

"Well, here then," Giles said and the Barrett roared.

The .50-caliber round entered the still open door of one of the A-Stars. It shattered the humerus of the copilot and punched through his rib cage, turning his heart and upper lungs to mush. It then blew out the far side of his body, clipping the back of his right arm before slamming into the pilot. After killing him, the bullet punched a hole through the right side window. Both bodies slumped forward. Dan turned an unbelieving stare at the sergeant, who was grinning and pushing himself back from the edge of their hide.

The response from the mercenaries was immediate. Every one of them in sight began running for cover and laying down rounds in the direction of the two snipers. Only two of them had seen the rifle signature of the SASR. Most of the rounds were off by twenty or thirty yards. But the two who had seen the muzzle blast began gesturing and directing fire toward them. The two snipers were already displacing from their hide and crawling along a slight depression when the sound of the other helicopter taking off caught their attention. As it rose off the parking ramp, it banked to the left and headed north toward the two men.

Giles rolled over on his back and was attempting to get a shot at the helicopter above him when a whooshing sound and massive explosion ended that endeavor. Flaming wreckage began falling in the woods between them and the runway. The burning jet fuel spread over a hundred-yard swath of woods, lighting the trees on fire. They were running for their lives away from the fire when the pilot of Tomahawk One called them on the radio.

"Mamba One, Tomahawk One, are you in the tree line north of the runway? Over."

"Tomahawk One, Mamba One, affirmative." Giles was starting to choke on the smoke.

"Mamba One, we have you on thermal, just barely, we'll run some interference for you."

The two Apaches swept over the airfield from east to west. Tomahawk Two slewed around and flew sideways directly above the two fleeing snipers. The *chunk chunk chunk* sound of its 30mm chain gun sounded right above their heads. Hot brass rained down through the trees all around them as a small series of explosions tore across the edge of the runway, causing the mercenary Quick Reaction Force to scatter. Two more bursts and there were no living bodies on the north side of the runway.

Dan and Giles began curving around to the west at a fast jog. They needed to get back in sight of the hangar and back in the fight. As they made it past the edge of the flames and were turning toward the airport again, Giles let out a *woof* of air and collapsed. The report of a heavy-caliber rifle echoed across the field. Only the fact that Dan turned to help his friend saved him from being killed as well.

As he turned to look at Giles, who was rolling around in agony, a bullet tore through his drag bag, shattering the Leupold scope mounted to his rifle and ricocheting into the left side of his back. The bullet tore a painful furrow across his scapula and exited his left shoulder. Dan dove to the ground and tugged Giles behind a tree. He was looking for a covered escape route when another round tore right through the tree and hit Giles in his back right below the shoulder blade. The deformed round crashed through the top of his lung and came out through his chest. The dead guardsman slumped to the side.

Dan rolled over three times, shedding his drag bag along the way. He had his M4 with a suppressor and his pistol. As soon as he was free of the now useless equipment, he made himself small and called in.

"Nomad One-Six, Mamba One, they have a sniper somewhere on the airfield. Echo Five Golf is KIA and I am WIA. Shooter location is unknown, but it is a heavy rifle. Repeat heavy rifle. I am in the tree line north of the runway and will need a medevac. Over." Dan was trying not to move too much, but it felt like his entire left arm and upper back was on fire. He could feel the blood seeping into the flight suit that was the base garment for his Ghillie suit.

"Mamba One, Nomad One-Six copies. Hold on; we're on our way. Over."

"I'm not going anywhere," Dan said and slid his right arm across his chest and applied pressure to the wound.

Across the runway and next to a maintenance shed, Adam Weir was studying the area where Dan had disappeared very carefully. He could see the one soldier he had killed quite plainly through the Schmidt and Bender scope mounted on top of his rifle. The custom rifle fired the .338 Lapua cartridge and was almost as deadly as the .50 carried by the Americans, and it had superior ballistics. After failing to see any movement, he turned his attention to the orbiting helicopters.

He was lining up a shot at one of the Apaches when movement at the edge of his field of view caught his attention. Shifting his aim to the right, he saw the first Black Hawk banking in over the east end of the runway. He took aim at the pilot and sent a match round streaking across the intervening space. The bullet impacted the glass at enough of an angle to cause it to deflect upwards slightly. The round smashed into the pilot's helmet next to his left ear. Fragments of the helmet were driven into the side of the pilot's head, wounding him but not killing him.

Adam was lining up another shot when the volume of helicopter blades around him increased dramatically. One of the Chinooks was hovering over the terminal building next to the shed he was hiding against. He rolled on his side to see if he had a shot at the massive helicopter but could only see its rotor arc. Realizing that an assault team would soon be above him, he decided to get off one last shot before trying to escape. He looked out to see three more Black Hawks had come in and flared out over by the operations hangar. He put his crosshairs on another pilot and fired. This round went through the glass more cleanly and hit the pilot in the chest. The bullet hit his M9 pistol in the grip, sending fragments of the gun and its ammunition into the pilot's vest. Only the deformed bullet made it through his armor. The pilot slumped forward in his harness as people began filling the radio with calls warning about the sniper.

Lieutenant Crowe was one of the men who got off the CH-47 that had touched down on the roof. He heard the sound of the sniper rifle and had a good idea where it came from. Running over to the edge of the building, he looked down but didn't see anything at first. He was just about to move on when he detected the movement of Adam slowly pulling his rifle barrel back under the boards that composed his hide. Crowe pulled out a grenade, thought about it, and put it back in his harness. He then leaned over the edge with his M4 and began peppering the woodpile with rifle fire. After about ten rounds, Adam attempted to roll out and fire up at the roofline with a pistol. The arm gave Crowe a reference point and he clicked his selector to full auto and began really hosing the pile. The hand holding the pistol flopped open on the ground.

Nelson jogged over to Crowe as he was reloading his rifle. He looked over the edge and asked, "Is he the only one?"

"Don't know, sir, but I sprayed the shit out of that wood pile! I don't think there's any more down there!" Crowe shouted over the noise as he reloaded his carbine.

The sound of gunfire had them jogging over to the other side of the roof. They eased up to the edge and looked over at the parking ramp. The infantry that had landed on the airfield was involved in a furious firefight with the mercenaries. Several of the planes had been hit and one was already fully engulfed in flames, sending a thick black plume of smoke boiling up into the sky. The sound of gunfire beneath their feet let them know that the assault team from their Chinook was having to fight its way down into the terminal building. One of the DDMs set up his rifle next to them and took a shot at something then rolled back behind the edge of the roof. He realized that the two officers were still looking out over the edge and marveled at their stupidity. He grabbed them and pulled them down behind cover as several rounds of return fire impacted along the roofline.

Nelson and Crowe gave the troop a thank you nod and then noticed that he was firing a nice hunting rifle. Before they could say anything, he had moved down the wall twenty feet and popped up to fire at something else. He then hunkered down and began reloading the bolt-action rifle.

"I wouldn't put my head above the lip for more than a second, sirs. I'm trying to get the sniper next to the hangar to show himself." With that, he began moving on all fours farther down the building. He popped up and let loose another round. A second later, the unmistakable boom of a Barrett sounded from below. Both Nelson and Crowe heard one of the other DDMs report a hit. "I think we got him, sir, but I still wouldn't stick my head up. Thar be bad men about!" The reference to the Pirates of the Caribbean was not lost on the two officers.

Nelson and Crowe went down the stairs to the interior of the building and met up with Master Sergeant Lovell. After a brief update, Crowe grabbed a fire team and went to check on the sniper at the side of the building. They made their way outside as the firing began to die down.

They approached the corner to the alley between the two buildings and peeked around the corner. Nothing was moving, so they approached the pile of bullet-riddled plywood and began pulling it apart. Several of the boards had bloodstains on them, and there was a small duffle bag with some equipment in it, but no body. And no rifle or pistol, either.

"Nomad Six, Nomad Two-Six, the sniper is missing from the west side of the terminal. There is no body, but there is a blood trail. Enemy sniper is wounded." Crowe was following the line of red droplets to the corner. He held up short of the corner and did a quick peek before stepping back and moving several feet away from the corner, knowing that the wood-framed structure would not stop a heavy-rifle bullet. When he didn't receive any fire, he had the Fire Team rush around the corner and take cover.

The blood drops began to spread out, showing that the enemy sniper was moving faster or he had treated his wound and wasn't bleeding as much. Crowe believed the former to be true. He didn't think the enemy sniper had time to treat what was obviously several gunshot wounds. They followed the spoor southeast into the tree line.

"Nomad Six, Two-Six, blood trail leads into the trees heading toward the BCA building. We're going to need to track him. He has lost a lot of blood. Over."

"Two-Six, this is Six, I need him accounted for. We're sending a team out to Mamba One. Break." Nelson had a map spread out on one of the ticket counters. "Bulldog Three, are we secure out there yet? Over."

"Nomad Six, Bulldog Three, two mikes."

"Nomad Six copies." Nelson turned to Lovell. "Can we get ready to get our guys?"

"We can go now, sir. If that guy takes a shot, we'll be on him like white on rice. I think he's running." There were ten soldiers behind him nodding in agreement.

"All right, go get him." Nelson pressed his mic boom closer to his lips. "Mamba One, Nomad Six, can you give us your exact location? Help is on the way."

"Nomad Six, just send them out to the wreckage. I'm sixty meters west of it." The bleeding had almost stopped with the direct pressure, but the pain was still evident in his voice.

The rescue team double-timed out onto the runway and spread out on line. They took off at a fast jog toward the far tree line, where the wreckage of the downed helicopter was still burning fiercely. Two of the trees were also going up like roman candles. The fire was spreading slowly but steadily.

"Bulldog Two, Nomad Six-Two, do you have that firefighting gear secured yet? This wood line is going to go up if we can't get some water on it. Over."

"Nomad Six-Two, we are getting started now, will be heading in your direction in one mike. Over."

"Nomad Six-Two copies. Break. Mamba One, your location? Over." Lovell was peering into the trees but hadn't entered them yet.

"Up here to your left!" Dan called out instead of using the radio. He tried to raise his wounded left arm while maintaining pressure with his right. The pain was intense, so he settled for lifting his head and moving it back and forth. Lovell saw the movement and seconds later, Dan was on a stretcher.

"Sergeant Giles' body is right over there," he said, nodding toward the downed man. "My drag bag is somewhere between here and there, if you guys could grab it, please."

Lovell made sure all the equipment for both men was gathered along with the body, and the procession set off for the terminal building. Lovell and one other troop covered the eight troopers who were carrying the stretchers back across the runway. They were halfway back across when an explosion off to their left had everyone diving to the deck. A few seconds of furious gunfire and then silence. They had just gotten to their feet when more gunfire sent them sprawling to the turf again. It was coming from around the corner of the east side of the terminal. The shouts of contact with an enemy came rapidly over the radio.

Dan had rolled off the stretcher this time and put his rifle to his shoulder. The action started the blood flowing again from his wounds. This time when they got up, he rose to his feet unsteadily with the rest of the team and hustled the rest of the way to the hangar, where he collapsed next to a tool chest.

"Medic!" Lovell pointed needlessly at Dan as the young soldier ran over from where he and three others had been working on the other wounded. He turned and looked at Giles, but Dan shook his head. Lovell looked down at the young sergeant for a moment, shook his head, and then jogged off in the direction where the last round of gunfire was heard.

"I need you to lie on your stomach so I can cut this off of you and get at your wound," the medic said, gently trying to push Dan down onto his belly.

"Stop! You are not cutting my Ghillie! I'll take it off; hold on!" The contortions required to get the flight suit off of Dan's shoulders had him sweating even more and almost made him pass out. He finally got the suit down to his waist and was lying flat on his stomach when a pair of boots pounded up and stopped right in front of his face.

"Is that the only place he's shot?" Scott asked the young man who was cleaning the area around the wound. "That doesn't look too bad! Shit, here, let me take care of that. You go take care of those other guys!"

"It looks like that is the only hole, sir." The medic looked up at the park ranger standing over him, holding a large first-aid kit. "It is going to need some stitches though. That's a nasty gash."

"Wait! Wait! Don't let him touch me! I'll look like fuckin' Frankenstein when he gets done with me!" Dan had grabbed the army medic's ankle. "Really! He'll do more harm than… urk!" Dan's pleading was cut off by Scott's hand coming down firmly on the back of Dan's neck. The first-aid kit *thunked* to the ground right in front of his face as Scott took a knee next to his brother's prostrate form.

"Go on, seriously! Don't listen to his whining. We are all EMTs or paramedics." Scott made a shooing gesture. "You can come back and check on me if you like."

"All right." The medic didn't sound too sure but went back over to tending to the troops, looking back over his shoulder a couple of times to make sure Scott wasn't amputating his brother's leg.

"Now… let's see here. What do we have for idiots who get shot? Ah, this will start us off!" Scott held up a bottle of hydrogen peroxide, which he promptly dumped onto the bullet hole in his brother's shoulder. As the liquid turned pink and foamed out of the wound, he set out a roll of medical tape and two tubes of liquid stitches. He took a gauze pad and wiped the blood away then peeled back the lips of the wound. Part of the bullet's jacket and several glass shards from Dan's scope were visible. Scott picked up a pair of tweezers and almost clapped his hands in delight.

"This is going to hurt you A LOT more than it is me!" The joy was evident in his voice. "Got some glass and the bullet jacket in here, and… it looks like part of your scope's turret. Damn, that thing blew a lot of shit into you, little brother."

"Just get it over with, you sadist!" Dan was gritting his teeth.

Scott used a syringe to irrigate the wound with Lidocaine, numbing it somewhat.

"Oh, yes sir! Right away, sir! You know something like this wouldn't even slow a Marine down!" Scott was enjoying himself immensely. Ever since the two of them were little they had always patched each other up. Sometimes the repair jobs caused more harm than the original injury, and they always involved a little extra pain. The shrapnel was dug out with a minimal amount of fuss since Scott didn't want to really make the injury any worse. Scott applied a piece of medical tape to each side of the wound.

He then used a cross-pulling motion to pull the edges together. Once the gash was closed, he used a bead of liquid stitches to seal it. He left the wound exposed to the open air so the Super Glue wouldn't stick to a bandage. After cleaning and bandaging some other cuts, he helped his brother to his feet, slapping him on the other shoulder just hard enough to cause a little pain.

"See, good as new!"

Dan, still wincing, glared at his brother and began stripping the rest of the way out of his suit. He got down to his underwear and went over to his pack, which the troops had left next to the tool chest. He pulled out some jeans and a flannel shirt, which he put on but didn't button.

"Fucker got Giles," he said, looking over to where several bodies were laid out covered in ponchos. "He almost got me. Then he went back and shot him through a tree."

Dan gingerly picked up the bullet fragment his brother had pulled out of his back. He turned it over in his hand and examined it closely.

"Doesn't look like a fifty. Probably one of the high power .30s, 7mm mag, or something… maybe a .338. The fucking thing sounded like a cannon. I could hear it over the firefight. Did they get the asshole?"

"I know they got one or two of them, I don't think alive." Scott gestured toward the terminal. "You'll have to ask Nelson or Crowe."

CHAPTER 39

West of Bemidji, MN

The soft thud of running feet and the ragged breathing told Barry Metzler that he needed to be quiet and stay hidden. The twelve year old had been making his way toward all the noise at the airport when a small pack of feral dogs had caught his scent. He wound up hiding in a toolshed behind an auto repair place just off of the main road into town. The dogs had sniffed around but became skittish with all the gunfire nearby. The young man had developed the patience of Job over the last several weeks. He climbed up onto the top shelf of the storage racks in the shed and was going to wait the pack out. The pack left sooner than Barry thought it would, so he decided to wait just a little longer.

Barry's family had lived on a small ranch west of Bemidji. The toxin had caused the deaths of his mother and two sisters, and his dad was missing. His brother didn't live at home, and Barry had no idea where he was. Barry had heard the warnings on the radio while he was in the fort that he and Andrew Petty had finished earlier that summer. They had stocked the fort's big Igloo cooler with bottled water and fruit punch, so Barry had enough to drink for the first couple of days.

Food, on the other hand, was scarce. The boys had two boxes of Pop-Tarts, a big bag of sunflower seeds, and a bag of teriyaki beef jerky stashed away. These supplies had seemed adequate to keep them alive during the zombie apocalypse… or when they were hiding out to avoid chores. The truth was that the meager supplies had kept hunger at bay long enough for Barry to make several short foraging runs into his neighbors' houses. He wound up hitting a goldmine when he found the cellar door to the Smith's house unlocked. Mrs. Smith was always baking stuff, canning stuff, and preserving stuff. The huge cellar had yielded up enough food to keep him alive for a month. He was tired of pickles though, that was for sure.

Barry found a few other things in the cellar that had allowed him to survive. A Coleman machete in a green canvas sheath that never left his side now, an old surplus military sleeping bag, a folding shovel in a plastic carrier, and a .22 rifle with four boxes of ammo. The rifle was a Marlin Model 700 with six little ten-round magazines and two big plastic ones that held twenty-five bullets each and looked really cool, like the banana-shaped magazines on the AK-47s the bad guys always used in the movies.

Barry had shot plenty of .22s in his day, and the range master at scout camp last year had taught him the importance of cleaning his weapons, so Barry had hunted around until he found a small self-contained cleaning kit up on a shelf right next to a pistol case. The case had contained an old Colt .45 ACP with two magazines. Barry searched like crazy but couldn't find any ammo for it. That didn't keep it from going right into his backpack though.

Barry had then faced the quandary of moving everything back out to the fort or just staying in the basement of the Smith's house. The door from the cellar up to the kitchen was locked from the other side, and the back door had been locked when he tried it. He hadn't made it around to the front of the house when Mrs. Allensworth had come snooping around. Barry knew she was one of the sick ones because she was walking funny and her face and very substantial bosom were covered in blood and guts.

Barry thought this was cool, since blood and guts were kind of cool. Mrs. Allensworth's chest had been the topic of many late-night discussions between Andy and Barry when they spent the night in the fort, thus making it *very* cool.

The whole thing lost some of its appeal, though, when she got close enough for Barry to smell her. Barry didn't think he would touch her even if she was wearing the bikini that she sometimes wore when she sunned herself in her backyard. The bikini and the fact that they had been peering through the fence were usually the conversation starters at the fort.

Barry had locked himself in the basement and secured the door with a bicycle cable lock that he found. He had only ventured forth to raid his dad's work shed, where he knew his dad kept several cases of bottled water for the field hands that worked the property. He could only carry one case at a time, and it took him five trips to get the supplies back to the Smith's basement. He had considered going into his house to get some stuff, but the carnage his mother had caused, especially when she had killed, Bert, their dog, was just too painful.

The water and other supplies were getting low, so Barry thought he could hit the Walmart that was just past the airport for some supplies. He had been working his way along the expressway toward Paul Bunyan Drive when he noticed the helicopters. He picked up the pace and had gotten a little careless, resulting in him having to take shelter from the dogs in the storage shed. The sounds of not too distant gunfire had sent the pack trotting off into the woods.

A few minutes later, as Barry was considering climbing down and continuing toward the gunfire (he had assumed it was the military cleaning up the crazies), he heard the sound of someone approaching. The loud footfalls and heavy breathing kept him from giving away his presence. These days, not everyone was your friend. A body thudded into the side of the shed, and the sound of breathing got louder. It was interrupted by the sound of whoever it was talking on a radio.

"They bloody took them all out. I need that extraction!" Adam gasped between breaths. "I'm east of the airport at an automobile repair facility. I don't know where those wogs got their intel, but the bloody Americans had full air support, and I think fighters. The air crews reported that they thought the helicopters were shot down by fighters!"

Barry remained perfectly still as the person on the other side of the tin wall whispered fiercely into his radio. The accent made Barry think of the Nazi bad guys he'd always seen in the movies. He was also afraid because the man had said *Americans* like it was a bad thing. He moved his head very slightly in an effort to see through a seam in the wall but couldn't make anything out. Whoever was on the other end of the conversation must not have had any good news because the man began to blow a gasket.

"I have six bullet holes in me, you ass! I'm not going to make it much farther down the fucking road! I need extraction now!" Adam began circling the building, looking for a way in. "I'm going to hole up here. You people figure it out!" He continued around the building until he reached the door, which Barry had secured with the simple latch and then barricaded against the dogs. Adam pushed on the door firmly but moved on when it didn't budge, not wanting to risk making any noise. He walked across to the building on the other side of the small lot and managed to slip inside one of the vehicle maintenance bays.

Barry waited a few more minutes before climbing down off of the shelf. He slowly made his way over to a small seam in the corrugated panels and peered out into the repair yard. There was nothing moving in the narrow field of view that he had. He was looking for other openings he could look through when the sound of a helicopter flying right overhead shook the shed so violently some of the parts fell off the shelves. The Apache had been so low that the rotor wash swirled the trash up off the ground. Barry cowered next to the door and made himself as small as possible.

The helicopter made several more passes and even slowed to almost a hover before moving on. A few minutes later, there was the sound of footsteps outside the shed and the sound of muffled voices. The door shook as someone again tried to get in. Barry was looking out of the seam when a face appeared right in front of him, looking in.

"Holy shit!" Corporal Maggio recoiled from the grimy face that was looking out at him. "There's a little kid in there! Scared the shit out of me!"

The troops gathered around and Lieutenant Crowe put his mouth to the door and said softly, "Hey there, are you all right? I'm from the National Guard and I'm here to help."

"I'm okay. Are you guys looking for another guy that talks like a Nazi?" Barry asked as he unlatched the door. "Cause he's in the building right over there." Barry pointed past the troops surrounding the door as he opened it.

"You mean someone with a German accent is in that building?" Crowe asked as he followed the pointing finger.

"Yeah, I heard him talking on a radio like you guys have." Barry's eyes were wide, staring at all the hardware strapped to the guardsmen. "He said he has six bullet holes in him."

Crowe shot a look at Lovell as he stuck his head in the shack to give it a once over. "Okay, let's get you somewhere safe, just in case there is a bad guy in the other building." He gestured everyone back around the corner. A few gestures, and the platoon pulled back and began to form a perimeter around the building, well out of sight. After a few minutes, one of the Strykers pulled up and Crowe used a bullhorn to hail the building.

Weir was sitting at a desk in what had been the office manager's office, trying to bandage his wounds. His broken rifle sat on the desk next to the open first-aid kit he had found mounted on the wall. He had been hit three times in the back of his right thigh, once in the left buttock, once in the back of his right arm, and once in the left side of the neck. The bullet that passed through his neck had missed both the carotid artery and the jugular vein. In fact, all the rounds had missed vitals, but they were painful and numerous. Plus, there were all the splinters the bullets had sent into various parts of his body. The amount of blood he had lost was minimal for that number of wounds, but the muscles were cramping all over, and he was in a lot of pain.

The sound of a voice telling him he was surrounded and to come out unarmed with his hands up, was almost the last straw. He considered putting his pistol to his mouth and just ending it. His waffling cost him the opportunity to do it, as a flash-bang grenade came through the window and landed right in the first-aid kit. His eyes couldn't help following the path of the explosive device, even as his pain-muddled brain was telling him to close his eyes and cover his ears. He got his eyes closed and his head partially turned away when the munition detonated. The bright white light blinded him through his eyelids, and his whole body felt the shockwave from only two feet away. He was bowled over in his chair and landed on his back. The entry team found him unconscious lying on the floor.

Lovell made sure he collected the wounded man's radio and immediately removed the battery. They had been equipped with an encoding chip that was rigged to self-destruct if a code was punched into the keypad on the front of the device. Somehow, all the prisoners and enemy KIA had managed to prevent the government forces from getting a hold of an intact radio. The radios could have the security feature triggered remotely and, thus far, had prevented the guardsmen from recovering an operable radio.

Barry was allowed to ride back to the makeshift base in the turret of the Stryker. This almost made up for the past few weeks' tribulations. He and Maggio were fast becoming friends, talking about X-box games and other matters of grave importance all the way back to the hotel. He became a little nervous when they tried to take his weapons away at the hotel. Maggio vouched for him, took Barry to his room, and showed him how to open his personal weapons locker. The rifle and pistol were placed in the locker and Maggio even promised to get Barry some ammo and practice time with the .45.

Weir was taken to a room and given medical treatment. The wounds were stitched up and he was cable locked to the bed. All told, the raid had killed over forty people and seventeen were taken prisoner. Only four of those were not wounded during the firefight. They were all kept separate until they could be loaded into one of the Chinooks and transported back to Camp Ripley.

CHAPTER 40

Coronado, CA

Naval Amphibious Base (NAB) Coronado is the home of Naval Special Warfare. Sailors who wish to join the elite ranks of the SEALs go through the challenging BUD/S course. It is also the location of the Marine Corps BRC (Basic Recon Course) Amphibious Operations training. These sailors have to endure the grueling training of BUD/S before heading off to SQT (SEAL Qualification Training), better known as "The Finishing School."

There were over 300 Special Warfare Operators who were able to make it onto the island when the outbreak started. They had helped secure the island and were now making forays across the bay to the 32nd Street Naval Station to secure the remaining ships there and get supplies back over to the island.

These operations had managed to recover several hundred other Navy personnel and civilians. Several more of the ships that were docked had been cleared and the access secured. Crews for these ships were being assembled and trained on Coronado. Others were added to the security team keeping the island secure. By the second week, limited air operations were underway at Naval Air Station North Island, on the other end of town. Flight ops had been re-established at MCAS Miramar and, along with Camp Pendleton, the three bases were beginning to swap materiel and personnel. It was only over the last few days that it was determined that the military had the manpower and resources to mount offensive operations across the country.

Lieutenant General David P. Moore was sitting at a conference table with several other senior officers and staff NCOs, listening as Colonel Neal brought every one up to speed. The briefing included the intel that was starting to be recovered by the interrogation of the prisoners.

"We finally have a positive fix on the compound that these guys are using to launch their operations from. It's an estate in upstate New York, There has also been some activity from another estate in Michigan. Both of them have large Muslim populations in the area. These are large multi-million-dollar estates with a lot of land. They both have private airfields and large hangars. SATCOM is going back over the coverage they have to see if they can figure out what was going on prior to the attacks. CIA also has uncovered some links to some incidents in Florida." Neal used a laser pointer to indicate spots on the photo overlays projected onto the screen. "We are ramping up the teams for assaults on both of these. We have four ODAs out of Bragg that will be hooking up with you gents for the drop on the Michigan site," he said, gesturing toward the Navy SEAL LCDR seated at the table. "They have four C-130s for your HAHO drop. This will be coordinated with the Marines' assault on the New York site. They will drop from MV-22s. The Green Beanies will have eyes on the ground tomorrow. Our recon Marines left Pendleton this morning and will hook up with a National Guard group out in Minnesota tonight. They will have eyes on the target site tomorrow. We hope to initiate within forty-eight hours of that."

A new picture flashed up on the screen. The overhead shot showed several burned-out aircraft, and battle damage was visible to some of the buildings in what was obviously a small airport. The burnt-out hulk of a HMMV in front of the terminal attested to the violence that had occurred.

"This is Bemidji Airport. It was supposed to be the jumping off point for the next wave of attacks. The terrorists were coming west past the Appalachians before branching out to the Southwest. A series of very fortunate events resulted in the National Guard element I mentioned earlier, along with some local law enforcement types recovering the airfield not once, but twice, from the mercenaries who were tasked with securing it. It is now firmly in our hands, and this will be the departure point for the Marines heading to New York.

"The Air Force is constantly updating their strike package capability as they are seeing a large influx of pilots and ground crew to their bases, which have been re-secured. This includes those A-10s, which I thought they had retired. Apparently, there is a behind-the-scenes network of Warthog lovers who keep them around. There will be air support available. Lots of it.

"Strategically, we have no one to shoot at. The toxin was distributed to almost every country. Even the Arab nations. The few governments that we have made contact with are all crying foul. It's hard to argue with them when they can point to 60 percent casualty rates. The mercenaries we have interrogated have only given up that their employer is Arab with a lot of money. NCA reports that you Navy folks have plenty of subs and ships with cruise missiles to eliminate a foreign power. We just don't know who to point them at." Neal gathered some papers and gestured toward the SEAL sitting to his right. "LCDR Milton will brief you on his team's op plan, Commander."

"Good afternoon, gentlemen…"

CHAPTER 41

South of Bemidji, MN

The MV-22 Ospreys swung around in a gentle arc, slowing as they approached the empty field. Because the enemy forces had tried to secure the airport and the Ospreys were capable of vertical take-off and landings, it was decided to land them at the grass field that the National Guard had set up as the FARP (Forward Air Refueling Point). The Ospreys had been refueled once in their flight from San Diego by a KC-130 from Edwards Air Force Base.

As the twin rotor birds settled to the ground, a small group of men and one small boy walked slowly out to meet the new arrivals. The Ospreys normally landed with their rear ramps partially open in case of an emergency, so it only took them a few seconds to complete the opening process as the rotors spun down to a stop. The welcoming committee consisted of Captain Nelson, Lieutenant Crowe, Master Sergeant Lovell, Chris, Scott, and Barry. Barry had become the official mascot of the unit. They had given up on trying to keep him restricted to the compound since he always managed to appear wherever the troops went. Several people suspected that Corporal Maggio had something to do with this, but nothing had been proven thus far.

Mark and Jake were the first ones to walk down the ramp of their Osprey and were mildly amused to see a boy who looked to be about ten years old with a .22 slung over his shoulder and a pistol holster on his hip that looked ridiculously large. Derry did a double take when he realized that the butt sticking out of the Bianchi holster was that of a Colt .45. They stopped in front of the boy, who came to attention and rendered a passable (for the Army, anyway) salute.

Mark and the Marines behind him, some carrying heavy gear, came to a stop while Mark came to parade ground attention and returned the salute. "Chief Warrant Officer Mark Norris reporting as ordered, sir!"

Barry, who was somewhat taken aback since he just expected to get a pat on the head, recovered quickly and said, "Welcome, Chief Want Officer!" He had no idea what a want officer was but he appeared pretty important. "I'm Barry and these are my Army guys!" he said, puffing out his chest.

With the ice officially broken, everyone shook hands and made introductions. Barry received the expected head pats, and they all walked over to the Hummers while the refueling team began swarming over the aircraft. The assault teams unloaded their gear while the STA (Sniper Target Acquisition) Marines left theirs on board. They would be leaving to jump into upstate New York in about two hours.

Scott walked up behind Mark and said, "I knew a young Marine corporal once who went by the name of Norris. I seem to remember him always being in trouble."

Mark turned around and stared at the man talking to him. As recognition dawned on him, a huge grin split his face. "Captain Prescott? Holy shit! How are you doing?" Mark was pumping his hand. "Christ, what's it been, twelve years?"

"That it has. I've been here for the last eleven." Scott had his hand on Mark's shoulder as they walked away to reminisce. Barry watched them walk over to a Hummer and turned back around to head over to the Osprey. He had never seen such a cool plane before. He didn't get all the way turned around before he was staring at a wall of magazines and pouches that had all kinds of cool stuff stuck to it. He almost reached out to touch it until he realized that the wall was part of the huge Marine standing in front of him. He took a step back and still had to crane his neck to look up at the man towering over him. Figuring that the salute thing worked once, he tried it again.

"Are you a Want Officer too?" he asked, waiting for his salute to be returned.

"It's Warrant Officer there, little man. W-A-R-R-A-N-T, and no, I'm a Sergeant," Jake said as he squatted down to the kid's level. "Where do you think you're headed off to?"

"I was jus' gonna look at that helicopter plane. That's cool!" Barry was stepping to the side to point it out to Jake just in case he had forgotten where it was.

Jake stood back up and kept his body between the inquisitive young man and the Osprey. "That, little guy, is called an MV-22 Osprey. It takes off and lands like a helicopter, but once it's in the air, the propellers tilt forward and it flies like an airplane."

"Can I check it out? Please!" Barry was literally dancing from foot to foot. "Dan promised me a ride in the plane." He gestured at the park ranger Cessna parked at the edge of the field. "But he got shot at the airport and isn't back to flying stats yet."

"He did, did he? Well, I think a tour might be in your future but not right now. They have to be refueled and then we're taking them on a mission. After that, I'll make sure you get to check it out."

"Aww, man! I always get told that!" Barry turned and sulked off toward a Hummer. Corporal Maggio was sitting in the gunner's cupola, watching the tree line. Barry was halfway there when he noticed some movement in the brush at the western edge of the field. Corporal Maggio slewed the turret around and was dropping the machine gun onto target when Barry's .22 let out two pops and the bushes began to thrash wildly. A third pop, and all the movement ceased.

Everyone on the field had brought their guns up at the first sound of gunfire. The locals quickly realized what had happened and returned to what they were doing. The Marines took slightly longer to lower their weapons and relax.

"That kid can sure take care of himself," Jake said to Lovell as the two of them continued to exchange personnel rosters.

"Shit! Barry was living out here on his own until just a few days ago," Lovell said, glancing at the kid as he climbed onto the hood of the HMMV. "He brought more supplies in with him than some of the cops we rescued. He has a survival instinct, that's for sure. We tried keeping him in the compound, but he just escapes and goes out looking for ferals. We'll hear that .22 of his popping in the distance, and our rooftop snipers say he gets a lot of them. The corporal he's talking to has taken him under his wing. Taught him how to use that .45 he's toting around too."

"Well sheeit! I guess I better stay on his good side." Jake turned back to the work at hand. He only looked up the next time the .22 barked.

CHAPTER 42

FL230 above Buffalo, NY

The rear ramp of the C-130 slowly sealed itself back up, and the plane banked gently to the right. Behind and below it, dark shapes hurtled through the night. After only a minute of free fall, the members of ODA 249 deployed their chutes and began steering them toward a specific set of GPS coordinates. The coordinates were the location of an open field on an estate two miles from their target.

The large CDAs that the team used allowed them to travel the four miles to their LZ with no problem. The night air was calm and the partial moon supplied just enough light to make the landing a piece of cake for the experienced operators. All four men came down within feet of their desired location and began to gather their chutes.

Each man was armed with a suppressed M4 carbine and had a large drag bag strapped to their backpack. After removing their canopy harness and stashing their parachutes in the shrubbery that ran along the stone wall that bordered the field, they immediately took off on a northerly heading. After crossing two estates, each of which was comprised of dozens of acres, the team split into two, two-man elements and began stalking to their final rally points. Here they switched out their ACU tops for their Ghillie suits and began to "veg them out," attaching pieces of the local flora to them. They also buried their large rucksacks under some more bushes and sprayed both the ground and bushes with pepper spray. They donned their slimmed-down daypacks and began their very careful stalks into their final hides.

"Rocketman, Gumball One, data upload." SFC Chris Preston was the ODA team leader.

"Gumball One, received."

It was another forty-two minutes before the radio came to life again.

"Rocketman, Gumball Two, data upload." Sergeant Miles "Smiles" Barton, had worked his way around the south side of the target.

Sergeant Julio Peralta, "Gumball Three," checked in about five minutes later.

Sergeant John Camden was the last to check in since he had to work his way all the way around to the north of the property. It took him another two hours to follow the wood line along the far side of the estate neighboring the target site. He encountered three ferals along the way—two human and one large dog. The first one he encountered was a teenaged girl whose muscles had been so overstressed that all she could do was lie on the ground and pant. She had crawled into the bushes and was lying there quietly. If she hadn't growled at him, John might have stepped within reach of her. He took out his silenced pistol and fired one round into her upturned face.

The next thing he ran into was a dog that had been tracking the girl he just shot. The huge Malamute had been following the scent of the feral girl ever since she and two others had attacked his pack. John had stopped to listen to his surroundings and heard the animal's approach. The dog became aware of John at the same time John saw it. It growled and began to charge, but the .45 ACP hollow point hit it on the end of its snout, destroying most of its face. The dog let out a yelp and jumped back. As it turned to run, a second 230-grain Federal Hydra-Shok punched into its side, breaking ribs and destroying the heart and lungs. The dog collapsed on its side and lay still.

The dog's yelp was heard by Antonio Savalas. Antonio had only been partially exposed to the toxin and was just plain crazy. He had been a landscaper at a nearby estate and managed to hide out in the stables while the world went crazy. Antonio had been exposed several times by small bites from rodents. He recovered from the first two exposures but was recently bitten again, this time by a large rat. The dose was substantially larger than his previous wounds, and he was in the throes of it when he heard the dog's cry. He immediately made a beeline for the sound, only to run smack into a bullet.

Camden had moved farther into the woods in hopes of avoiding what was becoming a crowded (to him) tree line. He transitioned back to his suppressed M4 and heard Antonio running toward him from quite a distance. John took a knee next to a tree and had the illuminated reticle of his ACOG scope pasted on Antonio's chest as he appeared through the trees. The rifle made a subdued *phutt-chunk* as the action cycled, but the round passed close to a tree and caused a sonic crack. The bullet struck Antonio in the sternum, but the 5.56mm round was deflected to the right of the heart and merely grazed the lung while traveling through the chest cavity. He fell backwards like he had run into an invisible wall but immediately began thrashing around.

Out came the MK23 Mod 0 pistol with silencer again, and one *phutt* later, all was quiet. Camden held still and listened to make sure this latest audible fiasco hadn't brought more attention to his location and moved off again. He called in to inform the rest of the team what had happened. He was more than an hour late to his OP, and it was light when he finally reached his hide. His luck changed for the better though, and he managed to get into the hide without being detected.

"Rocketman, Gumball Four, data upload."

"Gumball Four, about time. Did you enjoy your midnight stroll?"

John was too professional to rise to the bait and talk unnecessarily. He began sketching out his range card and modifying his hide. He would be here for two days minimum; he might as well get comfy.

CHAPTER 43

Buffalo, NY

"Rocketman, Kingsnake One, data upload," Art Sanchez whispered into his mic.

"Kingsnake One, Rocketman copies."

"Rocketman, Kingsnake Two, data upload."

"Rocketman copies."

"Rocketman, Kingsnake Four is on line."

"Kingsnake Four, copy."

"Rocketman, Kingsnake Three, data upload."

"Kingsnake Three, Rocketman copies."

Two more STA elements checked in from New York as Grubbs rubbed the stubble on his face. They were getting water for hygiene purposes, but the grooming standards had become very "modified" in the control center. Lack of sleep and unending stress had virtually made the wearing of the Class B uniform a joke. Those airmen and women who had utilities were authorized to wear them, but Grubbs had finally told the troops to wear jeans if they had 'em.

"I don't know why these things always have to kick off at zero dark thirty, sir," Lieutenant Simmons said with her stockinged feet up on the chair next to her. "They really need to re-evaluate the whole 'cover of darkness' thing. It's playing hell with my beauty sleep!"

Grubbs almost said something about the troops on the ground not getting any, but held his tongue. Simmons had found out that her boyfriend was killed at the very beginning of the outbreak, and she was still here doing her job. She really did look like hell, but he believed that the extra work was keeping her mind away from dark places, and that was a good thing. His had been spending too much time there lately, and he didn't wish it on anyone.

"I'll make sure to tell that to the ops guys next time, Lieutenant."

"Thank you, sir. I appreciate it." She leaned forward and began typing on her console. The images from the observation teams were being displayed on the huge digital displays on the wall. Different analysts were calling the snipers and asking them to zoom in on various features at both sites. Every once in a while, a small group would gather and an impromptu discussion would break out about something on the screen. Sometimes a tech would march up to the display and point something out while stomping his foot in anger. *Intel weenies is right*, Grubbs thought as he watched a tech push his glasses up on his nose with one hand while scratching his chest under his pocket protector with the other. *But they're my weenies.* He grinned and began typing out e-mails.

In Michigan, ODA 625, ODA 612, and SEALs from Team Three all jumped into a commercial parking lot that was several miles from their target site. The jump had been delayed because of air traffic from the site, and the C and C elements didn't want to risk even the slightest chance of being discovered. Once on the ground, the elements formed up and began the long trek to their final departure points.

The same thing was happening in New York, except the landing zone was the field that the Marine snipers had used for their insertion. The Marines had jumped from the Ospreys, which had flown back to pick up follow-on forces. Two of them flew a few miles away and actually taxied under freeway overpasses so they would stay hidden from flying eyes but would be available for medevac if needed.

The Ospreys from the medevac flight had just shut down and the crew chiefs were lowering the ramps when the pilot of Victory One heard a thud from on top of the aircraft. He looked up through the Lexan panel overhead and saw a gore-smeared face looking in at him. The feral began beating and scratching on the glass, trying to get in.

"Miller, we've got a crazy on top of the bird! Get him off without putting a hole in the plane!" The pilot was yelling but he wasn't panicked yet.

"Roger that, sir. On my way." Sergeant Miller unplugged his helmet from the comm station and pulled his M4 from the rack. He walked down the rear ramp of the aircraft and started to walk around the right side of the plane. He stepped under the wing next to the engine nacelle and pointed his rifle at the top of the aircraft. Not seeing anything, he began to walk farther away from the plane to be able to see up top better. He looked at the copilot and made a "what gives" gesture. The copilot pointed over his shoulder toward the rear of the plane.

Miller turned toward the back of the plane and took two steps when the sound of gunfire made him jump and spin around. The copilot had opened his side window and was aiming at a teenage girl who was shambling toward him. Just as he raised his rifle to shoot her, the feral from on top of the plane jumped from the wing and crashed into his back, driving him to the ground. Miller tried to roll over and get the man off his back, but the feral had straddled him and was scratching and pulling at his helmet.

Corporal Moon, the other crewman, came around the back of the plane and immediately fired two rounds at the female, who was almost into the fray herself. She fell into the male feral, who was distracted long enough to let Moon close on him and deliver a vicious butt stroke to the head. The unconscious man slumped to the side.

Miller shoved away from the two bodies and stood up. They both stank to high heaven, and more than a little of the odor had rubbed off on him. It was so bad that Moon took a step back away from him.

"What?" Miller said, looking at the retreating corporal. "I didn't get bit!"

"Dude, you stink!" Moon was waving his hand toward the dirt-encrusted Marine.

Miller was about to say something when he realized that Moon was absolutely right. The body odor from the feral was bad enough, but the stench of rotting meat and feces was overwhelming. He started to strip off his flight suit, but then thought better of it. They were walking back to the ramp when another feral jogged down the embankment of the overpass and began running at them. They both fired two rounds, and the body spun to the ground. They walked into the back of the Osprey and Miller immediately stripped off his flight suit.

"I hope we don't have to stay here long," Miller complained as he used baby wipes to clean the exposed skin that had gotten smeared with God knows what. "Those fuckers will be all over us with the noise we made getting in here."

"That's for sure." Moon was standing in the open ramp, scanning the other side of the underpass. "I hope those Fast Company guys have their shit together."

"Well, we'll know in about ten hours…"

CHAPTER 44

Dearborn, MI

The security patrol was good. They were alert and professional. They kept their heads on a swivel and stayed quiet. The four of them maintained a good interval, stopping every twenty yards or so to listen and scan the terrain. Their team leader, Ian, wished they could have brought dogs along, but their employer wouldn't allow them on the property. The team had taken a left turn out of the gate on the random whim of the patrol leader and had made it halfway around the estate when Ian decided to take a break. They pulled back into the wood line at the perfect spot to look out over the estate. They all took a knee facing outwards and sipped water.

Ollie gestured to his crotch and stepped over to a bush to relieve himself after receiving a nod from Ian. As he was unzipping his fly, the stench of rotten meat drifted up to him. He ignored it for the most part as he finished his business, but the smell got stronger as a slight breeze wafted the sickly sweet odor toward him. He made eye contact with Ian and touched his nose then gestured upwind. Ian took a few steps toward Ollie and caught the smell.

He gestured for the team to form up and they began walking toward a clump of bushes. The dead feral was easily visible under the brush. The team noticed the hole in her head. Ian leaned down and rubbed his gloved finger in the blood that had leaked from the entry wound. The blood was thick and tacky, as it had not had a chance to dry completely. That and the fact that no animals had gotten to the body yet indicated that she had been killed in the last day… probably within the last several hours. The team began carefully looking around the area when one of the men pointed out the brass shell casing. Ian used his clean hand to pick up the .45 shell casing and examine it. None of the mercenaries used .45s. They had all been told that only 9mm ammunition would be available to them.

Ian looked around some more and noticed a pebble pressed into the ground. The ground didn't appear scuffed, but the moist dirt around the pebble's edge didn't match the shadow cast by the pebble itself. A few steps in that direction, and a second casing was found, with the third shortly thereafter. Another puff of wind and the smell of dead flesh again wafted into their noses. They all turned and saw the dog lying on its side. A quick examination showed the two bullet wounds on the animal. A brief search revealed the body of the third feral and the last of the shell casings. Ian noted that they were 5.56mm, an almost sure indicator of an American military presence.

"Base, patrol, we have possible visitors here. I have one dead woman and one dead male feral and a dead dog that have all been shot in a very proficient manner," Ian whispered into his radio.

"Patrol, any other signs in the area?"

"Base, we have not begun tracking them yet, but it doesn't appear to be more than one or two. The ground is not disturbed enough for more than that." Ian watched as Steven took a knee and began examining something on the ground. "I have .45 caliber and 5.56mm shell casings. These are new and shiny. The wounds observed are recent and none of the lookouts reported gunfire in the last day. I believe whoever did this is using suppressed weapons."

"Patrol, we are sending out a second squad to your location. They will help you sweep the area."

"Roger. We will hunker down here." Ian walked over and looked at the patch of ground that Steven was staring at. "What'cha got there, mate?"

"It looks like just one set of prints. Athletic shoe tread, maybe one of the tactical boots. Definitely not a military-type lug sole. Not that it matters with their special ops guys. Moves off in that direction." He pointed east, further into the trees.

"Okay, we'll wait for the others to get here then we'll begin tracking this fellow down. If he stays close then we'll find him. If he's wandered off, then it's no problem. But either way, I don't like having this fellow around." Ian kept his head turning in all directions. *I am not comfortable with special ops types in my area. They bring trouble with them,* he thought as they all took a knee again and waited to talk the other team into their location.

"Gumball team, Rocketman."

"Rocketman, Gumball One, send it." Preston was on the west side of the property, where the main gate was. He was making sure that his window count was good on the front of the building.

"Gumball, we just intercepted radio traffic from the security patrol that is on the east side of the property. They found the dead ferals that Gumball Four engaged last night. The Tangos are sending out another patrol to conduct a sweep of the area. I would also imagine that if they have any kind of optics on the estate, they're scanning the woods." Tech Sergeant Willis looked up at the digital display of the Michigan estate. "They already passed by G-3 and are to the north of him. If they are able to track G-4, then things will get real interesting. Over."

"Rocketman, we will track them. Please have our on-call air ready for interdicting fires and light up the Predators. It will definitely get interesting if we have to break contact under fire. Break. Gumball Four, how good is your hide? Over." Preston tried to see if he could visually make out the hide. But even though he knew the exact GPS coordinates, he couldn't make out Camden's position. But looking through a spotting scope from almost a mile away and being on the ground fifty meters away are two different things.

"Gumball One, Gumball Four, I copied all. I am betting my life on this spot. I am under a patch of ivy, and I'm vegged out pretty good, Sergeant. I don't think even their best could find me. All bets are off if they have dogs though. Over." Camden was under a mat of ivy that had grown among some of the granite boulders, which were common in the area. He had been able to cover the last forty meters of his stalk on top of clean boulders (no moss to get scraped off). He had then been able to lift the plant and, using a pair of Fiskars snips, cut the roots away enough to crawl underneath. Some of the plant would start to turn brown in a few days, but he would be long gone by then.

Camden's Ghillie suit had several colors of burlap fibers tied to the square netting that was attached to the base garment. These fibers were of various greens and browns. Before crawling under the plant, Camden had tucked most of the brown fibers under the netting and pulled the dark green ones out. After attaching some of the ivy to his suit, he crawled under and made sure that the thick leaves were all oriented naturally.

After setting his M49 spotting scope on the short tripod, he set up his rifle. This involved darkening the tape on the stock and barrel and attaching some short pieces of vegetation. He could now push the rifle slightly forward into its shooting position, in which case, only the last inch of the barrel would stick out beyond the ivy. He then began ranging target reference points and making his notes.

"Gumball Four, well, you may be betting all our lives on it." Preston was staring really hard at some boulders with ivy laced between them. "I'm looking at your area, and I can't see you. I just hope your back trail is good and these guys aren't that good at tracking. Over."

"One, I see you looking right at me." Camden had swiveled his scope to look at his team leader's hide.

"Rocketman to all teams, we may have a situation developing with Gumball. If they are compromised, we will initiate a drone strike for them to break contact and then try to contain the compound. All Kingsnake units, continue your movement unless activity at your objective changes. Thumper, Mongol, Skunk, and Otter teams, you may need to hustle it up to get into position if we have to jump off early. Break. Mongol One, we will breach the front gate with a Hellfire if you cannot provide the breach per plan. I need ETA for all teams. Over."

"Rocketman, Thumper One, LD in twenty mikes." First Sergeant Barnes and the rest of ODA-625 were coming up from the south.

"Rocketman, Mongol One, LD in fifteen mikes. We'll make it."

"Rocketman, Skunk One, we're up."

"Rocketman, Otter Two, we're up in three mikes." CPO Dan Pike answered for his lieutenant, who was relieving himself.

"Titan One-Six, Rocketman, I show you in position." Willis saw the green triangles that represented the Marine teams in their briefed assault positions. "There is a possibility that we will have to initiate early. Over."

"Rocketman, Titan One-Six, we will be good to go in three mikes. Over."

"Rocketman copies all. Out." Willis turned toward General Grubbs, who was talking to a lieutenant colonel. "Gentlemen, we will be good to go in about twenty-five minutes. Our Predators and Global Hawks are on station and the assault teams are almost in position. The Jarheads are ready to go and the Green Beanies will be ready in about twenty."

"Very good, son. We'll be up in the loft when things kick off. How are the National Guard and law enforcement guys doing with the Gyrenes?"

"By all reports, sir, they just folded them right in, and they haven't had any problems. They're operating under their call signs."

"Very well, I am going to get a cup of coffee, and then I'll be ready to kick this pig."

"Yes, sir."

The estate had its own private airfield with an actual tower built into the back of the main residence. Jake could see movement on top of the turret and he suspected an observation post at the least, and a sniper at the worst. Art had also observed movement up there from the other side of the property. Since the mercenary teams had already shown that they had capable snipers, no one was taking any chances. They had been keeping the roofline under intense surveillance for the last four hours and it finally paid off when Art was able to see a rifle being moved on the roof.

"Rocketman, Kingsnake One, I have a shooter position on the roof of the main house. If I designate, will you be able to keep a lock on that section of roof? I would like to designate and have that be the first area engaged. Over." Art already had the laser pointed at the roof.

"One, Three, I can designate from this side with a straight LOS. Over." Jake had the better view of that section of roof.

"Kingsnake, Rocketman, stand by, I am consulting with the Predator drivers." Willis had one of the drone drivers in the room as a liaison and, after a brief discussion, got back to the Marines. "Kingsnake, you there?"

"Rocketman, Kingsnake is standing by. Over." Willis could almost hear the Jarheads' eyeballs rolling back in their heads.

"Sorry 'bout that. Drone ops says they can re-lase the target after you lay the pipper on it. The drone will maintain orbit with that spot targeted until it is engaged. Over."

"Kingsnake Three copies. When can I designate? Over." Jake had his PBL pointed at the target already.

"Kingsnake Three, Rocketman, anytime."

"Rocketman, Kingsnake Three, designating target code 105. Over." Jake hit the button and sent the beam out to "paint" a dot on the fascia right below the roofline.

"Kingsnake Three, Lollipop One, ground contact return, Code 105. Standby… target lock. We have the target designated with our laser. Thank you. Over." The voice over the radio sounded like a peppy high school cheerleader, which is exactly what Sierra Lasky had been before joining the Air Force.

Tech Sergeant Willis looked over at the drone pilot standing next to the general and mouthed "Lollipop?" with an incredulous look on his face. The drone pilot just shrugged and smiled.

"Lollipop One, Kingsnake Three, I am off target. I have a detectable laser bloom on the target though. Is that going to stay that way until we engage? Over." The laser was invisible to the human eye, but the "bloom" or light splash of reflected rays would be visible to anyone looking through an NVG device.

"Kingsnake Three, Lollipop One, as soon as the GPS syncs to the target, we will only have to intermittently re-lase to verify that we are on target and will not illuminate for more than a second until weapons deployment."

"Lollipop One, Kingsnake Three copies. Break. Rocketman, I have the hangar doors visible. I am designating code 111. Over."

"Kingsnake Three, Rocketman copies all. Out."

CHAPTER 45

Dearborn, MI

Khaled was sitting in his room, looking at the reports that had come in before contact was lost in Bemidji. The garbled transmissions indicated that the U.S. Military was in a lot better shape than it should be. This had him very concerned, as the entire plan hinged upon them being able to spread the toxin to rural areas and reducing the population to a manageable level.

He was staring intently at the screen to his laptop, when movement outside his window caused him to glance up. A small white dot was approaching rather quickly and was leaving a smoke trail behind it. His brain only had a second and a half to process this before the Hellfire Missile slammed into the roof of the ATC room that was only one floor up and twenty yards away. The blast was so violent that he was thrown sideways off his chair and painfully into the footboard of his bed. The entire south wall of his room was blown in. The cloud of dust and debris was so thick he couldn't see a thing. His laptop was blown closed and flew onto the bed and slid right underneath a pillow, where it would be moderately safe.

Khaled didn't lose consciousness, but he came close. His ears were ringing and he had blood running from his nose and right ear. He tried to stand up, but his balance was off and he wound up having to lean on the wall to make it to his feet. He looked out his window, which was now devoid of glass, and could faintly hear the sound of gunfire. He began searching for his laptop but could only find the power cord. He was on his knees searching through the rubble when two more violent blasts knocked him back down. Although these were more distant and did not blow him over again, they did knock him flat on his stomach.

More debris fell on him and an interior wall stud made of several two-by-fours nailed together landed across the back of his legs. More dust and smoke blew into the room, making it nearly impossible to breathe. Khaled wrapped his hands over his head and cowered as the ceiling partially collapsed on top of him. He was lucky that he was next to the bed instead of under it or on it, as the frame collapsed with the slab of masonry still attached. The bed kept the slab from crushing him. He did, however, get a sliver from another wall stud driven into his side. With all the destruction around him, Khaled forgot about the laptop and began screaming for help. This lasted for less than a minute since it required him to inhale huge lungfuls of the dust-laden air. One long coughing fit later, and he just sat there in a miserable ball.

The attack was coming along nicely as the estate was struck several times by missiles from the unmanned drones. The precision-guided ordinance had penetrated every exterior wall of the main house and destroyed all the targets, which had been designated by the Marines or selected by the analysts. The only wildcard was the now reinforced patrol, which was somewhere on the northern side of the property. The target acquisition teams had lost track of it, and the satellite team was too busy to notice when they could no longer follow them through the woods. Their last position had them some 300 yards from Sergeant Camden's hide. Because of this, the sniper was not engaging targets, fearing that the sound of the massive .50 would bring trouble down on him.

The assault teams were in no hurry to rush in until the target had been softened up. Although speed was necessary to recover the intel on the site, the teams were loath to risk taking casualties to get it. Human life had become a lot more precious in the last few weeks. The snipers continued to engage any targets that presented themselves, which caused the occupants to take cover instead of being able to fight the fires, which were cropping up around the various buildings.

One building was completely flattened by Hellfire strikes. The large hangar next to the airfield was hit by two of the AGMs. The structure was large enough for the two Lear jets and the single Bell A-stars helicopter that was in it. By the time the missiles stopped streaking out of the sky, three of the building's walls were blown out, and the fuel truck that had been parked next to it was fully engulfed in flames. When the truck blew, it sent a black swirling cloud five hundred feet into the air. Burning fuel from the explosion covered the front of the barracks building, which had also received a missile of its own. There were only six people from the nightshift, who had just gone to bed in the building, but when the two survivors of the missile strike tried to run out the front door, they ran into a wall of flame. They turned around and began crawling back through the collapsed structure.

The security team managed to get a little coordination going but anytime anyone appeared outside the buildings, they dropped to the ground with a rather large hole in them. After six minutes of the worst "Shock and Awe" they could imagine, there was a tremendous secondary explosion as the ammunition in the armory went up. The blast was so violent that it actually blew some of the other fires out. Several more of the security team were killed and the northern end of the mansion collapsed.

The first white flag appeared a few minutes later at the south end of the mansion. Art had the teams hold their fire but did not send anybody in to make contact. After another few minutes, the first head appeared, looking cautiously around. Several of the house staff then carried out two wounded people and sat down on the lawn. A few minutes later, a few more came out, one of them carrying a rifle. It was a bad decision because a .308 match round impacted the bridge of his nose right below his sunglasses and blew out behind his right ear. The body fell to the ground as the rest of the people on the lawn sprawled flat and put their hands behind their heads.

Finally, the entry team approached from the south. They entered the grounds from a hole that had been blown in the wall by a drone strike. A squad rushed over and secured those who had surrendered—searching and segregating them. Then they were flex-cuffed and escorted back out through the same breach in the wall. Additional entry teams came in through the same point and went straight to the hole that had been blown in the south wall of the main house. After everyone had stacked next to the wall, the teams "bumped up" and carefully, but quickly, entered the structure. Two sticks went to the upper floor and roof and two began clearing the ground floor in the fluid grace that experienced operators called CQB. Their movement had almost a ballet-like quality as they moved from one room to the next, sweeping and clearing. The only hang-up came when they reached the communal dining room.

Almost twenty people had been in the room having breakfast when the attack started. Several of these were experienced mercenaries who recognized the attack for what it was and began barricading the doors and approaches. After two attempts to make it to the armory had failed with members of the security team falling to sniper fire, an attempt was made to get to the basement through the kitchen, but a missile strike there had collapsed the stairway down to the storage areas and the connecting tunnels.

Knowing that they faced execution if caught and taken prisoner, the remaining staff tried to hold off their attackers while they attempted to clear the stairway down to the basement. They pushed large oak tables to create a barricade at the door, and then used other furniture to reinforce it. The survivors took cover the best they could as several of their party worked at clearing the obstructed stairway down to safety.

When the third squad of the entry team came to the barricaded door, they tried to push on it and were met with a hail of gunfire, which wounded two of their team, one seriously. Fourth Squad, with Master Sergeant Lovell, arrived and they all pulled back around the corner of the entry hall. The wounded were extracted and the teams reorganized. After referring to the sketch in his pocket, he got on the radio.

"Titan Four to any Kingsnake unit, does anyone have eyes into the room that is to the north of the main entry door by about fifteen meters? We have resistance and the door is barricaded."

"Titan Four, Kingsnake Three, I have eyes into a room from the rear of the house with activity inside." Jake had an intermittent view into the room. There wasn't a window left in the entire structure but the breeze was blowing the torn and tattered curtains across the window openings. "I have maybe ten people behind some furniture pushed up against the door. I can see weapons. If you can get someone with a '203 to put some forty mike mike in there, you should be able to soften it up. I can provide covering fire, but I wouldn't be able to engage them all before they were behind cover. Over."

"Titan Four copies, sending out a '203."

A few seconds later, two troopers and a Marine came out a back door and began working their way along the wall to the window opening. All three had M203 grenade launchers slung under the Barrels of their M4s. The men stopped short of the window and looked out toward Jake, even though they had no chance of seeing him.

"Kingsnake Three, Titan Four-Four, any activity? Over."

"Titan Four-Four. Negative, will advise if they head toward the window. Over."

"Kingsnake Three, we are going to work our way past the window to get a better angle on the door inside then put our grenades on the barricade from the backside. Over."

"Titan Four-Four, I copy all. Will provide cover fire as needed. Over."

The three men crawled past the window then they loaded 40mm HEDP (High Explosive Dual Purpose) grenades into their launchers. They got far enough away that the grenades would arm, then stepped away from the wall and got on line, pointing their weapons at the window. They counted down, and then fired all three grenades through the window. One of the grenades clipped the crosspiece of the multi-paned window and was deflected slightly to the right. The other two flew straight through and impacted the barricade. The two blasts killed seven of the defenders and sent the rest sprawling, most of them wounded to some extent or another. The grenade that had been deflected actually slammed into the back of one of the security team members and detonated. The force of the blast sent body parts flying across the room.

As soon as the explosions were heard by the entry team, they sent two grenades into the doors from down the hallway, blowing them both wide open. A machine gunner laid down a quick burst of totally unnecessary cover fire and the team entered the room to find everyone either dead, unconscious, or so disoriented that their attempts at resistance were futile. The ones who tried, died.

The team cleared the room and a fire team set up on the kitchen door. The door was kicked open and two fragmentation grenades were thrown into the room. These were very hard throws, which sent the bomblets ricocheting off of walls and countertops, giving the occupants of the room no time to chase down the small steel balls as they were bouncing about. Both detonated with muted thumps from the other side of a countertop from the door, and then the squad made entry. There was only one person in the kitchen and she was unconscious and bleeding from a multitude of fragmentation wounds on her body and face. She was searched, flipped on her stomach, cuffed, and left there as the team stacked up at the door to the cellar.

Again, two grenades were thrown through the door and it was slammed back closed. This time, shouts and a mad scramble could be heard briefly before the grenades went off. Two more crumps, and the team opened the door and sent a couple of bursts of automatic weapons fire down the stairway. Four more bodies were strewn about on the stairs with another lying on the small landing in front of a pile of debris. After checking and searching the bodies, the door was secured into the kitchen and the team moved on.

Clearing the rest of the house was relatively easy with only two other holdouts offering resistance. One Marine was hit in the upper outside of his thigh and another in his vest. Both of the mercenaries were killed. The Marines began rounding up the prisoners and searching for intel. It was while searching through a collapsed upstairs bedroom that they found a Middle Eastern man curled into a ball under some debris, whimpering piteously. A further search recovered a laptop that was still on, stuffed under a pillow. The squad leader looked at the files, half of which were in

Arabic, and after grabbing the power cord, carefully carried the laptop down to Mark Norris.

The clouds of smoke drifting up in the air, along with the noise of the explosions, acted like a dinner bell for the ferals in the area. Both humans and animals began heading toward the noise. Some ran into each other and violent encounters occurred. Since the estate was located in a somewhat rural area, the population was not very dense. But the noise and smoke attracted them from a broad range.

Slowly, a ring began to tighten around the estate.

CHAPTER 46

Dearborn, MI

Ibet and Satif were running through the underground tunnel as fast as their out-of-shape legs would allow. Both of them had been on the eastern side of the house getting ready for morning prayers. They usually conducted them on a small patio that faced east then took their breakfast in a private salon. The first explosion sent them sprawling, the second knocked them down again before they had gotten all the way back up. Deciding that crawling was the wisest course of action, they both scuttled to the main corridor and were able to make it to a basement stairwell before another blast shook the house.

Once down in the cellar, they made their way to the door, which opened into the tunnel connecting the main house to the armory building. They stopped at the base of the stairs leading up to the armory and were debating going up to see what was happening and get a few guns when the building took the hit from the Hellfire. The blast blew the door open and, once again, they found themselves knocked flat on the floor.

Every building on the estate had access to an underground network of tunnels. Some of them were present when Satif purchased the estate, some were added after. There were three escape tunnels that led off the property. One led to a concealed exit next to the front gate from a panic room that a previous owner had built. The logic being that if he had to escape a home invasion, he would wait at the front gate for responding authorities. The other two led off the property, one to the estate to the north and the other came out in the woods to the east.

After picking themselves up again and dusting off, they began the hike that would take them to the estate north of them. They had a cache of weapons and supplies as well as a vehicle stashed on the property. It was a two-mile hike to the tunnel exit and they would have to wait until the coast was clear before attempting to leave the area. With the amount of missiles dropping out of the sky, any movement above ground would surely be observed and receive some very unwanted attention. It took them over an hour to make it to the end of the tunnel. This included stopping and arming themselves at the cache.

They decided to wait in the tunnel and rest. They had only been there for fifteen minutes when they heard labored breathing coming from back in the tunnel. Fearing that it was their pursuers, they both took up firing positions, with their rifles pointed back down the tunnel. The dust had settled for the most part by this time, but there was still a faint haze obscuring vision beyond about seventy-five feet. As the sounds came nearer, the two exchanged nervous glances. The sound of footsteps slowed then stopped. They could hear a muffled conversation. A black shadow appeared in the dust cloud moving slowly then it stopped and shrank. Then another shadow emerged, and the tension was too much for Ibet. He activated the red laser sight attached to his rifle and jerked the trigger.

Moun Etama was one of the mercenaries who had been guarding the estate. He and Charles Berkoff had managed to crawl down into the tunnel and escape the inferno that the barracks had become. The two seasoned fighters were a bit singed but had managed to re-arm and put together a bit of kit. They started out through the tunnel after gathering what equipment they could and were almost to the end when they heard movement up in front of them. They began to advance in overwatch. Just as Charles was rounding the last bend he saw a red laser, which was clearly visible, cut through the haze and hit Moun on the chest. Gunfire immediately followed.

Charles sent several rounds back toward the source of the laser and turned to see Moun backing away carefully, untouched by the shots that went wild. They both backed around the bend in the tunnel and regrouped. They heard some more frantic whispering, and, recognizing Arabic, Charles called out to them.

"Kief Halleck! You idiots!"

"Who is there?" Ibet asked.

"It's Charles and Moun! You almost hit him!"

"Why did you not identify yourselves?" Ibet was becoming more calm and confident as he realized that it was merely two of the mercenaries down the tunnel and not the U.S. forces.

"We were approaching quietly! At least we weren't spraying rounds all over the tunnel!" Charles was restraining himself from just shooting what he considered his former employers.

"Very well, we did not know who was approaching. You may do so now."

Moun and Charles exchanged a look then began advancing up the tunnel again, still keeping their rifles at the ready. They saw Ibet and Satif nervously standing in the room at the tunnel's terminus. After they all warily told their stories to each other, they decided that remaining where they were was the best course of action. The tunnel had been rigged with explosives to collapse it and they did so. The QRF that eventually followed the tunnel they had used found a wall of rock and dirt. They set up a watch—comprised of Moun and Charles—and waited.

CHAPTER 47

Colorado Springs, CO

"Guns up…"

Grubbs listened as the snipers from the Michigan site checked in. The assault teams were in place and the A-10s and Predators were getting lined up for their initial passes. Otter One had shifted a little north and stopped well short of its planned line of departure, or LOD. The Zoomies at SATCOM had been able to guide them in such a way that they stayed unobserved by the mercenary patrol.

SATCOM had tracked the second patrol as it entered the wood line to the east of the estate. Visual contact, supplemented by IR cameras, allowed them to track the patrol's movement until it stopped about 130 yards from where Gumball Three was hunkered down. The team had stopped, backtracked, stopped again, and then started a spiral search pattern.

Ian was getting a tingly feeling. He didn't like tingly feelings because it usually meant someone was watching him. They had followed the intermittent signs until they had gone about fifty yards past the last sure sign. They retraced their steps and went back to the last sure sign. Whoever they were tracking was good. If there hadn't been just enough leftover morning dew to allow them to see displaced water on the ground, they probably would have lost him/them long before. Because they had found so little sign, Ian was beginning to think that they were only tracking one man. Ollie and Steve agreed.

"Well, what do we think this gob is doing?" Martin Price was the leader of the second patrol sent out. "If he's trying to make ghost then he went north along these rocks and out of here. From what we've seen of his fieldcraft, we'll be all day looking for him that way. If he's snooping about, then he's around here somewhere."

"I think we should sweep toward the compound. If he's run away, fine." Ian gestured back along the broken line of rocks. "But if he's trying to get some intel on us, he's that way." Ian pointed. "And he's hidden well. I wish we had Adam here to find him out. Those sniper fellas have an eye for this. A dog or two would be nice as well since I seem to be in fantasy land."

"Well, let's go have a look about and see what we can see." Martin told the team to get on line with only five meters between each mercenary. "I'll call it in and see if any of the observers see anything."

"Right."

"Base, Patrol, we are almost due north of the compound and have lost the trail. Can you have the lookouts keep an eye out in this direction for anything that looks like someone trying to hide?" Martin was walking along the line of broken rocks as he spoke. "Look for brush that has been displaced, glare, straight lines in places they shouldn't be, and have them look for a washer."

"Patrol, what are you talking about a washer? Like for clothes?"

"No, you fool, like the kind you put on a nut and bolt!"

"Patrol say again your last; it's not making any—"

"Have them look for the end of a sniper rifle barrel, you idiot! It will look like a washer when seen from the end!" Martin rolled his eyes at Ian.

They walked until they were spread out along the tree line. Martin scrambled down off of the rocks he had been walking on and walked out into the open. He then turned around and looked back toward the woods. He slowly let his gaze travel over the line where the ground met the trees. He stood there for almost three minutes before moving off to his left.

Twenty-seven feet behind him, Camden was doing his best to be invisible. He had received word from Rocketman that the patrol was on its way, and he had done his best to become one with the earth. He'd heard the approach of the patrol and now could just hear one man moving around in front of him.

Back in Colorado, the entire team was fixated on the drama being played out on their screens. Tech Sergeant Willis was hovering over his microphone, ready to tell the SEALs from Otter One to bail out Gumball Three. He watched as one man broke from the tree line and walked to within ten yards of Gumball Three's indicated position.

"Gumball Three, he's right in front of you, but he's moving east. The rest of the patrol is still in the tree line," Willis whispered, not wanting his voice to somehow give away the sniper's position.

Camden broke squelch twice to acknowledge.

"Tell him we are hitting the compound in thirty seconds." Grubbs wanted Gumball Three to be ready to provide supporting fires once the Otter team took out the patrol. As Willis was doing this, the man wandered back to the tree line. Everyone in the room watched as the first Hellfires were launched. The explosions rippled across the entire compound. The front gate was blown completely free of its hinges, with one of the panels slamming through the front wall of the house. Seven missiles blew three holes in the estate walls and collapsed the entire south side of the main building.

The security patrol all turned and looked at the immense devastation that occurred in a matter of seconds. Most of the team immediately moved to cover. As soon as the missiles stopped falling out of the sky, they could hear rifle fire from the southeast. They heard several *chunks* as grenades were fired into the structures surrounding the main house. The loud report of a heavy rifle told them a sniper was back that way.

Martin and Ian were debating whether or not to ambush the attackers when the decision was taken out of their hands. Two of the security patrol who were kneeling next to a tree toppled over. A second later, a grenade flew through the air and landed next to another group. The small explosion wounded three men. As the team members started shouting to each other to re-orient to their rear, a .50-caliber round hit Martin in the waist. The 671-grain match bullet hit him at the top of his left hip pocket and crushed his pelvis before blowing out the front of his lower torso. It didn't kill him immediately, but the shock left him unconscious until he bled out.

Ian realized that the shot had come from the west side of the property and knew they were surrounded. More silenced rounds from their rear made leaves and small branches fall as they ripped through his team's area. He had just gotten the men all turned and facing north so they could assault in that direction when a grenade attack flattened everyone. When he got up to begin the assault, he was only joined by two others; everyone else was wounded. Before he made it three steps, a round punched through his thigh, sending him crashing down. Both of the other men fell before they could take their fourth.

The screams of the wounded men trying to surrender drowned out his calls for help on the radio. It didn't matter, anyway, since a Hellfire had hit the CP in the compound. He was screaming into his mic when a rifle butt impacted the base of his skull. He was too well muscled to die from the blow, but it stunned him so badly that when he got his wits about him, he was flex-cuffed and hogtied. All of his equipment and most of his clothing was cut off and stacked in a pile. Then the bound prisoners were laid out in a neat row and instructed not to move. One of the men decided to test the boundaries and was shot for his troubles.

The man standing over him spoke into his radio.

"Gumball Three, your backside is clear if you have things you need to do."

Immediately, there was a loud boom as Camden went to work with his M107. Everyone was startled at how close the sound was. After ten loud booms, there was a pause and then two more. After a two-minute pause, the vegetation a few yards away rippled as Camden backed out from his hide and walked over to the group. He looked over the prisoners and turned to Chief Pike.

"Thanks, gents. They would have kept me from getting my stick time in." Camden looked at the KIA. "Well, shall we go check out the digs?"

The estate compound was a wreck. Resistance was light since most of the mercenaries had been outside the wall when the attack started. The lone sentry on the roof had been taken out and only one person put up any resistance as the buildings were cleared. The teams had to be on the alert for ferals that were showing up in ones and twos to investigate the noise. Radio antennas on the roof had been shot to pieces with precision rifle fire. The teams cleared the outlying buildings and the C and C element gathered at the front of the house as the intel guys were sorting through the wreckage. A perimeter security team was stationed along the estate wall and were engaging the occasional Feral that came into view. Everything in the area had been attracted to the noise and movement.

"Hey, skipper!"

LCDR Milton turned as SCPO Don Waring jogged up. "What have you got, Senior Chief?"

"The entire estate is sitting on a tunnel complex. We still have teams clearing them but we've found an underground storehouse full of chemical canisters. Our brief said that they used 250-plus aircraft last time. And the Minnesota guys said that they were putting together a little armada of crop dusters. Well, you need to see this, sir. There's enough chemical to poison almost every square mile of the continental U.S. and Canada too."

As Milton and Waring were heading down to check out the find, Captain Dale McCreeson was debriefing the snipers of ODA 249. The "Gumballs" had all come in except for Peralta who had taken a long-range overwatch to the southeast. The shooters all briefed the info on their engagement cards and a sitrep was called in to SATCOM.

Down in the tunnels, Milton walked through a hatchway and stood in awe of the enormous storage room in front of him. There were four thousand metallic containers stored in racks twelve feet high. His attention was drawn to the side of the room where his XO and the First Platoon leader, Lieutenant Joe Diehl, were standing next to a desk with a body lying close to it. He walked over and noticed an overturned trashcan surrounded by burnt papers dusted with white powder from an extinguisher. He bent over and gently picked up some of the charred documents. The shipping manifests still had dates, times, and ports of origin clearly visible on them.

"Yemen?" Milton asked as Diehl turned to look at him.

"Yes, sir. Achmed there," he pointed to a body off to the side, "was trying to destroy this stuff when we came through the door. He refused to stop, so Pravek put a couple through his ten ring."

"Anything on the computer, XO?"

"Yes, sir! I think we have enough intel here to figure out where the money and brains are hiding out." Perry was dragging files over to the drive icon on the computer screen. He had a USB cable plugged into the computer tower that went to a small external zip drive. "I'm backing everything up right now on a secure drive because I know they had Trojan programs to scramble their com encryption. I'm sure these guys got the word off about us hitting them. I just wish we had the ability to act on this stuff in a timely manner. Those fuckers will be gone by the time we can get over there."

"Well, let's get this off to Rocketman and we'll see what comes of it." Milton turned back to Waring. "How extensive are these tunnels? I don't recall anything more than a basement when we looked at permitted plans." The assault teams had raided the local county clerk's office prior to the attacks to give them a little extra intel. They had used the building plans to help them formulate their plan of attack.

"Shit, sir, all the basements are connected and expanded. We haven't tripped any booby traps or IEDs yet, but we aren't taking any chances. I can't give you a timeline on clearing them, sir, because we don't know the extent of the tunnel system." Waring had one of the raided plan sheets out. Some rough sketches of the tunnels underlying the complex had been drawn to show what had been cleared so far.

"Well, don't let them get spread too thin. No bypassing rooms unless they are cleared and secured with eyes on them. I don't want teams to be getting cut off because they bypassed an area and Hadji pops out behind them." He looked at the drawings one last time then turned to Diehl. "I'll have every other asset come down to assist with the clearing."

"Aye, aye, Skipper!" Diehl got on his radio and began relaying orders.

CHAPTER 48

Bemidji, MN

Barry was bored.

Corporal Maggio had the duty, and the other kids his age were all playing kids' games that he found really stupid now. *Call of Duty* just didn't do it for him anymore. Not now that he had been out hunting real people, well maybe not *people* so much, but real bad guys… things… whatever. Halo still rocked and he and Maggio played a lot of that.

He wandered up to the roof and talked to Chris and Yavi for a little bit. The bushy eyebrows and comical expressions on Yavi's face always made him smile. He was heading back downstairs when a commotion in the CP caught his attention. He sidled up to the doorway and eavesdropped as one of the soldiers reported to Captain Nelson that the mission to New York was returning and would be arriving at the airfield in about forty minutes.

Barry turned and made a beeline toward his and Maggio's room. He always carried his machete with him but got yelled at by Mrs. Waller, one of the schoolteachers, when she saw him walking around with his .45 on his hip and his .22 rifle slung over his shoulder. So far, the soldiers had stuck up for him, but he didn't want to push it. They let him come and go as he pleased now, and he didn't want to have that change. He pulled out his "Hunting Harness," a modified shooting vest that Maggio had helped him make, that carried all his essential stuff. It held all his magazines for the rifle and pistol—he had a bunch of those now; Maggio had gotten them from a gun store they'd raided—a two-way radio that the CP monitored all the time, some food (MREs were still cool to him), and a camelback hydration system.

After putting it on and doing his "Battle Rattle" check, he opened the safe and got out his two guns. He slipped the belt clip for the pistol through his belt on his right hip and threw the .22 over his shoulder after inserting the magazine, chambering a round, and putting the safety on. He had forgotten to do that once and Master Sergeant Lovell had chewed his ass so bad that he almost ran away and hid under his bed for a week. That man was scary when he was pissed.

Barry was standing next to the building, looking out into the parking lot, wondering which vehicle he was going to sneak into when Lieutenant Crowe walked up behind him, grabbed him by his vest, and nearly lifted him off of his feet as he strode to the Hummers.

"I wouldn't want someone to think that we left you behind by mistake." He grinned down at the young boy who was walking on his tiptoes as he was being pulled along. "I remember you were promised a ride in an Osprey. Today might be your lucky day."

"Thanks LIEUTENANT! I won't get in the way, and I'll scout the edge of the field for ya." Barry straightened his vest as Crowe let him go.

They climbed into the lead Hummer, and they let Barry ride in the gunner's copula on the way to the airport. The M240G didn't have the ammo belt fed into it, so Barry was allowed to swing the gun around and practice aiming at whatever caught his fancy. He even pointed out a Feral to the gunner in the Hummer behind them. The man was bent over some dead animal, ripping it to shreds and stuffing the bits of flesh into his mouth. The convoy was traveling too fast for the second gunner to get his gun around in time. Barry made a mental note of the location and continued to enjoy the trip.

The Bemidji Airport was now a secondary base of operations and was staffed full time. Dan Preston was the de facto boss and spent his time flying the park service Cessna around, scouting the countryside, and learning to fly the Bell helicopter they had gotten from the terrorists. He didn't do too much though, as he was still healing from the gunshot wound on his back.

The west end of the airfield had become the junkyard where all the damaged aircraft had been towed or pushed after the last fight. The tower was up and running with several of the old tower crew coming back to work. Several of the air traffic controllers and other staff had perished during the outbreak, but enough remained to operate the field in a limited manner. There wasn't that much traffic, anyway.

The convoy pulled out onto the parking apron and everyone got out and waited. Dan came out and was shooting the shit with Crowe when the

Ospreys buzzed the field in formation. They went into the break as their engine nacelles began to rotate into their helicopter mode. After circling the field, they settled down on the runway and taxied over to the ramp. The Marines began trooping down the rear ramps to a round of applause by those gathered there.

Barry recognized the big Marine who got off the second plane and walked right up to him. He saluted and said, "Hi, Sergeant Derry! I'm here to keep you safe on the way back to our base if you need it. But I'm also ready for that ride too!"

Derry looked down at the kid standing in front of him and grinned.

"Bud, you're gonna have to talk to the man over there," he said, pointing to Mark. Norris and Colonel Neal were talking to one of the pilots. "That shit is above my pay grade."

"Okay." Barry turned and walked over toward the two Marines standing at the rear of the Osprey. One of the crewmen walked by, and Barry wrinkled his nose at the smell. The Marine saw this and scowled at him. Barry didn't say anything since he didn't quite know who was who with the Marines. He was pretty sure that the want officer was pretty important though. He marched right up and did the whole saluting thing again.

"Hi, Chief Want Officer Mark! I'm your scout today. If you need anything, let me know. And I can go for a ride whenever you're ready!" he said, nodding toward the ramp of the Osprey.

Mark turned and came to the position of attention and rendered a parade ground salute. Then he reached down and punched Barry lightly in the shoulder.

"You are? Well, that's good because I need a good scout. We just got landed here, bud, but how would you like to go to Virginia with me? The colonel here is going to need a couple bodyguards while we go pick up some important people. Jake and I are pretty tired but I bet you could cover for us while we're flying and we'll have you back in a day or so." Mark looked at Crowe, who shrugged. "We have to take them to Michigan, and then we'll be back here by the day after tomorrow. Is that cool?"

Barry's head was already nodding as he glanced back and forth between Crowe and Norris.

"This is Colonel Neal; he is the boss of all of us. So you need to make sure you're on his good side, okay?"

Barry turned and saluted Neal, who burst out laughing.

"So you're the famous Barry? I heard about you from some of the National Guard troops," he said, returning the salute. "So you think you can keep me safe for this trip?"

Barry stared at him hard, then not sensing that the colonel was being patronizing, he nodded his head.

"Yes, Mr. Neal, but you have to listen to me when I tell you not to do something. The crazies are fast and can be very dangerous." He patted his rifle as he spoke. " You'll need a gun too, because I can only cover one direction, and if Mark and Jake are each covering one then you'll need to cover as well."

Neal barely kept his mouth from falling open. He listened as the kid gave him a set of detailed instructions on survival techniques. When he was done, the pilot took him into the cockpit and began showing him around.

"I can't believe I just got schooled by a fourteen year old who knows more about surviving these things than I do!"

"He could definitely teach a few classes, sir, and I think he's only ten or twelve." Mark was chuckling. "So we go to Quantico, pick up this CDC team, take them to Michigan, and then stop back by here on the way home, right, sir?"

"That's the word."

The ground crews were attaching fuel lines and performing maintenance on the birds when gunshots broke out at the edge of the airfield. Two of the security team members were overrun by ferals, who tackled them to the ground and began tearing into them. Several more troops began firing in the direction of the pack. There were almost fifty of them and they fled back into the western wood line.

Mark got up from the kneeling position he had assumed to fire at the ferals and noticed that Barry was lying on the ramp of the Osprey with his rifle smoking. As he watched, the young man fired three more times toward the trees then stood up. He looked back at the colonel and walked over. He changed magazines in his rifle as he came.

"They'll head north and east," he said to Mark. "The smell of all this human activity will draw them from a long ways off. I usually try to thin the packs out before they get too close to town, but I don't come this far north. It was the noise from the planes that drew them here."

Neal gave Norris a WTF look. Mark just smiled and shrugged his shoulders. They watched as the airfield's reaction team trotted over to the casualties. The two bodies were placed on stretchers and carried back to the terminal building. Barry kept his eyes on the tree line as he walked with everyone back to the terminal building.

"Lieutenant Crowe, is it okay if we take the young man here with us to Michigan and back? I would say that we'll keep him safe but I fear that the opposite will be true, and he'll take care of us."

"Yes, sir, Colonel. Barry there is his own man, but I will let the folks back at the CP know that he's off on a mission of national security." Crowe was grinning at the young boy. Barry's well-muscled but skinny chest was puffed out about two miles past his belt line. *National Security*, he thought. *How cool is that!*

Mark took the young man over to one of the aircrew and gave him instructions on making sure that Barry had a headset for the flight. After showing him where he could store his gear for the flight, he left Barry with instructions not to go anywhere because they were leaving in about ten minutes.

Barry, who never took off his gear when he was outside the compound, walked to the last seat at the back of the Osprey's cabin and sat down, looking toward the wood line. He would maintain a vigil until it was time to leave.

Norris and Neal went over to one of the other Ospreys and checked the boxes of material that had been recovered from the raid. After ensuring that the proper material was offloaded and everything was organized, they headed back to the command bird and got ready to lift. Barry was literally hopping from foot to foot as he followed everything that happened during their liftoff preparations.

As the aircrew made their final checks, a freshly showered Sergeant Miller, smelling MUCH better in Barry's opinion, held up a gunner's harness and looked at Mark while nodding in Barry's direction. Mark nodded assent.

The rear door of the Osprey had a Gatling gun mounted on a tripod off to the side of the cargo ramp. There was an overhead attachment point for the gunners to hook into while the aircraft was in flight. After hooking both Barry and himself into their harnesses, Miller began showing Barry how to "sit" the gunner's position. As the Ospreys lifted away, several ferals could be seen to the north of the field. Miller received permission to engage, and Barry reached the highpoint of his life thus far when he was allowed to fire the mini-gun. Miller was suitably impressed with how quickly the kid learned to lead the targets.

CHAPTER 49

Quantico, VA

Anna and Gary stood a little apart from General Branson and Admiral Huff as they watched boxes of papers and crates of materials and instruments being wheeled or carried into the hospital. She did a double take as what had to be the smallest bodyguard in history escorted a lean Marine Corps colonel into the facility. The colonel marched up to Huff and saluted. The child next to him noticed the salute and rendered a passable one but didn't wait for it to be returned before turning around and facing the open doors.

"The Marines are recruiting them kind of young these days, Colonel," Huff said, smiling.

"I think he's a Minnesota National Guardsman actually, sir," Neal said as he shook the admiral's hand. After introductions were made all around, the group retired into one of the conference rooms to discuss the raids. Barry stood guard outside the door to the conference room scowling at anyone who approached. This included Branson, who had gone to his office to get his laptop. He harrumphed at the fact that Barry saluted the Marine warrant officer but not him. He refrained from saying anything because the six-foot-three-inch Marine sergeant standing next to him did render a salute but did not look in the least bit friendly.

The meeting took the rest of the afternoon and lasted well into the evening. Branson was more than a little taken aback when he finally stepped out of the conference room to see both the large Marine and young boy still standing watch.

"Have you two had a chow break?" Huff asked as he followed Branson into the hall.

"No, sir," Derry said, nodding in Mark's direction. "We were waiting for the Gunner. He gets lost easily in unfamiliar places."

"I'm gonna lose you in a minute… Forgive the sergeant, sir. He has an over-inflated sense of self-worth." Branson shook his head and frowned at the unmilitary-like behavior of the two barbarians. He would have said something if it weren't for the fact that Huff was laughing right along with them.

Barry, whose head had swiveled back and forth during the exchange, finally said, "Do you know where you are sleeping tonight, Colonel Neal? I'd like to check it out before you get there."

Huff laughed and turned to Neal. "Well, I guess we should do as your security specialist suggests. We can give you a lift over to the transient barracks."

"Thank you, sir. We'd appreciate it." Neal turned toward the two government sedans, which Barry was eyeing with some trepidation. He hadn't ridden in a regular car since before the attacks and had seen many victims who had been trapped in their cars. He even avoided riding in the rangers' trucks. "I'm sure we'll be all right there, bud. We have some firepower to cover us," Neal said, gesturing toward the Hummers in front of and behind the staff cars.

"Ohhh kayyy…" Barry looked at Jake and Mark, who both nodded. They all climbed in with Barry riding in the front passenger seat of the sedan Neal was in. They drove to the barracks with Barry's .22 out the window and Neal still in awe of how focused the young boy was on the surrounding landscape. They managed the three-minute drive without incident and were climbing out of the vehicles when another staff car pulled up. They watched as the attractive lady from the CDC climbed out of the car and gathered her things, shooting a smile at them as she turned to enter the hotel-like structure that had once been the Transient BOQ.

The appeal was somewhat lessened by the fact that there were still boards and other debris from the makeshift barricade that had been set up when people first started going crazy from the toxin. The boards had been set aside but were still pushed into place at night. Everyone trooped into the foyer, where a young lance corporal was on watch. After verifying who everyone was, he issued room assignments and the appropriate keys. He eyed Barry and was going to say something when Jake gave him a shake of the head. The guard shrugged, not really wanting to even engage Derry in conversation, and they all scattered to their rooms.

Barry opened the third floor door to Neal's room and gave it a good once-over. He went to the windows and opened them, but made sure to lock down the setscrew so that they could not be pried open. Neal went to the bedroom and began to unpack his meager belongings from his duffle. When he was done, he walked out to find Barry flopped on the couch.

"Do you want to clean up?" he asked "There's a bucket of water in there." He nodded toward the bathroom.

"No, sir. I like to clean up just before bed so's I can sleep clean."

"You are wise beyond your years, young man." Neal grinned. "Shall we rustle up some chow?"

"That sounds great, sir. Sergeant Jake and I didn't get to eat during the meeting."

"Me neither; let's go."

As they walked out into the hall, they saw Mark and Dr. Napolitano talking a few doors down. They headed in that direction.

"Sir." Mark nodded as the colonel approached. "Jake went off to search out the Lance Corporal Underground and see where the good food is."

Anna got a confused look on her face and said, "Lance Corporal Underground?"

"It is commonly believed that officers run the military. The NCOs let us believe this to be true; however, the mafia-like organization that can usually scrape up the best goods is known as the 'Lance Corporal Underground.' It is composed of the most seasoned junior Marines who have made the burden of tolerating us officer types an art form. They are usually the best informed people on any military installation and know where the best places are to hide to avoid onerous duties, as well as which chow hall has the best grub."

"Ahh." A look of understanding came across Anna's face. "Well, I've just been eating at the cafeteria at the clinic. I didn't know we had options."

"There's always options!" Jake was striding toward them from the stairwell. "We will be dining in a top secret location, gentlemen and lady!" The last was said with a bow toward Anna.

"There is a Sergeant Newcomb whose parents owned a BBQ place out in town. Said sergeant managed to get his folks and a good portion of their equipment onto the base. They have an eatery set up and supposedly, it is the best chow around." Jake gestured down the hall. "If our esteemed security specialist will allow the good colonel to join us, we can head that way now. The lance coconut downstairs will be leaving in a few minutes."

They all went downstairs, where the door guard was just turning over his shift to a relief. He smiled nervously at the colonel and warrant officer, then after introductions, led them outside, where they all piled into a big white government van. Barry took shotgun for the seven-minute drive to one of the abandoned mess halls. There were a few vehicles parked out front and a few people standing around the entrance foyer. The smell wafting around from the side of the building had everyone salivating before they got up the front steps. They noticed a few very vigilant sentries who were keeping well away from the edge of the trees.

"The ferals still make it onto the base, and the smell here draws them from miles around," the young lance corporal said when he noticed everyone looking.

"You should cover the windows so the light doesn't attract them also," Barry said, walking past the young Marine. "The smell only brings them from downwind; the lights will attract them from every direction that they are visible from."

"He does have a point." Jake shrugged as he continued to hold the door for the rest of the party.

They were seated at a big bench table and were introduced to Sergeant Newcomb and his parents. The facility was only about a third full, and they had plenty of time to talk about what was going on. A young girl brought out a huge plate of both BBQ beef and pork ribs. Fresh, soft rolls were laid out with butter, and a bowl of coleslaw was plopped down in front of them. They tore into the best food any of them had eaten in a long time. Norris and Neal used the time to get a better understanding of the toxin from Anna, while Jake and Barry talked guns, girls (just starting to not be yucky to Barry), and video games.

At the end of the meal, Sarah Newcomb caught Barry in the kitchen wrapping the last few ribs in paper towels and stuffing them in his pockets. She scolded him about that not being the proper way to transport her cooking and wound up sending them off with a big box filled with enough food to feed the rest of the base. Barry was staggering toward the door when Derry took pity on him and grabbed the box.

The van dropped them off at their quarters, and they were passing through the lobby when General Branson came stomping out of the stairwell. He was about to tear into the guard on duty about the lack of TP in his room when he stopped and took a deep breath through his nose. The odors wafting out from the box that the little boy was carrying were enough to make him lose his train of thought. Barry just smiled at the man and ducked into the stairwell. Neal and Norris nodded politely, and Anna just grimaced at him. This last was enough to discourage him from trying to find out what was in the box.

He settled for grabbing a few rolls of bath tissue and returned to his room.

CHAPTER 50

Bemidji, MN

Glenn had just looked in on Dan as he slept in his hospital bed. They were on the third floor of the hotel. The survivors had launched a recovery operation at the hospital to gain access to some desperately needed supplies. A feral had jumped on Dan's back and re-opened his wounds from the airfield and, in fact, had torn them open further. The damage to his shoulder and back was extensive. The entire group of original survivors was feeling a little down. The guardsmen had lost several good men, and it just didn't seem right without Barry poking around and sticking his nose into everything.

Scott walked in and looked at his brother sleeping soundly. He gestured to Glenn, and they both moved out into the hall, trying to close the door quietly. They walked a few feet away so as not to disturb Dan. Scott pulled out a notebook and began referring to some notes.

"You're watch commander tonight. We're expecting the mission back from the East Coast in the morning." Scott rubbed his bloodshot eyes. "I have to rack out for a bit."

He went back inside and began pulling a second chair to face the one Glenn had just left. He collapsed into it and put his feet up. He allowed his head to flop back and he looked up at Glenn.

"I'll be right here if you need me."

"You got it, boss."

Glenn went down the hall and stopped at his room to grab his gear before heading upstairs to the communications room. Once he had received a briefing from the person standing the radios, he settled in to read the after-action reports from the various units that had been involved in the raid on the airfield and hospital. He was three pages into it when the radio operator sat up straight and unplugged her earphones so that the transmission she was listening to could come over the speakers.

"...three men down and we can't get to them! The ferals are using weapons!"

Glenn sat up straight and stared at the radio.

"Who is that and where are they?"

"I think it's Patrol Three over on the southwest side of town."

"Unit sending, identify yourself and your location!" Glenn had taken the three steps to the console and had picked up the desk mic.

"Central, Patrol Two! We are trapped away from our vehicles about a mile north of the university." The voice was panicked. "We are under attack by an unknown force that we originally believed to be ferals. The people attacking us are armed though; they're using sticks and spears!"

"Central, Patrol Three, we're heading in that direction." Corporal Maggio's voice came over the radio. "ETA is seven mikes."

"Patrol Three, Central copies." Glenn turned toward one of the guardsmen. "Get the response team ready. If P3 can't handle it, we'll have to get out there."

The specialist picked up his gear and hustled off to gather the troops. Glenn turned back to the radio. Contact reports showed that Patrol Two had been checking out a grocery store when they were ambushed by a group of people using improvised clubs and spears. The six-man team had taken shelter in the manager's office. The ferals numbered over forty individuals, and they had decided to wait for a relief unit to help them deal with the problem.

Out in the store, several members of the pack grabbed cans off of the shelves and threw them through the window. The pack members also had some pieces of short rebar from a construction site. They had used them to try to pry the door open. A few rounds from the defenders inside sent them scampering away, but not for long. They maintained their bombardment until a lilting scream had them all stop and rush to the front of the store.

Maggio and his three vehicles pulled up next to P2's Hummers and got ready to cover them. He was just calling them on the radio to tell them that they were in position when a flood of bodies exploded out through the front door. Maggio was startled but still managed to get the 240 around and start firing. It was too little, too late, as he was hit by a piece of thrown rebar that knocked his hand away from the machine gun. He was reaching for it again when three ferals that had climbed up on the Hummer began hitting him with the steel rods. Although his helmet protected his head as he crouched down in the gunner's cupola, the savage beating he was receiving resulted in both of his shoulders being broken.

"Go! Go!" he screamed at the driver as he tried to cover up. "We need—" The statement was cut off as blood exploded out of his mouth. One of the attackers had stabbed downward with a piece of rebar. The spike tore through Maggio's neck and into his chest cavity. His body slumped down in the gunner's harness as the last two attackers continued to cling to the vehicle as it accelerated away from the storefront.

The other two Hummers had a crossfire angle and were able to break up the pack as it rushed toward them. The mutually supporting fires formed a wall that prevented them swarming the two remaining Hummers. The members of P2 burst out of the door, shooting as they rushed to their vehicles. The Hummers were okay, but the lone pickup they had been using had two flat tires on the passenger side. One of the ferals had used the rebar to break the rubber valve stems off. Roy looked down at the flat tires then hustled over to one of the Hummers. He had to make a running jump into it as it was pulling away.

"What's up with your truck?" Chris asked as he realized they had almost left his good friend.

"They broke off the fuckin' valve stems to flatten the tires!" Roy was pulling out a magazine from his vest to reload his rifle. "They flattened both right side tires! Those bastards are getting smart!"

"Central, Patrol Three, we are coming home with one KIA. Echo Four Mike is KIA."

"Central copies all, Godspeed."

Glenn turned away from the radio and shook his head. He made sure that there were people ready to receive the battered group of survivors. Then he sat down and wondered how he was going to tell Barry.

CHAPTER 51

Northeast of Bemidji, MN

Barry was having the time of his life as the Osprey began its descent toward the airport. It was shortly after takeoff and right before landing that the crew chief lowered the tail ramp and allowed Barry to man the mini-gun. The young man was holding on to the gun's handles and leaning out almost into the slipstream. They were approaching the Bemidji Airport from the northeast when Barry leaned way out and started gesturing for Sergeant Miller to look downward.

Miller grabbed the overhead attachment point and leaned out to see what the kid was pointing at. Down below, a group of survivors had pulled several vehicles into a knot on a road. They were surrounded by an overwhelming crowd of ferals that were circling them, throwing rocks and sticks.

Miller told the pilot to inform the other aircraft in formation and they began a descending turn to get closer. As soon as the surrounded group saw the approaching aircraft, a white sheet with "SOS" on it was displayed. The other crewmember had Neal and Mark put on headsets and informed them of the situation.

"Well, let's go sort this out," Neal said into the intercom.

"Aye aye, sir!" The pilot banked the tilt-rotor into a steep descending turn after telling the other aircraft in the formation what they were doing. The Marines and Barry all got their gear ready while Miller took over the mini-gun.

The Ospreys circled to the right to give the gunners the easiest field of fire. Short bursts of fire began to chew up the attackers on the ground. The planes didn't even get to circle the fight once before ferals broke and ran for the surrounding woods. The three MV-22s set down 100 yards from the vehicles. Mark, Jake, Neal, and Barry all walked down the ramp and waited for someone from the cars to approach. It took a few seconds before a large bearded man stepped out from between two cars and approached. He stopped about twenty yards away when he noticed that not all the guns were pointed at the ground.

"You all from the government?" he asked, keeping his eye on Miller, who was not doing anything to hide the fact that the mini-gun was now pointed toward him and the vehicles behind him.

"We're from several different branches, yes, except for Barry here, which makes him the only honest one among us." Neal gestured at the young man standing next to him.

This brought a chuckle from the man who seemed to relax.

"Well, thank you very much for your assistance. We probably would have been able to hold them off, but it would have cost us some ammo and maybe even a casualty. Something we can ill afford. We're looking to get to Bemidji." The man stepped forward and stuck out a hand the size of a baseball mitt. "Name's Seth Adams."

"As in 'Grizzly Adams'?" Barry asked, stepping forward with Neal.

This time Seth broke out into a full-blown guffaw as he shook first Neal's hand, then Barry's.

"Yeah, I've been told that a time or two!"

They finished making introductions as more members of the convoy came over to meet their saviors. Once everyone was comfortable with each other, Neal and Mark pulled Seth aside and asked him a few questions.

"What do you need in Bemidji?"

"Well, first of all, we heard that the medical center there had been recovered, and we have several pregnant women with us who we would like to see cared for. Secondly, we had heard that the National Guard had re-established an operating base there, and I was going to see if I could get in touch with the CDC. I used to work for them, and I have a few ideas about this toxin."

"Well, you heard correctly. The National Guard has been clearing and securing the city. We have one of the CDC's top scientists with us." Neal gestured at the parked Osprey. He was about to walk Adams over to the plane when Barry grabbed his arm.

"Colonel, we need to get a move on. The ferals are regrouping in the tree line, and I don't want them damaging one of the planes if they attack with rocks and spears." Barry was gesturing toward the trees.

"Miller!" Mark yelled at the crewman leaning on his mini-gun. "Movement in the tree line!"

Miller, who had been eyeing several of the women who had come out from behind the cars, snapped back to awareness and swiveled his gun toward the tree line. He saw the movement that Barry pointed out and sent a stream of rounds across a fifty-yard section of woods. He was rewarded with several screams and some violent shaking of the underbrush. Then he sent a second burst until all was still again.

"Perceptive young man there," Seth said in admiration.

"Yeah, he keeps us safe," Mark said in a very serious tone.

"How about we take your folks who are in need of medical attention with us. We'll leave a few of our shooters with you and have a gunship come out and fly cover for you the rest of the way," Neal suggested, getting the conversation back on track.

"Wow! That would be great!" Seth said. "I'll get my people ready. And the sooner I can get with that CDC scientist, the better."

The pregnant women were loaded into two of the Ospreys and several of the Marines and a park ranger were left with the convoy. One of the Apache gunships flew out to escort the convoy the last forty miles into town. Seth got into the Osprey with Neal and was introduced to Anna.

"Seth Adams," he said, shaking her hand as he settled his massive frame into the jump seat next to her. "I used to be a chemist at CDC. You look familiar to me. When did you start at the center?"

"I've been there almost twelve years now. I started straight out of school." Anna was staring at his face. "There was a Dr. Adams there when I first started."

"One and the same." He tilted his head in acknowledgement. "I have family in Duluth. I retired and moved there to help take care of my mother just over ten years ago. I'm still a consultant of sorts."

"Well, I'd love to go over my notes with you," Anna said, pulling out a three-ring binder. "I've figured out the transference vectors and…"

Barry walked down the hall and paused outside the room that he had shared with Corporal Maggio. Everyone had been walking on eggshells around him since they landed, and now he just wanted to be alone for a while. He pushed open his door and walked over to the weapons locker out of habit. He put his rifle away and then stood there staring at Mag's stuff. His rifle and tac vest were missing, but most of the rest of his gear was still there. He leaned in and pulled out a calendar that they both kept.

There were notes about significant things that had happened recently as well as little reminders of everyone's birthdays. He flopped down on his bed and flipped back two months. He had been reading the informal diary for about ten minutes when there was a knock on the door. He set the calendar on his nightstand and opened the door to see Jake standing there with two beers in his hand. Barry smiled and stepped back.

"I know you're a little young for a beer, but in my book, you sure as hell have earned the right to toast your friend with one," Jake said, handing him one of the cold bottles as he walked over to the small table in the corner. "I didn't know your buddy very well, but I heard good things about him."

Barry took the beer and eyed it for a second before taking a sip. Jake almost choked on the face he made at the taste.

"Yeah, it's an acquired taste."

"Why in the hell do you guys drink that stuff? My dad gave me a shot of brandy once. It was worse than this," he said, lifting up the bottle.

"Like I said, you get used to it." Jake raised his bottle and an eyebrow. "You want to say something about your buddy?"

Barry raised his bottle and sighed.

"He was like my older brother, but way cooler and nicer than my real one. He was awesome at Halo..." He gestured with the bottle toward a game console next to the TV. "And he was always teaching me about his guns and stuff. But he made sure I knew all about my guns first. And he stuck up for me when the other adults tried to get me to stay back here with the little kids." He looked Jake in the eye. "He knew I could take care of myself, and I can!"

With that, he tilted the beer to his lips and took a big swallow. He put the bottle on the table and put his head in his hands with his elbows on his knees. He sat there for a few minutes before looking up at Jake.

"My dad and brother are missing; I'm almost positive they're dead. My mom ate my sisters and my dog." He shook his head. "My best friend from school and his entire family are dead, and now Mag is gone too. I don't think I like this place anymore, but I don't know where to go."

"Yeah, you've caught some shitty breaks. I lost my folks in a car accident when I was just a little older than you. Had to live with my aunt and uncle until I was seventeen and joined the Corps. Found a family here though." Jake leaned back and took another pull as he eyed the kid in front of him. "I know I can't replace your friend. I suck at video games. But I promise you, if you want to learn how to shoot, I'll teach you everything I know."

"Thanks, Jake." Barry got up and flopped on his bed. "I would like to learn how to shoot an M4 better, but the women around here keep trying to get me to go to these tutoring classes. I was going to go loot an AR-15 from one of the sporting goods stores. I can scrounge up magazines and ammo."

"Don't worry about that, little man; I'll make sure you get the proper gear."

They sat and talked until Barry's eyes started getting heavy, and soon he had nodded off.

Jake picked up the calendar and looked through it. When he flipped to the current month of August, he saw that Barry's birthday had been that day.

CHAPTER 52

Dearborn, MI

Moun jogged up the slight rise and took a knee as soon as he could see over the crest of the hill. Satif joined him a moment later, and they waited impatiently as Ibet waddled up, huffing and puffing like he had just run a marathon. He was bent over, breathing heavily when Charles jogged right up and squatted down next to the others.

"There are several following us." He gestured back the way they had come. "Two of them attacked each other, but there are lots more closing in. If I'd had a silenced weapon I could have thinned them out a bit."

Moun just nodded and looked down at the map. They had waited two days before leaving the tunnel complex. The noise and commotion of the attack by the Americans had been like a big dinner bell for every affected mammal, human or otherwise. They made it seven miles on foot. Ibet had argued vigorously to take the car, but they had seen one of the American planes on the second day, right before leaving and none of them wanted to be the recipient of another missile attack. Moun was considering just killing the two men and trying to re-establish some form of contact with society. He had a very marketable skill set.

"If we can make it to this industrial park," Moun gestured to a point on the map, "we can find a place to hole up and try to establish communications with the other sites."

"That's a good tab right there," Charles said, pointing out the distance. "Another ten or twelve kilometers, depending."

"Yes, we have some running to do." Moun gestured back along the way they had just come. Down in the depression below them, two males were crossing an open area. They kept a bit of distance between them but didn't attack each other. This behavior usually led to mutual hunting and pack formation. The one thing they did not want, was a pack focusing on them.

Moun and Charles had just stood up and were adjusting their packs when Moun noticed Ibet taking his pack off. He stalked over and confronted the man.

"What are you doing? They are right behind us," he whispered fiercely while gesturing back the way they had come. "We have to move now!"

"Just kill them; you have a gun!" Ibet pointed at the AK-47 slung from Moun's shoulder.

Moun noticed that Ibet's rifle was missing. He moved to the man's side and felt his pack. It was suspiciously light.

"Where is your rifle? And what gear is missing from your pack? We packed very specific items." Moun hefted the almost empty pack while it was still on Ibet's back. "If we fire a shot it will allow the rest of them to localize on us!"

"Do not touch me!" Ibet's voice rose to almost a shout as the others began to shush him. "You should be carrying this not me! It was too heavy. You gave me the most to carry."

Moun almost raised his rifle to shoot the man, but he saw Satif start to raise his rifle in defense of his friend. Now was not the time for a Mexican standoff, so he turned on his heel and began jogging. Charles, who was supposed to bring up the rear, trotted after him.

"That was not wise!" he said as he hustled the man into a shambling jog. "We need these men in order to survive."

"They should not speak to me so," Ibet huffed. "I am the one who pays them."

"I do not think they are worried about a paycheck now. Where did you leave your rifle?"

"Back along the trail." Ibet waved his hand over his shoulder. "And the ammo too. I have a pistol and plenty of ammunition for it. Wait until we are picked up by the other base. Then we will see what happens. I should have them shot for their arrogance."

Moun and Charles both overheard Ibet's little rant and exchanged knowing glances. They both picked up the pace and had soon outdistanced the other two men. They kept a brutal pace and managed to put over half a mile between them. Once they were sure they were out of earshot, they began to make plans of their own.

"Well, do we peel off and leave them to die of their own stupidity, or do we kill them and take their kit?" Charles finally asked.

"I doubt Ibet has much left other than his iPad, but that would be useful." Moun kept scanning their surroundings as they slowed to a walk. "Satif has a full load though, and we could definitely use that."

"We should do it quietly and leave them for the ones following us. That will keep them occupied while we get away."

"Let's stop just before the highway and do it there. I will take the fat one." Moun was ready peel the skin off of the idiot.

They kept a walking pace so that the two lagging men could catch up. When they did, Moun noticed that Satif was carrying Ibet's pack on his chest. Both men were out of breath and were easy to subdue. Ibet did not struggle at all, while the exhausted Satif could barely muster the strength to fight back.

"Traitor pig!" Ibet started in with the threats. "I will have the skin stripped off your body for this!"

"Shut up, you fool!" Moun took out some riggers tape and wrapped it around the fat man's head several times. Satif just glared at them as he had just a single wrap put around his head. "You should not plot against the people saving you while they are in earshot. As for getting paid, I think your friends will compensate me quite well for this." He shook the iPad in Ibet's face.

It was then Ibet realized that Moun did not intend to let him live. That realization took the wind out of his sails, and he seemed to shrink down into himself. Satif got a panicked look on his face but was not as much of a coward. He continued to glare at his captors.

Charles was already pulling apart the two packs that Satif had carried. He split the useful items between his and Moun's packs, making sure that everything fit right. He refilled their canteens and then he and Moun took turns drinking what was left over until they were both sloshing in their stomachs. He then walked over to Satif and pulled off his tape. He held the canteen and allowed the man to drink. Satif stopped when the remaining water was half-gone.

"You might as well drink it and be comfortable in your last hours. We hold no ill will against you, but we do not trust you. Your friend will not be getting any."

"Why have you betrayed us like this?" Satif started. "We have done you no harm, and we have always paid you quite well."

"Give it a rest," Moun said over his shoulder. "Your friend here would have done us plenty of harm. He endangered us with his reckless behavior out here, and he would have pulled something if we were ever rescued by people he had control over. No, your friend has uttered his last words, and while I respect your loyalty to him, it is a threat to us, so you will share his fate."

Moun nodded at Charles, who wrapped more tape around Satif's head. Both men were stood up and tied to trees facing each other. Moun and Charles put on their packs and picked up their rifles. As they were about to walk away, Charles went back and slit the tape off of both men's mouths.

"Now you can tell your friend what you really think of him," he told Satif.

Ibet started back in with the threats. They got louder as the two contractors walked away. Finally, they could hear Satif yelling at him to shut up because the ferals would hear them. They both chuckled and were turning to continue their hike when Ibet let out a scream. Since they had not covered more than fifty yards, they both spun around to see one of the ferals that had been following them smashing a large stick into the side of Ibet's face. Charles instinctively raised his rifle when a noise caused him to spin around.

Three ferals plowed into them at a full sprint. Charles was able to get off two rounds while going over on his back. Moun had a young male jump on his back and bite him on the head above his left ear. He ignored the pain and shot the two that were tearing into Charles, before attempting to dislodge the attacker on his back.

Charles scrambled to his feet and picked up his rifle. He had just shot the feral off of Moun's back when a dozen more swarmed them. Although both men gave a good showing, it was only a minute before they were both dead and being consumed by the cannibals.

Satif watched in horror as the man finished beating in the side of his friend's head. He struggled vainly against the paracord wrapped around his wrists, to no avail. He looked over at the two contractors just as they went down among the sounds of vicious blows and snarling. He turned back to see the blood-smeared stick swinging right at his face. The stick only partially connected with his head as he ducked the blow the best he could, the stick smacking solidly into the tree. He looked up through the blood flowing in his eyes and his last thought was: *I'll know the pain of my enemies.*

CHAPTER 53

Bemidji, MN

Barry finished brushing his teeth and walked downstairs to the operations center. It was oddly quiet with just the on-duty communications officer there. He nodded at Barry and told him that there had been some survivors brought into the courtyard, which was where everyone was. Barry figured them to be the group from the previous day, so he took his time going down there. He wandered by the kitchen first and grabbed a muffin and carton of milk. Next, he went to the drying racks, where some venison jerky was being dried. He pulled a strip off the rack and headed to the courtyard.

A sheet had been hung over the breezeway, obscuring his view of the courtyard. He started to get an uneasy feeling and was reaching for the pistol at his side when Jake stuck his head around the sheet.

"There you are!" He gestured the young boy forward. "The Colonel has some questions for you."

"Uhh, okay," Barry said and stepped into the courtyard.

"HAPPY BIRTHDAY!" Almost every person in the community was there. The entire place was strung with birthday banners and presents were overflowing and stacked around one of the tables. Newly promoted Captain Crowe, Colonel Neal, Mark Norris, and a large contingent of the National Guard troops were standing off to the side. Barry just stood there, frozen in place, staring at all the smiling faces.

"Come on, son! Let's get this party started!" Crowe walked over and took him by the arm. A cake was brought out and candles were lit. The whole crowd began loudly singing "Happy Birthday." The cake was huge and the candles were spread around the outside. It took him several puffs to blow them all out amidst the catcalls and hootin' and hollerin' going on. The kitchen crew began cooking breakfast, and pretty soon, an all-out party was going on.

Barry was led over and parked in front of the table with the presents on it. The gifts varied from military gear, which included a brand spanking new M4 with an ACOG scope and tac-lite, to a homemade Popsicle stick man made by one of the children whose family he had saved and led back to the compound. Homemade cards matched the store 'looted' cards in number. Almost everyone recounted how Barry had come to their rescue or aid in some way.

The young man stood there and gazed around at all the people laughing and smiling at him. He was speechless as he picked up the little Popsicle stick man and turned it over in his hand. The figure had been painted green and had little bobble eyes and a plastic gun glued to its hand. On the back was written "Barry–our hero." He stared at the small piece of wood and plastic as a tear rolled down his cheek. He looked up to see little Abilene Ramos staring at him. He had found her and her parents trying to make their way out of the city several weeks before.

"Do you like it? I know it's not cool like the other stuff, but I wanted to make you something to say thanks." She looked down at her shoes bashfully.

"This is my absolute favorite thing ever!" Barry said, hugging the girl. He struggled to keep the tears in check as he was reminded of KK, his little sister.

Jake caught on to the scene and stepped up.

"How cool is that!" he exclaimed, looking at the little figurine. "Hey, Gunner! Check this out! Barry has his own Army man named after him!"

Mark and several others gathered around and began to fuss over the present. Abilene was taken aback by all the attention and huddled next to Barry. He smiled at her and made a production of threading a piece of para-cord through the figure and wearing it around his neck. Abilene smiled and ran back to her mother, who mouthed "thank you" to Barry.

The party lasted more than two hours, with Crowe finally calling a halt to the festivities so they could get the Marines back home. Barry took his new equipment and secured it in his room. After the hustle and bustle of the morning, he took a little while to himself so he could set up his new vest and gear. He thought about the morning's events and how he had been feeling lately. The convoy to the airport was loading up when Barry walked out of the hotel with a duffle bag and all of his gear.

He marched up to the truck that Jake was standing next to and tossed the bag in the bed. He then turned and faced the giant man in front of him.

"I need you to keep your promise and teach me how to shoot. Like you. With this," he said, hoisting the M4 on its sling.

"Oh Christ!" Jake said, realizing what was happening. "Uhh, you may have to wait a little on that, bud. I have to get back to California. Things are going better here, but San Diego is a lot bigger, and LA is a huge mess. I have to go back and help out…"

"I know." The direct stare made Derry more uncomfortable than being chewed out by a drill instructor. "I'm going with you. I can be more help there."

"Ahh shit!" Jake looked around hopelessly. His eyes finally settling on the group of officers by the front of the hotel. "Uhm, I would have to have permission, and the Colonel would…"

Jake stopped talking to Barry's back as the young man marched up to the group of men. He jogged over just as the group of men turned to face the young man who had come to a halt a few feet short of them.

"Hey, Barry. Are you coming to the airport with us?" Colonel Neal asked, taking in his rifle and tactical gear.

"Colonel Neal, I would like to go with you to California, sir!"

Neal looked at Crowe, who looked at Norris, who looked at Derry, who just shrugged.

"Uhh, sir…" Derry began. He fumbled with words for a second before standing up straight and looking the officers in the eyes. "I promised Barry I'd teach him how to shoot. I didn't think about how soon we'd be leaving, and he, well, he would like to come out to California and help!"

"What about your friends here?" Norris was aware that Barry had no family left.

"I'll be back, sir." The young man met everyone's eyes, one at a time. "Jake promised I could get trained and that's what I want."

"Why do I have the feeling I've had this conversation before?" Mark asked, looking at Jake.

"Because he's just like Jim," Jake said, smiling.

"I'm just asking for a ride," Barry said, surprising them all. "I have a compass and can walk; it would just take me a long time."

Neal's mouth dropped open for a second as he realized the kid probably could make the trip. He pulled his mouth closed into a grimace and turned to Crowe.

"Well, it looks like he may be riding with us some more."

"We did say he is his own man," Crowe agreed.

"Gunner?"

"I have some rules that my kids have to live by. Do you think you can abide by them?" Norris asked, returning the young man's stare.

"Yup." The grim determination on the boy's face was a portrait of a warrior.

"Where's your gear?" Neal asked.

"In the truck, sir."

Anna, Seth, and Lovell came out to the vehicles. The burly Green Beret had his arms full of luggage, which he easily tossed into the bed of the truck. He took in the serious looks on everyone's face and frowned.

"What's going on, Captain?"

"Mr. Metzler here is going to California, apparently," Crowe answered.

Lovell looked down at Barry and smiled.

"Well, they probably need him more than we do, now."

Barry turned a smug look at the Marines as if it was the final word and marched back to the truck. Derry looked at the colonel, who nodded then followed him. A few minutes later, the convoy rolled down the street headed to the airport.

CHAPTER 54

Over the Pacific Ocean

The Ospreys flew out over the Pacific Ocean and made a descending left hand turn. The Navy ships that were supplying power and water to the base were anchored in an even line to the south as the late afternoon sun cast a gold and red sunset against a few high-level clouds. The planes in the formation peeled off one by one and landed. The lead bird parked closest to the base operations building.

A large crowd was gathered behind a set of barricades. As the Marines began to troop down the ramp, a cry of "Daddy!" was heard. Neal's head snapped up and he looked around as a young woman ducked under a sawhorse and sprinted toward him. Neal picked his twenty-year-old daughter up in his arms and spun around with her.

"Cori! Oh my God, honey! We went to your dorm and looked for you! I thought you were gone!" Neal had tears running down his face.

"I went to Blake's house…" The Colonel walked off with his daughter under his arm.

"Dad! Jake!" Terry was waving as everyone ignored the barricades and pushed out onto the field. Jim, Jen, and Mel all rushed out to swarm Mark. They began to include Jake in the hugs when Mel stopped and stared at the young boy standing off to one side.

"Who's that?" Mel said in a quiet voice, suddenly becoming quite shy.

"Mel, this is Barry." Mark gestured for the young man to come forward. "He's going to be staying with us for a while."

Barry, who had not taken his eyes off of Mel since the second he saw her, stepped forward and mumbled, “Hi.”

“Oh my God!” Terry exclaimed. “He is sooo cute! Can we keep him?”

“He’s not some puppy, Terry!” Mel snarled over her shoulder at her sister, before turning back to Barry. “Don’t let her bug you; she’s a butthead!”

“Uhm, okay,” Barry said as the prettiest girl he’d ever seen took his hand and led him off the tarmac. Jake looked at Mark and Jen, then just shrugged. Things were about to get interesting in the Norris household.

The End

ACKNOWLEDGEMENTS

No one writes a book without some form of input from others. I take credit only for the errors and mistakes in this book. The idea for this novel was conceived in a bar with me drinking and arguing with a friend, who is a fellow Marine and is now a water safety engineer. We watched the news as some guy ate the face off of some other guy on a freeway overpass. My buddy says, “That’s my worst nightmare. We use a positive chemical indicator to detect toxins. These new ‘one-off’ drugs go right through our scanners sometimes. You could get that from a public water fountain…” And there you go. *Gone Feral* was born.

There are two organizations I have joined in my life: The United States Marine Corps and The Kappa Sigma Fraternity. Both of them changed my life forever. So to my brothers, both Jarhead and Fraternal… Semper Fi and AEKDB.

To every person I made read this thing before it came out, thank you for your time and criticism. Two people were the most helpful—Charles Hume, who was always positive and supportive, and Brian Woeller. I wrote the sequel just because you (and twenty other people) wanted to see more of Barry. The preview follows immediately after this…

The inspiration for the kids in this book were my own children and their friends. It is a rare weekend when my house doesn’t have a slew of teenage bodies covering every horizontal surface. Some of the humor in here came from my daughter, Abigail, who took me to task for claiming that a truly creative writer can write about anything. She immediately said, “Oh yeah? Put ‘crime fighting pickles’ in your book!” She then turned to Kyle, one of the neighborhood kids, and said, “Give him something hard!” The kid looked at me and said one word: “Nosferatu.” The pickles were easier, trust me.

To every zombie/horror/thriller writer who ever put to pen the coolest books ever, thanks. I enjoyed your works; I hope you enjoy mine.

And to my small but growing fan base (all eight of you at last count), thanks for buying my book; it was written for you, after all!

Keep reading for a preview of the sequel:

Barry's Walk

PROLOGUE

Camp Pendleton, CA

The sun was getting low in the western sky as the young man crested the hill and stared down into the valley in front of him. He could see the backs of the four classmates in front of him as they followed the trail back down to the schoolhouse. A glance behind him showed a line of fellow classmates struggling up the hill to his location. He dragged a dusty sleeve across his brow to wipe away the sweat that was running down his face and dripping off his nose. The young man hitched his pack a little higher and fingered the small figurine hanging from a piece of paracord around his neck. With a look of grim determination on his face, he made sure his M4 carbine was secure on its sling, but readily available, and began to trot down the hill, while a .45 in an old canvas holster bumped against his hip.

As he picked up speed, he began to gain on the classmate in front of him. He had almost caught up when the man he was gaining on turned with a startled look on his face. Seeing the determined look on the younger man's face, he began jogging as well. Soon there was a small knot composed of the second through fifth place students bearing down on the leader. Try as they might though, they couldn't catch him. As soon as the leader hit the road with a half-mile remaining to the finish line, he took off like he wasn't carrying a forty-pound pack and rifle. His scarred face was set in grim determination as his ground-eating lope easily kept a safe distance between him and his fellow classmates.

Rounding the last bend in the road, Jim Norris trotted across the finish line and checked in with the class' lead instructor. After that, he moved back to the curve in the road to cheer on his classmates. He watched as the next two people to come into view bore down on the finish line in a dead heat. He was surprised to see the smallest member of his class pumping his legs madly to try to get second place. It just didn't happen, as Barry Metzler came in third, having passed two classmates since his pause at the top of the ridge. Both men crossed the line breathing like locomotives. Barry turned and staggered over next to Jim to lend motivational support while Ernie Wright collapsed on his back, not even bothering to remove his pack.

It took over two hours for the rest of CCTC-1 to cross the finish line. The final stragglers crossed the line, followed by the Medical HMMV with two students in it. The class had just finished its final hump before graduation, which was two days away. The first class of the Marine Corps' Civilian Combat Training Course would graduate eighty-two students, the oldest being a fifty-six-year-old former carpenter, and the youngest, a fourteen-year-old orphan from Bemidji, Minnesota.

CHAPTER 1

14 Months Earlier

"You can't doooo that!" Andrew Petty complained as his older brother, Will, turned the hose on him, easily overpowering the Super-Soaker Andrew was aiming at him. The rules stated that the hose was neutral territory. The squirt gun fight had elevated to a water balloon fight, which then devolved into a mud-wrestling match. "We get to fill our guns too!"

"This is my gun, butthead, and if you want some water, come and get it!" Will yelled as he sprayed Barry before he turned the hose back on his younger brother. Barry used the distraction to dodge in and grab the Igloo ice cooler that had been the ammunition depository for the water balloons. It was now half full of water and the remnants of several popped balloons. He picked it up and heaved the contents at Will, drenching him thoroughly and ending the water fight with a resounding victory for the underdogs.

Will, who was a poor sport in victory, became an absolute bully when shown up by his younger brother and Barry. He lunged at Barry with a balled fist and a curse on his lips, which changed to a yelp of surprise as he tripped on the cooler that Barry threw at his feet as he nimbly skipped away. Will went down hard on the muddy lawn, giving Barry and Andrew the opportunity to run away.

The two friends took off for Barry's house, knowing that it wouldn't be safe at Andrew's house for quite some time. They cut through the woods, making sure to stop and look down into Ms. Allensworth's backyard. The sixth-and-seventh-grade social studies teacher was immensely popular with the students, especially the boys. The 5’9” blonde had worked her way through college as a model and was stunningly beautiful. This was not lost on the male population, and a lot more fathers began showing up at PTA meetings.

Peering through the trees, the boys saw a towel on the chaise lounge in her backyard. The boys exchanged a knowing grin and immediately went into stealth mode. They dropped down onto their hands and knees and began to crawl down the slope toward her fence. If they could get there unobserved, they would be able to get a near perfect side-on view as she was getting a tan.

Movement at the kitchen window caused both boys to freeze as Justine Allensworth finished making a tall glass of sweet tea and headed to the back door. The boys watched as she made herself comfortable and picked up her Kindle to read. The two twelve year olds got comfortable and just stared at what had to be God’s most perfect creation for a while.

Andrew was really feeling the sun on his neck and was starting to fidget when Barry gave him an elbow to make him be still. Their clothes had quickly dried in the summer sun and they were now beginning to sweat profusely. Their discomfort paid off though as she stood up and laid the lounge down flat. Both Barry and Andrew were coiled tight as springs as she undid the strings to her bikini top and lay down on her stomach. The brief glimpse of her magnificent chest would be the subject of both boys’ fantasies for some time.

The boys watched for another half hour before Justine got up and went inside for some reason. This provided the boys with one last look at her chest and then allowed them to slip away to the fort, where they would talk for hours about how they would propose to her as they worked at putting the finishing touches on their hideaway.

Their fort was located almost exactly halfway between Ms. Allensworth’s house and the back fence line of Barry’s farm. The entrance was a cleft between two rocks on the side of the hill overlooking the farm. This was camouflaged by dragging some vines across the opening and attaching them with a piece of rope to a wooden frame. Both boys were avid science fiction and war movie fans, so they had developed a super-secret protocol for getting to the entrance unobserved. This protocol involved looping back to check their back trail to see if anyone was following them. While watching out for any spies trying to follow them, the boys talked about various horror films and discussed defending the fort in case of a zombie apocalypse. Once sure that they weren’t being followed, they slipped past the vines and entered their sanctuary.

Once past the boulders, the cleft in the rocks opened out into a space twelve-feet wide by fifteen-feet deep. This immense cavern had a set of shelves along one side, which held various items important to fort defense, including an old battery-powered radio and a pair of old binoculars. A small red Igloo cooler provided food storage, while two lawn chairs completed the furnishings. The boys had scavenged a small A-frame ladder that allowed them to climb up onto a small rock shelf that looked out over Barry's farm in the distance. This platform would eventually be used for mounting a hyper speed turbo-laser to be used in defense of the zombie hordes.

Neither of the boys knew it, but that was exactly what they would be facing by the end of the week.

DON'T MISS BOOK TWO OF THE GONE FERAL SERIES

TED NULTY

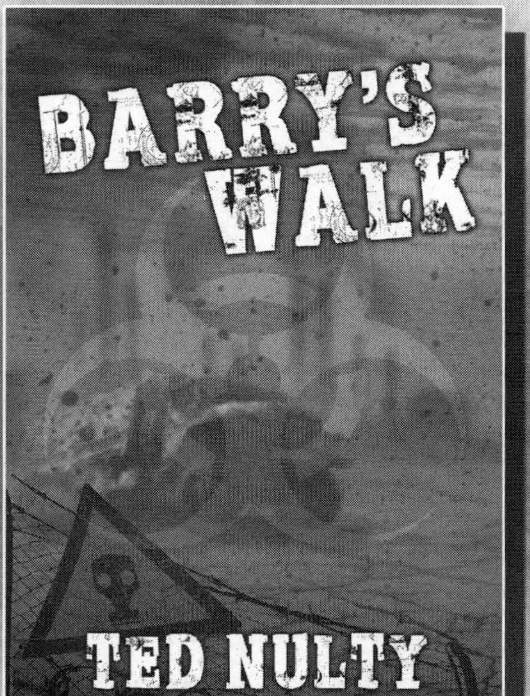

Where were you when the world ended?

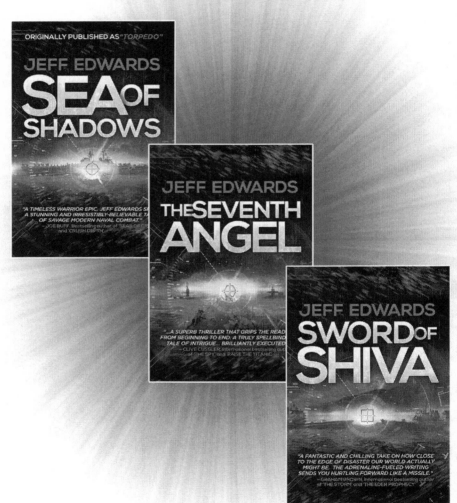

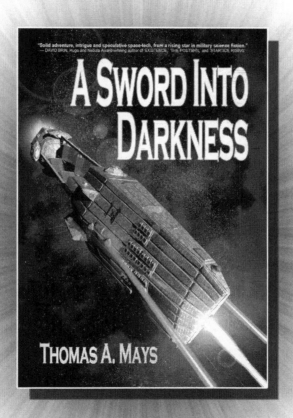

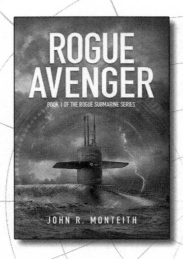

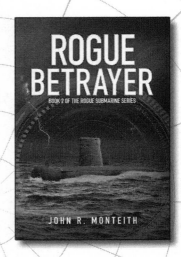

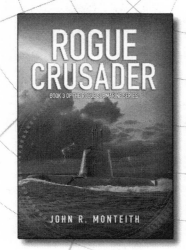

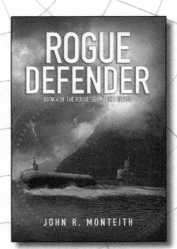

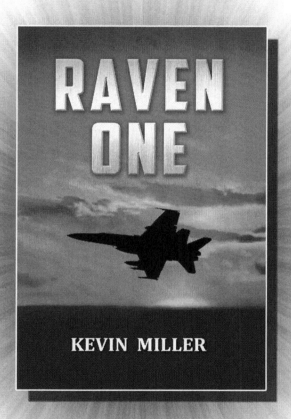

72892045R00174

Made in the USA
Columbia, SC
29 June 2017